Consort's Glory

The New Protectorate: Book One

Abigail Kelly

Author's Note

For those who wish to see them, content warnings for this book can be found in the backmatter and on my website.

~Abigail

For 13 year old Abigail.
For 17 year old Abigail.
For 21 year old Abigail.
You made it.

Chapter One

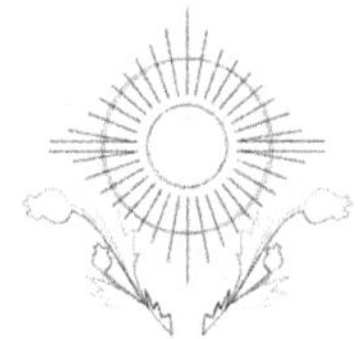

February 2045 - San Francisco, the Elvish Protectorate

Margot Goode was a practical sort of person — particularly when it came to her death.

Healers were no strangers to Grim's tithe, nor to suffering. The clasped hands of life and death belonged to the same being, after all, and healers could no more separate the two than they could change the inexorable current of time.

Even so, Margot's death took her by surprise.

It didn't come for her in the shape she always feared it would. It didn't come for her in the smothering dark, reeking of madness, piercing with claws and teeth. It came slowly, first through the tips of her fingers and then upward, over slopes of muscle and rigid bone, to steal her life before she got the chance to live it.

Burn out. The affliction all witches of her caliber suffered late in life, when the magic coursing through their veins began to damage its host beyond its ability to repair itself. It came for her too soon, and every day it got harder and harder to hide the symptoms.

What began as fine tremors after a long healing session

became hard shakes and frequent migraines. Fatigue. Lack of appetite. A peculiar sense of vertigo, like the world was slipping out from under her feet at a steep angle.

Cold practicality finally pushed her to leave the Coven. It compelled her to put in the transfer request to the Healing House in a sleepy, well-to-do San Francisco neighbourhood. That clear knowledge that her death pressed closer every day and a compulsion she just *couldn't shake* brought her to San Francisco to look for the person who could save her life.

And it pushed her to accept the dinner invitation from the alpha of the local shifter pack, the risks be damned.

The Merced coyote pack was not the largest in California, but it was the most powerful pack in the Bay Area. They had to be both smart and ruthless to win any sort of autonomy under those who ruled the Protectorate, the swath of tightly controlled land running from Arizona to the top of Oregon.

After several healing sessions with their trouble-making teenagers, Margot knew many of the Merced pack well. Even so, the risk of stepping into shifter territory was enormous. It always was when she dealt with predator races. Not because she couldn't take care of herself — healers were the people with the most intimate knowledge of the body and how to break it, after all — but because one slip-up, one good whiff of the scent buried beneath the layers of protection she slathered on every day, and her closely-guarded secrets would be exposed.

Margot dealt with Viktor Hamiliton and his pack enough to trust them not to hurt her, but there were breathtakingly few she would *ever* trust with all of herself.

So it was a risk to join the pack for dinner at the edge of marshy Lake Merced, but even the familiar anxiety of discovery wouldn't stop Margot from going. She *wanted* to go. She liked Viktor, she liked the pack members who had taken to dropping by her house on a weekly basis, and she missed the familiar chaos of a family dinner.

And Margot was desperate.

Of course I'm desperate, she thought, tightening her hands on the steering wheel of her car. *I'm dying.*

Margot drove down darkened streets, back to the Healing House with a full stomach and covered in the scents of a dozen young, single coyote shifters eager to see if she'd feel any magical tickle, any chemistry at all, when they touched. They were eager in a way that might have made her uncomfortable if she weren't currently suspended over the knife's edge of her own mortality.

Besides, she couldn't blame them. Bonding with a Goode witch, a *real* gloriana? The curiosity of it was like an aphrodisiac to the quicksilver minds of the coyotes.

Rolling her shoulders back to relieve some of her tension, Margot decided she needed another shower. The coyotes didn't smell bad, but they weren't *right,* and it grated against her nerves to have the scents of so many strange men in her pores, rubbing that niggling compulsion in the back of her mind the wrong way.

None of them were the reason she felt so compelled to step out of the safe stranglehold of the Coven to move to San Francisco. She knew it in her bones. She knew *he* was out there somewhere, but not in the Merced pack.

They were attractive, certainly, with their wide coyote grins and lean, powerful bodies. They generally leaned toward cheerful humor and quick to ignite and even quicker to die tempers. But not even the alpha of the pack, the razor-sharp Viktor, who'd managed, against her best efforts, to become a friend, inspired so much as a twitch in her magical *or* romantic instincts.

Viktor was gorgeous, intelligent, and clearly a man who cared about the people under his charge more than he cared about personal power. Even if he didn't have lush, sandy blond hair, skin of burnished copper, or baby blue eyes, she would have been drawn to his air of responsibility, his quick tongue, that easy smile.

She *liked* him. They were friends — could have even been more if only her damn magic would *cooperate.*

Why? Why can't it be one of them? Any of them?

Margot unclenched her hands on the steering wheel, fighting the tremors that came with so much more force when she was alone.

No one else has this problem. No one else needs to be so selective. Why can't I just choose?

But no one else hit burn out so young, either. And no one was what *she* was; could explain how the differences would change things, how her body might react if it didn't get what it needed. She was a witch, but she was also more.

That *more* was killing her.

She was supposed to have time. Years to figure herself out. Decades, maybe even a century. Years to settle down, date, find the right one in her own time, just like every other gloriana.

Her own grandmother didn't start feeling the symptoms until she was nearly *one hundred and fifty,* and by then, Sophie already had Noni Tula, so there was no question about who she would bond to, nor who would carry the weight of Sophie Goode's considerable magic when it turned on her.

It fell in line with Margot's consistently shitty luck that she barely made it past twenty-five before her body turned against her.

Exiting a roundabout with a tastefully lit, burbling fountain at its center, she drove with her windows down to let in the cool, eucalyptus scented air. Luckily for distracted witches everywhere, the entire Protectorate had an m-grid, allowing the sigil-lined, exhaustless engines of even the oldest vehicles to lock onto the streets and nearly drive themselves. It brought the chances of a collision to nearly zero.

Passing large, mostly arrant-owned houses with their sprawling lawns and huge, old growth trees made into silhouettes by the dark, Margot considered just how much time she had left.

Six weeks at maximum, her healer's training helpfully supplied. *With symptoms first appearing last year and increasing in severity approximately every four to five weeks, I'm looking at total burn out in two months — if I'm lucky.*

There was no use wondering what would become of her then.

She was a gloriana, the most powerful caliber a witch could be born into. If she were only a minor witch, a brightling or a brilliant, she might have just suffered permanent nerve damage or the crushing loss of her abilities.

But she wasn't, and that meant there was only one way things could end: Nerve damage. Internal bleeding. Loss of neurological function.

Death.

The only way to save her pitiful, squandered life was to find a bondmate, someone to filter her power through to diffuse the damage done to her cells every second of every day; a sort of magical dialysis that would bind her very soul to another. It was a bond that would save her life and make her partner incredibly powerful in return.

If only I could find *him.*

So far her search only revealed what Margot always feared: her bondmate couldn't just be *anyone.* There would be no hasty, ill thought out, shotgun bonding for her. Margot Goode's bondmate would be one man and one man only.

Unfortunately, the compulsion to find him, that prickly sense of knowing, pulled her towards San Francisco for nearly a year, but gave her little else to go on. She was certain he lived in the city, but so did nearly a million other sapient beings.

Even if she had all the time in the world, the chances of running into her bondmate were slim to none.

Margot pulled into the driveway of the Healing House and killed the engine of the zippy little m-car, a thing that, like the house, belonged to the neighborhood. The Healing House and its amenities belonged to the people it served. It, along with everything within and without, wouldn't miss her when a blood vessel popped in her brain and the lights simply... went out.

Feeling suddenly, immeasurably tired, Margot let out a long sigh and leaned her forehead against the steering wheel.

I'm running out of time. And... damn it, I miss my family.

She knew it was foolish to keep her impending death from her grandmother, to lose precious time with her family. Sophie Goode wouldn't be able to fix Margot's problems, but she would do everything in her power to try. Even before Margot left Washington, the matriarch of the Goode family had begun shoving eligible men in her direction — young and mature, powerful and less powerful, witch and shifter, hybrid and even an arrant or two.

But that was why she took the job in San Francisco — that urge to *find him,* to satisfy that clawing need to hunt him down and clutch him to her chest and never, ever let him go. Even if she could explain it, Margot wasn't sure her family would understand that the normal rules didn't apply to her and never had. They couldn't. They weren't like her.

No one was.

They would never understand the compulsion to be exactly where she was, and if she confessed about her condition, she feared they would hog tie her and drag her back to the Coven to force the issue of her bonding to the first willing partner.

Because they love me, and my death will hurt them in ways I can't imagine. Uncurling one hand from the steering wheel, Margot rubbed at her stinging eyes. *Get home. Get in shower. Get to bed. You aren't giving up right now, in this stupid tiny car.*

Forcing herself to move, Margot popped open the door and swung her legs out into the chill of the February evening. Her light jacket and floral print dress did little to seal in warmth, so she hustled up the path through the small garden, through the traditional iron gate, and up the low ramp to the covered stoop. Like always, the slight bounce of her steps surprised her.

Every time she thought she was used to the way magic settled into the sidewalks and soil of San Francisco, she had to consciously adjust her gait once more. The sponginess of the ground tended to change day by day, hour by hour, like the temperamental weather the city was so famous for. It was just another quirk of the old, strange city, like the sentient fog and water teeming with bloodthirsty waterfolk.

Natives had no trouble changing the way they walked at a moment's notice, giving them the famous *San Francisco Gait,* but Margot still occasionally struggled with the loping, bouncing movements necessary to walk down the street on a magic-heavy day.

Stepping lightly toward the door, Margot didn't need to fish for keys in her purse or pocket. The doors to a Healing House were always unlocked, even when the resident healer wasn't in.

The Allied Charter listed all Healing Houses as sacrosanct. Not even the lowest criminal would stoop to stealing from one, not simply because doing so was the quickest way to spend a lifetime in a miserable, sigil-lined prison, but because they were declared holy sites after the Great War nearly wiped out healers altogether.

The gods Glory, Grim, *and* Blight claimed healers for their own. To harm one, even indirectly, was blasphemous in the extreme.

That was why Margot didn't think to check her home for intruders when she stepped through the door and dropped her purse onto the little entryway table.

Only her bedroom was warded against outsiders, her sigilwork painstakingly etched into the walls and door frame to keep out anyone who might wish her harm. A normal healer would never think to take those kinds of precautions, but Margot wasn't anywhere close to normal.

Moving to close the door, one hand extended to flick on the light. The hair on the back of her neck, exposed by her neat chignon, rose with sudden, prickling tension.

Margot turned her head slowly, her senses on high alert as she scanned the entryway and the darkened rooms that made up her living room, as well as the sterilized clinic just beyond it.

Her hearing was better than the average human's, but she heard nothing. No squeaky floorboards, no foreign breathing. There was a thread of scent, something sharp and chemical, but this was the city, not her home in the lush forest of the Pacific Northwest, and that wasn't necessarily unusual.

The only thing she could sense was a low-level hum of magic in the air. Not so strange with neighbors so close, but—

The blast hit her in a single, percussive wave, throwing her back into the yard. The heavy front door followed, its splintered bulk sailing over her in a wide arc to land with a crash against the iron gate.

Margot landed hard on her side against the smooth brick path that led to her home, her head cracking against it with a teeth-rattling crunch.

Blackness, filmy and terrifying, engulfed her.

Time stretched in a strange way. The seconds pulled long, thin, until they were overstretched in a mind shocked to stillness by both injury and surprise. She wasn't quite unconscious, but drifting. There was no sound in the darkness, but she could feel heat on her skin, the rasp of acrid air in her lungs — *knew* that something had gone horribly wrong.

Margot didn't hear the following explosions as the gas line ruptured, but she could feel them as they punched through her. One after another, two blasts that rolled through tissue and bone like m-lev trains.

Her vision swam back in a haze. The filmy darkness lifted enough to reveal chaos: falling debris, the roar of flames, the twisted wreckage of what was once a pillar of the neighborhood.

Too dazed to do much else, Margot could only raise her arm to cover her eyes as glass and shrapnel pelted down from the upstairs windows. Her coat took most of the damage, but her legs were bare beneath her flirty dress. Her ears rang, but she could hear nothing besides the high whine of injury and her harsh breathing.

Easy repairs, she thought, only distantly recognizing the sounds and crackling heat of a building inferno. *Blown eardrum, surface lacerations, bruising to my cheekbone, and possible hairline fracture to my skull. Nothing difficult.*

Margot could comprehend injuries. What she couldn't grasp was the way the Healing House, her responsibility for a paltry six months, was destroyed; flames licking from deep within its belly to make the gaping holes where there were once windows glow with sinister light. The black film swimming across her eyes granted her only a fleeting glimpse of the wreckage before it dragged her under again.

There was an odd sensation of fleeting hands on her throat, skimming down her body, the awareness of strange people around her, but Margot couldn't open her eyes to look around and see who was touching her. The sensation only lasted a moment, anyway, and when she could finally muster the ability to clear the spots from her eyes, there was no one there.

Blackness again. Her head screamed at her as the bricks rushed up to greet her battered cheek.

Hands on her shoulders — a small, hard shake. Margot tore her gaze away from the burning building to see the shadowed face of a neighbor above her, his lined face covered in a thin layer of perspiration.

"...*Goode!* Can... move?"

His voice went in and out, but Margot couldn't tell if it was due to her damaged ears, her head wound, or the shock.

She did a cursory scan to make sure she didn't have any spinal injuries or unnoticed bleeding before offering her neighbor — *Adam,* she recalled, *father of two boys in middle school, registered arrant with no magical ability, works in m-tech finance* — a tight nod.

He was helping her up in a moment, strong hands clasping her elbows to lever her onto her feet. Margot's head swam as her hearing came back to her in a rush of roaring flames, car alarms, and frantic yelling.

One ear worked, at least. The other was screaming at her, a trickle of warm blood sliding down her cheek and neck to pool in the dip of her collarbones.

Sirens squealed in the distance, and she could hear the frantic chatter of dozens of voices as her neighbors exited their homes wrapped in robes. Adam gently but urgently guided her toward the curb, his voice rising behind her as he yelled out to someone to call for m-vac.

Margot wanted to assure him that she didn't need a magical lift to an emergency clinic, *couldn't* get one, actually, but the words were glass in her throat, her mind stuck in the deep rut of a single question.

How did this happen?

A stone of cold dread settled into the pit of her stomach. *Was it me? But why? Why a bomb? If someone knows, wouldn't they just expose me?*

It was premature to assume it was a bomb, magical or mechanical, but Margot couldn't imagine this sort of devastation was an accident. *After all, if it was some sort of gas leak, wouldn't other homes be blown up too?*

When she looked around, Margot saw damage — the homes directly opposite hers had their front windows blown out, their mailboxes toppled, and several appeared to have lost their front doors — but nothing like the devastation that struck the Healing House. It was a relief, however minor, to see no glow of flames in the stately homes.

The screech of tires drew her eye to the street as Adam pushed her down onto the curb a little ways away from her front yard. Another neighbor — *Kimmi, early thirties, lawyer, diabetic, married to a woman who owns an Italian restaurant in Lakeside, brightling and hybrid harpy respectively, no children* — ran up with a throw blanket. Her fellow witch's face was starkly white under the streetlights.

"Healer Goode, the fire squad is here," she rushed out, voice pitched high as she wrapped the blanket around Margot's shoulders. "And Patrol is coming, too. Annie called."

Margot could do little more than offer a dazed thank you as she watched a sleek, top of the line fire engine come to a sudden stop in front of her home. People dressed in m-enhanced fire suits leapt out of the back, their bodies weighed down by the heavy-duty foam blasters that would stop the flames before they engulfed the entire neighborhood.

She could feel the heat of those flames at her back. There would be no saving any part of the Healing House.

Margot didn't cry for the loss. It wasn't her home, not really, but she'd been entrusted with its safekeeping, and she felt the shame of that failure far more than she felt her injuries.

She squeezed her eyes shut. *I'm a Goode, for Glory's sake, and I failed the first thing I tried on my own.*

Voices rose and fell as the fire squad worked. Margot caught only snippets of conversation over the flames and the buzz of the foam blasters. Time passed slowly on the curb, punctuated only by the frantic snatches of conversation and the crackle of her home being destroyed.

"...a Healing House! I can't believe—"

"Do you think it was an accident? I heard—"

"She's a Goode, isn't she? Do you think it might have been political or—"

Sometime later, the cold bit at Margot's exposed legs even as Kimmi carefully tucked the blanket tighter around her shoulders. "You need medical attention," she worried, chewing her lip, "I'm going to—"

Kimmi cut herself off. Whatever she meant to say died as her eyes fixed on something behind Margot's back.

Warm hands on her knee and the back of her head made Margot tense. A familiar, if slightly unwelcome scent in her nose, half-hidden by the acrid smoke and the chemical stink of the fire retardant foam, eased the tension away.

Margot turned stinging eyes to the man crouching down beside her. When she looked up, she found a handsome face and eyes of clear baby blue staring back at her.

Her voice cracked. "Viktor."

The coyote shifter held her gaze for a long moment, his lips pressed thin, before he turned to give Kimmi a sharp order. "Go get her some water. We don't know that she didn't inhale some of the smoke."

Kimmi didn't waste time arguing. Faced with a force of nature like Viktor, few would dare.

When her neighbor scrambled off to follow his orders, Viktor crouched beside Margot on powerfully muscled legs, his well-loved blue jeans stretched tight over his knees. "Hey now," he crooned in that coyote-smooth voice as he stroked her hair back with one gentle hand, "if I'd known what you were headed home for, I would have been even more inclined to invite you to my bed. Hindsight's a real bitch, isn't it?"

A startled laugh bubbled out of her, raw and raspy. "I still would have said no."

His smile was wide and easy, but his startlingly blue eyes were hard, his protective anger breathtaking in its coldness. "You sure? Maybe you need to take me for a test drive before you really put me out of the running, pretty witch."

Margot found herself leaning into him when he put his arm around her shoulders. Touch hunger, a weakness she could very rarely indulge, crested in a great, selfish wave to overtake her good sense.

She had only known Viktor a few months, but even with his relentless flirtation, she found comfort in his steady presence, his unwavering calm. He was a man used to leading a massive pack of coyote shifters. He *had* to be a bastion of calm confidence. She was drawn to that sort of competence, that easy authority. It reminded her of home and satisfied something in her she didn't want to think about too hard.

He was also kind, with an unswerving sense of loyalty to his people, and Margot happened to enjoy his flirting, even if they both knew by now that nothing would ever come of it.

"Why are you here? This isn't your territory," she croaked.

Viktor nudged her a little bit away so he could examine her face, his fingertips gentle under her chin. The hardness in his eyes solidified into a cutting thing as he took in the damage. "You're not pack, but you're as good as," he rumbled. "You've saved the life of one of mine at least three times in six months. That puts you under my protection. Besides, this is the edge of my territory. You think I wouldn't investigate?"

Margot blinked hard, her eyes smarting with the threat of tears. She had a mile-wide streak of Coven pride, of course, but to *belong* to a people, to never have to hide or pretend for them — Margot had never experienced that.

Staring up into the handsome angles of Viktor Hamilton's face, she asked herself again, *Why can't it be you? I'd kill to belong to someone like you.*

Not because he was handsome, but because he was *kind,* funny, and fiercely protective of those he loved. With him, she would never have to worry about what the world would do if her secret got out. He would keep her safe. He would love wholly, without shame or boundary. He would accept her. *All of her.*

Margot's lower lip trembled as the shock finally began to wear off, stripping her of the protective barrier that blocked out both fear and pain. Breathing faster, her heart hammering, Margot was humiliated to feel Viktor brush a tear from her grimy cheek. "Oh, no tears," he grated, something wild in his coyote-bright gaze, "I can't stand it when women cry. You stop it now, pretty witch. That's an order from an alpha. *No tears.*"

"I'm a healer," she rasped, "we don't cry."

They were trained to only do that in private. No one wanted a weepy healer when they were wrist-deep in viscera, after all.

Viktor cupped her cheek. His palm was warm, roughened by work and the time he spent outdoors. The skin contact fed the greedy thing inside of her, the part of Margot that screamed for someone, anyone to touch and *care* in the way it needed.

"Then stop crying, witch. How am I supposed to take care of you if I've got a blubbering healer clinging to me?" His smile was crooked and terribly charming. "I can think of better reasons to cling, if you're amenable."

Margot's laugh was watery, her punch to his t-shirt clad

shoulder without any true force. "Making a healer mad is a bad plan. I know where all your organs go, rem—"

The peculiar feeling of something snapping hard against the surface of her subconscious stole her breath. Margot's head snapped up and turned in one fluid move that was pure instinct; unerring compulsion.

The screaming thing in her stood at attention, waiting, watching, as the very air seemed to shift.

In the same instant, Viktor was up and in front of her. A growl, so deep it was almost inaudible, rumbled over her sensitive skin, cutting through the competing sounds of the fire squad and the people gawking in their doorways.

Except... all that chatter from her neighbors had gone mysteriously quiet. Margot darted a glance along the street just in time to see several black-clad figures ushering people into their homes. They wore no Patrol emblem on their backs, but their height, the way they moved— there was no mistaking *what* they were.

Elves.

Her gaze swung back to Viktor, who stood ramrod straight, his legs spread and his sturdy, tanned hands turned deadly with coyote-sharp claws. Behind her, she could feel the wild energy of another coyote shifter moving closer; a man she knew as Benny, one of Viktor's packmates, watching his alpha's back.

There was someone else near, too. Blocked from sight by her coyote bodyguard, Margot could *feel* him change the air in her lungs, the current of magic that ran through every cell in her body. A force of nature stepped up to the curb in shiny black shoes tipped with deadly silver.

She was surprised to hear the high note of astonishment in Viktor's voice when he demanded, "The fuck are you doing here, Teddy?"

"What makes you think you have any right to ask that question?" Recognition was a sharp *twang* in that hungry, neglected part of her. The voice was cool, tightly controlled, deep with an authoritative rumble that sent a wave of goosebumps over her skin. Magic fizzed in her veins at the sound of the rich baritone, so smooth and familiar.

"Now," the stranger continued, "step away from the healer, Vik, before I *move* you."

A warning growl rumbled behind her, distinctly coyote and deeply territorial. Out of the corner of her eye, Margot caught two black-clad figures moving with unnatural grace towards them, their metal clawtips glittering in the glow of the streetlights. The glamours over their faces cast them in smoke and shadow, obscuring features until they were nothing but clawed wraiths, ready to defend this man Margot couldn't even see properly.

She stared at the figures, unable to process what she knew to be true. *That's the Sovereign's Guard,* she thought. *Why... are they here?*

All elves were trained to fight from birth. It was one of the few aspects of their lives they actually liked to talk about publicly. But the *guard* — they were in a league of their own. No one crossed the Sovereign's Guard and lived to tell the tale.

Whatever was happening, things were about to get *much* worse.

Margot reached up to grasp Viktor's belt loop, using it to help herself stand. Even using him to leverage her full weight upward, he didn't sway, his defensive stance unchanged.

The blanket around her shoulders slid away, exposing her battered skin to the cold, wet air. Viktor's arm swept backward, attempting to keep her behind him. "Margot, no. Let me deal with him."

More scared of the approaching wraiths than whoever could possibly be standing in front of Viktor, she pushed against him to peer around his broad shoulder. "Viktor, the Sovereign's Guard is—"

All the air squeezed out of her lungs.

The man standing just a few feet away was huge — easily two full heads taller than she was, with an added hundred pounds on him to boot. Almost everything about him was thick with muscle except for his waist, which was a finely tapered angle sliding into narrow hips, accentuated by a simple black belt, slacks, and heavy, calf-length coat. His shoes, now familiar to her, gleamed with black leather and silver accents in the low light.

He was all black and white: Black hair, a mess of waves on top and trimmed neatly on the sides, accentuating the elegant points of his ears. A white button-down with starched arrow collar up to his chin, pinned in place by twin, intertwined thistles cast in silver. A black elvish suit jacket, perfectly pressed, stretched over broad shoulders. Black leather gloves with wicked silver clawtips covered large, deadly hands. He even had skin that appeared bleached white in the yellow glow of the street lights, but which she knew was actually the palest sapphire blue.

Catlike black eyes framed by thick, sooty lashes, and set in a hard-edged face almost too pretty to be real, stared back at her.

Margot's foolish heart skipped a beat, her magic bubbling like champagne in her veins, before it caught another, faster rhythm.

No one who lived in the Elvish Protectorate could mistake the man before her for anyone else.

He was Theodore Solbourne, *Sovereign.*

Chapter Two

The news of his consort's brush with Grim didn't put Theodore in a good mood.

Arriving at the scene to find said consort in the arms of a notoriously charming coyote alpha put him in a *really* fucking bad mood.

Theodore tried to think past the immediate burst of protective rage that came with his first full inhale of Margot's scent; to reason past the initial, blinding burst of chemicals now infusing his bloodstream; to quell that first, furious urge to clutch her to his chest and never, *ever* let her go.

Calm except for the churning, volatile hormones sinking their teeth into his psyche, he forced himself to look away from Margot with sheer, teeth-gritted will. He wanted— *needed* to drink in the sight of her. It was a need he'd forced himself to satisfy with surveillance shots sent in by her guard until this moment, but now that he was faced with her, Theodore knew he could not go on the way he had.

Still, he had to focus.

Wrapping his authority around himself like a cloak, Theodore arched a brow. "Stand down, Vik." He kept his gaze locked with

Viktor's. "This situation is under control. Go back to your territory and stay there."

Viktor's eyes went from vivid blue to deep, menacing amber in an instant. "She's a friend of the pack. Might as well belong to—"

"No, she does not belong to you," Theodore replied, the whip of command in his voice. A blue flush darkened the tops of his cheekbones and the tips of his ears as he struggled to restrain every protective, possessive instinct. "If she had joined your pack, I would have heard of it."

Margot Goode was *not* under Viktor Hamilton's authority or protection. Theodore knew for certain that the responsibility for her protection belonged solely to *him.*

And I failed her.

He didn't need to glance at the burned husk of her home to feel the acid of shame that ate at his insides. It joined the elemental crush of his instincts to make a potent, bubbling fury.

But the recriminations had to wait until Margot was safe, and definitely until she was no longer holding onto the coyote shifter and looking at him with that battered, stricken look, like *he* was the one who would take care of her in her hour of need.

Taking in a deep breath through his nose, he said, "If you do not stand aside so that I can assess the situation and see to Healer Goode's welfare, Vik, I will be forced to use my claws." Theodore slowly canted his head to one side, assessing the man he once called a friend. "I think we both know how that will turn out."

Viktor's grin was all coyote — sharp-toothed and cunning. "You wanna start a war over a girl, Teddy?"

He would. In a heartbeat, he would.

He allowed himself a single look at Margot's pale face before he answered, with the utmost sincerity, "*That* is up to you, Vik."

Theodore could feel the commander of his guard a little ways behind him, as well as the shadows that were his elite unit hovering just out of sight, ready to defend him at a moment's notice.

Kazimier knew better than to interfere, though. If Theodore truly needed the back-up, Kaz and his guards would be by his side in a heartbeat, but there was no way Theodore couldn't subdue two coyote shifters on his own. He wouldn't even break a sweat.

"No, no, no." Margot elbowed her way out from behind Viktor. The shifter made to grab her, but one venomous look from those copper-colored eyes put him in his place. Not even an alpha wanted to piss off a gloriana.

And then Margot Goode, the bloody center of his universe, stepped forward.

Theodore's heart squeezed hard. His lungs expanded in a huge inhale, the scent of her skin burning a path through his chest, sizzling through every vein, every capillary, until it branded him from the inside out. Theodore's heart hammered against his nearly unbreakable ribs as sweat slicked down the length of his spine.

He could *feel* his body kicking into overdrive, making him into something new, something just for her.

My consort. Finally.

He imagined their meeting a thousand ways. In the six months since she snapped into focus in his mind, Theodore became even more obsessed with their meeting than he was the past twenty-five years. He planned it down to the minute and inhaled every scrap of information about her that existed so he could get the moment *exactly right.*

Nothing had gone according to plan, but the impact of it, the enormity of seeing her in the flesh, was as he expected: Margot Goode knocked his entire world sideways.

"No war. No fighting," she said, her prim voice only slightly roughened by her ordeal. The sound of it sent a rush of adrenaline through his system, sharpening every one of his senses to her and her alone. "I'm fine. Just— what exactly can I do for you, Sovereign?"

For a taut moment, all he could do was stare.

Margot was awfully small compared to him. All five feet and

three inches of her fell well below the elvish average of seven feet. Her bones were fine; her features delicate, breakable, *almost* fey. Her hair, full of plaster dust and half-fallen out of a twist, was a red that leaned closer to gold.

Her eyes were a deep copper, almost red. Despite the head wound, they were clear, focused, guarded in ways that made him want to stroke the tension out of her spine with slow, gentle touches.

Theodore watched, rapt, as blood trickled down the elegant column of her throat, marking the place where he would — Glory willing — use his fangs to subdue her, gentle her, make her his.

The part of him that was not in any way civilized let loose a howl of rage as fresh blood dribbled down her throat to stain the sweetheart neckline of her ruined dress, breaking the sensual spell.

His own blood rushing hot and furious in his ears, Theodore shoved his hands into the pockets of his slacks before she could see the way his claws flexed hard. The instinct to hide anything that might make her fear him could not be ignored.

Put her at ease, his rushing blood told him. *Gentle her.*

Instinct both muddied his thoughts and made them more clear. The demands of his blood whipped across his psyche with ruthless confidence, honing his focus to a claw's edge.

Make her see you'll take care of her, instinct pressed, a force of will and a want so furious it felt barely under his control. *When she's well, let her use her claws on you, then pin her down and lock your jaw on her throat and—*

Theodore cleared his throat. *Not yet.* "A healer was attacked in my city," he finally answered her, his voice a touch rougher than normal. "The granddaughter of Sophie Goode, no less. Of course I came to investigate."

Margot stood very still, only stray strands of her hair moving in the damp breeze. "I... didn't realize anyone paid attention to who I was."

He gave her a quizzical look. "Didn't you wonder why you got approval to be in the Protectorate so quickly? Your grandmother made it very clear that the Collective would view your residency at the Healing House as a sort of... diplomatic exchange." He fought a grimace. "A trust exercise, if you will."

"Oh." Margot swallowed hard. "Have I been under surveillance this whole time?"

He didn't bother to lie. "Yes. Your safety has been a top priority for Patrol since your arrival."

Theodore knew he should blink. Look away. Let her think, for just a moment, that he was not utterly consumed by the sight and smell and presence of her, but he couldn't. He could barely stop himself from closing the distance between them when he finished, "This is going to be investigated to the fullest extent of my power, Healer Goode. Whoever or whatever did this will not get away with it."

Attacking a healer was breathtaking in its audacity; an act of unrivaled stupidity. Considering the rarity of healers and the fact that they were under the direct protection of whoever controlled the territory, it also carried the weight of a slight against *three separate gods*.

Theodore could only imagine the kind of desperation that went into committing such crime. What could possibly compel someone to attack a *healer*, of all beings?

Even if his elite guard didn't already confirm the scent of explosives from the back of the Healing House, Theodore knew it was no accident. It couldn't be. Not when Margot Goode was the granddaughter of the most powerful witch in the United Territories and Allies, and not when she had been connected to him from her very first breath.

Margot was far, far too important to be the focus of simple bad luck. Someone targeted her.

If that someone had a motive related to politics, they would be dealt with in the traditional elvish fashion — with tooth and claw. Attacking a healer in his territory was a high profile hit to his image, a challenge to his ability to keep his territory safe.

Attacking a *Goode* was an even ballsier move, since her very presence in the Protectorate acted as an expression of tentative trust between the Protectorate and the Coven Collective. Damaging that relationship could have dire political consequences.

But if that motive turned out to be about her very personal, if currently unacknowledged, connection to *him,* then Theodore had much more to contemplate than a clear challenge to his power.

Margot raised a hand to her bleeding ear as she replied, “We don’t know it was an attack, though, do we? It could just be an accident. There’s no reason for anyone to target me.”

The back of Theodore’s neck tingled with unmistakable warning. His stomach sank. *She’s lying.*

Theodore took careful note of the distance between them. Seven or eight feet, he guessed, stood between him and the woman he’d thought of every day since he woke from a dead sleep in a cold sweat twenty-five years ago.

It would be the easiest thing in the world to close that distance, scoop her up, and throw her in the m-enhanced town car that waited by the curb inside the now fully cordoned off block. It would be so easy to whisk her off to safety, social niceties be damned, where he could force her to tell him exactly why someone might want to harm her.

He couldn’t do that, though; not without making her an even bigger target. It was the same reason she wasn’t immediately swarmed by her guards after the bomb went off. As soon as it was determined she wasn’t mortally wounded, they backed off, following strict orders to be wary of drawing unwanted attention to their charge.

Until their bond was secure, and until Theodore sniffed out the traitor in their midst, that kind of attention could — *would* prove deadly.

So he couldn’t do what he wanted to, which was mainly throw her over his shoulder and hide her away in his suite until the world was a safer place for her. He couldn’t even *reassure* her, not in front of so many witnesses, even though it went against every instinct now thrumming in time with his pulse.

"Why haven't you healed yourself yet?" he found himself snapping. His temper couldn't be checked when warring impulses were shredding his composure. "You're bleeding."

Those copper eyes narrowed. "I've been healing myself for the past several minutes, Sovereign. I can multitask."

Her tone was flawlessly polite, measured in a soothing, very *healer* cadence, but the small flash of temper in her eyes was unmistakable.

The elf in him loved the bite of her verbal claws, the whisper of challenge she presented, but the man wanted to wrap her in blankets and shove her into a padded room as quickly as possible. He had no patience for watching her suffer.

He opened his mouth to direct her towards his waiting vehicle, but Viktor's drawl cut him off.

"I know you're a top-notch healer, but you took a real hit." A hand, tanned to a deep gold, skimmed an undamaged swath of her cheek. "You need to go to a med center, sunshine? We've got one not too far from here. You can come stay with me—"

"No, thank you." Margot took a single step back, her expression warming even as she rejected his offer. "I'll find accommodation elsewhere. I'm sure the Collective will have somewhere I can stay the night and recuperate. I'll be fully healed by morning."

Without meaning to, both Theodore and Viktor donned identical looks of thunderous disapproval. When Viktor opened his mouth to argue, though, Theodore decided he had given the coyote shifter too much leeway.

"Vik, go back to your territory. Healer Goode is none of your concern."

They locked eyes, Viktor's coyote amber connecting with Theodore's midnight blue in the sickly glow of headlights and street lamps.

Theodore made sure Viktor could see the seriousness in his expression, the sheer implacability he felt toward the subject at hand. In this, he was not only the sovereign of the Protectorate, but an elf whose consort bled in front of his very eyes. It made every vicious instinct surge to the fore, shredding the thin veneer of icy sophistication all elves wore, the pretense that they were not apex predators but rational, cool-headed people, until he stood on the precipice of real violence.

It was a jealously guarded secret that elves were a singularly savage race. They were more vicious, more territorial, more possessive than any other — and when it came down to it, not even the carefully curated image of chilly reserve would stop an elf from tearing out the throat of one who dared threaten what belonged to them.

It was this brutality, perhaps, that finally convinced Viktor to back off. Not because he feared Theodore, not even close, but because the animal in him recognized the beast in Theodore. That beast wouldn't be satisfied until the threat was shredded beneath his claws, something the coyote alpha understood and approved of.

Still, the aggravating man turned to give Margot a searching look, giving his back to Theodore in a deliberate display of dismissal. "You want me to stay, sunshine?"

Sunshine. The pet name made Theodore roll his eyes. They hadn't spoken properly in five years, but Viktor was the same incorrigible flirt he ever was.

Reaching back to sweep her hair into a tight coil, Margot gave Viktor a deadpan look. "I can take care of myself, Viktor." Her hair secured by some unseen means, Margot reached out to press a single fingertip to the coyote shifter's tanned cheek. Her voice was softer, almost yearning, when she added, "Thank you, though."

Viktor nodded once before his sombre look slid into something more playful. "I'll come check on you. Maybe you'll need me to change your bandages, or help you into a bath."

Theodore was relieved when Margot only huffed and paced away to peer grim-faced up at the smoking shell of the Healing

House. As she drifted down the quiet block, Viktor turned back to Theodore.

Serious now, his voice was a rumbling growl when he said, "You'll catch who did this, Teddy —*fast,* or we'll take over."

"Why do you care?"

Raging instincts aside, Theodore knew that Viktor didn't truly have any designs on Margot. The only person Viktor ever truly wanted was, at least in his mind, out of his reach.

His flirting was and had always been incorrigible, his friendship just as much. But he rarely showed any sort of protective instinct outside of his pack, and despite his earlier claim, Margot definitely wasn't that.

Viktor stepped closer to Theodore than most sentient and lower beings would have dared. Only the years of friendship between them allowed that sort of proximity.

"It may not mean anything to you, but she's hiding something awfully soft under that tough Goode shell," he explained, amber eyes studying Margot's profile as she drifted over to speak to one of the fire squad. "That one's got a huge heart. She's been working in the Underground, treating people for free almost every spare minute she has. But she's private. Wouldn't ask for help if she was trapped under a ten-ton boulder." He *tsked.* "Healers. All the same."

Theodore knew that his healer made frequent trips to Underground hotspots and back alleys most wouldn't venture into, but his guard had never been sure exactly what she was doing there. Their job was to keep her safe, not spy on her.

Gaze sharpening on the man who was once his closest friend, he asked, "How do you know?"

Those keen, coyote eyes held his. "She didn't tell me, if that's what you're bristling about. She likes me, but we haven't known each other long enough to swap secrets." Viktor shook his head, sandy hair falling carelessly around a handsome face. "But I know people, and even the Underground talks. I know she's been using the Market as a clinic. The weres have seen her more than a few times. In fact, they like her enough to have put a protection order out, though I don't think she knows it."

Everyone liked healers, but it said something about Margot that it was the most notoriously violent of the factions within the Protectorate — the coyotes, the weres, *himself* — who were actively looking out for her.

Viktor's warning was clear: If Theodore didn't find whomever threatened her, not only would he have the Coven Collective howling for his blood, but half of San Francisco's most vicious power players.

It was a good thing Theodore didn't scare easily.

Tearing his eyes away from the diminutive figure of his consort, Theodore shared a hard look with Viktor. "She's coming back to the Tower with me. No one will get another chance to hurt her."

A keen intelligence was Viktor's greatest, and most underestimated, weapon. "You going to lock her up, Teddy?"

Theodore shook his head. "No, Vik." He paused, gaze lingering on the woman who was the center of his universe, before he quietly admitted, "She's my consort. I'd die before I hurt her."

Viktor was silent for a beat. His voice was tight when he replied, "You gonna..."

"Yes."

The shifter let out a harsh exhale. "Publicly?"

Theodore straightened his shoulders. "Yes."

"I'll be damned. Good luck, Teddy." Viktor turned to walk away, his second prowling behind him, but stopped after just a few steps. He didn't turn to face Theodore when he asked, "Is... is Cam doing well?"

Theodore crossed his arms and tried to squash the flare of old, protective anger that came with the mention of his cousin's name. "Why don't you see for yourself? She's in town for the Summit."

He watched Viktor's shoulders bunch, every muscle in the shifter's body tightening until he nearly vibrated with tension.

His voice was harsh when he whispered, "You know I can't do that."

"Right." Theodore felt a familiar bubble of disgust burst in his gut. "Because you're a coward."

Viktor didn't take the bait. He didn't whirl around to snarl. They were both men now, both responsible for too many lives to snap and claw at one another as they used to. But Theodore knew he *wanted* to.

"Don't you fucking do that," Viktor hissed.

Theodore shook his head, disappointed in the man he once saw as a brother and furious on his cousin's behalf. "The world is about to change, Vik. Maybe think about that before you let fear steal more from you than it already has."

Viktor nodded, a single jerky movement of his head, before gesturing for his second to follow him back to their vehicle. Neither commented on the eerie silence of the street now lined by stiff-backed shadows in sleek uniforms.

Theodore turned back to the house, now only a smoking ruin. His eyes found Margot immediately.

She looked terribly small as she stood on the sidewalk, her arms wrapped around her middle and her face tilted up to stare at the shattered windows and curling tails of smoke rising from the Healing House.

As the fire squad began their final sweep over the property to ensure that none of the blaze had been left to smolder unchecked, Theodore could not escape the impression that Margot Goode seemed very alone.

His heart beating fast, he thought, *No, she's not alone.*

He was closing the space between them before he'd even thought it through, his long legs eating up the sidewalk until he stood by her side. In an instant, the slump of her shoulders vanished; replaced by a rigid chill that kept her spine straight, her chin up.

She turned and took one precise step back. "Thank you for

coming, Sovereign. I'll be sure to convey your concern to my grandmother when I get the chance. I—"

"You can call her and tell her that you are now formally under my protection from the comfort of the Tower," he smoothly interjected, his temper strung taut by her proximity, her injuries, and the wild suggestion that he was *ever* going to let her out of his sight again.

Sweeping an arm towards the car Kaz procured after their hasty transport from the emergency m-gate in his office, he added, "You will be guarded and taken care of there. You will rest so your injuries can heal properly. Everything you need will be provided for you."

He expected her to hesitate, but Margot didn't even *look* in the direction of the car. Her eyes, red-brown like new pennies, fixed on his face with the sort of politely mulish look only medical professionals could master.

"I appreciate the offer, *sir,* but I must decline. I'd prefer to stay with my kin."

Her defiance should have made him bristle. He was at the top of the hierarchy — people simply *did not* say no to him.

When the Families gathered for the Summit, they might collectively vote against him, but one on one? They might simper, they might lie, they might find other ways to get what they wanted, but they didn't just *refuse* him. It would have been taken as a direct challenge, and that challenge would be met with the instinctive bloodlust that sang in his blood.

But this was *Margot.* Instead of bloodlust, he felt his claws sink backwards into his fingertips, retracting beneath the leather and silver of his gloves. Instead of his muscles clenching with the promise of violence, they relaxed. Even the frantic beating of his heart began to slow.

It *was* a challenge, but the sort that his body knew instinctively would not be won with tooth and claw.

Keeping his voice low, soothing, he took a small step closer and said, "I cannot guarantee your safety with your kin. I can guarantee it in my Tower."

Something rippled across her expression, a flash of naked fear, before she shook her head. "No."

"No?" Glory save him, but he wanted to pet her and bite her in equal measure. "No... what?"

"No, you can't guarantee that."

That made his spine lock. "You don't think I am capable of protecting you?" Theodore was painfully aware of the smoldering building to his right, just as he was aware of the blood drying in iron-rich tracks on her delicate skin. "I wasn't here for this," he ground out, "but I *will not* let anything harm you again, Healer Goode."

Those penny eyes searched his face. He watched, fascinated, as her round pupils blew up to eclipse all but the finest ring of copper iris.

"I am not important enough to warrant that sort of attention," she replied, the slightest edge of panic breaking through her calm. "If anything, that may put me *more* at risk." She swallowed. "Besides, you're the sovereign. You have better things to do than keeping an eye on one insignificant witch. I'm not one of your people. The responsibility for my safety doesn't belong to you."

He choked back his incredulous scoff and carefully leaned down, bringing them nearly nose to nose. She didn't move. Didn't blink. Didn't even *breathe.*

"Darling witch," he murmured, daring to trace a wicked silver clawtip down the straight line of her pert nose, "*I* decide what is important and what is not; what belongs to me and what does not. As of this moment, your welfare, your happiness, your safety, your comfort — *all* of it belongs to me. Are we clear?"

Her lips, lush and rosebud-shaped, parted as if to speak; intent even now, with his claws so close to her throat, to argue. The temptation to silence her with a swift nip of his fangs was overwhelming, but Theodore settled for the lesser pleasure of pressing the tip of his silver claw against the cushion of her lower lip.

Mercy, he thought. But there was no mercy in Margot's excruciating softness.

Infusing his voice with as much authority as he could muster, he told her, "No. I am not changing my mind. So long as you are in the Protectorate, you agreed to live by my laws, under my protection. It's not my problem if you did not expect me to handle those things personally."

He pressed his claw more firmly against the delicate skin of her lip, watching with rapt attention as her mouth opened ever-so-slightly. Sucking in a breath brought her scent into his lungs — luscious, with the bite of green things and something deeper, familiar. It was dampened by what he recognized as over-the-counter scent blockers and the competing smells of fire retardant foam and ash, but he would recognize the scent of her anywhere.

"If it disturbs you so much, you can leave my territory immediately," he bluffed. "Go back to the Collective right now and never come back. I'll arrange for an m-gate for you. You could be back in your grandmother's cold embrace by midnight."

It was a dare he had no intention of letting her take, of course. If she left the Protectorate, he wouldn't have even the slimmest chance to win her back to his side. Worse, she would be outside the reach of his protection.

But he wanted to see what she would do. He knew so little about the woman who was his heart, the reason he'd done everything; built what he had, taken the seat of power so young. Was she the type of woman who would fall back, regroup, gather her allies? Or was she the sort who stood her ground, fought back?

He had his answer when an arc of electricity jumped from the rosy flesh of her lip to the silver tip of his claw. He jerked his finger back reflexively, nerves smarting, and bared his upper and lower fangs with a hiss of warning.

"I'm not leaving San Francisco," she answered, annoyingly unaffected by his flash of fang.

"Watch it, darling," he warned, flexing his fingers. "That little shock could be considered an act of aggression. I usually demand blood for that sort of thing."

She didn't blink. "Don't use your claws on me if you don't want me to use mine on you."

Glory save me.

It didn't matter that she was covered in dust and blood. He was suddenly painfully hard.

Showing her his fangs one last time, he turned to curl his fingers around the nape of her neck, enclosing her in the warmth of his leather-covered palm. "In the car, Healer Goode," he growled, steering her towards the sleek black vehicle half hidden beneath the shadow of a massive eucalyptus, "before I bite you."

She stiffened. "The sovereign would never—"

"Oh, the sovereign would." He breathed deep. "Don't tempt me, darling."

She was tense under his hand, but didn't fight him as he guided her around the fire engine and towards the car. Kaz leaned with deceptive ease against the hood, his hulking form nearly blending into the shadows.

He felt it when Margot caught sight of Kaz. A little jolt ran through her, the delicate muscle and bone under his palm stiffening with surprise. Giving her nape a gentle, reassuring squeeze, he nodded to the man whose size made even Theodore look average.

"Healer Goode, this is Kazimier Roine." He watched Kaz straighten and step away from the car, into the pale orange pool of light from the street lamp. "Kaz, this is Healer Goode. We're taking her home."

Kaz was the same height as Theodore, but broader, every muscle and tendon honed to deadly perfection. He had a beautiful, aristocratic face at odds with his usual attire of jeans and t-shirts and a beaten leather jacket, and skin of strikingly luminous green. His hair, raven black, was long and pulled back into a loose braid.

Unlike Theodore, he didn't bother with gloves to hide his

natural claws. Those claws flexed against the leather of his jacket's sleeves as he uncrossed his arms.

Theodore wondered what Margot saw in Kaz that made her first tense, then, hardly a second after he stepped into the light, relax. Most people didn't have that sort of reaction to orcs, half-blooded or not.

In a voice that held an irritating amount of relief, she said, "It's a pleasure to meet you, Kaz."

"Likewise, Healer Goode."

She peered up at him. "Are you from the Orclind?"

Kaz tilted his head in a small nod. "My mother lived in Boise, but her family followed the migration around the borders."

Margot's smile was small and a little sad. "The Goodeland is on the border. I grew up around a lot of orc families."

Kaz offered her a slow blink — his version of a smile. "You might have met my kin, then."

"Maybe."

Theodore scowled at his brother, who only arched one heavy black eyebrow in response. Gritting his teeth against the need to draw her attention back into him, he steered her towards the passenger door.

Opening it for her, he reluctantly released her nape to usher her in. When Margot's scratched legs swung inside, he checked to make sure her coat and dress wouldn't be caught before he gently closed the door.

Theodore turned to eye the man currently hiding his amusement under his usual grim expression. "How come *you* got a warmer greeting than *I* did?"

Kaz didn't miss a beat. "Because I'm the handsome brother, remember?"

Theodore showed his fangs. "Fuck off."

"Do I get to take your pretty witch with me?"

Only years of rigid self-discipline and a lifetime of dealing with Kaz's dry humor stopped Theodore from shoving his brother into the side of the car. Walking around the trunk to grasp the handle of the other passenger door, he shot his brother a narrow-eyed glare. "Drive, Kaz, before I decide I don't need two brothers anymore."

"You could try, but then Sam would be the handsome brother."

Seeing as he had a beautiful consort waiting for him in the backseat, about to be tucked into the protective cocoon of his Tower, he didn't bother with a reply. Yes, Kaz and Sam were the pretty ones, but Theodore had Margot.

He didn't need anything more.

Chapter Three

As Theodore slid his big body into the backseat with her, Margot forced herself to ignore the ensuing panic that threatened to bubble over into hysteria. She'd managed to go her whole life without ever being in the same room with an elf — a necessary, life-saving precaution — and now she was wedged against the door of a car, sharing the same air, the same *seat,* as the sovereign himself, headed toward his fortress.

Where I'll be surrounded by elves twenty-four/seven.

Her hands were shaking so violently that she had to shove them into the pockets of her ruined coat as she closed her eyes, trying to find the focus to speed up the instinctive healing already taking place in her cracked skull.

Closing her eyes didn't mean she wasn't hyper-aware of both the elf seated to her right, his thigh a bare six inches from her own, or the orc currently guiding the m-enhanced car along the meticulously maintained streets. She wasn't lying when she told Theodore she could multi-task.

Margot was perfectly capable of freaking out and sealing cracked bone at the same time.

The orc, Kaz, didn't scare her nearly as much as Theodore, though. She was used to orcs. The Coven, and most of the Coven

Collective's land on the West Coast, butted up against the Orclind. Growing up, she'd spent many a lazy summer afternoon cavorting with orc children.

But when puberty hit, her playmates gradually disappeared. Their parents would cast her uneasy looks, and after one of the boys she shared a clumsy kiss or two with asked his mother why Margot "smelled that way", they steered clear of her altogether.

That was when her grandmother handed her that first bottle of Noscent, and the isolation of the Goodeland changed from a childhood paradise to walls that edged closer, loomed larger, every day.

The reminder of that bitter memory forced Margot to open her eyes. Cold sweat dampened the skin of her palms. Had the sharp scent of adrenaline and blood already washed away her layers of protection?

Her eyes darted around the dim cabin of the car, trying not to linger on the sharp profile of the elf as he looked out of his window. Neon light and the flash of headlights illuminated hard, angular features and curling lashes.

She was also painfully aware of Theodore's scent, so much so that she barely noticed Kaz's.

It was spicy, like cinnamon crossed with bright cedar, with a rich undertone that reminded her of drowsy summer nights by the bonfire. It settled in her lungs and made a home there. It was impossible to ignore and luxurious; a slow caress to her senses.

Margot was painfully aware of how quickly scent could permeate even a big room full of people. In the confined space of the car, she didn't stand a chance.

Panic fizzed across every nerve.

Fresh air would help. Daring to pull one unsteady hand from her pocket, Margot reached for the switch to lower her window.

Her finger barely touched the switch when smooth leather, warm and inherently dangerous, slid over the back of her neck. The faintest prick of metal claws kissed the vulnerable skin of her pounding pulse.

"You shouldn't roll the window down. It's cold," Theodore rumbled, like it was *normal* for him to stroke the pad of his thumb up and down the curve of her throat.

The panic flared brighter, hotter, and yet the clasp of his hand didn't make her want to thrash, to scramble away. It should have awoken every survival instinct she had.

Instead, the muscles of her neck and shoulders loosened under the steady heat and pressure of his kneading fingers and heavy palm.

Touch wasn't rare in her line of work, not when she needed skin contact to heal, but *affectionate,* intimate touch... No, she rarely got that.

Only her covenmates were ever allowed that close. Other intimacies, the ones she craved in the deepest, loneliest parts of her being, were completely impossible. The trust it would take to let a partner that close for that long was the kind she could only give to her bondmate.

Even at her loneliest, her most touch-starved, Margot knew the risk of taking that chance with anyone else was simply too high.

It was that touch-starved, screaming part of her that allowed Margot to melt into Theodore Solbourne's confident hold for a single, breathless moment. The feeling of warmth, the heaviness of his palm and the slow strokes of his thumb, momentarily soothed an ache that never really went away.

"I need fresh air," she lied, turning her head to try and break his hold.

Theodore's hand slid away from her nape, but it didn't leave her. Instead, it settled on the curve of her shoulder as he replied, "Fine. Kaz?"

There was a flash of movement as Kaz fiddled with the dials on the dash, and then the hum of air through the vents filled the luxurious interior of the car. A moment later, warmth blew gently against her bruised skin as her window lowered a third of the way, letting in cool, wet air.

The air helped clear a little bit of the shock that stubbornly hung on, fogging up her normally razor-sharp mind.

Every cell in her body hyper-aware of Theodore's hand on her shoulder, Margot forced herself to breathe deeply through her mouth before asking, "Shouldn't I have stayed to talk to Patrol? I didn't give anyone a statement."

"No need," Theodore answered. His voice was a living thing that filled up the limited space between them, wrapping itself around her until all of her focus, every one of her senses, belonged to him. "You can give me your statement."

Margot swallowed the hard lump of panic clogging her throat. She had no idea what the protocol for her behavior was supposed to be. Usually she understood the best way to navigate a social situation to keep herself as unnoticed as possible, but there was no way to escape the sovereign's notice now. How could she, when he seemed incapable of keeping his hands to himself?

But she didn't dare shrug it off, and not only because the desperate, tactile creature in her cried out for the steady touch of another. What if he took it as a sign of defiance? Theodore didn't truly seem to mind her lapse in judgment earlier, but how would he react if she kept pushing him? Would he chalk it up to a witch's reputation for cattiness, or would he suspect something deeper, more dangerous?

The risk of exposure and the forbidden yearning for contact kept her still under his claws.

Secretly, below even the yearning for simple touch, there was a heady thrill, too. A dormant part of her stretched out in languid pleasure at the feeling of his claws pressing against her delicate skin. Heat, low and unacknowledged, simmered in her belly.

Margot held herself rigid as she explained, "I don't have much to say. I came home and didn't sense anyone in the house. The explosion caught me just as I was stepping through the threshold."

Theodore's face was half in shadow. Only a streak of orange light sliced across his features, highlighting a lush mouth and the faintest hint of dark stubble on his jaw. Those deadly claws pressed just a bit harder into her skin, sending a lick of flame down her spine. "Where were you before the explosion?"

On any other night that might have been a tricky question to answer. She usually spent her evenings and days off in the poorer, shadowed parts of the city, using her skills for some *real* good. It wasn't illegal to serve the Underground, of course, but she wasn't exactly supposed to use the Healing House's resources on people outside of her neighborhood jurisdiction, either.

Grateful that she wouldn't have to admit to pilfering medical supplies to the sovereign's face, Margot answered, "I was invited to dinner with the Merced pack. After I finished my shift—" during which she healed only a *single* sprained ankle, a profound waste of abilities that could repair hearts, excise tumors, cure *cancer* "—I drove to the lake and stayed there until eight-thirty."

What she could see of Theodore's face showed not a hint of surprise. But why would it, when he already admitted to having her under surveillance?

"Do you spend a lot of time with the coyotes?"

She shrugged. "They prefer healing to going to the medical center, so I've seen quite a bit of them recently, but I'd never been in their territory before tonight."

No, they usually came to her in small packs of two or three. And after she made Viktor's acquaintance, he was almost always one of them, but Margot recalled the tension between the two men and tactfully refrained from mentioning that.

Theodore nodded. "What about your wards?"

"What wards?"

"The ones protecting the Healing House." His thumb drew lazy, distracting circles. "Wouldn't you have been notified that a stranger had crossed your threshold?"

She made to shake her head, but stopped quickly when the movement made her temples pound. Her skull was almost totally healed by now, but the bruising would take a more natural course in order to conserve her energy.

Blinking hard to correct her swimming vision, she answered, "Sovereign, there are never any wards placed on Healing Houses. They're open to everyone."

Her bedroom, on the other hand, was a different story. Her magic was too crude, too wild, for most complex sigilwork, but her grandmother had been ruthless in her training for self-defense. The warding on her personal space was air-tight and nearly impenetrable.

Unfortunately, whatever happened to the Healing House probably didn't take place in her bedroom.

There was a curious note of strain in the sovereign's voice when he asked, "So you sleep in a house with unlocked doors *and* no wards?"

A deep rumbling came from the driver's seat.

Margot flicked a glance at Kaz, whose huge, clawed hands were white-knuckled on the steering wheel. It occurred to her, briefly, that she had never heard of an elf employing an orc. They were born adversaries. Even their creation myths put them at odds.

But she didn't have the luxury of ignoring Theodore's question for more than a second, so she carefully put aside her curiosity about their relationship for later. "It's traditional," she insisted, trying not to react defensively to his incredulous expression. "Everyone is welcome in a Healing House. Locks and wards would imply otherwise. Besides, it's not like it's ever really been a *problem*. I've always felt..."

She caught herself before she could say the word *safe*. Margot hadn't felt truly safe since the day her grandmother handed her that bottle of Noscent.

Clearing her throat, she finished, "I've always felt secure in the Healing House."

Margot watched, fascinated, as Theodore closed his eyes and took a deep breath. When he opened them again, it was with a grimace that put both his upper and lower fangs on terrifying display.

"Right," he flatly replied. "That changes now. I will be speaking to the Healer's Guild in the morning and instructing them that every Healing House in my territory should have wards put up immediately."

Margot reared back with surprise. Without missing a beat, Theodore's hand followed her retreat. A deep frown cut the handsome lines of the sovereign's face as a pair of headlights flashed through his window, illuminating expanded vertical pupils of his dark, almost black eyes.

Margot gawked at him. "You can't do that. The Healing Houses are sacred. Glory's Temple would never allow—"

"If they wish to stay in the Protectorate, they will damn well do as I say." He didn't blink. Theodore's stare remained locked on hers as he raised his hand from her shoulder to press the tip of a claw against her battered cheek. He was so gentle that she barely felt it, but she *knew* it was there, every nerve attuned to his nearness.

More of that curious heat slid down her spine to pool low in her stomach, as if the very *threat* of him was enough to make her burn.

Continuing in a low, hard voice, he said, "You were nearly killed tonight. If anything had gone differently, you would have died in that house. The threat against a healer is bad enough, but the insult to *me* is utterly unacceptable. If I can't protect the healers in my territory, how can I be expected to protect *anyone?*"

The fine hair on the back of her neck prickled. Margot hadn't considered the wider implications of the explosion, but he was right.

Theodore had only been the sovereign for eight months, after all. His power was far from settled.

Delilah Solbourne's abdication had been shockingly smooth, considering how young her little brother was and the rumors of the Families opposition to his ascension. Even Margot held her breath for the first few weeks after the abdication. It felt like the whole world waited for a challenge, for blood to spill across the video feeds.

It didn't occur to her that the explosion, if it *was* a bomb, might have been a targeted attack intended to shake the public's confidence in the sovereign. It made a sick kind of sense. If healers were supposed to be sacred, their spaces open to all, Theodore's inability to keep them safe would be a damning indication of his lack of control over his territory.

The fact that the healer in question was a Goode, even one intentionally kept out of the public eye, could escalate things even further.

In the UTA, perception of power was everything. If Theodore couldn't prove to the world that he could hold his territory, someone else would.

Margot paled. "But we don't know if it was a bomb, do we? This whole thing could just be one big coincidence."

"Our squad picked up the trace scents of both accelerant and explosives."

Kaz's voice was a smooth glide against her senses, low and smoky. Orcs were renowned for their lovely voices, and Margot might have sighed with homesickness at the sound of such familiar richness if he hadn't thrown cold water all over her paper-thin hopes.

Theodore's eyes, the slitted pupils expanded to swallow nearly all of his dark irises, never wavered from her face. "This was done deliberately. Whether it was intended as a blow to my power or not is irrelevant. The outcome is the same."

Margot swallowed around the lump in her throat. "And what will that be?"

"I'm going to hunt down the perpetrators until I have them under my claws." The flash of headlights as another car passed illuminated the savage set of his handsome features. Steadily, with the conviction of a man unused to being told *no,* he continued, "And I am not letting you out of my sight."

~

In theory, the Protectorate was a federation comprised of every prominent elvish family, each with their own sovereign territory and seat of power.

The elves controlled the west coast as well as Arizona and most of New Mexico. Working as a unit, the elves were a merciless, efficient machine — they invested heavily in finance and technology, meticulously maintained infrastructure, and kept their secrets locked up tight amongst themselves. What information about elvish private lives and anatomy existed was unreliable at best, leaving them plenty of room to craft an image that was as ruthless as it was outlandish.

In practice, of course, everyone knew that the Solbournes were at the top of the precipitous food chain. The Solbournes held the title of Sovereign for the past three generations and ran San Francisco from their fortified island just off of the coast, where the best and brightest technological and magical advancements were made. Rumor had it that they kept a stranglehold on power by maintaining control over the treasury and rarely seen Protectorate military.

No one outside of the elvish hierarchy could prove it, though. For all that the elves took good care of their citizens by granting them guaranteed basic income, housing, and food, the elves never, *ever* broke rank.

Which was why it was extraordinary in the extreme that Margot Goode, a witch, was about to step foot in Solbourne Tower.

A single road connected Treasure Island to the rest of the world. From her position in the backseat of the town car, Margot peered out the window as they passed through the heavily fortified gate that blocked that connection from unwanted visitors. She held her breath as the tires glided smoothly over the last feet of the bridge and then onto the island itself.

Her wide-eyed gaze held fast to the looming skyscraper she had only ever seen cutting a harsh shape against the horizon.

The Tower and the elvish-made island it sat on was iconic — more iconic than the Golden Gate. More than the UTA Congress. More than the brutal, haunting structure of the Dragon Roost on Drummond Island.

It stood as a monument to the entirety of elvish power, a building both brutal and beautiful that reminded all who saw it that elves were the masters of their domain.

Her eyes traced the familiar black stone of the skyscraper, the carved gold lines, illuminated by hidden lights, that ran like sigils through the darkness; the shape that hearkened back to the stone monoliths humans once carved for the elvish Sovereigns of old.

There were so many more of them then, she mused, chilled to her core, *back when we bowed and scraped and hoped we wouldn't end up on their feast tables.*

Margot turned her head to glance back toward the jagged line of San Francisco's twinkling skyline, now barred to her by a swath of blue-green water that was both ice-cold and filled with predators — only some of which she could name off-hand.

Even if she could swim that far, and even if the cold or the predators didn't get her, Margot knew that the encroaching fog, thick as brushed wool, would obscure and confuse until she simply lost the ability to keep her head above water.

Trapped, her mind helpfully supplied her. *You're trapped.*

She was without the security of her Coven, her protective layer of scent blockers wearing off by the minute, and about to enter an elvish stronghold from which there would be no escape.

Staring up at the rapidly approaching monolith, Margot was curiously calm despite the clear knowledge that she would probably not make it out of the Tower alive.

I'm dead anyway, she thought. *At least now I'll get to satisfy some of my curiosity before I go.*

What were elves *really* like? What did their homes look like? How did they interact with their family, when foreign eyes weren't watching? Never before could she have risked trying to answer any of those burning questions, but *now*...

Theodore's hand closed over the back of her neck as Kaz steered the car toward what appeared to be the entrance to an underground garage. They stopped momentarily at the gate that blocked the entrance, but the guards manning the station took one look into Kaz's open window and ushered them in.

As Kaz navigated a shockingly ordinary parking garage full of shiny vehicles, some more obviously m-enhanced than others, Theodore held her rigid attention with a single, languorous stroke of his clawed thumb down the side of her throat. The touch sent a sizzling awareness across every nerve, and Margot came to the conclusion that she had to stop him from making any more contact with her before she did something unforgivably stupid.

Stiffly turning her head to catch his eye, she said, "Sir, while I appreciate your concern for my wellbeing, I'm going to have to politely request that you stop touching me."

His fingers flexed. "Why? You seemed perfectly content with Viktor's paws all over you."

Margot didn't rise to the bait. "He's a friend. You are not. I am not in the habit of letting strangers put their claws on my neck." No matter how much they secretly thrilled her.

Whatever she was expecting, it was not for Theodore Solbourne to snort with laughter. Immediately, the gloved hand disappeared, leaving the back of her neck exposed to the cold air filtering in from the lowered window.

Dryly, he noted, "Well, it's good to hear you have *some* sense of self-preservation at least."

Kaz pulled the car to a smooth stop in a parking space and killed the engine. Without a word, he slid out of the driver's seat and closed his door, leaving Margot and Theodore in the quiet darkness of the cooling vehicle.

Warmth glowed in her stomach, foreign and unsettling, as she listened to the soft rustle of Theodore's clothing, smelled the luxurious scent of his skin, felt his presence in the soft darkness of the car.

Adrenaline spiking for reasons she couldn't honestly attribute to fear, Margot reached for the door handle with trembling fingers — only to freeze when she felt warm breath on her cheek.

She didn't dare turn her head to see, but she could feel him move. Margot could hear the telltale rustle as he positioned one arm along the seat behind and the other across her front, not touching but close enough to feel the heat of him, so he could grasp the handle.

Margot was caged against the door, frozen, her instincts in a riot.

The buried part of her that keened for touch, that could never, ever be free, was a temperamental thing. It bucked against his obvious intimidation, his audacity in cornering her. It wanted to rake its claws over all that smooth blue skin and show him that he would have to do much more than invade her personal space to win her attention. It wanted to dance with him, to make him *work*—

Margot breathed deep, pulling more of him in without thinking. Her blood rushed, strangely fizzy, in her veins. The muscles of her abdomen tensed.

Something in her that had long remained still began, at last, to stir.

His whisper burned hot across the skin of her cheek. "Tell me, Healer Goode, do you want to use your claws on me?"

Her answer came hard and fast.

Yes, the secret part of her wanted to tear at him, to see what he would do if she snapped her teeth, but the other part of her that had always kept steely control over her baser impulses would not let the words out.

Staring at the headrest in front of her, she found herself answering his question with her own, "Why? Do you want me to?"

He was close, his big body surrounding hers but carefully,

intentionally keeping an inch of space between them. Still, she felt the air change when he tensed. His voice was unchanged, but she could swear there was the hint of a growl under the words when he said, "Only if you're prepared for the consequences."

"Beheading?"

A soft huff against her sensitive skin. He shifted infinitesimally closer. "No, I like your head where it is." There was a note of softness in his voice that was at once baffling and familiar, as if she'd heard it a thousand times. "I like your claws, too. I wouldn't mind it if you used them to challenge me." He paused, huffing an amused breath that was not quite a laugh. "Fair warning, darling: Elves love a challenge — but I *always* win."

A cold whip of fear cut through the spreading glow of warmth in her blood. Was *that* what the secret part of her wanted? Was it fucking *suicidal?*

Horrified by the disturbing flash of insight, Margot could only manage a mute nod to acknowledge the warning.

The door handle clicked as Theodore unlatched it, but he didn't open the door right away. Instead, he leaned forward to breathe against her ear, "Feel free to sharpen your claws on me any time, darling."

The bite of a fang nipping the lobe of her ear elicited a gasp. That terrifying heat, no longer a secret thing, blazed to life as Theodore pushed her door open and rumbled, "After you, Healer Goode."

Margot was hyper-aware of both Kaz and Theodore as they ushered her into a discreet elevator, her nerves strung too tight. She tried to take in everything, just in case she needed the information for an improbable escape, but there was only so much she could absorb. Focusing on the well-worn wrinkles in Kaz's leather jacket in front of her, Margot found the solid core of her focus and held it tight.

She was a healer. She could compartmentalize. There was no reason to think about Theodore's scent in her lungs, or his fangs sliding against her skin, or the bite of his claws. None.

Margot watched, reluctantly fascinated, as Theodore's lightning fast fingers typed a code into the keypad by the row of ordinary buttons. A retinal scanner came next, then a small green light blinked as the elevator began to rise.

When he turned back to her, Theodore explained, "We have extremely tight security on the private floors, Healer Goode. No one can get in or out without an escort keyed into the system — yourself included."

She eyed the keypad. "Will I get a code?" *Will you ever let me leave?*

Theodore didn't touch her, but she felt him step closer, his arm nearly brushing hers. "When I can be assured of your safety, yes." Ignoring her arch look, he added, "It's for your protection. Once you are on the family floor, you will be under some of the most extensive security in the UTA. You will be safer than you have ever been in your life. As soon as I have assembled a permanent guard for you, there's no reason you can't go in and out at will. But your safety comes first."

Safety, surrounded by elves? Maybe, if she were normal. Maybe, if her magic wasn't frying her from the inside out. Maybe, if elves didn't once suck the marrow from the bones of witches for an after-supper treat.

The elevator glided to a smooth, almost soundless stop.

The doors slid back, revealing a narrow, white-walled hallway. It was shockingly barren except for the tiny black lenses in each corner.

Cameras? But that wasn't much protection. If someone was determined to get to the armored door on the other side of the hall, what would cameras do to stop them?

They were already halfway down the hall before she bothered to glance up.

Red. Not evenly spread out, not uniform in color or consistency, but *red.*

Sigils, she thought, the breath sucked out of her lungs. Thousands and thousands of sigils — all written in blood.

The room carried no tell-tale scent, but there was no mistaking it. The heart of her, the part full of incomprehensible power, recognized the threat in those bloody, overlapping lines.

Most protection spells were done with one's own blood, but Margot knew that wasn't Solbourne blood painting the ceiling. It couldn't be.

Elves bled blue.

Her stomach turned. Whatever those sigils did, she was certain it was too gruesome to contemplate. No one made so many sacrifices, painted with that much gore, without packing as much menace into their spells as possible.

Just passing under it made her hair stand on end. An enemy would never make it through that hallway in one piece.

The hallway wasn't long, but by the time they made it to the imposing metal door on the other side, she felt like the bloody sigils had migrated from the ceiling to live beneath her skin.

When she glanced at Theodore, she found him watching her, his expression solemn. "My father," he explained, gesturing to the ceiling. "Paranoia is a remarkable thing."

Margot barely contained a shudder. *Yes, that makes sense.* She didn't know anything about Theodore Solbourne, but she didn't get the feeling that he was the blood-sacrificing kind.

Thaddeus Solbourne II and one of the key players in the Great War, however, very much was.

There was a pause, then the whirring of gears and dull thud of bolts disengaging from deep within the door. It was more of a vault than anything, but Margot didn't care. She just wanted to get out of that hallway. The buzz of cold, hungry magic in her ears was enough to make her look at even the most sinister decor as welcoming.

The door swung open on its own, revealing what she expected

the interior of the Tower to look like — rich woods, high ceilings, low, tasteful light to illuminate massive oil paintings. The air held the faint traces of scent, stale but numerous, all with that rich undertone that was purely elvish.

Still, *still,* she picked him out immediately.

Spicy cinnamon and cedar. A thin, golden thread for her to follow — if only she wanted to end up on the business end of his claws.

The fact that she didn't immediately recoil at the prospect made her question just how much damage the bomb might have done to her brain. Her steps stuttered. "Is this... Am I in your personal quarters?"

She watched in dismay as Kaz tilted his head toward Theodore, silently communicating something, before he stalked off, his huge body moving with terrifying grace.

Theodore glanced down at her. "Yes. I told you I was going to keep you safe, didn't I?" A coil of tension pulled taut in her stomach when he added, "You're stuck with me now."

"I can't stay in your personal quarters," she insisted. "That's not... That's *improper.*"

"Improper?" He bit his lip with a single, deadly fang. Releasing it slowly, he said, "There's nothing improper about it. However, if you'd like me to show you what *improper* really means, I'd be happy to."

Vividly recalling those fangs scraping against her ear, Margot flushed hot with embarrassment. "That's not what I meant."

"I know, but I'm not changing my mind. You're staying with me." Margot couldn't decide if it was her imagination, or if there was a real note of finality in that statement.

Theodore waved her forward with a flick of his claws. "Come along, darling."

When he started walking, her only option was to follow, and she had to hurry to match his long-legged stride. He guided her through a twisting series of corridors and past finely crafted doors, all of them shut, before they entered what felt like the center of the maze.

An octagonal foyer, marble-floored and covered by a domed ceiling of dark glass, stretched out before her. Pairs of double doors marked the edges of the octagon, and in the precise center, a mosaic of the finest craftsmanship took pride of place.

Crossing thistles, their thorny stems and leaves intertwining, their rich violet blooms standing proud against a rising sun — the Solbourne crest blazed against the white marble.

Theodore stepped up to the edge of the crest, the silver tips of his shoes barely nudging a thorny stem, and turned his head to offer her a sharp-toothed smile. His gaze was hot, intensely focused, when he breathed, "Welcome home, Margot."

Chapter Four

The moment Theodore closed the door to her guest suite, Margot sprang into action.

She wasn't the most gifted warder, and her concentration was torn to shreds, but there was no way she could sleep in a place not thoroughly warded against intruders — especially with Theodore Solbourne just down the hall. The Healing House came with generations of inlaid spellwork in its beams and insulation, each resident healer laying their own layer down, but like she explained to Theodore, none of it was for protection.

No, only her bedroom was impenetrable, and that was because Margot spent hours slaving over the spellwork to make it so.

There was no such protection on the small suite Theodore Solbourne provided her.

She could feel the hum of old elvish magic in the walls, but it wasn't *hers.* It raised the hair on the back of her neck in the same way the sigils in the hall did. It was a deep, elemental sort of magic — something that wouldn't necessarily respond to her in a moment of need.

Unbuttoning her coat, her chest heaving with harsh breaths, she moved toward the closed door on quick feet.

A small piece of white chalk from her pocket, something no self-respecting witch left the home without, and then a string of murmured words that were less language and more distilled intent compelled her hand to move on its own, scrawling sigils over the door in neat rows.

Her tutors once praised her for her perfect penmanship, even if her spellwork wasn't always... conventional. It couldn't be. Her magic just didn't work with the normal methods. It didn't want to conform to the hard lines and rigid structure of the spellwork taught to so many witches, their craft honed over centuries until it could be taught from a textbook.

For all that she was a nurturer by nature, hers was a wild sort of energy, implacable and aggressive. It was pure, elemental electricity that at once allowed her to communicate flawlessly with the cells of a body and yet could also be used to burn flesh to crisp. It struggled with the finer elements of warding and cursework. It was a raw power that could not be mistaken for anything other than the mark of a gloriana.

Blessed and cursed by the goddess Glory, Margot could heal the most complex wounds, understood the body on a level even the most experienced healers struggled to comprehend, and yet she could erect only the flimsiest of barriers between herself and the outside world. She could turn that howling energy inside of her into an electrical storm furious enough to wipe out a city, and yet that very same power was destroying her cell by cell.

But a flimsy barrier was better than nothing, and a howling storm at least took a bastard or two with her.

Margot was raised by a woman whose ruthlessness and paranoia were legendary. Sleeping in an unfamiliar environment without *some* barrier was incomprehensible. She had no desire to wake up with those silver claws on her throat, those black eyes reflecting the lights of the city from the shadows.

So why did the muscles of her abdomen clench when the image presented itself?

Because I'm dying, she thought, her bit of chalk making soft scratching sounds as she laid the final sigil down. *My brain is collapsing. My neurons are frying. I wouldn't think Theodore Solbourne was attractive otherwise.*

Not that he *wasn't,* of course, but under normal circumstances, Margot knew she would never, ever get close enough to him to have any sort of reaction, let alone the shocking curl of lust she felt in her belly when those terrifying fangs slid against her ear.

Yes, he was beautiful in the hard, primal way that so many elves were, but he also represented a lethal threat. That overruled even the most attractive body.

Not to mention the attitude.

Yes, the *attitude.* He hadn't said anything unforgivable yet, sure, but something about his high-handedness, his intensity, made her skin itch. Sovereign or not, he filled up a room too much, she decided.

His voice was low and silky, carrying the unmistakable weight of command, and his scent clouded her senses until she couldn't think or see or concentrate on anything but him. It was an unacceptable, dangerous reaction.

Stepping back from her work, Margot watched with a critical eye as the sigils flashed once, a vivid electric blue, before fading to a charred black.

The spell was not particularly sophisticated, but she had infused enough raw power into it that it would do the trick. A quick glamour and the sigils faded from sight entirely, leaving anyone who entered none the wiser.

Unless, of course, they were foolish enough to try and enter with malicious intent.

Stuffing the chalk back into her pocket, Margot paced away from the door to explore the rest of the suite. It contained a sitting area, a small, fully furnished kitchen, a gleaming bathroom with an overflowing basket of toiletries, and a single, decently sized bedroom with an empty walk-in closet. The colors of the walls and furniture were muted, ranging from cream to deep gray, and the design of the space was sophisticated but plain in the way that suggested it rarely, if ever, housed guests.

It made sense. Elves weren't exactly the sociable sort — and even less inclined to let strangers into their homes.

After repeating her spellwork on the bedroom door for redundancy's sake, Margot sank onto the edge of the sharply made bed. A fluffy robe lay waiting for her, a single lily and small, folded card resting beside it. Gritty chalk dust smeared the creamy cardstock as she flipped it open.

Welcome to Solbourne Tower, Healer Goode. I wish it were under happier circumstances. Myself and my staff are at your disposal, day and night. Please let me know if you need anything at all. Best wishes, Andy Yadav-Coran, Solbourne Houserunner.

A phone number and instructions on how to use the fancy intercom by the bed followed, each word written by a neat hand.

Margot's hand dropped to her lap, deeply disconcerted.

Why all the courtesy?

She wasn't a guest. She wasn't staying in some fancy hotel. She was a witch in an elvish stronghold — a place her kind had only ever been welcome as breakfast, lunch, or dinner. At best, she was a now homeless low-level political prisoner.

The idea, the preposterous *suggestion,* that the head of Theodore Solbourne's staff would treat her with the deference suggested by the note was...

Well, she had no idea what to make of it.

All her life, she lived by the rules her grandmother set out: Be quiet, keep your head down, and never, *ever* attract the attention of an elf.

The understanding had always been that one stray glance could spell disaster for her and the parents she didn't know, the families they had both gone on to have without her. Her very existence was a liability, and so she had to do everything in her power to mitigate the risks she took.

Margot still wasn't sure that Theodore Solbourne wasn't playing some elaborate trick on her. Would it not be in character for someone of his unimaginable power to reel her in with promises of security, to trap her in his gilded walls, only to wring her neck when she was lush with the feeling of safety?

I would have to become complacent to let that happen, she reminded herself. As it stood, she couldn't imagine ever coming to trust him, or feeling a sense of safety in his home, no matter how much instinct demanded she melt under his firm touch.

The thought brought back the memory of his hot, leather-covered palm on the delicate skin of her neck. Margot shuddered, a potent mix of trepidation and lust sending electricity skating down the column of her spine.

Suddenly acutely aware of her body, Margot could no longer ignore her various aches and pains, nor the dirt and dust and dried blood caked into her usually smooth skin. For someone whose cleanliness was not only a matter of professional pride, but some thing on which her very life depended, her current state was utterly unacceptable.

Still, she couldn't throw herself into the huge, glass-walled shower she glimpsed on her inspection of the suite. Not yet.

Duty first.

Turning to eye the bedside table, she momentarily shoved her discomfort to the back of her mind. The table held a modern lamp, all chrome finish and hard lines, and a cordless ball she recognized as a fancy in-home intercom system. The Solbournes were at the cutting edge of magic and tech, so it didn't surprise her that they had the best money could buy.

The unit, cheekily named Met — a play on *magically enhanced tech* — was a soft blue ball with a rubbery finish. Discreet and powerful, her grandmother had an older version in every home in the coven for ease of communication and security, so Margot was passingly familiar with them.

The Met could do all sorts of things, like send messages and search the web, but it could also emit low-level spellwork to help with sleep, lay down basic perimeter wards, or do simple house chores like scrubbing the floors or making the bed. It could also, in the wrong hands, wreak havoc.

The Goodes had access to some of the best and brightest sigilworkers in the world. Ruby Goode, Margot's second cousin, had personally upgraded, hacked, and boosted every Met in the Collective, ensuring their safety from outside sigilhackers. They were totally secure and worked on an isolated, Coven-run network, eliminating the possibility of outside surveillance.

The Met in her suite was more advanced than the ones in the Goodeland, but it was also almost certainly rigged to record anything she said or used it for. Unfortunately, Margot did not have an ounce of Ruby's skill or know-how. Not that many did, considering Ruby was rapidly building a reputation for herself as a genius with both tech *and* magic.

Margot rubbed her stinging eyes with a long sigh. Healing and electrical energy were all well and good, except they were limited in their usefulness. She wouldn't have given up her ability to heal for anything, but another minor skill in something *adaptable* would have been awfully nice.

Resigning herself to the fact that any call she made on the Met would be overheard, but lacking any other option now that she was fairly certain her cellphone was destroyed, Margot scooted closer to the bedside table.

"Met."

A pulsing blue light glowed around the base of the sphere, followed by a pleasant chime. Dreading the coming conversation, Margot instructed it to call her grandmother's private number.

It wasn't late enough for Sophie to be in bed, but even if it was, she would have answered the call. Part of being the Matriarch was being available at all times to her family. Sophie *never* missed a call.

Despite the fact that the caller ID must have shown an unknown number, Margot's grandmother picked up on the second ring.

"Sophie Goode speaking."

Margot's throat seized. Her grandmother's cool, crisp voice, always tightly leashed, sent a wave of homesickness through her.

"Grandma," she forced herself to say, her voice raw despite her best efforts to keep emotion out of it. "It's Margot."

"Margot?" There came the tiniest pause before Sophie's voice hardened into brittle ice. "What's wrong, Granddaughter?"

Everything.

Everything was wrong. She was dying, her house was blown to bits, and now she was some sort of indecipherable political prisoner. Margot couldn't rightly imagine how things could be *worse.*

"I'm okay," she forced out, very aware of listening ears, "but things have gotten complicated. Someone blew up my Healing House tonight. We don't know who, but it's been confirmed that there were explosives."

There was a beat of stunned silence, then, "Where are you calling from?"

Sharp as a blade, Sophie never missed anything. She couldn't afford to.

Margot sucked in a fortifying breath. "I'm calling from Solbourne Tower. The sovereign has taken me into... protective custody while they try to figure out who planted the bomb. And why, I suppose."

She could practically hear her grandmother sifting through the information, plucking out every risk, every possible motive, every way it could harm or help the Collective. There was no need to warn Sophie that they were certainly being listened to, nor that Margot was standing on the edge of a knife, her chances of discovery ratcheted up a thousandfold.

In a calm, cool voice, Sophie asked, "Are you injured?"

"Not anymore." Of her initial injuries, only surface bruising and soreness remained.

"Are you comfortable where you are?"

Margot's gaze flicked around the luxurious, if sparse

bedroom. She knew what Sophie was really asking. *Are you being held prisoner?*

"The sovereign has been kind enough to lend me a suite," she answered. *I'm not in a cell. Yet.*

"I'm grateful you're being taken care of, but I'm surprised Mr. Solbourne did not send you to a Collective household for safekeeping. Did his people give you a reason for holding you in protective custody?"

Margot pressed her clammy palms against the tops of her scraped knees, trying to calm her racing heart. "The sovereign has taken me under his personal protection."

As of this moment, your welfare, your happiness, your safety, your comfort — all of it belongs to me.

Theodore's voice, low and bursting with unbridled authority, rang louder in her memory than even the explosion. What it *meant,* she had no clue. Even knowing the political ramifications of the attack, Margot failed to wrap her head around why *Theodore Solbourne* would come running to her aid, let alone declare her under his protection.

And more, her mind whispered, recognizing some deeper claim that she could not consciously acknowledge.

Margot didn't understand it, but Sophie might. Even with their stilted conversation, she had faith that her grandmother would understand the things Margot could not.

"I see." Sophie's voice was entirely neutral, but Margot knew her too well to read it as disinterest. "I will have to call Mr. Solbourne in the morning to thank him for his dedication to your safety. Of course, I will also insist that you be turned over to Collective hands immediately. If you are being targeted, the safest place for you is home."

Every muscle in Margot's body seized. Words tumbled out of her mouth before she could stop them. "No, Grandma, I—" She licked her lips, her eyes swiveling around the unfamiliar room like she could find some perfect excuse there. "I mean, *yes,* you should speak to him, but I won't be coming home. It wouldn't look good for a healer to run scared, and even worse for a *Goode* to do so."

Some of the remoteness fell away from Sophie's tone when she tightly replied, "Margot, you were nearly assassinated. If you think I will tolerate a threat to your safety, you are mistaken."

They both knew that she wasn't talking about the bomber.

Sweat dewed along her spine and in the creases behind her bent knees, but Margot knew better than to let Sophie cow her.

No, Margot would never be in line to be Matriarch, not with the burden she carried. The mantle would pass to her cousin Alric, who would see the Coven into a brighter future when his time came. But Margot was still raised to be a leader, to shadow Sophie as she navigated politics and family tangles. She was no shrinking violet. She was a *Goode,* and on the subject of leaving San Francisco, she was utterly implacable.

He's here. I'm going to find him.

Keeping her voice firm, Margot answered, "I am not asking you to. I am handling the situation." A necessary lie. "If I were to run scared now, it could damage our relationship with the elves *and* make us look weak. Denying the sovereign's offer of personal protection would be an insult to the entire Protectorate, Grandma. The sovereign was adamant that my being here was a *trust exercise.* Your idea, I believe."

And even if there were no dire political ramifications, Margot had to stay. Her last chance at life resided in San Francisco. She could almost feel him, a presence pushing at the gauzy curtain of the back of her mind, so very close but infuriatingly out of reach.

She could not, *would* not leave before she found him.

Margot could hear the strain in Sophie's voice even under the sharp bite of her displeasure. "I will speak to Mr. Solbourne in the morning," she reiterated, equally implacable. "And I will send out an alert through the Collective — although they will probably already have heard the news by then."

There was no getting around that. Even if Margot wanted to

keep things quiet, the news of an attack on a healer would travel fast.

Sensing Sophie's desire to get off the call and gather her allies, Margot hastily added, "Before I go, Grandma, you should know that the sovereign is going to put out an edict for all Healing Houses in his territory to be warded."

Sophie's only indication of surprise was a small pause. "He wants to pick a fight with Glory's Temple?"

Sophie Goode found most of the world outside of the Collective and its lands suspect, but Margot knew she *despised* Glory's Temple with an uncharacteristic intensity. It used to surprise her, back when she assumed everyone worshipped Glory the same way the Coven did, but the truth of Sophie's own childhood took those rosy glasses off early.

There were valid reasons for the Collective's cold refusal to do any business with those who claimed affiliation with the Temple — and Sophie Goode had more reasons to hate them than most.

Shaking her head, Margot answered, "I warned him that they may take it as a breach of their autonomy, but he worries that more healers may be targeted, so he won't back down." She recalled the hard set of Theodore's jaw, the appearance of real worry in his dark eyes. "He... seems sincere."

"Indeed. Mr. Solbourne and I will have a lot to talk about tomorrow."

Dread was a lead weight in her belly, but Margot did her best to ignore it. "Please tell Noni and Alric that I'm fine, Grandma. I don't want them to worry."

"Of course. I'm sure Tula will call you anyway, though."

Yes, of course she would. Sophie Goode's bondmate was as fierce in her softness as Sophie was in her cool intelligence.

Homesickness made her throat tight when she whispered, "Good night, Grandma."

"Goodnight, Granddaughter. We'll talk soon."

~

Margot kicked off her covers.

One thing she learned after leaving the Coven was that she had trouble sleeping in unfamiliar places. Any bed that wasn't *her* bed felt wrong. Any room that wasn't *her* room was full of suspect shadows. Any blankets that weren't *her* blankets were too rough, too silky, too heavy, too light.

Of course, becoming an apprentice healer in the Ward as a teen meant she had long perfected the art of falling asleep wherever she stood, but that wasn't the kind of rest the body truly craved. It was just enough to allow a person to slog through another rotation, not to provide any meaningful recuperation.

Even that paltry rest eluded her.

Margot stared up at the darkened ceiling of the unfamiliar bedroom, her heart beating hard against her ribs. Her skin was clammy under the borrowed pajamas. A current of... something buzzed just under her skin, making her itch for movement, for relief from the tension that made the muscles of her neck and shoulders lock.

Removing the sheets and down comforter didn't provide any relief. Getting up to splash water on her bruised face didn't either. Even after she gave up the pretense of trying to sleep in favor of pacing the bedroom, Margot only felt that strange tension increasing.

Restless, she left the confines of the bedroom to make herself some tea in the small kitchenette. The water bubbled in the instant heater as she fished a small box of assorted teas from a nearly empty cabinet.

Just some chamomile and then I'll...

Her skin prickled. Magic surged to the surface, passing along a warning.

Someone touched the door.

Margot set the box of tea down onto the counter without a sound. Flicking the instant heater off with a touch of her negligible telekinesis, she turned to face the door. Cinching the waist of the too-big robe, Margot stared at the door and considered her options.

Stay inside and watch them try to break through the sigilwork, or open it and see who's on the other side?

One was safer, marginally, but the other held no prolonged suspense, no fear of being cornered by someone able to break through her crude spellwork.

Facing the monster on the other side was, she decided, far superior than waiting for it to get you.

Setting her chin, Margot ignored the fear crawling through her to stride through the sitting room. It was exposure she truly feared, not a fight. No, she *knew* how to fight. It was instinct hammered into the DNA of every witch, of every being who was once prey. She could fight. She *would* survive.

Closing her clammy fingers around the knob, Margot sucked in a harsh breath through her nose, gritted her teeth, and threw open the door.

...And found no one on the other side. The hallway beyond her door was empty.

Margot blinked, her adrenaline leaving her in a great rush as she stared at a massive painting of a desert landscape. There was no intruder standing in front of her door. There was only the heady scent of the sovereign and—

She looked down. Dark eyes with wide, vertical pupils stared up at her. "Why are you sitting in the hallway?"

Theodore shrugged, apparently unconcerned that he was caught sitting against the wall by her door, his forearms propped up on his bent knees and his suit jacket gone.

"This is my home," he answered. He tilted his head back until the messy black waves of his hair touched the wall. "I can sit in a hallway if I want to."

"Well, of course you can." Margot eased backward, at once confused and relieved to see him there. Her heartbeat slowed. A little bit of that insistent pressure eased with every inhale of the cinnamon-cedar laced air. "I'm just confused as to why the sovereign of the Elvish Protectorate would sit outside my door in the middle of the night."

He tilted his head to one side. Between his bent legs, he loosely intertwined his gloved fingers. "Does it bother you?"

Margot opened her mouth to answer in the affirmative, but the words stuck in her throat. *Did* it bother her?

It was weird, sure, but something in her relaxed at the sight of him there. His presence was huge, overwhelming, but it also felt reassuring, like nothing could get to her if he kept his post.

Which was absurd, obviously, but instinct couldn't be reasoned with.

"No," she finally answered, perplexed. "I don't think it does."

Theodore's smile was slow, his eyes heavy-lidded in a way that made her bare toes curl against the hardwood floor. *Oh,* she thought, watching a lock of oil-slick hair fall into his eyes. *Oh, he's...*

Stripped of his suit jacket, casually posed on the floor, his hair a mess and his gaze almost drowsy, Theodore Solbourne wasn't just handsome. He was *disarming.*

"Are you going to invite me in?"

Margot flushed. "No."

Theodore let out a long breath as he adjusted his position against the wall. "Worth a shot." His smile softened. Gesturing to the door, he told her, "Go back to sleep, darling. I won't let anything happen to you."

"I thought you said I was safer here than anywhere else in the UTA."

His fingers curled tighter around one another. "You are, but I thought that after everything you might not feel that way tonight. So I'm keeping watch."

Margot felt the air wheeze out of her lungs. "To... make me feel better?"

"Yes." Theodore looked away. She thought his throat might have bobbed under the high, starched collar of his shirt. "It's important that you feel safe."

She was too tired, too *confused* to see past any machinations. Was this a game? An elvish cultural practice she had no way of knowing? Was it just *him?* Margot couldn't make heads or tails of it on her own, so she didn't bother withholding her questions. "Why? Why does it matter? You don't even know me."

Theodore shook his head. "Sleep, Margot. You're safe. I promise." As if he couldn't stop himself, one hand slid away from the other to dart towards her. Without looking, he gave her calf a gentle squeeze through her robe. *"Rest."*

Unsettled by the sight of him, by his touch, by his baffling concern for her comfort, Margot didn't dare argue anymore. Nodding mutely, she shuffled back into the suite and shut the door.

Abandoning her tea, Margot dimmed the lights, fetched a blanket from her bed, and curled up against the door. *Just in case,* she thought. *Just in case.*

~

"I can't sleep knowing you're out here."

Theodore looked up from where he was very deliberately focusing on a nearly invisible seam in his gloves. He took in her rumpled state, the comforter hugged tight around her shoulders, and her loose, waist-length hair with a small appreciative sigh. Even bruised and annoyed, Margot Goode was just... perfect.

Even so, Theodore didn't like the idea of robbing her of rest. The wan set of her cheeks and the livid bruising around her hairline were vivid reminders that his consort needed coddling. And *gods,* he wanted to coddle her.

Flattening his palms against the floor, he began to push himself up. "Do you want me to—"

"Sovereign, I..." Margot looked away from him, her gaze briefly fixing on one of his sister's behemoth paintings on the opposite wall. With the quick, nimble fingers of one hand, she smoothed her hair back behind her round ears. Her eyes darted back to meet his. "Come in for tea."

Theodore was halfway up when he froze, leaving him hunched against the wall as he stared up at her with open surprise. "What?"

"Come in for tea," she repeated, firmer. "I don't feel good about you sitting out here all night to make me feel better. Maybe if we... if we just talked a little, I'd feel more comfortable, and you and I could finally get some sleep."

He straightened to his full height. "You inviting me to bed, darling?"

Margot cast him a surprisingly withering look. People didn't often look at him like that. Very few could get away with it. His consort, though... She could look at him any way that pleased her.

"You know that's not what I meant."

Theodore smoothed a hand down the front of his button down and watched, pulse thundering, as Margot's eyes tracked the movement. *Maybe not so far from what you meant, then.*

"Tea," he said. "Just tea."

"Just tea." Margot turned to shuffle back into the suite, her small hands hitching the comforter higher around her shoulders.

He frowned. "Are you cold?"

That didn't seem possible, considering the sensors in the walls were programmed to change the air conditioning to the ideal setting depending on the body temperatures of its occupants, but the way she hugged that comforter around her slight frame had his instincts roaring.

"I'm always cold." One small hand appeared from beneath the folds of the comforter to click on the instant heater. Everything about her was small and fragile-looking, but Margot appeared especially breakable as she hovered near the instant heater, her bare toes curled up against the cold tile. When she reached for a plain ceramic mug on a high shelf, he rushed to grab it for her.

Those luminous eyes swung in his direction. "You didn't have to do that. I could have reached it."

He fought the impulse to drape the blanket more securely around her shoulders. "I wanted to help."

Theodore was *desperate* to help, actually. If one half of the pull was the animalistic need to provoke, to *challenge,* the other half was brutal tenderness. It clawed at him, this need to see her safe, to know she felt cared for. For no one else would he stand guard outside a door. For no one else would he hover, begging for a chance to do *anything.* Only for her would he move mountains and remake countries — or fetch mugs from high shelves.

Margot was quiet as she delicately thumbed through the selection of tea bags in the sample box. Plucking out two paper packages of chamomile, she slowly admitted, "You're... not what I expected you'd be, Sovereign."

He leaned his hip against the counter. Watching a lock of red hair slide out from behind her ear to brush her cheek, he asked, "What did you expect?"

"I never expected anything before tonight." Placing the mugs under the spout of the heater, Margot waited until they were both full of steaming water before continuing. "But if I did expect anything, it wouldn't be someone who sits in hallways all night. What if someone saw you? Wouldn't that be considered strange for the sovereign to do?" Her eyes flicked in his direction; just a flash of copper. "Unless your staff is used to you spying on people, I suppose. Or sitting outside of unsuspecting women's doors."

Theodore gently accepted the mug she offered him. He didn't often drink tea, but he would have gladly swallowed a mug full of motor oil to just be in her company. "I wasn't spying."

"I know." She lifted her mug to her lips and turned to press her back against the lip of the counter, her gaze somewhere in the sitting room. "Maybe I shouldn't be so sure of that. I *know* I shouldn't be so sure of that. But you don't feel like a liar."

Swallowing a piping hot mouthful of flower water, he rasped, "I'm not. Never have been." His abilities might have made him an exceptional one, but Theodore never had the patience for deception. "And you can call me Theodore, you know. Or Teddy."

"You're the sovereign." She shook her head. Taking another long sip, Margot peered at him from over the rim of her mug. "Hardly seems proper to call you by your first name when you outrank me so thoroughly."

Theodore set his mug down but didn't release it. Holding onto the heated ceramic reminded him that he *shouldn't* reach for her instead. "I've only been Sovereign for eight months," he insisted, sensing that this was important, that she *needed* to see him as a man first and Sovereign second. "I'm still Teddy underneath the title."

Margot cast him a strange look, as if she couldn't quantify him in the way her quick mind wanted to. "You've never been Teddy to me, though. We just met, remember?"

Right. That was... getting harder to remember. No wonder, with the pull drawing him to her like a magnet and twenty five years of yearning threatening to make him spill his heart out at her feet.

Swallowing, he replied, "I don't see why we can't disregard titles."

"I don't see why we'd want to."

"Maybe for the same reason you didn't want me to leave earlier." He dared to lean closer, to breathe in more of her heady scent and feel the warmth of her radiate through layers of fabric. Margot didn't move. She didn't breathe. She simply stared, her pupils expanding to make the copper iris a thin ring around a fathomless black center.

"I honestly have no idea why I said you could stay." She breathed deep, her chest rising and falling slowly, as if she wanted to get as much air in her lungs as possible, to keep it there for as long as she could. "My grandmother would be appalled. *I'm* appalled."

Theodore couldn't stop his grin. Was she always so proper? It tickled him to think so. In all his daydreams, never once had he pictured she'd be so very prim. It was a good thing he didn't. Imagining what it would take to get her to shed that stiff, polite exterior would have driven him to madness.

"What's so appalling about it?" He pressed closer, his tea abandoned. Theodore dared to tug on a fold of her comforter-turned-cloak. "That I'm Sovereign, or that I like you even when you don't do as I say?"

Margot's lips parted. Goddess, but she looked so soft and delectable and open. He would have given anything to have free rein to kiss her then, when she looked at him like he was the center of the world.

The softness vanished almost as quickly as it arrived. In its place came a bristling indignation. "I have no reason to do as you say, sir," she shot back.

"No," he agreed. Heart hammering, he gave in to the impulse to skim her cheek with the backs of his claws. "But it might be fun."

It was a tease, a bit of flirtation, but the moment he caught the thinnest thread of her desire in the air, Theodore was lost. His claws, hidden beneath his gloves, retracted instantly. His pupils blew up to absorb the entirety of his irises. His cock throbbed with a painful, insistent beat in his slacks.

Theodore swayed forward, one hand gripping the edge of the counter in a futile attempt to hold himself back. *Softness,* his instinct whispered. *She's all softness until she bites. Oh, goddess, I want her to bite.*

"Margot, I..." He sucked in a ragged breath. What did he want? What could he *say?*

"I've finished my tea." Her cool voice, devoid of the warmth that had begun to color it, was a knife blade through the haze of the pull.

His voice was tight, strained, when he answered, "Right. I should let you sleep."

"Yes."

She held herself so still, he wondered what she was trying to accomplish. Did Margot fear he would lunge at her if she moved like prey? Or did she worry that she too would sway, bending under the electric current pulsing ever-stronger between them?

Glory, let it be the second, he prayed, forcing himself to leave her for the second time that night. *I'd rather not be the only one suffering tonight.*

Chapter Five

In general, Theodore didn't get much sleep. He wasn't one for sitting still, and since he spent every spare minute of the last twenty-five years of his life as his sister's protégé and getting the shit kicked out of him in surprise combat training, Theodore was used to going days without sleeping.

What he *wasn't* used to was the keen awareness that his consort slept in the adjacent suite. It should have soothed him, knowing that she was finally under his care and close at hand, but it did the opposite.

Unable to trust himself so near to her after their encounter in her suite, he paced half the night, wearing a track into the expensive carpet of his study, and fought the impulse to stand guard at her door once more.

It turned out to be a good thing he didn't bother trying to sleep. Almost as soon as the clock struck five, calls and messages started pouring in.

Most of the media inquiries and lower level contacts were filtered through his two steely-eyed assistants, but there were several interested parties with direct access to his private lines.

The first message was from Valen Yadav, General of Patrol and the man who was Theodore's grandfather in all the ways that truly mattered. He had dispatched a tech unit to piece together any evidence not destroyed by the fire and had several shadow teams chasing down whispers of discontent.

Theodore made it clear when he took the seat of power from his sister that he would not reinstate their father's reckless use of the shadow teams to enforce compliance from the Protectorate's citizens. That didn't mean he underutilized them, however. If there was some plot to undermine his claim to power, it was the shadows who would uncover it.

After going over Yadav's report and giving his approval for a full investigation into the attack, he sorted through the various statement requests and flagged articles forwarded by his assistants. Despite their efforts to quarantine the blast site, Theodore was not surprised that news of the attack had already made headlines.

His lips thinned with displeasure as he scrolled through an article from *The San Francisco Light* with not only Margot's name printed in bold letters, but a grainy photo of her sitting on the curb with Viktor, her scraped knees tucked close and her blood still running fresh rivulets down her throat.

> **HEALING HOUSE DESTROYED IN LATE NIGHT BLAST** — *At roughly 9:30 PM, an explosion rocked the well-off neighborhood of St. Francis Woods, shocking residents and injuring the local healer, Margot Goode, 25, who took the post only six months ago. Although there has been no official statement from Patrol or the EVP government, witnesses speculate that it was a targeted attack.*
>
> *"I can't believe someone would go for a Healing House," says Antony Cleeve, arrant investment banker who lives three houses down from the Healing House. He claims to have seen the explosion as he took his dog out for his evening constitutional. "And the healer— we've only had her for a few months, but she's really good at what she does. Friendly. A really nice girl. I just don't get it. Who would want to hurt a healer? Aren't there laws to protect them?"*

We at the Light are in full agreement with Mr. Cleeve. If the explosion is proven to be deliberate, it will mark the first attack on a Healing House since the Healer Protection Act passed in 1917, and will undoubtedly send waves across the UTA.

The ramifications of the attack might prove more far-reaching than simply spawning outrage, however. The rumored target, Margot Goode [pictured above beside Viktor Hamilton, alpha of the Merced coyote pack, who could not be reached for comment], is not just a little known member of the Goode Coven, but, according to the records unearthed by the Light staff, the only granddaughter of Sophie Goode herself.

We at the Light and much of our readership wonder what this act of violence, should it prove to be so, will do to the sovereign's reputation. Only in power for eight months, Theodore Solbourne is rumored to have been challenged for his position upwards of four times by high ranking elves. With his hold on power so precarious and the apparent attack on a healer in his territory, the upcoming Summit could prove to be the most politically volatile one since Thaddeus II declared his total rule in...

Theodore skimmed the rest of the article, his bare claws digging into the flesh of his palms as it went on to speculate about Margot, why she may have been targeted, and just what her relationship was with the Merced alpha. Without statements from his government, Sophie Goode, or Viktor, all the *Light* could do was throw Margot's identity out into the populace for them to chew on.

Theodore stabbed his claws through his hair and blew out a furious breath.

It wasn't how he wanted to introduce her to the world. It wasn't how he *planned* it.

Twenty-five years he'd known his consort was Other. Twenty-five years he knew that keeping her by his side would take careful planning and the seat of power under his control. In one night, all of the steps he mapped out to ease Margot into life at his side were blasted to bits.

His plan to introduce her to the world and his people *after* their bond was solidified lay in shambles, the destruction no better illustrated than in the scorched remnants of the St. Francis Woods Healing House.

Not all was lost, though. Not even close.

He didn't like being forced onto the defensive, but Theodore knew when to take advantage of a sudden change in circumstance.

No, this was not how he wanted things to go, but he was clever enough to see certain benefits to the situation. Mainly, Margot was close at hand and would not be leaving his protection. There was also the benefit of the world seeing her as a victim. If she had the public's sympathy from the start, it was good groundwork for building her into something not even the elves could tear down.

Even if that didn't work, Theodore knew there was no going back. Their fates were intertwined, had *always* been intertwined, and he was not about to let her go now that he was finally so close to the life he dreamed of.

Besides, it wasn't like either of them had a choice now. Theodore knew the consequences of coming into contact with Margot when he stepped through the emergency m-gate. They had a matter of days before the pull, the chain reaction of chemicals and magic in elvish blood that pushed consorts together, would become irresistible.

Shooting off a message to his head of PR to field the statement requests with firm reminders that the investigation was ongoing and the safety of Healer Goode their main concern, Theodore glanced at the time and sent another message, this time to the Met in Margot's room. The rest of the messages, which included emails from nearly half of the families in the Parliament *and* a mocking personal note from the insufferable dragon Taevas Aždaja, could wait until after he'd seen his consort.

No, circumstances weren't ideal, and he would need to draft a joint statement with Margot to give to the press while they hunted for her attackers, but he could overlook all of that in favor of the joy he felt when he got to spend any time with her.

Rising from his chair, Theodore darted into his bedroom to take a brisk shower before changing into fresh slacks and a button down. Fixing his starched collar at his throat, he eyed his flushed cheeks and wet, tousled hair with the bubbling happiness of a man ready to greet his destiny.

Breakfast. With Margot. *His* Margot.

His breath came faster, his pulse hammering under his fingers as he pinned the double-headed thistle against his throat.

Margot.

Her name was a luxury he'd only indulged in for six months. For nearly twenty-five years, she'd simply been '*my consort*'. His dream. The cool touch in the back of his mind, always there, soothing him even when he felt there was no continuing on. The soothing tether he clung to when his body took a beating or the frustration of dealing with his sister and brothers got to be too much.

A whisper of a mental link he touched obsessively, *hourly,* just to reassure himself that she was still there.

Theodore was incredibly lucky that he was able to sense her at *all,* considering most elves didn't recognize their consorts until they came face to face.

But *he* knew. He had always known.

Margot was his. More importantly, he was hers, and *had* been hers since the night she was born.

Theodore wasn't given his family's hit-or-miss gift of Foresight, unlike both his sister Delilah and his older brother Sam, but he was blessed in another way: long range psychic connection. It was a rare and valuable skill, but Theodore only really used it to keep his link to Margot open.

He didn't read her mind, of course. That would have been a deeply immoral breach of her privacy, and ran the risk of opening him up to far more than his mind could handle. But he could *sense* her, could feel the general tenor of her mind, the flavor of her personality, every day for the past twenty-five years.

The link sprang into being when he was ten. He always suspected — and after cross-checking Margot's intake forms knew for certain — that it manifested mere minutes after her birth.

It was the bond that told him that she was not an elf, and it was that knowledge that changed the course of his life.

By the time they were finished, it would change far, far more than that.

Margot was Other. Yes, she was different, and *yes,* she was perfect. He would change the world to have her. The alternative was unthinkable.

Theodore self-consciously smoothed his unruly hair back against his scalp and peered at his reflection in the mirror above the bathroom sink. He was Sovereign, but he didn't feel like the title lived in his skin, reflected in his looks. Theodore was just Theodore — Teddy, to his friends and family.

He was attractive by elvish standards, but those had less to do with looks and everything to do with power: physical, mental, and political.

Physically, he trained hard and could take down any challenger who presented themselves. Mentally, he was clever, passably charming, and had a sneaky psychic ability that would always keep his enemies one step behind him. Politically, he stood at the very top of the food chain, the *only* position that would allow him to live the life he dreamed of.

Unfortunately, none of that guaranteed anything with Margot.

Despite his two and a half decade long relationship with her, Theodore was in the dark about what she liked in a man; what she found attractive, what would win her.

While he didn't doubt that he *would* win her, he would have preferred more preparation for the campaign.

He wanted to know what books she liked to read, what side of the bed she slept on, what made her laugh. He needed to know what made her happy and what made her cry.

He wanted to know the joy of kissing her and being kissed *by* her.

Calm down, Teddy, he inwardly coached himself. *Slow. She needs slow. She doesn't fucking know you, idiot.*

Straightening his spine, Theodore snagged his gloves off of his bedside table and tugged them on with a scowl. He usually didn't mind the social obligation to wear them, but he loathed the idea of having the barrier between himself and his consort. Only skin contact could soothe that raging beast in him, whipped to a frenzy by the presence of his consort.

But forgoing them wasn't a choice he could make yet. They hid the one outward sign of the *pull,* the physical reaction elves underwent when they found their consorts, and it was something no elf would miss if they saw it.

He was just shoving his cell phone into his pocket when it began to vibrate in his hand. Knowing it was either his family or his direct subordinates, Theodore didn't bother to check the ID before he raised it to his ear.

"Go."

"You, Mr. Solbourne, are a tough elf to reach."

Theodore paused halfway through the doorway of his bedroom, his gaze locked on the furniture of the sitting room. "Madam Goode," he answered slowly, "for what do I owe the honor?"

Sophie Goode's voice, familiar to him from her many, many media appearances and speeches on the UTA Congress floor, came through the receiver with a crispness that chilled the blood.

"I've been trying to reach you for over an hour, but your assistants refused to give me your personal number. They were very insistent that you would get back to me in due time, but seeing as you are holding my granddaughter prisoner, I'm sure you can understand why I refused to wait."

He muffled a snort. Theodore doubted she was a woman who waited for *anything*. It was a good thing that he wasn't one to bend under intimidation, otherwise the force of the Goode Matriarch's seething disdain would have buckled his knees.

"Margot is not a prisoner," he replied, affecting the cool, imperious tone of the sovereign with ease. "She is being given every courtesy and has been honored with my vow of personal protection. In fact, we are about to have breakfast."

"A prisoner is still a prisoner even if the locked door is a pretty one." She was a direct sort of woman, apparently, and Theodore found himself begrudgingly admiring her lack of obfuscation. Sophie Goode did not pussy-foot around.

"While I appreciate your concern for her wellbeing and understand the position this attack puts you in, it would be best for all parties involved if you turned her over to her kin immediately," she continued, every word chilled with undisguised menace. "She should be with her family, where she will be cared for and protected."

While the beast in him did not like the implication that Margot wouldn't be sufficiently cared for by him and him alone, Theodore understood the urge to protect his people. That did not mean he was about to pull his punches, though.

Margot was *his* consort. That neatly overrode any claim Sophie Goode had on her.

"Madam, Margot was given the choice to return to the Collective land last night. She refused." He paused, allowing his words to sink in. "Seeing as she wished to remain in my city, your granddaughter agreed to follow the laws of the Protectorate — which includes my own edicts. I declared her under my protection, and so here she remains."

A chilly silence reigned for several long seconds before Sophie replied, "Margot is young. She doesn't always know what's good for her. Whatever game you're playing, she has no reason to be a part of it. She doesn't involve herself in politics."

Theodore's hackles raised. His claws, diamond sharp beneath

the silver claw-caps of his gloves, flexed. "She seemed to know her own mind well enough to me, Madam."

"Yes, she knows her own mind," Sophie agreed, "but she is young, and out in the world on her own for the first time. Now she's been blown up — nearly killed, if the reports are accurate. I worried something like this would happen to her if she left the Goodeland, but I allowed her to sway me because I thought she was unknown enough to be safe. Now I see that was a mistake."

The witch, being the experienced negotiator and politician that she was, paused for just a moment before adding, "I know you of all people understand the importance of protecting one's family. Would your sister not do the same for you if she were in my position?"

Despite his unbending stance on letting her leave, Theodore was willing to give his consort's kin a lot of leeway, but mentioning his family's bloody history *and* questioning his ability to protect her? *Unacceptable.*

The glass and sleek metal of his cell phone creaked ominously with the tightening of his grip. He made sure she could hear his reaction to such an insult in his voice, his tone dropping until it matched hers in chill and sharpness when he replied, "The Protectorate is the safest territory in the UTA."

Was there panic when he first took his seat? Yes, but he held onto his power and kept the Protectorate from bloodshed. He would continue to do so until the day he died.

Sophie was soon to be his kin by consort, and she was a ruler in her own right, but he would not let her mistake him for being below her. He was *Sovereign.* He protected what was his, whether that was his family, his consort, or his territory. No one had the right to question that.

Baring his fangs at an enemy he couldn't see, he grated, "Why did you think it was so dangerous for her? What threat are you concerned would follow her into *my* territory?"

A prickling sensation swept across his mind, his psychic senses on high alert, as Sophie Goode answered, "Margot is a beautiful young woman with extreme magical talent. There are many types of people who would take advantage of her at the first opportunity."

Scenting something suspicious, Theodore felt his internal danger sensors ping an alarm. Dropping all pretense of civility — or what little remained — he said, "Madam Goode, if there is an active threat against Margot, I'll hear it now. If you choose not to share it with me and she comes to harm because of it, I will hold you *personally* responsible."

"My granddaughter is not your—"

"The threat, Madam," he snapped, "or this conversation is over."

"You."

Theodore blinked twice in quick succession, too surprised to be offended. "Pardon?"

"You and your kind represent a threat to her," Sophie answered, each word lodging hard and heavy in his chest. "Your kind used our finger bones as toothpicks. You savage your own for minor insults and upward mobility in the hierarchy. Your very nearness to her is a threat. I will not tolerate my granddaughter being used as a political pawn, and I *absolutely* will not allow a single one of you to lay a claw on her."

Where an elf might have gone hotter, their voices louder, Sophie Goode only got colder, each word arrowing across the connection like shards of brittle ice. "You are a young ruler. Do not make the mistake of underestimating the Collective, Mr. Solbourne. Others have, and all of them have regretted it." She paused to let her threat sink in. "There is no reason for us to be enemies. Return her to us now, before I am forced to make this ugly for the both of us. When she's in safe custody, perhaps we can discuss the fight you're picking with the Temple. I might even be willing to side with you."

Again, the prickling. Whatever trust he might have had in Sophie Goode's connection to her granddaughter perished under her refusal to tell him the truth.

He didn't think that Sophie Goode was lying outright, but rather leaving out something crucial. It went beyond a gut feeling. It was certain knowledge, his gift shining through when he needed it most.

Whatever it was, Theodore would discover it. No threat against Margot would be suffered to exist.

Theodore kept his voice even when he replied, "Margot may leave if she chooses to go. If not, she remains with me." Baring both pairs of fangs in a vicious grin, he added, "And as a parting note, Madam Goode: You should know that elves are intensely covetous creatures. We do not give up what is ours unless it is ripped from us by tooth and claw. Margot is mine. If you want her back, you'll simply have to *take her.*" His fingers flexed and the glass screen of his phone cracked like brittle ice. "You are welcome to try."

He made it to his private dining room a bare minute before Margot stepped through the doorway. It was lucky that every room on this floor of the Tower was connected by a series of hidden hallways and security exits, or else she would have seen him power walking from his suite like a fool.

As it happened, he slid through the discreet staff door hidden behind a great flowering plant and situated himself at the set table with forced nonchalance a few seconds before she arrived.

He wasn't sure what he expected, but seeing her again, in the flesh, in his *home,* was a punch to the gut.

Margot stood in the doorway, her back straight, her red hair swept up in a tight coil, her creamy skin glowing in the early morning sunlight streaming in from the wall of windows to his left. Keen, intelligent eyes flicked over him and around the room, assessing every inch of the space with a cool reserve at odds with her fey features, her delicate build.

She was indescribably lovely.

He was so distracted by the thundering of his heart, by the rasp of his lungs sucking in huge, gulping breaths to bring her scent closer, to haul it into his very cells, that it took him a second to wrap his brain around several key facts.

First: Margot's creamy skin was marred by mottled bruises around her forehead and left cheek. A thin red line slid from above her temple and into her hair, the only remnant of the gash that oozed sluggishly the previous night. When his gaze ran down her bare throat — *Glory save me* — and down her finely shaped legs, he spied several more scratches, more bruising; all of it obscene on the skin of a healer who should heal herself as easily as breathing.

Second: She wore the same clothing as yesterday, except this time he was treated to the sight without the bulk of her coat in the way. The dress was pretty, a soft blue with clusters of blooming flowers, and shoulder straps that tied into bows that kissed the smooth curve of her shoulders. The neckline was heart-shaped, revealing just a hint of cleavage; her slight build accentuated by the curving cut.

The overall effect would have been pretty enough to stop his breathing, if only there wasn't a deep, rusty stain running along one side of the neckline.

Theodore tensed, his claws scraping at the insides of his claw-caps, every instinct, every damn cell in his body attuned to a single emotion: protective fury.

Someone harmed his consort. Someone spilled her blood, bruised her soft skin, and he would not rest until that person's throat was between his teeth.

"Good morning, Mr. Solbourne," she said, like everything was normal and he wasn't about to come out of his damn skin.

Theodore stood up from his chair, his right hand automatically moving to button his suit jacket. Only when his fingers grazed the crisp cotton of his shirt did he realize he'd forgotten to put it on. *Fuck.*

"Call me Theodore," he replied, hoping she didn't notice the aborted movement of his hand as he lowered it to his side or the rough growl in his voice. "Or Teddy. Please."

He circled the small table to pull out her chair, his pulse thumping beneath his high, protective collar. Her gaze followed every movement, and although she tried to hide it, he caught the flicker of unease in her penny-bright eyes.

From the doorway, she said, "We talked about this last night, remember?"

"Yes," he allowed, "but the matter isn't settled. I want you to use my name."

"Why?"

He swallowed. *Because it would mean the world to me if you did.*

But he couldn't say that. Instead, he shook his head and quirked a brow, gesturing to the table.

Margot slowly peeled herself out of the doorway to make her way across the cozy dining room. It wasn't even half as large as his study, and the formal dining hall where he hosted all of the heads of the elvish Families in his territory twice a year was bigger by thirty times, but it was where he spent his evenings with the people who meant the most to him. Those people were Valen and Andy. They were Delilah and her world famous consort, Winnie. They were his brothers Kaz and Sam, when he could be compelled to leave his hermitage in the desert.

And now Margot, of course.

The dining room was intimate. Private. Perhaps a risk, if she secretly enjoyed luxury, but he knew instinctively that Margot would not have been impressed by a grand dining room.

Besides, he relished being close to her.

As Margot cautiously slid into the chair, he sucked in a deep breath, hunting for the sharp smell of her. It was almost entirely smothered by the smell of expensive soap, but it was *there,* cloying and delicious, with that intriguing base note that tickled the back of his mind like a reminder. There was something there he couldn't put his finger on, but he didn't dwell on it. If things went well, they would have hundreds of years to unravel all of each other's mysteries.

As he gently pushed her chair closer to the table, he murmured in her ear, "Keep talking like that and I'll start to think you don't want to be friends with me."

He didn't need to touch her to feel the tension pulling every one of her delicate muscles taut. Unbidden, Theodore was reminded of the way she melted into his touch the previous night; how she relaxed, almost against her will, into his hold; the way desire curled through her scent when he teased her.

Following the memory, and the accompanying flash of instinct, he clasped her bare nape and gave it a single, proprietary squeeze.

Beneath his gloves and claw-caps, Theodore's diamond-hard claws sank backwards into his fingertips, instinct and chemistry paving the way to making it easier to knead the tense muscles of her neck. For no one other than his consort and their offspring would his claws retract. It was instinct to soothe, to gentle, to do no harm.

Margot felt incredibly fragile under his hand, but he knew she had her own claws, her own fangs. *Perfect. Absolutely perfect.*

"Mr. Solbourne," her voice was strained, but her shoulders were slumping, losing their rigid posture as Margot's body recognized something her mind had not yet put together. The *right* response, and one his own body recognized immediately. "I am very sensitive to touch, and I don't believe I gave you permission to handle me."

No, she hadn't, and he was raised by two of the fiercest elvish women alive. Delilah and Winnie were his mothers, and they adhered to the strictest, most elvish ideal of consent: If you wanted to touch, be prepared to ask or lose a hand.

But Theodore, like all elves, also understood the duality of that ethos. Elves viciously guarded their personal space, their bodies — even their clothing was designed to provide maximum protection to vulnerable areas — but the flip-side of that was the unalterable truth that they loved to fight, to touch, to *fuck.* The finding of a consort was as much a fight as it was a courtship, a union blessed by Glory and forged by biology-altering magic. It was constant provocation; the invasion of space and the proving of one's worth.

With an elvish consort, Theodore was *expected* to invade her space. He was expected to push her boundaries, just as she was expected to unleash her claws on him for doing so. It was in the furious clashes that *true* courtship lay.

It was his job to provoke, but also to soothe and coax, to win her trust and prove his worth by never, ever reacting to her challenges with violence or anger. Margot might be Other, but the drive in him, the beast at the heart of every elf, didn't care. It would prick her until she fought back, and then it would subdue her with teeth and tongue and every other sensual weapon at his disposal until she surrendered.

"What would it take to earn permission?" he heard himself rumble, only half aware of anything beyond the heat of her skin through the leather of his gloves and her scent in his nose.

Instead of answering the question, she shot back, "I'm uncertain as to why the sovereign would want it in the first place."

Theodore dared to brush his cheek against the silk of her hair. He was titillated to discover it was cool, the strands not yet entirely dry from her morning shower. What would it be like to run his claws through those damp strands? What would it feel like to have them draped over his bare skin?

His chest felt too tight. A shudder raked itself down his spine.

The pull was intense, the chemical reaction to her nearness and the unfinished bond making his blood increasingly volatile, but the satisfaction of *knowing* her, having her with him, after twenty-five *long fucking years...*

It was almost too much.

"I should think that's obvious," he answered, fighting the urge to press his lips against her unbruised temple, to simply breathe her in and never stop. He was so touch-hungry for her it *hurt.*

Margot was quiet for a beat. Only her breath, somehow even despite the jagged rhythm of her pulse beneath his thumb, and the low whir of air through the vents broke the quiet.

Finally, in a voice that was oddly flat, she said, "As flattering as the attention is, Sovereign, I must decline any advances you make. Not only is it politically unwise to pursue even a fleeting sexual relationship between us, I have no desire to end up gutted and floating face down in the bay for the pleasure."

A lash of pure protective fury struck him, followed immediately by the acute sting of rejection. Why on Burden's sweet Earth would she assume anything of the sort? What had he done to give her that impression?

His hand tightened on the back of her neck, but before he could open his mouth to disabuse her of any notions of *"fleeting"* and *"gutting"*, she continued, "Beyond that, if this is the cost of your personal protection, I cannot pay it." She turned her head, as much as his grip allowed, to meet his gaze with a look so fierce, so beautiful that it made him ache. "I am waiting for my bondmate."

Chapter Six

Margot's pulse was a hot, electric rhythm under her skin. Each beat was a lightning strike; a bright, biting force of nature that threatened to make her reckless, to push her into something she couldn't undo.

The part of her she kept so tightly leashed, the half that Sophie spent years smothering, training out of her with rigid discipline and over-achievement, roared to life in her blood.

It raked at her mind. It bellowed. It strained toward the elf caging her in against the edge of the table even as it hissed and spit at him.

Only that drilled discipline and years of hard apprenticeship under Head Healer Mason kept Margot perfectly still in his hold. The strain of her two natures, never, ever quite so at odds before, made cold sweat break out across her skin.

Having him so close, *touching* her, his rich scent in her nose, was opening doors in her mind that had remained firmly locked for twenty-five years. Her magic arced through her, lacing the air with stinging ozone, and Margot felt suddenly that she was unmoored when she wasn't looking; tossed out into a roiling ocean to drown, no hope for rescue in sight.

Even through the chaos in her mind and body, Margot sensed

the barely restrained violence in the man at her back. She held her breath, expecting a scathing rebuke for daring to reject *him,* Theodore Thaddeus Solbourne, son of Thaddeus Solbourne II, head of the Solbourne Family and Sovereign of the Elvish Protectorate.

Theodore, whose attention surely, surely would get her killed, no matter how much her body wanted to bend to his will.

Instead, his voice was smooth, calm in a way that she didn't expect when he replied, "It appears we have a lot to discuss, darling."

Abruptly, the hand at her nape disappeared. He was sliding into his own seat across from the small, round table not a moment later, his expression shuttered.

Margot stared at him, once more taking in the way his white shirt stretched over ropes of muscle and broad shoulders, the way the daylight streaming through the floor to ceiling windows changed the color of his pale blue skin.

Of course, she got a good look at him the night before, but Margot couldn't tear her eyes away from Theodore in the light any more than she could in the half-dark of the car or the dim glow from the lights in her suite.

A curl, black and shining with all the colors of elvish iridescence, fell across his brow as he reached out to pluck the silver lids off of their plates, his own silver claws tapping musical notes against the domed metal. Theodore wasn't wearing a suit jacket this morning, and the tiny hint of stubble on his jaw was gone, making him look somehow younger, less intimidating.

He was gorgeous. She could admit that. No sane person would deny it when faced with the full force of Theodore Solbourne's presence. The hard lines of his face, the elegant pointed tips of his ears, the deft, leather-covered hands — he was finely wrought down to the smallest detail. Even his *lashes* were perfectly curled and sooty against his skin.

Electricity arced through her again, hot and settling low in her belly. *Desire,* her mind helpfully supplied. *This is desire.*

Not the kind she had ever felt before, though. This was urgent, explosive, *needy.* It made her want to get up from her chair and sit in his lap just so she could be closer.

Terrifying. It was terrifying, this change that swept through her, and Margot couldn't reconcile it with any experience that came before. The closest comparison she had was her darkest memory: That week of endless black, of madness and agony and fear so great it haunted her still. She hadn't been in control then. She wasn't in control now.

What was happening to her?

"Eat," he commanded, gesturing to the uncovered plate in front of her.

She glanced down to find an artfully arranged array of breakfast foods. Sliced fruit, a fresh croissant, a small ramekin of oatmeal sprinkled with melting brown sugar, and, with a subtle sniff, she discovered an omelet made not of eggs, but almost identical plant-based protein. Considering her usual breakfast involved a bagel and a protein shake carefully calibrated for her needs, it was far, far more than she would ever have bothered with for herself.

Margot flicked her gaze back to Theodore and then down to his plate. Elves went out of their way to keep their habits and physical needs secret from the general public, so it had taken her years to discover what they actually ate. Theodore's spread was as different from her breakfast as any food could possibly be.

The elvish diet, she remembered grimly discovering, was almost one hundred percent protein. *Raw* protein.

Theodore's plate, while equally artfully arranged, was made up entirely of strips of raw meat run through with thick, creamy veins of fat.

Margot yanked her eyes away from the sight, her stomach twisting hard. In another life, the sight wouldn't have bothered her, but in this one she was a healer first, and when she looked at meat, all she saw was flesh.

Swallowing hard, she dropped her eyes to her own meal. "I thought we had a lot to discuss."

A rumble of indiscernible feeling came from his side of the table. "We do, but there's no reason we can't also eat. You're under my care now, and that means you will *not* go hungry."

She didn't dare look at him directly, but she caught his movements out of the corner of her eyes as he shredded a hunk of meat with his clawtips and flicked bloody pieces into his mouth. Margot sucked her lips between her teeth and bit down.

Oh Glory, I was not raised to handle this.

Unable to stomach anything even if he wasn't going to town on an extremely rare filet mignon, Margot reached for what looked like a cup of coffee. There was a small pitcher of cream and a bowl of sugar perched close to her plate, but she didn't bother with it.

She liked cream and sugar in her coffee, but one look at the rippling liquid in her cup told her she was trembling too much to successfully manage the fine movements necessary to accomplish it without making a mess.

Lips thinning at the reminder that her time was rapidly running out, Margot took one sip of bitter coffee before carefully putting the cup back in its place.

The shaking would soon be uncontrollable. Not that she had much control of it now, of course. Even when she wasn't healing, like she wasn't just then, Margot suffered waves of tremors.

Next, she would begin losing control of her limbs, their motor function destroyed by the magic frying the connections between cells, alongside rupturing blood vessels to set off crippling spasms. If a brain bleed didn't kill her, then the building magical storm in her cells would simply cook her brain until it stopped working altogether.

She could already feel the buildup of energy in her body. It was part of the reason she still hadn't healed the cuts and bruises from the blast. Her internal eye was so focused on repairing the constant damage done by her magic that she couldn't spare any attention for the little things. Soon, she wouldn't even be able to do that.

As if hearing her thoughts, Theodore took a sip of his own drink before abruptly asking, "Aren't you a bit young to be looking for a bondmate?"

"Not necessarily," she hedged, wary of this man who never did what she expected and who made her hunger for touch more fiercely than she ever had. "I'm a gloriana — I'll need one eventually, so I figure, why not now? I'd like... I'd like to meet someone and think about starting a family."

Not *soon,* really, but her approaching death had a way of putting certain wants into perspective. If Margot was lucky enough to stop the demise coming for her, she damn well would pursue the path she'd always wanted: her own home, her own life, her own family.

Theodore's sudden stillness caught her eye. Margot glanced up, her breath freezing in her lungs.

He sat there, one forearm braced against the edge of the table, the tips of his claws dripping with blood, and stared at her with eyes so black it was almost impossible to make out their slit pupils as they focused unerringly on her face.

In a measured, pleasant voice, he informed her, "That was your one."

"Excuse me? My one what?"

"Lie." Theodore blinked slowly, his dark green tongue snaking out to lick away a drop of blood from the corner of his mouth. Her stomach muscles tightened even as instinct urged her to leap out of her chair and *run.*

"You get one lie," he continued, "but no more. Understand that I will *always* know if you lie to me, Margot. Don't try it. It's a talent I have, being a living lie detector, and not one I want to use with my witch." His expression was hard but earnest, beseeching her not to let him down. "You and I, we must *always* be honest with one another."

His witch?

She fisted her hands in her lap. "That wasn't a lie."

"It was a half-truth." He smiled, but it was grim, lacking the wicked charm he previously deployed on her. "Trust me, I know the difference."

Was this just another thing about elves she didn't know, a hidden sense they had, or was it something specific to Theodore? It was possible he was simply very good at picking up micro-expressions, body language and inflection, but the gleam in his dark eyes, along with his utter certainty, implied it was something more.

Fuck.

Changing tactics, she straightened her spine and baldly replied, "Maybe, but it's also none of your business. Sovereign or not, you aren't entitled to the details of my personal life."

Theodore blew out a breath, eyebrows raised, and leaned back in his chair. She watched his bloodied right hand scrape against the pristine white table cloth, leaving red tracks in its wake.

"Now that's where you're wrong."

Her eyes darted back up to find him watching her. "Why's that?"

"Because," he answered, eyelids falling to sultry half-mast, "you've already found him."

Margot could only stare at him blankly, utterly mystified.

Seeing her lack of comprehension, Theodore grasped the edge of the table with both hands, leaned forward, and announced, "*Me,* Margot. It's me."

A bomb going off in her coffee cup would have seemed less outlandish, less shocking, than Theodore's utter certainty of something entirely, completely *impossible.*

Margot leaned backwards slowly, her eyes fixed on his face, and tried to find words in a mind that had simply stopped working. "That is... I'm really not..." She cleared her throat. "That's not a very funny joke, Sovereign."

And not simply because it was objectively preposterous. The sovereign of the Protectorate and *her?* Nonsense.

For one thing, elves did *not* mate outside of their race. Their population numbers were the lowest of all the races in the UTA. The excuse given to the public for the lack of interbreeding was because they were doing their best to avoid extinction and not "sacrifice their elvish legacy".

The general consensus of the public was that it was simply to keep a hold of their power and an aversion to diluting bloodlines — a myopic choice that other races made in the distant past with disastrous results. The dragon clans were *still* recovering from their own enforced isolation, and were the most vocal group decrying the practice because of it. Despite his playboy image, Isand Taevas, lord of the dragon clans, always backed laws in the UTA Congress that promoted intercultural communication and cross-pollination.

But elves apparently hadn't learned the lesson. They stuck to their own, passed their wealth onto their own, and only bred with their own.

At least, they were supposed to.

Margot knew for a fact that not every elf abstained from liaisons with other races, but none of them were *Theodore fucking Solbourne.*

Slow down, she firmly instructed her racing mind. *Slow down. There's no way he means that, and even if he did, that's not how this works. It's definitely not how it works for me.*

Yes, his presence and his touch did... things to her that it absolutely should not do, but she wasn't about to forge a bond with him. Knowing her magic, when she met the right person it would simply snap into being, anyway, so her bondmate certainly couldn't be *him.*

A large part of her was glad he wasn't. Bonding with him would save her from death, but for how long? Her very existence was... well, not quite illegal, not quite an abomination, but close. If word got out about her *and* she was bonded to the sovereign?

Memories of that dark, padded room, of that all-consuming terror and pain made her shudder. *Disaster.*

Bonding to Viktor or someone like him would have been ideal. He never would allow her to come to harm, and would be open minded enough to accept *all* of her. But Theodore Solbourne? No. Even if she could believe for half a second that he actually wanted her *for* her, she could never, ever trust him with both parts of herself.

"I'm not joking," he replied, shaking his head. The curl resting against his brow fluttered with the movement. "Just like I wasn't joking with your grandmother this morning when I told her the only way she's getting you back is by tooth and claw — *after* she refused to tell me what exactly the threat against you is."

Theodore tilted his head, a very cat-like movement, before lowering his voice to ask, "I wonder... does it have something to do with your search for a bondmate? That would explain her reluctance to tell me, I suppose."

Margot felt like she'd gotten verbal whiplash. "I— You spoke to Sophie already?" All the blood rushed away from her face. "You told her to *fight* you?"

"She told me you were in danger and then refused to tell me the truth as to why. And like I said, I *know* when I'm being lied to." He shrugged, but nothing about it seemed casual. Every movement Theodore made carried the sensual lethality of a predator. "Now, are you going to tell me, or am I going to have to uncover the truth myself?"

The swiftness with which this encounter with the sovereign got out of hand left her reeling. Margot had no idea what to say. For once, her genius intellect and her overly intensive conditioning failed her.

Theodore had her trapped neatly between those terrifying claws.

No matter what she said, she would be forced to reveal information she couldn't risk getting out. Margot hadn't even told her family that she was on the hunt for her bondmate — she certainly didn't want to tell this incredibly powerful man, a dangerous stranger with undefined motives, that she was actively dying. He could use it against her and her family; perhaps even blackmail her by threatening to reveal it to her grandmother.

Neither could she tell him the truth about the threat that hung like an axe over the back of her neck every day of her life. But explaining that her search for a bondmate had nothing to do with that threat confirmed that it existed in the first place, which would demand the explanation she *could not* give.

Margot sat in her seat, paralyzed.

Theodore watched her for some time, his half-lidded gaze so focused on her face that she imagined he was trying to crack open her mind with the look alone. When the minutes ticked by and her throat did not stop its panicked constriction, he finally broke the spell.

Letting out a frustrated breath, Theodore skimmed the pads of his fingers over the back of one hand, then the other. Two tiny flares of magic later and the blood on his claws disappeared. *Sigil lined gloves,* she noted numbly. *Expensive. Must be custom made. I wonder why he wears them.*

Pushing back his chair, he stood up to circle around the table. With apparently no effort, he grasped the back of her chair, pulled it a little ways out from the table, and spun it slightly to the side, angling her toward him. Margot sat frozen, her heart hammering against the cage of her ribs, and waited for violence, for coercion, for the charming facade to fall now that he knew he wouldn't get his answers so easily.

But Theodore Solbourne didn't wrap his fingers around her throat or bare his fangs terrifyingly close to her face. He didn't rage at her at all.

Instead, he dropped down into a kneeling position by her feet and gently cupped her tightly balled fists, his gloved hands engulfing hers in gentle warmth.

Margot stared down at the sovereign, one of the most powerful men in the world, as he knelt at her feet, and watched her world narrow into a pinprick. Her breath rasped in her nose.

She couldn't understand what was happening, who he was, what he *wanted.*

"This is not how I wanted things to go," he quietly admitted, eyes down. Deep lines of discontent formed between his heavy brows and at the corners of his mouth. "I had so many plans. I had a strategy. I thought..." He sighed, and she could feel it against the pebbled skin of her arms.

"Fucking Blight," he swore, tightening his hold on her fists, "you're *shaking.*"

Margot opened her mouth to tell him it wasn't because of him, but nothing came out. Her throat was closed, her ability to process language obliterated by the sight of the sovereign on his knees before her.

Theodore lifted his head to look into her face. His expression was strained, hardly the cool mask of controlled contempt he showed to photographers and politicians, making him something entirely new.

A self-deprecating smile curled his lips and deepened his dimples. "You don't have any reason to trust me. I'm a stranger with an infinite capacity for harm. I know that. I really do. My siblings have warned me for years that I might come on too strong."

He lifted her balled fists to his mouth, and for a strained moment she thought he would kiss her knuckles, but he simply hovered there, his breath puffing against her sensitive skin with a wispy caress.

He looked up at her through his lashes, so long that the light caught the tips and turned them green, violet, and yellow with that peculiar elvish iridescence. "I don't hold your caution against you, even though it feels like a knife to the ribs every time you look at me like you're waiting for me to claw you."

A single word managed to squeak through her closed throat: *"Why?"*

Theodore was quiet for a moment, his eyes moving slowly to trace a path across her features, searching for something. "I don't think you're ready to hear that yet. I've pushed you far enough for a morning after a bombing." Giving her a lopsided grin that made him look unforgivably boyish, he continued, "I'm going to earn your trust, Margot Goode. I *am.* A decent place to start would be seeing to your comfort. Glory knows it'll make me feel better, at least. We should probably get on with that, don't you think?"

Slowly releasing her hands, Theodore stood up to his full, impressive height and gestured toward her untouched plate. "Eat, Margot. I'm going to make some calls in my study before the rest of the world descends on us. I'll have someone point you in my direction when you're finished."

He turned to go, and he was nearly to the door when her voice returned to her.

Sounding painfully croaky, she asked, "You're just going to drop it? Just like that?"

"It?"

The words felt like sand on her tongue, gritty and coarse and *strange.* "My bondmate. The threat. Either. Both."

Theodore turned to give her a steely-eyed look. "Oh, I'm not done. I *will* find out what you and your grandmother think is so dangerous about you being here. I might give you time to tell me on your own because I want you to trust me, but if it comes down to your life, Margot, I will force the issue." A muscle in his jaw ticked. "And we don't need to discuss who your bondmate is. We already know."

Again, she asked, "But *why?* Why do you care? Why does it *matter?*"

His lashes swept down, concealing the look in his dark eyes as he once more turned to leave the dining room. Sweeping his claws over his shoulder in an expansive gesture, he answered, "Eat. You're going to need your strength, Margot."

And then he was gone.

~

She was only alone in the dining room, left to reel, for approximately ten minutes.

Most of that time was spent staring blankly out at the rippling waves as sunlight began to break through the dense fog between Treasure Island and San Francisco, trying to wrap her mind around the strategy Theodore was playing.

It was useless.

Margot felt as though he was challenging her to a game she didn't know the rules for or even have enough hands to play.

Nothing about her was important enough to warrant this sort of attention, let alone the bizarre machinations he seemed intent on. Even being Sophie's granddaughter wouldn't earn her this sort of multi-layered political maneuvering. The only thing she could come up with was the chance that he already knew her secret and planned to use it against people she had never so much as spoken to — but if that were the case, he would have just *said* so already.

I'm not fit for this, she thought, staring at her half-eaten fruit with loathing. *At this point, I'd rather just have it out in the open and be done with the dancing around and lying. I'm dying. I don't have time for politics.*

No, she didn't want to die, and she certainly didn't want to see any harm come to her parents, but she also didn't know how to handle Theodore's talk of bondmates, his hands on her, the way her stomach tightened when he smiled at her, combined with the constant fear of exposure.

Better to have a threat announce itself clearly than play her for a fool.

Realizing she was gripping her fork so tightly she could no longer feel her fingers, Margot carefully set it down and pushed away from the table, her breakfast hardly touched.

"Oh, did you not like your meal?"

At the sound of the soft, lilting voice, Margot's head snapped up. Her eyes landed on a tall elvish woman in the doorway, her lithe frame swathed in a crisp gray uniform and her mass of auburn curls half pinned behind her head. She was beautiful, with an air of age about her that lent her a sophisticated mien.

Margot took in the amethyst cast of her skin, her height, and the tips of her pointed ears peeking out from beneath her curls in one single look. She forced herself not to tense, but every muscle in her body wanted to lock in place at the sight of yet another predator, another one of the beings she had gone *her entire life* trying to avoid.

The exercise in self-control sharply illuminated a truth she wasn't ready to face: that she had, at some point without her noticing, stopped tensing in Theodore's presence.

"No, it was lovely," Margot managed to say. "I'm just not particularly hungry at the moment."

The elf drifted into the room on long legs, her movements catlike and graceful except for the smallest hitch in her gait. *A problem with her hip,* Margot's years as a healer immediately supplied. *It's rotating incorrectly. Either a ligament issue or a problem with the joint. An old injury maybe. Could be a developmental issue, but that's less likely.*

Interesting that this woman would have such a high rank, as the gold Solbourne pin on her breast implied, when she had such a visible imperfection. Margot was under the impression that any outward sign of weakness was unacceptable to elves on the whole.

Eyes of pale gray settled on Margot's face with a small, barely perceptible frown. "That won't do. Look how thin you are — and all those bruises! How are you going to get stronger if you don't eat enough?" Those eyes flickered toward Margot's plate, her frown deepening. "I specifically instructed the cooking staff to make a good meal for a healer. Was their research on the subject incomplete?"

"It was perfect," Margot firmly answered, smothering the flare of irritation she felt when the elf mentioned her size.

It raked up old, painful memories of playful jabs that struck too close to home, as well as the very real, very painful facts of her life. She might have been taller, a sturdier weight, with a period that came at an earlier age, more *normal,* if only—

No. Do not travel that road again. Resentment gets you nothing but misery. Move on.

Margot stood up from her seat and carefully placed her napkin next to her plate. Striving to sound normal, like the feeling of being alone in a dining room with a strange elf wasn't about to make her hyperventilate, she said, "I'm sorry, I don't think I caught your name. I'm—"

"Healer Goode, I know." The elf had her hands on Margot's upper arms before she could even think to step out of her reach. This time, there was no helping the way Margot froze, her fight or flight instincts battering against her rational mind.

"I'm Andy," the elf said, a warm smile creasing her lovely face, "the Houserunner. I'm in charge of taking care of the entire Solbourne Household, which now includes you. Isn't that wonderful? I'm so happy to finally meet you. Welcome!"

Margot made a reedy sound of opposition, but Andy didn't seem to notice it. "Now, I believe Teddy has someone out sifting through the Healing House for your belongings — I am *so* sorry to hear about what happened, by the way! *Goodness,* an attack on a Healing House? Who would do such a thing?" She shook her head with a grimace that revealed delicate fangs. "But that may take some time and we won't know the condition of things besides. In the meantime, Teddy asked me to arrange for a private shopping trip to get you the necessities." Andy waved her hand with a jaunty wink. "And whatever else you like, I'm sure. Sweet boy does love to spoil us."

Andy gave Margot's stiff arms a gentle squeeze and leaned a bit closer to ask earnestly, "What do you need in the meantime? I have the basics, of course, but I've never had to think about a witch before. I don't want to miss anything." Her eyes wandered to the ruined dress Margot wore. "A change of clothes for the trip is in order, of course."

Despite opening her mouth to deliver a laundry list of

protests, starting with the fact that she was *not* a member of the Solbourne Household and ending with the fact that she could buy her own clothing, *thank you very much,* Margot stifled the urge.

For one thing, Andy had the air of soft earnestness that reminded Margot very much of her Noni Tula, and she knew from experience that saying no to that kind of person always left her feeling like a monster. For another... Well, so what if Theodore wanted to buy her clothing on his own dime? She was already a de facto prisoner. He might as well clothe her.

Besides, she did have one very specific, extraordinarily pressing need Andy could fix.

"That would be amazing," Margot answered, forcing a smile. "Thank you so much for thinking of me, Andy. I mostly only need the basics that you've already given me. But if you could get me a couple bottles of Noscent body wash, I would be very appreciative."

Andy's auburn brows rose with surprise. "Noscent? The scent blocker? Whatever for?" She leaned forward, nostrils flaring, and Margot couldn't help her instinctive need to move backwards, her heart leaping into her throat.

"You smell lovely, Healer Goode. Like a summer storm." Her smile was warm, if a bit baffled, when she added, "And something else, too, though I can't quite put my finger on it. I wonder..."

It was a miracle that Margot's voice didn't come out shredded when she replied, "It's a healer thing. Please, I would really be much more comfortable if you could get me some, Andy."

"I..." The elf made to lean in again, her expression growing more confused by the second, but Margot took a quick step backward and out of her loose hold before she could take a closer whiff. Blinking quickly, Andy cleared her throat. "Of course. A few bottles of Noscent. You're sure that's what you—"

"Yes," Margot answered, swallowing a jagged lump of fear in her throat. "I'm sure."

Chapter Seven

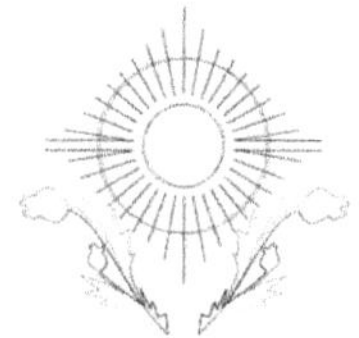

Margot stood in front of a heavy wood door and smoothed her trembling hands down her thighs. Andy quickly procured several pieces of borrowed, very elvish clothing for her, but only a handful fit her significantly shorter-than-the-average-elf frame. A soft, fitted gray dress with a high cowl collar and black tights weren't exactly exciting, but Margot was happy to have them. Anything was better than her bloody dress.

But the change of clothes and second, scalding shower didn't wipe away the nerves she felt when confronted with the door to Theodore's study.

Margot finger-combed her hair back behind her ears self-consciously, her throat bobbing. It was impossible, but she swore she could feel him just beyond the wood, his energy buzzing against her hypersensitive nerves.

She *wanted* to go in. Desperately. She wanted to open that door and see him behind some fancy glass desk, his head bent over a file or a tablet, and...

And what?

She didn't have the answer. Margot didn't have the answers to anything anymore. Her whole world went up in smoke with the Healing House. Now nothing made sense, and the only thing that felt *right* was being near Theodore — even when she wanted nothing more than to snap her teeth at him.

It was an impulse she didn't understand, but Margot was smart enough to know that instinct had a mind of its own. Perhaps, under all the trappings of his position, her instincts understood what she didn't: that Theodore truly didn't wish her any harm.

Either way, she needed to knock on the door.

Sucking a deep breath, Margot straightened her spine and gave the door two sharp knocks.

"You're always welcome, darling."

Darling. The endearment made her flush to the roots of her hair. People had given her nicknames before, of course, but she usually endured them with a stiff smile. *Short-stuff. Pixie. Sunshine.* All of them cute, but with the edge of something patronizing that she couldn't quite get past.

But *darling...*

Darling was old-world. Classy. It was what a besotted husband called his wife in one of those ancient entertainment feeds, and for reasons she couldn't parse, it made her want to bite her lip and hold her breath until the butterflies in her stomach stopped their flapping.

Margot wasn't about to let him see that, though. Who knew what havoc a man like Theodore Solbourne could wreak with that kind of knowledge?

The door opened silently, its hinges perfectly oiled, and revealed a room that made her forget all about butterflies.

"Oh," she breathed, stepping inside. The toes of her flats nudged a thick, expensive carpet as she admired the floor to ceiling bookshelves that framed the room. They were crammed full of rare printed books — not the recycled kind that everyone else had, but the real, virgin-paper kind. The kinds with old-school leather and thread bindings, too. All of them were lovingly encased in glass panels, keeping out anything that might damage their delicate and infinitely precious contents.

"I should have guessed you like books."

Theodore's voice drew her attention to the far end of the room, where a behemoth, live edge desk dominated. It stood out sharply against the massive windows. Outside, a gloom had settled over the choppy waters.

Theodore cut an imposing figure against the backdrop of dark clouds and white-capped waves. His hair was mussed, disheveled in ways that spoke of fingers and frustration, but a smile lingered around his lush mouth as he leaned back in his chair to watch her take in all his treasures.

"Of course I like books," she replied, for the moment ignoring the way his gaze made every bit of magic in her veins buzz. "Who doesn't?"

"Only fools." Theodore rested his chin on one of his palms. His expression was warm, indulgent. "Do you want to look at some of them?"

Margot took half a step toward the nearest shelf before she managed to stop herself. "No, I couldn't. They're too delicate. I'd hate to damage them."

"You won't."

He rose from behind his desk slowly. The wheels of his luxurious office chair made soft clicking noises over the hardwood floor as he pushed it backwards and circled the huge, polished desk. "This is a small part of the Solbourne Archives, you know," he told her. "Just the stuff that has sentimental value to me. If you'd like, I can show you the whole collection."

If she'd *like?* Margot would have killed to see that collection — and she took an oath to never do that sort of thing!

Heartbeat stuttering with excitement, she crept closer to one wall, her eyes darting as she tried to read every title at once. "That'd be a dream come true. I swear I've read everything in the Collective's library, and I've never had the chance to go to any of the big collections before, so if you could..."

The sentence died on her lips as she felt Theodore's heat radiating behind her. One huge, dangerous hand settled on the curve of her lower spine. His voice was pitched low when he said, "You cannot imagine the satisfaction it would give me to make one of your dreams a reality."

Margot swayed backward into his hand as she tried to breathe past the sudden constriction of her lungs. "You said these were the books that had sentimental value to you. What's special about them?"

Theodore bent slightly, putting them nearly cheek to cheek when he answered, "They were my mother's."

Margot's eyes widened. *Oh.*

No wonder he kept them close by, locked up safe in glass and polished wood.

There was no official statement on what happened to Raina Barbieri-Solbourne; only that she passed away in the chaos surrounding Thaddeus II's execution. Margot knew her recent history well enough to put together that Theodore must have been only a baby then. At thirty-five, he was only just considered an adult under elvish law. It was entirely likely that he had no memories of his mother.

Just like her.

Margot turned her head just enough to see him out of the corner of her eye. Any more and they would have bumped cheeks. "You're lucky to have something of your mother's to remember her by. I wish I did."

Theodore rubbed his hand up and down her spine in a slow, comforting circuit. "Was your mother called to Grim, too?"

She shook her head. "I don't know. I don't even know her name."

"Does that make you angry?"

Margot pulled back to look at him more fully, surprised by his question. Most people asked if the fact that she didn't know her parents made her sad, or begged off talking about it altogether for fear of upsetting her. But Theodore asked if she was *angry.* It was the kind of question only someone who understood would ask.

"It used to," she answered, looking into his somber expression with open wonder. Just who *was* this man? "And I suppose it still does, deep inside, but you have to let go of that sort of thing eventually. It'll poison you if you don't."

Theodore skimmed the pad of one leather-covered thumb over her cheekbone. It spoke to how much he handled her, and how much she craved that handling, that Margot barely noticed it beyond the usual thrill it inspired.

"Or, if you're very lucky, you can have something come along that forces you to put aside that anger so you can take what you really want in life." He fell silent, his expression achingly soft in ways she didn't understand.

They stood in that silence for several long moments. There was no sound in the room besides the low hum of electronics and their own steady breathing. They looked at one another unabashedly, each amazed by the other for reasons all their own, and wondered what it would be like to close the short distance between them.

The sound of a cell phone vibrating on his desk broke the spell. Making a disgruntled noise, Theodore gave her cheek one last lingering touch before he stepped away to check his phone.

Margot turned away under the pretense of examining the books. She licked her lips and thought, *Margot Ellouise Goode, you've lost your damn mind.*

But now the thought was lodged in her brain and wouldn't be dismissed. What would it be like to just... let Theodore kiss her? He clearly wanted to. Whether his reasons for wanting to were genuine or not remained to be seen, but no one looked at a person like that and *didn't* want to kiss them. More disturbing than that revelation was the one that came after it.

Margot wanted to kiss him, too.

I'm dying. She squeezed her eyes shut and tried to get her breathing back under control. *I'm dying and that's why I want to touch him so bad. I'm dying. My brain is one electrical charge away from oozing out of my ears. There's no other reason.*

It had nothing to do with his striking features, the way he

moved, the confidence that seeped out of his pores, the way he looked at her like he wanted to get on his knees and beg her for something she didn't know how to give. Absolutely not.

"That was my PR team." Theodore's voice shattered her train of thought. When she turned to look at him, Margot found him fiddling with a control panel on the edge of his desk. A clear screen flickered to life in front of his face, but she couldn't see what streamed across it from where she stood, only the flashing light that reflected off of his high cheekbones and dark eyes.

"The news got out that the Healing House was destroyed," he explained, tapping away at a projected keyboard. A thread of anger replaced the previous softness in his voice. "There's no information out about the situation, obviously, but someone leaked your name and photo to the press. They're speculating."

Cold fear washed away the warmth in her blood. "They... Does everyone know who I am now?"

Theodore met her eyes through the screen. His expression was grim. "Yes, darling."

Oh, goddess. Margot swallowed the acid swell of bile that crept up her throat. Her relative anonymity had been her greatest defense. Now that it was gone... *It's only a matter of time before people find out.*

Margot met his hard look with one of wild-eyed panic. For the first time in a very, very long time, all her training vanished. "That's bad, Sovereign. That's— I can't— No one should know who I am. That's *bad.*"

"Only if we don't nip it in the bud. We will." He braced both hands on the top of his desk and leaned forward, his expression unbending. "You are *safe,* Margot. I'm never going to let anything happen to you again. Whether you believe me or not is irrelevant — it's the truth. We are going to fix this together." Theodore's voice was sure, soothing in its unbending authority.

Margot's spine straightened in response to that steel, a little bit of her panic falling away. The core part of her, the hidden, dangerous thing, knew without a shadow of a doubt that he would not let anything happen to her.

Instinct, she acknowledged. It was instinct and intuition that told her Theodore would take care of things. She just had to make the choice to trust it.

Feeling a little more calm, if not entirely on board with the idea of handing him the reins, Margot walked around the two plush armchairs in front of his desk to rasp, "What do you need me to do?"

Theodore gestured for her to circle his desk, allowing her to step into his intimate space. Never in a million years would Margot have pictured herself standing *behind* the sovereign's desk. But there she was, circling it to stand fearlessly beside the sovereign as he laid a heavy hand on the curve of her hip like it was the most natural thing in the world.

With his free hand, Theodore nudged the clear screen toward her. Viewing it from the correct angle, she could see great swaths of information running across the glass: newsfeeds, emails, messages, data streams, stock tickers. Displayed most prominently, however, was a single message from his PR team.

Theodore squeezed her hip. "How do you feel about putting out a joint statement with me, darling?"

"I've only ever helped Sophie with hers before." She glanced up at him warily. "What do you want us to say?"

"Well..." He shot her a lopsided smile. "You could start off by telling everyone you're having a great time as my guest."

Margot arched a brow. "That I'm not a prisoner, you mean."

"Exactly." Theodore peered at her closely. "You don't still feel like one, do you? Because you're not. If you'd like to leave, I'll let you go." His hand tightened on her hip, sending another swarm of butterflies flapping in her stomach and a message at odds with his promise. "Can't say I won't follow you, though."

Margot shook her head. She still couldn't believe that this man wanted anything to do with her — so soon after they met, and when she was the wrong species? There was no way he wanted her *that* way.

But she didn't think he wanted to hurt her, either, and at least in this, she believed he actually wanted to help her.

"Okay," she answered, moving her attention back to the screen so she didn't feel compelled to actually answer his question. "Let's write a statement."

By the time they finished crafting a statement that both soothed the public and yet gave nothing away, it was late afternoon. Margot was shocked by the ease with which they worked together, how flawlessly their thoughts meshed as they collaborated. She was even more surprised to find herself enjoying the lunch Andy and her staff brought into the study for them.

Theodore was... charming. No, not just that. He was attentive, focused. He appeared to hang on her every word even when he firmly disagreed with something she said. He was quick to tease and equally quick to push more food across the desk for her. She lost track of the number of times he quietly refilled her glass of water when she wasn't looking.

He hovered, but not in the way that made her feel caged. It was as if Theodore got his greatest pleasure out of taking care of her, and jumped at any opportunity to do so, no matter how small the task was.

Margot had no idea what to make of that.

She had even less of a grasp on how to handle him when she found herself in a hastily cleared out luxury department store a few hours later, a fleet of black and glamour-clad guards manning all the exits as Theodore pawed through a rack of dresses.

"Why did you put this one back?"

Margot set a soft white sweater onto the small pile of clothing she had gathered. "I was only looking at those," she answered, trying to get past how bemusing it was to see the sovereign picking through silky cocktail dresses worth a fortune. She couldn't decide if the scene was more or less bizarre without the background buzz of other shoppers.

"Don't you want this one?" Theodore pulled a violet dress off of the rack, and then a soft, backless dress in cream that made her sigh with pleasure when she touched it. "Or this one? I saw you look at both."

"Exactly, I was just looking." Margot turned away from him to look at her neat bundle of essentials on the low sofa just outside of the dressing rooms. "I don't have any occasion to wear anything like those dresses, and I'm not about to ask you to pay for things I don't need."

"You didn't *ask* me to pay for anything," he smartly replied, much closer than before. Not a second later, both dresses drifted down to cover her pile of sweaters and skirts and jeans and all of the practical necessities she now lacked. "I want you to get everything *you* want, darling. There's no limit."

She looked up to find Theodore standing beside her with his hands perched on his lean hips, a mulish look on his face. The sovereign was stubborn, but she could be, too. "There is a limit when the gift comes with strings."

Theodore's lips thinned. "There are no *strings.* I'm taking care of you. It makes me happy. Consider this... compensation for my lack of adequate protection. You wouldn't have lost all your belongings if I'd been there."

Margot rubbed her forehead. "We've been over this, Sovereign. There was no reason for you to be there in the first place. You're not my—"

His voice carried across the cavernous department store when he announced, "Get what you want, Margot, or so help me, I will buy the entire women's department and *you* will have to deal with the fallout."

Exasperated and reluctantly flustered by his insistence, Margot crossed her arms. Her first instinct was to respond to his challenge in kind, her hackles raising at his imperious tone, but she had to move past that urge.

For reasons beyond her, she knew that this *meant* something to him. And fighting Theodore on it would only dig the hole deeper. A night and a day in his company and already she understood that the sovereign was a man unused to hearing the word *no,* and when he did, he took it as a signal to do *more,* not less.

"I already agreed to let you buy my clothes," she said, most of the annoyance smoothed out of her voice. "But I really *don't* need the dresses, Sovereign. Where am I going to wear them? I've never even been to a party before. I don't go to fancy dinners. It would be a waste of your money and a waste of two beautiful dresses." Against her better judgment, she cast a wistful look at the dresses. "I've *never* worn anything like that before."

And I probably never will. A grim thought, but a truthful one.

Theodore's stance relaxed a little. His expression, previously hard-edged and stubborn, smoothed into something softer. Canting his head to one side in a gesture she had come to recognize as his "time to quiz Margot" tell, he asked, "You've really never been to a party? What about a nice dinner? A symphony?"

Her throat constricted around a jagged spike of grief and old bitterness. "No," she answered shortly, turning away to fuss with the pile. "Grandma never let me the few times I was invited."

Not even her own graduation gala, the party thrown to honor all the apprentices of her year at one of the most advanced hospitals in the world. For Margot, there were no symphonies. There were no club nights with her cousins. There was no prom or festivals or fairs. There was only the Goodeland, the hospital, and her own shriveled potential.

Too many people in too tight quarters, her grandma always told her. *You never know who could be standing next to you. Why invite the danger? It's not like you don't have friends to spend time with here at the lake.*

Except she had cousins, not friends. Acquaintances, not confidants. Fellow apprentices, not comrades. Cold distance, not embraces or kisses or—

A leather-covered finger curled under her chin. Theodore guided her face up until she could not avoid his gaze even if she wanted to. "You know, the more you tell me about your grandmother, the less I like her. What possible excuse could she have for caging you like that?"

"She had her reasons." Good ones. *Very* good ones.

Margot gently extracted her chin from his loose grasp. Her stomach twisted with a mixture of guilt and dread. "I'm surprised she hasn't threatened to storm the Tower yet," she told him, only half joking. "Grandma is... very protective of me. Always has been. Knowing I'm with you must be making her tear her hair out."

Well, metaphorically, anyway. Sophie Goode didn't lose her cool *ever.* No matter how dire a situation, no matter how riled Sophie was, she never, ever let on. Stoic was the name of her game, and if she had ever been any other way, Margot wasn't aware of it.

Sophie felt things, though. She felt deeply. No one in the Coven or the Collective could deny that. Every single one of her actions, no matter how coldly calculated they might initially seem, were aimed at protecting the people and Coven she loved above all things. Margot only hoped that what she did that afternoon, that publicly aligning herself with Theodore would make her grandmother think twice before trying to forcefully remove her from the EVP, inadvertently causing Margot's death.

Theodore picked up the white cocktail dress, mindful of the wicked tips of his claws, and held it out to her with a smile that was all challenge. "I would very much like to see her try." His smile melted into a look so warm it glowed. Pressing the wispy, achingly pretty gown into her hands, he softly added, "Take the dress, darling. I promise I'll find a reason for you to wear it."

Margot slowly closed her fingers around the fabric. Her mouth was strangely dry when she asked, "You're sure?"

"Yes. Now hurry up and get more." He grinned, huge and delighted. "We have a dinner reservation, remember?"

Oh, she thought, her ears buzzing as the world narrowed down to just Theodore: his little eye crinkles, his dimples, his four terribly dangerous fangs. *Oh, he's... I don't think anyone's ever smiled like that before.*

Perfect. That was the word she couldn't find.

When Theodore smiled like that, he was perfect.

Dinner was dreamlike. There was no other way to put it. Only in a dream would Margot find herself tucked into a private room at a restaurant whose name she couldn't pronounce. Only in a dream would she sip fine fey wine from some obscure corner of Europe and catch sight of a handsome elf through the crystal of her glass. Only in a dream would Theodore Solbourne sit across a tiny table and ask, "Will you answer a question for me?" in a voice that made everything in her stand at attention.

Margot toyed with the stem of her glass, her stomach full and heavy with a luxurious dinner of delicately sautéed greens and angel hair pasta. She knew that she would need to ask Andy to procure some of her special protein mix tomorrow, as she had gone too many days without it, but the beautifully made meal would hold her over until the morning, surely.

The golden wine made her a little sleepy, but not enough to wipe away her wariness when Theodore cocked his head to one side. His own meal — a raw slab of white-veined Wagyu beef drizzled with some sort of dark sauce she couldn't identify — was long gone.

"Depends on the question," she hedged. "If it's not too personal, sure."

Theodore raised his eyebrows and looked away. "Well, see, that's going to be a problem." He took a long sip of his own wine before turning his gaze back to her. In a low voice, he said, "Everything about you is personal to me."

Margot flushed. Had he caught her watching his lips on the glass? The way his jaw moved? The tantalizing glimpse of his throat his high collar allowed her?

No, that's the wine talking, she firmly reminded herself.

"Just ask, Sovereign."

Setting her half-finished glass aside, Margot tore her gaze away from his face to focus on the flickering candles between them. What was she doing, letting herself drink with him? Her size made her a natural lightweight, and the burn out meant she couldn't filter the alcohol out of her system as efficiently as she usually could.

Margot knew she needed to be sharp to keep up with whatever game Theodore wanted to play with her, so the wine — delicious fey honey wine that cost a fortune — would just have to wait.

"Why the Healing House?"

She glanced up, surprised. "What?"

"Why the Healing House?" Theodore leaned an elbow onto the table and casually traced the tip of a claw over the curve of his lower lip, his eyes locked on her. "I saw your intake form and your application. You are enormously over-qualified for that kind of position. That's for low-level brightlings and retiring healers, not someone who performed groundbreaking neurosurgery at *sixteen.*"

The air left her lungs in one great *whoosh.* "I..." Margot sat back in her chair, suddenly acutely uncomfortable under his intense scrutiny. "How did you even know about that?"

It was one thing to understand he'd been surveilling her — she was, after all, the granddaughter of the Goode Matriarch in foreign territory — but to find out about her work at the hospital... That went a step beyond normal background checks. *Many* steps, actually.

"I'll answer your question with one of my own, since you

keep dodging me," he replied, smiling that slow, challenging smile that made her pulse race. "How come you went under a pseudonym when you published the paper after the fact? Don't you want people to know what kind of healer you are? What you can do?"

Margot winced. Theodore had no way of knowing how mercilessly he picked at wounds, old *and* fresh. Throat tight, she answered, "It's complicated."

"I promise I can keep up if you explain it to me."

"I already told you that my grandma is protective." Margot folded her hands in her lap. They shook. "I meant it, Sovereign. She... I wasn't allowed off of the Goodeland until I got into the apprenticeship at Luminous General. The only thing that convinced her to let me do it was its reputation, but even then I wasn't allowed to..."

Make friends. Sign her name to groundbreaking research. Take credit for the work that might have made her one of the most respected healers in the world.

All this power to save lives, she thought, *squandered.*

Either way, Glory's blessings meant nothing. If she exposed herself, there would be no more healing. If she lived by her grandmother's rules, there would be no more healing. If she died, there would *definitely* be no more healing. No matter which way she looked at it, Margot was stuck; her power to do good smothered to death by circumstance and an inability to change it.

"That paper made headlines all over the world." Theodore dropped his arm onto the table with enough force to rattle the dishes. "Luminous General was lauded for it. Got grants for it. I watched a feed of the Head Healer accepting an award for that surgery — and then I found out most of the work was done by an apprentice only identified by the initial *M.*"

Margot didn't know what to make of the budding outrage in his voice, nor the fact that it seemed to be directed at everyone except her.

Brows slashing downward in a thunderous scowl, Theodore

continued, "You reconstructed brain tissue that was functionally *dead,* Margot. For Glory's sake, why wouldn't Sophie want you to get the credit you fucking earned?"

"No, it's not fair," she replied. "But I understand why she wanted me to stay anonymous. The world isn't safe for people like me."

Theodore's expression sharpened. Like a great cat sniffing blood, he leaned forward slowly, his claws digging tiny furrows into the tablecloth. "What do you mean by that?"

"I mean, I—" Margot waved a hand, as if she could wipe the statement from his mind with a gesture. No, there was no way she could hope to explain it to him without lying. She had no desire to test his ability to pick up deception and dig a deeper hole. "I just mean that it's not, okay? And to answer your question, I chose the Healing House because I came here looking for my bondmate, like I told you. Working at Laguna Honda or Solbourne General wouldn't have allowed me the freedom to do that."

Not that she didn't *want* to. San Francisco's premier medical institution, unfortunately named after Theodore's family, was in league with Luminous. Their Healing Ward was phenomenal. Their contributions to the field of healing were renowned.

Margot would have loved to walk those halls, to work with those healers, to do the research that might save so many lives — but that kind of high profile position was out of the question.

That might have made her grit her teeth before, her wasted talents and intellect grating like ground glass under her skin, but now Grim's soft hands rested on her neck. Margot didn't have the energy or the time for that old, all-consuming bitterness. Death had a way of putting that sort of thing into perspective.

But of course, Theodore's keen eyes didn't miss a thing. "Do you *want* to work in the General?"

There was no way to answer that without revealing too much or lying outright, so Margot decided not to answer at all. Throwing caution to the wind, she snagged her wine glass and took another long pull of the sweet, richly flavored fey concoction. It was potent stuff — so potent that once upon a time it was rumored to turn non-fey into Changelings with only a few sips.

That wasn't true, of course, since Changelings were fey children who simply looked and acted like humans until they hit puberty, but Margot could see why it had a reputation.

Not that drinking it would actually stop Theodore now that he was on a roll, though. Margot hadn't known him long, but it didn't take her genius intellect to pick up on the fact that he was a doggedly determined sort of elf.

Margot watched him warily from over the rim of her glass when he offered, "I could talk to the Head Healer and—"

"You *will not,*" she snapped. The wine went a long way toward loosening both her tongue and her temper. "It's one thing to buy me some clothes, Sovereign, it's quite another to get me a *job.* Please, I have some pride left!"

Theodore's smile returned, but this time it had an edge to it that made her insides knot. "I'll get you whatever I like," he shot back, "and I'll keep doing it even when you swipe at me. You know why?"

Margot sat up straight in her chair so fast she swayed. She fisted her hands in her lap, her jaw set in a hard line. Were all sovereigns this insufferable, or was it just him? "Why?"

"Because I *like* it when you claw at me." Theodore's eyes, so dark, framed by those lush, sooty lashes, promised all sorts of things she couldn't take him up on. "The more you fight it, the sweeter it will make the moment you give in, darling. Just wait."

She sucked in a livid gasp. "You are the single most *arrogant* elf on Burden's ba—"

A shrill beeping cut her off.

Theodore's hand snapped to his breast pocket, the place she knew he kept his phone, in the same instant that he lurched out of his chair so fast it tumbled onto the floor with a *bang!*

She didn't get a chance to ask him what was wrong. One moment she was fuming, and the next a burning wall of magic opened up behind her. Margot clutched at the armrests of her chair as it rocked forward, pushing her stomach into the edge of the table hard enough to knock the breath out of her.

M-gate, her mind helpfully supplied as Theodore lunged across the table to haul her chair out of the way. He tugged her out of it just as quickly. *Who would open an m-gate in a restaurant?*

The initial burst of light and energy from an m-gate was legendary — they were, after all, one of the most complex and energy-consuming magical feats — but Margot had only ever read about them before. Theodore turned his body to shield her from the worst of the light, his arms locked tight around her and his shoulders curved to shelter her, but Margot still managed a peek at the dazzling break in reality that consumed the far wall.

Two figures materialized in the shattered brilliance of the m-gate just as it began to fade. Two *familiar* figures. Margot unconsciously shrank into Theodore's chest. "Oh no."

Theodore palmed the back of her head as he straightened, his fangs bared in a display that would have sent a saner person running. Turning only enough to look at the newcomers, he bit out, "Madam Goode, you have *impeccable* timing."

Chapter Eight

Any other time, any other place, with anyone else, Theodore might have been impressed by the sheer, jaw-dropping audacity of Sophie Goode's trespass in his territory.

As it stood, however, Theodore was *furious.*

Pushing his consort behind his back, he turned to confront the woman who, by means he couldn't fathom, had circumvented the portable wards that his guard carried at all times.

Sophie Goode stood by their abandoned table. Dressed in a slim black pants suit, her graying hair pulled back into an elegant knot at the base of her neck, she looked like she was on her way to a business meeting, or about to make a speech on the UTA Congress floor. Her expression was utterly impassive, her hazel eyes cold. Even her scent radiated chill; a crispness that seared his nostrils when he breathed deeply. A weather witch by birth, everyone knew that Sophie Goode's main ability was *ice* — in politics *and* magic.

Her companion stood half a step back. Theodore identified him at a glance: Alric Goode, Sophie's protégé. He was tall for a human, his build thick in the way that implied frequent use of his arms and shoulders. His features were aquiline, his eyes hooded and his skin tone a rich golden brown. Scrawled across his skin in white ink were sigils too numerous to count. Power thrummed off of him in waves — hot and barely contained, the polar opposite to his Matriarch's disturbing chill.

A gatekeeper. Alric was rarest of the rare: a glorian who could tear the very fabric of time and space with his bare hands.

In the same instant that his guards threw open the door to the private dining room, Theodore thought, *No wonder she could get past the wards. She has her own damn m-gate on speed dial.*

"We're fine!" Theodore threw up a hand, forestalling his guard's instinctive response to eliminate the intruders. They were a fiercely protective unit, one that he was proud to call his own, but this was not a situation they could solve with violence. Meeting the eyes of the captain of his guard through the haze of his glamour, Theodore shook his head. "Close the door, Laurence. I'll handle this."

There would be a furious conversation later, though. His guard took their responsibilities as a matter of life and death. This kind of blatant mistake, no matter how unavoidable, would hit them hard.

Feeling Margot attempt to step around him, Theodore grit his teeth and shifted to block her from sight. Logically, he knew that her grandmother was no threat, but his instinct was to protect, and the rest of him wasn't exactly inclined to give Sophie Goode the benefit of the doubt.

When the door clicked shut, Sophie had the gall to arch a brow at him. "And how exactly do you plan on *handling* us, Mr. Solbourne?"

"By throwing you back the way you came," he snapped, "before I take my due for this blatant disregard for both my borders and my privacy."

"Both your borders and your privacy became moot points when you decided to hold my granddaughter hostage." Sophie's gaze slid to one side, no doubt taking in the sight of Margot leaning around Theodore's arm. "This all could have been avoided if you had turned her over to the Collective this morning, but here we are."

"Grandma, he's not holding me hostage." Margot ducked around him, but he didn't let her get far. Snagging the back of her dress with the tips of his claws, Theodore prepared to haul her backward if she made to run to Sophie's side.

Except she didn't run. Margot halted only two steps away from him, putting herself solidly in the middle of the fuming parties. "I *told* you," she continued, "I don't need to be rescued. I am doing fine."

"Fine?" Sophie's eyes skimmed Margot's face. There was no visible change in her expression, but something in her eyes got impossibly colder. "Explain to me why you're covered in bruises. Or perhaps why you've gotten so thin again. Have you not been taking your supplements since you left?"

"Supplements?" Theodore frowned as Margot shrank ever-so-slightly backwards. Curving his fingers over her shoulder, he gently guided her closer. "What supplements?"

Margot's gaze didn't settle on his face for more than a moment. "I have a protein deficiency. It's not a big deal."

"It absolutely *is* a big deal." Theodore glared at her, the temptation to bite almost too much to overcome. "Are you telling me that you've needed something for your health this whole time and you didn't *ask* for it? Is that why you haven't healed yourself yet?"

She didn't respond, but the way she pursed her lips and wouldn't meet his eyes was answer enough.

Theodore sucked in a huge breath. *Calm. Calm. We will discuss it later.* When he could bite her in private.

"I knew this was a bad idea," Sophie interjected. "I knew it, and I let you and Tula talk me into it because I'm too soft with you. I see that now. I should have put my foot down the moment you floated the idea of coming here." Turning her head to look at Alric, whose gaze slid slowly between Margot and Theodore, she commanded, "Open another gate, Alric. We're taking her home."

Margot and Theodore reacted at the same time. *"No."*

Sophie was already turning, clearly expecting Margot to follow without question. "No?" She turned back around. "Have you lost your mind, Margot? You know what he is."

Each word came faster than the last, sharper, until he could feel Sophie's furious disapproval like tiny shards of ice piercing his skin. Theodore drew Margot closer. If it was bad for him, he couldn't imagine what it must feel like for her.

"No," his consort answered, unyielding. "No, I'm not going. I know what I'm doing, Grandma." His neck tingled. It was a lie, but one he wasn't about to call her on. "I didn't ask you to come rescue me because I don't need rescuing. I'm an adult. I can handle myself."

Sophie arched a brow. "Since when, exactly?"

Theodore tensed, a snarl lifting his lip to reveal aching fangs. *No one* got to speak to his consort like that.

Before he could say anything, however, Margot broke away from his hold to stand in front of her grandmother, her hands on her hips. "Since *now,*" she bit out. "I'm not just your granddaughter, remember? I'm a Goode! I have some damn pride — and I can take care of myself. I didn't need you to come rescue me and I definitely don't need you to humiliate me."

"Humiliate you? How?" Sophie didn't raise her voice, but her eyes glittered with ice. "By trying to protect you? By doing everything in my power to keep you safe?" She didn't give Margot time to respond before turning her head sharply toward her protégé. "Alric, the *gate.*"

"By not trusting me!" Margot raised a hand as if to gesture sharply. He noticed, in the bare second before she curled it into a tight fist and lowered it once more, that it shook.

When she spoke next, her voice was quiet and layered with old pain. "Am I not a witch, Grandma?"

Sophie stiffened. "Of course you're a witch. When have I *ever* made you feel otherwise?"

"Right now." Margot took half a step backward. "Any other witch in the Coven, Grandma. Any other witch you would trust to take care of themselves. But me? I'm different, right? I don't get that trust. Because to you I've always been a liability."

Theodore's chest constricted in one agonizing lurch. There was a wealth of pain in his consort's voice; a lifetime of sorrow that he had only seen the shadow of until now.

Sophie's response was stiff, tight with restrained feeling. "I have only ever wanted to keep you safe." Her gaze flicked toward Theodore. "From *everything.*"

Margot rubbed her forehead, her shoulders rolling forward in a defeated pose that made him want to tear something apart. His proud consort, a woman who wore dignity like a cloak, who could bring the dead back to life with her bare hands, should *never* look like she'd lost a battle of wills.

"I've never been safe," she quietly replied. Her tone was stark, almost bland. "You and I both know that. I'm asking you to trust me, Sophie. That's all."

There was a taut silence as both women stared at one another, communicating things Theodore couldn't begin to understand. He glanced over Sophie's head to meet the eyes of her protégé.

Alric kept his eyes locked with Theodore's. It was impressive, considering most sentient beings couldn't withstand his direct stare for more than a handful of seconds. When his eyes finally slid away, Theodore got the impression that it was not because he couldn't handle it anymore, but because he had something more important to look at.

Addressing Margot, Alric asked, "Is it him?"

Margot flushed. "Is *what* him?"

"The reason you want to stay." Alric shrugged. "It's okay if it is, you know."

Theodore's heart beat an uneven rhythm. *Was* that why? Did she finally believe what he'd been telling her?

"Of course it's not him," Sophie answered for her, utterly self-assured. She turned a withering look on her companion. "Margot is far too smart to do something like that. Besides, if she wanted a relationship, there are plenty of eligible beings I can introduce her to."

Alric's hooded gaze traveled slowly around the room, taking in the candles, the half-finished bottle of wine. "I don't know, Sophie. This looks an awful lot like a date to me. I guess I shouldn't be surprised. I knew you had a reason for wanting to go to the Protectorate so bad." His full lips quirked. "Cousin, are you seeing the sovereign? Is that why you want to stay?"

Every eye settled on Margot. "I..." She cleared her throat. Drawing herself up into her usual prim pose, she answered, "Well, that's really not your business, is it? And so what if I am?"

It wasn't a yes, but it was close enough for Theodore to send Sophie a slow grin. "Yes," he purred, stepping up to mold one hand around the curve of her waist, "so what if she is? Do you intend to force her to leave my side when she so clearly wants to stay?"

Margot tossed him an exasperated look. "Not helping!"

He shrugged. "Never said I would."

No, the beast in him had only one goal, and it wasn't to soothe Sophie Goode's worries. It was to win Margot, to bind her to his side, to gentle her and run his hands over her skin and let her claw at him to prove his worth. Not even the logical part of him cared what Sophie thought, though.

"Margot," the Matriarch began, "do *not* do this. You cannot imagine what kind of risk this—"

"I'm not *doing* anything except staying in San Francisco." Margot held her grandmother's stare unblinkingly. "I love you, Grandma, and I appreciate the concern, but this is... I *have* to do this. I am not going back with you. I don't need rescuing. You are just going to have to live with that. And if you can't... I guess you'll just have to force me."

"Margot, in three days every important elvish family will descend on this city for the Summit." Sophie gestured sharply to the room at large. Her voice didn't change, but the temperature in the room dropped several degrees as her composure finally began to unravel. "Do you really want to be here when that happens?"

"I can handle it." Margot didn't bow under the heavy weight of Sophie's disapproval. "In fact, we put out a statement today that told the public I'm staying with the Solbournes as an act of goodwill and friendship. You have to have seen it. I know that's why you snuck in here instead of going public to get me back. What would it look like for the Coven — for the *Collective,* if I left now? Tell me."

The answer was obvious to everyone in the room: *Bad.*

It would look like the Goodes, and Sophie in particular, didn't honor friendships, and that would severely hurt their image as collaborators with the other territories. The shifters in particular would take it as a mark against the Collective, and that sort of thing could tank any trade deals or business agreements they had. And whatever else Sophie Goode was, she was a dedicated and ruthless ruler.

The fact that Margot had neatly laid a trap that pit Sophie's wishes against her loyalty to the Collective was a masterful bit of manipulation. The Matriarch had been thoroughly outmaneuvered.

Sophie knew it. Theodore could see it in the subtle tightening of skin around her eyes as the silence stretched.

The only way this plan of hers would have worked involved Margot quietly returning to the Collective or, as she suggested, being forced. Theodore would let neither scenario happen. *Not that she appears to need me to fight her battles,* he thought, gritting his teeth against the pounding desire in his veins. *Godsdamn if it doesn't make me want to clear off that table and just—*

"Fine." He braced himself for something scathing, but when Sophie continued, he was surprised to hear how quickly the woman could pivot. The remoteness returned to her expression. "Since you've given me no choice, I will play it the way you want me to. You'll stay."

He smothered a sneer. "How very magnanimous of you, Madam."

She turned her attention to Theodore. All business now, she said, "I'll send out word that the Collective thanks the Protectorate for the special care you've taken with our healer." She blinked once, slowly, as if even that small movement was a concealed threat. "And you *will* take care of her, Mr. Solbourne, or this will not be the last time you see me."

"Believe me," he muttered, "I don't want that."

"The feeling is mutual." Sophie looked at Margot. Despite her rigid control over her expressions, Theodore got the impression that this was costing her much. He wondered if, in some small, shriveled part of her chilly soul, she was actually proud of Margot for so elegantly waltzing out of her control. "You *will* call if you need me, Margot. No Collective witch walks alone. I will not let you."

Margot's smile was small, heartbreaking. "I'll call, Grandma. I promise."

"That's settled, then." Sophie turned around to face Alric, who was already raising his sigil-tattooed hands in the air to open the gate in the wall. If he hadn't just witnessed the intense battle of wills between the Matriarch and her granddaughter with his own eyes, he wouldn't have believed she felt anything at all. "Look for a copy of my statement in the morning."

There was an enormous, teeth-rattling tearing sensation in the air as Alric opened the m-gate. Before she could leave, however, Theodore raised his voice. "And Madam Goode?" He waited until she met his gaze to finish. "Don't ever fucking trespass in my territory again. Next time, not even being kin will protect you."

He meant it, and he made sure everyone in the room knew it, too.

They stared at one another, leader to leader, for several tense seconds before the Matriarch nodded once. Turning her head back around, Sophie stepped into the blinding light with the confidence of a woman used to such power. She glanced back only once, for a split second, to meet Margot's eyes before disappearing from view.

Alric tipped his head in a nod. "You know how to reach me if you need anything, short-stuff." He cast an appraising look in Theodore's direction. There was a keen intelligence in his eyes, as well as a familiar, distinctly *Goode* hostility that made Theodore bare his fangs. "I sure hope you know what you're doing."

As soon as Alric stepped through the gate, it collapsed in on itself, reality and blistering energy coalescing back into its preferred shape.

Margot slumped against Theodore's side, muttering, "Me too."

~

The car ride back to the Tower was a long, quiet one. Margot stared out her window, every line of her expression and her body language telling a story of exhausted defeat.

Theodore didn't understand it. She stood up to her ice queen of a grandmother with a stubbornness that made him proud. What did she have to feel defeated about? As far as he was concerned, she won a challenge that few would have escaped unscathed.

But he didn't want to push her when she looked so fragile, so he carefully withheld the urge to tug her closer and tell her how proud he was of her, how much he admired her spine. He could give her space.

Until they got to the Tower, anyway.

When they got to the door of her suite, Margot turned to offer him a quiet goodnight, but Theodore wasn't about to leave her. Realistically, he *couldn't.* The pull was only getting worse the longer he held himself back from the skin contact he craved. Asking his strained nerves to take total separation was too cruel to contemplate.

Theodore Solbourne was a proud man, but not fool enough

to forgo a bit of begging when it suited him. "Let me stay with you tonight," he pleaded.

Margot stared up at him with wide eyes. Exasperation finally brought some color back to her face. "I don't think that's— I'm not going to sleep with you!"

"I'm not talking about sex." Although just the suggestion made him ache in ways he couldn't acknowledge in polite company. "I'm talking about staying with you tonight. I can tell you shouldn't be alone, and I— fuck, Margot, I don't want to spend another night in the hallway. Let me keep you company tonight, darling."

He watched, rapt, as she gnawed on her bottom lip. Shifting warily from foot to foot, she asked, "You won't expect anything?"

Theodore leaned into the doorway, drawn by her orbit. "Not even a kiss."

She waffled for a moment longer, but the very fact that she didn't immediately reject him gave him hope. So did the way she swayed, ever-so-slightly, and the glazed look in her eyes. Fey wine was notoriously strong, and his delicately built consort had plenty of it before *and* after Sophie's appearance.

"Okay," she finally answered, glancing away. "I need to take a shower first, but if you come back in fifteen minutes maybe we can have another cup of tea."

"Another shower?" His brain might have short-circuited over the image that presented, if he didn't so vividly recall her damp hair from breakfast. "Didn't you already take one?"

Her endearingly shy expression shuttered. "Do you want to spend the evening with me or do you want to criticize my bathing habits, Sovereign?"

Theodore threw up his hands in surrender. "Fine, fine. I'll wait."

Roughly twenty minutes later, he sat on the couch in the suite's sitting room, his suit abandoned in favor of the breathable, much more comfortable workout clothes he wore when he sparred with his guards. He didn't own pajamas, and although he was titillated by the idea of showing up in her suite nude, Theodore knew that saving her the heart attack was the more merciful route.

There would be plenty of time for those things later.

Margot set a steaming mug on the coffee table in front of him. "You look like a cat burglar."

"A what?"

She gestured to his clothing. "All that black and the turtleneck. You look like you're about to go rob a high security bank, except you're missing a balaclava."

He watched her sit down, deliberately keeping one cushion between them, and gave her a bemused look. "All banks are high security."

"Not the point."

"These are my comfortable clothes." Theodore glanced down, trying to see what she saw. Nothing looked out of the ordinary to him. A high-necked, long-sleeved athletic shirt and comfortable black pants that wouldn't get in the way when he fought. There was nothing abnormal there. "Do you not like them?"

Margot avoided his eyes as she took a long sip of her tea. Her hair was loose and wet down her back, and her pajamas hung off her frame in ways that made his cock pay close attention. All of that was deliciously distracting, but he couldn't focus on it. Not when her scent was... *gone;* washed away under the subtle, astringent smell of Noscent.

He wrinkled his nose. Why in the world would she keep using the stuff? He could understand it in a Healing House, where anyone with a sensitive nose might wander in and it was best to be prepared, but in private? He couldn't wrap his brain around it.

"Why would that matter?" Her eyes darted to meet his before he could open his mouth to respond. "You know what? Don't answer that. You look fine."

Theodore leaned back into the cushions. Looping an arm behind her, he waited until she wasn't drinking before he slowly dragged her across the empty cushion between them.

Margot clutched her mug with both hands. "Hey!"

"What?" He settled her under his arm.

"You said you wouldn't try anything," she accused, her cheeks flushed bright red. Despite her protestations, he could tell that she was flagging. A blow-out confrontation with her grandmother and nearly an entire bottle of rich fey wine, finished *after* said confrontation, left Margot looking like she might keel over at any moment.

It was a good thing he was there to soften her landing.

Theodore dipped his head to breathe in the scent of her hair. This close, not even the Noscent could totally wipe it away. Relaxing now that his beast had her in its lungs and in its arms, he replied, "I made no such promise. I said no sex and no kissing. I very deliberately did not say *no touching.*"

Margot huffed. Eyeballing the gloved hand draped over her shoulder, she remarked, "You know, for such a touchy-feely guy, you sure wear your gloves a lot."

"You sure look at them a lot." He playfully pricked at the fabric of her pajama top with his clawtips. "I wonder why."

Unsurprisingly, Margot didn't answer him. Not that it mattered. As soon as she melted into his side, her little feet drawing up to tuck themselves under her thighs, he didn't care about anything else.

"Comfortable?"

She set her mug next to his with a sigh. "Yes." Tentatively, like she wanted to stop herself but couldn't, Margot turned to rest her undamaged cheek against his chest. Her voice was a painfully soft whisper. "This is... this is really nice."

Heart hammering, Theodore curled his arms around her and shifted slightly so he was leaning against the armrest, allowing her to stretch out along the cushions. "You sound surprised."

"I don't get much physical contact," she admitted. "I've never done this." Her voice dipped even softer, as if she were speaking to herself. "I shouldn't do this. I don't even know why I want to."

He peered down at the top of her head. It didn't even bother him that her damp hair soaked through his shirt. The satisfaction of *holding* her, of knowing she *wanted* to be held, was indescribable. "That's a shame." He lifted a hand to begin sifting his claws through her hair. "Elves love to cuddle."

"I didn't know that. I thought elves were one of the more solitary races."

"That's what we like to make people think." He stretched out his legs alongside hers, tangling them until they were both more or less horizontal on the elf-sized couch. Turning his nose into her hair, he added, "But we're not. We're pack animals just like shifters or orcs. We need touch to thrive. We're just selective about who gets to do the touching."

"...Oh."

Sensing a change in her mood, Theodore took in a deep breath and let it out in a long, slow purr. Margot jumped a little. "What was— Are you *purring?*"

Instinct pressed close. *Gentle her. Make her see you can be soft.* He purred a little louder and cupped the back of her head, urging her to relax. Within seconds, the stiffness disappeared, leaving her languid and soft against him.

She was quiet for a while, so Theodore pulled her closer and asked, "Do you want to talk about what happened with Sophie?"

"Not particularly."

"Do you want to explain to me why you didn't let me or my staff know you needed protein supplements?"

"No."

He nodded. "Do you want to talk about us?"

She made a low sound of disapproval.

"Darling, you're laying in my arms." He gave her a small squeeze. "You can't say there *isn't* an 'us'."

"Theodore." His name slid off of her tongue in a rebuke, but it still made every muscle in his body stiffen. "I told you, you're not—"

Curling his claws into her hair, he gently fisted a handful and used it to tip her head back. Margot sucked in a sharp breath and met his hungry gaze with wide eyes. Her round pupils were blown up into huge, black discs.

Roughly, he demanded, "Say it again."

Margot licked her lips. *"Sovereign."*

"You must really want me to bite you."

He could feel her heartbeat against his chest. It was fast, almost birdlike, and the feeling of it made him ache so much worse. His cock was a hot bar in his sleek pants, his hormones a raging storm in his blood. It would be so, so easy to drop his head and kiss her until neither of them could breathe. It would be even easier to flip her over, cage her in, and close his fangs over her vulnerable throat like his instincts screamed at him to do.

As if sensing his intentions, Margot's lips parted, inviting him closer. Still, she rasped, "You said you wouldn't kiss me."

Theodore squeezed his eyes shut. *Why the fuck did I say that?*

Because he was trying to give her as much time to adjust, to get to know him, as he could. Because he *wasn't* that ravaging beast that howled inside of him. Because he wanted Margot to want him as much as he wanted her.

Even so, *not* kissing her was one of the single most painful tasks he had ever encountered.

"This is torture," he muttered, hauling her onto his chest so that her head was tucked under his chin. If he couldn't see her, maybe the temptation would lessen.

Except that meant having her slight weight draped across his body — including her soft thigh, which was currently pressed against his erection. Theodore tipped his head back and opened his eyes to stare at the ceiling.

Mercy, he prayed. Perhaps Glory would listen, but it was more likely that Tempest, the god of wind and love and ceaseless, changeable lust, would hear him and *laugh.*

Margot shifted, unintentionally rubbing her thigh against him. "What's wrong?"

He breathed deeply, but it didn't help when the air was saturated with the scent of her, with that golden thread of desire that made him want to tear her pajamas off with tooth and claw.

"I'm doing my best to keep my promise," he tightly explained. "Now relax and go to sleep, darling." *For both our sakes.*

"I never intended to use you as a pillow." It was cute that she would say that even as she settled more heavily on his chest, her cheek resting just above his heart. One soft hand curled into the fabric covering his side, anchoring them together in her own way.

Husky, he said, "I like being used as a pillow."

"Does everyone know that the sovereign likes to cuddle?" Her voice was delightfully drowsy.

"No." Theodore smoothed his claws through her drying hair, his heart a huge, aching thing in his chest. "Just you."

Margot's breath began to even out, but just before sleep could claim her entirely, she whispered, only a touch slurred, "Good. I like that you're mine."

Mercy.

Chapter Nine

"She's fucking lucky to be alive."

Kaz leaned forward in one of the supple leather chairs on the visitor's side of Theodore's desk, his forearms braced on his knees and his huge green hands dangling between them. His hair, Solbourne black, was loose today. It hung in thick waves over his massive shoulders, inky against the jewel tone of his skin.

In the other chair sat Valen Yadav, General of Patrol and the man all three Solbourne sons aspired to be like. Military somber, with a steely spine and head high, Valen watched the two boys he helped raise with dark eyes, his expression stormy.

Like the rest of the Solbournes, he considered Margot one of theirs. The fact that she was harmed under *his* guard was a blow to his professional and personal pride. To Valen, Margot was a charge he failed to protect, and that was unacceptable to both the man and the general. The events of the previous night, when Sophie Goode so neatly humiliated the Sovereign's Guard, was yet another blow.

Valen had just finished outlining the facts of the preliminary report on the bombing and the new security measures they would be implementing within the Guard, and although he didn't say it aloud, Theodore could see his agreement with Kaz's assessment in his eyes.

Theodore stood at the corner of his desk, one hand braced against the edge, and tried to get his breathing under control. The mere suggestion of how close Margot came to death made his gorge rise. "And there has been no evidence of dissent? No threats slung around beforehand? That's not normally how these kinds of things work."

Separatist groups, rebels, zealots against the Temple, or magic, or the EVP government — they all *loved* to talk. Never, in the history of the Protectorate, had there been a politically motivated attack that didn't come with a declaration before or immediately after. They *couldn't* keep silent, not if they wanted their violent statement to mean something.

Valen shook his head, his close-cropped salt and pepper hair standing out starkly against his deep, sapphire-hued skin. "That assumes this was a politically motivated attack. We have no evidence of that yet."

"But the political ramifications are huge," Kaz replied, his voice a deep, sonorous rumble. "Just days before the Summit? And come on, a *Healing House?* You might as well accuse us of not being able to protect our young, too."

Considering how fiercely they guarded their children, it was an insult that would have sent any elf into a frenzy. One simply *did not* threaten children. They were too precious, too few, and family too much the bedrock on which the entirety of the elvish hierarchy lay to ever allow a threat against them.

Forgetting that absolute fact was when Thaddeus II finally crossed one line too many — and the reason Delilah slit his throat with her own claws.

"Yes, but there's been no statement. We're nearly forty-eight hours out from the blast. If it was political, it's a sneak hit — and probably the first of many. The city is on high alert and the bomb squads are on call just in case there's more." Valen scrubbed his claws against the white stubble on his hard jaw. There was no sign of strain in the hard, blocky planes of his face despite the fact that he probably hadn't slept a wink since the bomb went off. "But there's no evidence either way. We need to look at everything, including the possibility that it could be solely related to Margot herself."

Theodore clenched his jaw and heard his fangs squeak against one another. Elvish fangs were self-sharpening, their position allowing them to lie against one another when the jaws closed and scrape against one another when they opened, honing their points to constant, deadly sharpness.

Theodore wondered if he could clench his jaw hard enough to snap them. He wasn't keen on testing the idea, but if they kept talking like that, he would.

"She was definitely the target," Kaz pointed out. He twined his fingers between his knees and looked at Valen from beneath the curtain of his shining hair, unintentionally reminding Theodore that Kaz was, in fact, the pretty one. "If she had gotten home from that dinner any earlier, she would have had her brain turned to jelly or her body torn to shreds by shrapnel. It was pure luck that she didn't."

Valen nodded. "Teddy, has she said anything about who her enemies are? Who might be after her?"

Reminding himself that he liked his desk and did *not* need to rake his claws across the fine polished surface, Theodore grimly answered, "No. She and her grandmother have been infuriatingly closed-lipped about any threats." He breathed deep, recalling the previous night's hours of bliss and torture. "But I'm making progress. She's starting to trust me. She won't tell me now, but I know she will soon."

"She won't tell you?" Valen let out a harsh breath and sat impossibly straighter. His affront was clear when he demanded, "Why? We're *elves.* There's no enemy we can't handle." He gave Theodore an assessing look. "Haven't you been courting her these past two days? What's taking you so long?"

Theodore scowled. "It's taking exactly as long as it needs to.

She's skittish and has no reason to trust us, remember? *We* are the ones who let her be blown up."

"That's exactly it," Kaz dryly pointed out. "Problem is that *we* might be enemies. Why would the Goode Matriarch, who notoriously refuses to do business with elves, and her granddaughter, who was just attacked in elvish territory, trust us with their secrets?"

The stern lines of Valen's face deepened with his frown. "I've met Sophie. She wasn't always that way. I still can't really believe she had the balls to drop into our territory like that. Back when she was just starting out as the Matriarch, I remember her pushing for more cooperation with us." A speculative light entered his dark eyes. "She wasn't head of the Collective yet, I don't think, but I remember she had close ties with the du Soleil family. I don't know what happened there."

Theodore shook his head, his nerves stretched taut. Every second away from Margot strung them tighter, until it felt like he was being slowly pulled apart from the inside.

No wonder they call it the pull, he thought darkly. *And it's only been less than a day. How bad are things going to get if I can't make any inroads with her soon?*

He was reminded of the hunted look in her eyes, the sharp tang of fear in her scent, and felt a cold wash of dread in his veins. Courting Margot was never going to be *easy,* but Theodore had a feeling that it was going to be like trying to climb a sheer wall with his claws retracted.

He could do it. He *would* do it, but the ticking clock of the pull put a pressure on their courtship that made everything a thousand times more difficult.

Every second he went without skin contact, without beginning the processes of binding them together, made his thoughts a little foggier, his temper a little less restrained. The sovereign couldn't afford that loss of control at the best of times, but *especially* when he had the Families coming to discuss the future of their entire race in a matter of days.

The mention of the Goode family's ties to the *du Soleil* family, of all people, only made his mood worse.

The du Soleils were some of his loudest critics, and one of the biggest voting blocks of the Parliament. They were proud, secretive, and deeply suspicious of his family. Delilah's petition for abdication was nearly rejected because of the lobbying of Olivier du Soleil, a man nearly the same age as Theodore and three times as arrogant, and his father, whose cool hatred of Thaddeus II hadn't abated with his bloody death.

"Do you have any friendly contacts with the du Soleils?" Theodore suspected he already knew the answer.

"We don't have any friends in that camp," Valen replied, mirroring the sour look Theodore wore, "but the line of communication is never closed. They're coming in any day now for the Summit. I can have a meeting with Marcus to see what he knows."

Theodore was quiet for a moment, considering the facts. His claws drummed a slow beat on the polished wood of his desk. "I know we don't want to talk about it," he began, low and pained, "but there is a possibility that Margot was targeted not because of anything *she* did. It could be because someone knows."

Valen scrubbed his claws through the short strands of his hair, more aggressive than before. In a voice heavy with warning, he said, "Only the family knows who she is to you, Teddy. Close family."

"I know." He shook his head. The pain of that kind of betrayal might break him. "But it's something we need to consider, even if it feels unthinkable."

Kaz shifted back in his seat, the leather of his chair squeaking under his considerable bulk, and crossed his arms over his chest.

His claws, naturally black, stood out starkly against the orcish skin-tone of his partially bare forearms. He was strapped with muscle, his body a weapon honed for protection, and his pretty face was almost always set in a neutral, borderline disinterested look both men and women couldn't seem to get enough of.

But he was an orc, so Theodore wasn't surprised. *Everyone* thought orcs were attractive.

In most ways, Kaz took after his mother. Almost no one would assume he was a halfling by looking at him, but Kaz was as much a Solbourne as Theodore, Delilah, and Sam — something he paid for again and again.

"That's a line of investigation that may have nothing at all to do with the bombing." Kaz pursed his full lips, his eyes narrowing as he considered the facts. "If we can't get relevant information out of Sophie Goode, we have to get it out of Margot. We don't know if she is actively in danger, or if this is a small part of a bigger plot. Until we know for *sure* that she's not the sole target, we can't rule out the fact that she could be hit again. We need to talk to her."

Theodore wrestled back the urge to snarl. "She's not being *fucking* interrogated, Kaz."

Kaz sent him a reproachful look. "Of course not. But if she's in danger, then so are *you.* We have to know the facts, Teddy, for all our sakes."

"We can't waste valuable resources tracking down every possible lead when we have the ability to rule things out right now," Valen chimed in. "I know you don't want to push her, but the Summit is nearly here, Teddy. We're already stretched thin. We can't afford to keep Patrol on alert for much longer. Eventually we'll be forced to stall the investigation to protect the Families."

It went unspoken that if something happened during the Summit, when all of the members of the elvish Parliament met, Theodore could not only lose his throne, but his life as well.

Not being able to defend his own territory was bad enough, but putting so many elves at risk, when their numbers were already so abysmally low? It would be grounds to unseat his entire family in the bloodiest possible way.

And then who would protect Margot? What would all of this be for? How can I change the world and save my people from themselves if I'm dead?

Theodore knew the answers to those questions, but it didn't make the idea of Margot being pressed hard for information she clearly didn't want to give anymore palatable. His instinct was to coax, *gentle,* not interrogate.

But being Sovereign wasn't about making things easier for himself. It was about making the hard choices to protect the people he loved, even if it hurt them in the short-term.

Forcing the tense muscles of his jaw to relax a fraction, he ground out, "Fine, we can talk to her."

Valen and Kaz shared a glance. It was the older of the two who started, "Teddy, I don't think you—"

Theodore lifted his lip to show off his fangs. "No. I will *not* let you interrogate my consort without me in the room."

Kaz sent him another long, reproachful look, his dark eyebrows arched high. "Do you think you can actually control yourself? I was in the car with you two, if you remember."

"What the fuck is that supposed to mean? I didn't do anything wrong in the car."

"No," his brother generously allowed, "but you also couldn't keep your hands off her. That was a few minutes after first contact. How are you going to be now that you're forty-eight hours into the pull? If we start pushing her, if she gets anxious, will you be able to stop yourself from lashing out?"

Theodore opened his mouth to reply, but Valen beat him to it. In his usual cool, rumbling voice, the old general said, "I remember the pull, Teddy. It makes even the sanest elves crazy — and most elves don't have twenty-five years of built up anticipation like you do." His voice dropped, slowed, until it was as gentle as a hard-edged man like Valen could make it. "Let us talk to her, Teddy. You know we'd never intentionally cause her any pain. She's ours too, remember? We just want to protect you both."

He knew that. Of course he knew that. But millennia old instinct couldn't be so easily subverted. Theodore's beast didn't view either man as competition — Valen's consort being Andy, a woman who was for all intents and purposes his grandmother, and Kaz being... well, *Kaz* — but the protective rage burning a hole in his gut could not tolerate even the suggestion that Margot might find their questioning uncomfortable.

It was one thing for *him* to push her. No one else could claim the privilege.

Theodore crossed his arms, his expression unchanging. Margot's trust was as fragile as an eggshell. He'd be damned before he let anyone do anything to damage it. "If you want to talk to my consort, you will do it with me present or not at—"

A knock on his study door, two light taps, cut him off. Theodore's head snapped towards the heavy oak door, polished to a luminous shine, that tightness in his chest unfurling in an instant.

Margot's here.

His heartbeat jackhammered in his chest and his blood rushed in his ears. Without a conscious thought, Theodore was across the room and opening the door in the span of a few seconds.

Wrenching the door open, he found his witch a pace away, her hands tucked neatly behind her back and her face already tilted upward to peer into his eyes before carefully averting her eyes. His stomach knotted up at the sight of a soft pink blush staining her cheeks, just the same as when he skimmed his knuckles over her skin by way of goodbye not two hours before. Her blush hadn't died down since she woke in his arms, delicious mussed and kissable.

Because he was aware of everything about her, Theodore noticed that she had changed since their leisurely breakfast in her suite, her pajamas replaced with a soft green sweater over a black skirt and tights, but he only relished seeing her in the clothes *he* gave her for a moment.

The surprise and delight of seeing her, of her seeking *him* out, usurped everything else.

Theodore could feel the heavy gazes of his brother and Valen on his back, but he disregarded them. Just then, only *she* mattered. "Is everything alright?" he asked, fighting the urge to reach out and cup her neck, to draw her close. The only reason he bothered was because he knew Margot was shy and might balk at such an open display of affection in front of strangers.

Unsurprisingly, Margot's copper eyes darted past him, taking in the two men sitting in front of his huge, natural-edge desk. The only sign of surprise she showed was the smallest bobbing of her throat as she swallowed.

"Everything is fine," she answered, steering her eyes back to him. "I'm sorry to interrupt, but Andy said I should."

I'll bet she did, he thought wryly. Andy was a hopeless romantic. Theodore had lost count of the number of times she'd pressed him on why he hadn't sought out Margot yet. The moment she was within range for him to get a lock on her location, and after the subsequent frenzied hunt for information on the new healer in residence at the St. Francis Woods Healing House, Theodore heard little *else* from his beloved Houserunner-turned-grandmother.

The rustle of clothing preceded Valen dryly remarking, "And I'm sure my consort had a very good reason for sending you."

A flash of confusion momentarily wiped away the carefully neutral mask Margot wore. She peered at Valen. "Your consort?"

Theodore cracked a small smile. It did something to him to finally hear her say that word. It almost felt as good as hearing her say his name.

"Yes." Pleasure made his voice a touch huskier than was appropriate. He skimmed the tips of his claws over her elbow. "That's what elves call their mates. Andy is Valen's consort and vice versa. You might call them bondmates, or spouses. It's all the same."

It was fascinating to watch Margot's lightning quick mind process information in real time. He could practically feel it through their nascent bond, a current of pure electricity through his mind. *Beautiful.*

Margot tilted her head to look at Valen around Theodore, her caution apparently overridden by her curiosity. "Not exactly the same," she primly replied. "A bondmate isn't always like a spouse."

Theodore's brows drew together. "What do you mean?"

"Witches don't always choose to bond with a romantic partner." Margot canted her head to one side, then the other way, as if weighing her words. "The bond is a necessary side effect of being a gloriana or glorian. We need it to survive. Its formation doesn't hinge on romantic or sexual interest, and it's not a necessary component of reproduction like some bonds are for other races." Her gaze flickered in Kaz's direction, but didn't linger.

She looked up at him through her lashes, hesitating. When he nodded, urging her to continue, she said, "Most witches can bond with anyone they choose. It's true that many people wait for their romantic partner, but I know several bondmates who chose siblings, friends, or non-romantic life partners to bond with. My grandmother and my Noni, for instance, are life partners who bonded later in life than most." She looked away. "It's about trust. Whoever you can trust with your life, your magic — that's what makes a bondmate."

Theodore got the sense that Margot was cutting herself off, no doubt because of his continued insistence that *he* was her bondmate. Theodore wanted to tell her to continue, to talk and talk and talk. Listening to her speak was a luxury he had no intention of taking for granted.

Still, something in her explanation niggled at him. Examining her closely, he said, "Most witches?"

"Most witches what?"

"You said *most witches* can bond with anyone they choose." Theodore narrowed his eyes. Was that alarm he saw tightening the skin around her eyes? "That implies there are some who can't."

If he wasn't so acutely attuned to her, he might have missed the way she leaned back ever-so-slightly, as if she sought to pull away, to put distance between them. Impossible now that she lived in his skin as well as his heart.

"There are," she answered stiffly. Theodore didn't need their weak psychic link to know she was remembering their conversation over breakfast yesterday.

He would have pushed for more, but Theodore heard Valen sidling up behind him and forced himself to step back. *Later.*

"Margot, this is Valen Yadav. He's General of Patrol." Glancing at the man who helped raise him, added a deferential nod. "He's also family."

"It's a pleasure to meet you, Healer Goode," Valen said, his critical eye sweeping over her bruised face and down, no doubt taking in her wispy build and lack of claws, fangs, or muscle with which to defend herself. Theodore could see the displeasure hardening Valen's already stony expression before his assessment was even through.

Margot's shoulders stiffened. "Likewise, General."

He winced. She noticed it too, but unlike him, she didn't have the context to understand that Valen didn't find her lacking, but saw the same fragility that made Theodore see red whenever he considered a threat to her. Valen didn't care what she looked like or what her race was. He worried about her ability to defend herself.

"Why don't you come take a seat?" Valen stepped aside and gestured to his empty chair. "We were just about to come get you. I would like to ask you a few questions about the bombing."

"That's actually why I'm here." Margot didn't make any motion toward the threshold of Theodore's study. It was a marked difference from the way she drifted, dreamlike, into the room the previous day. "Andy was dropping off my supplements when she got an alert that someone was trying to reach me."

Theodore's spine stiffened. His claws, hidden under the silver claw-caps of his gloves, flexed hard, sending a sharp bite of pain-pleasure up through his fingertips. "Who was it?"

"Angelique Batacan. She says she has a lead on who planted the bomb."

Valen was too disciplined to rear back with surprise, but Theodore could tell by his sharp exhalation that Margot had shocked him. "Why in the world would the leader of the *weres* be looking into this?"

Theodore could only shake his head. "Viktor mentioned last night that they have a protection order out on her."

"What?" Margot looked just as surprised as Valen. "What's a protection order? And why would she do that?"

Eyeing her bruises and mindful of the fact that she had apparently been disregarding her health, Theodore stepped halfway out of his study to slide a hand behind her back and usher her through the doorway. "You should sit," he growled, making a mental note to ask her why she hadn't just finished healing herself already.

A healer with *bruises?* It was a sight so strange it was almost obscene, and one he was well past tired of seeing.

Margot let him propel her towards Valen's vacated chair, but in the stiff-legged way that implied great internal sacrifice on her part. When she was sitting stiffly on the edge of the leather cushion, he continued, "You're the only one who can tell us *why* Angelique might put a protection order out for you, but I can tell you that it is exactly what it sounds like. She put out the word that if you are harmed, the weres will take it personally and seek out retribution on your behalf. It's quite the honor."

"If you consider the protection of a bunch of half-trained, mostly-feral weres with criminal records honorable," Valen groused.

Theodore was amused to see Margot shoot Valen a look full of bristling temper. "They're good people. And if they *were* that bad, why would you let them stay in your territory? I thought elves booted troublemakers to the New Zone, no questions asked."

It was Kaz who replied, his voice thick with quiet laughter. "They serve their purpose."

"Right," she drawled archly, "just like all the rest of the Underground community. Cheap labor and illegal goods when you need it."

Kaz lounged in his chair, his expression openly intrigued as he assessed her. "Spend a lot of time in the black markets, little witch?"

Margot didn't take the bait. Instead, she merely arched a red-gold brow. "Do *you?*"

"Yes." Kaz flashed her a grin full of fang, an expression that was as notoriously charming as it was terrifying. "Maybe we can take a tour together sometime."

Theodore put a hand on the back of Margot's chair and glared at his brother. "Enough, Kaz."

Valen came to stand by Kaz's chair, his scowl focused on Margot like a stern spotlight. "How do you know Angelique?"

It was curious to watch the byplay between Margot and Valen. Instead of trying to avoid Valen's notice like many weaker souls, she locked eyes with the general and held his stare, her expression calmly impassive. Serene.

It was the smart choice. Any hint of deception or false meekness and Valen would have scented weakness. Nothing except for the steeliest will could deter the general from doing what he decided was his duty.

Theodore watched with begrudging admiration as Margot lifted one delicate shoulder in a shrug. "I'm a good healer. Word gets around and people come to me."

He didn't need his abilities to know that was a fib. "Viktor told me you have been spending your weekends and evenings in the Market." Margot's bright eyes swung around to stare at Theodore, her expression pinched with disbelief. "He said you've set up a sort of temporary clinic there."

She looked away, but not before Theodore caught the gleam of real hurt in her eyes. "That traitor. Why would he tell you that?"

It didn't sit well with him that he felt compelled to *defend* the handsome asshole he caught petting his consort, but Theodore felt a pang of guilt nonetheless. They had been friends once, after all, and if he could soothe away that little bit of hurt in his consort's eyes, he would do it.

Moving his hand from the back of her chair to the warm, smooth spot between her shoulder blades, he gently explained, "Viktor and I have a long history. We were... friends as kids. Mostly." Theodore shook his head, shaking loose the memories of a past that could not be recaptured. "He told me about the clinic because he trusts that I have your best interests at heart. He wants you *safe*, Margot. Just like I do."

Margot said nothing, but something in her eyes changed. She scrutinized him openly now, her eyes no longer skittering away from his, and open confusion and wonder brought her angular brows together. When she looked at him like that, it felt like she was really seeing *him*.

Theodore's heart pounded. That hint of vulnerability got a little bigger every time he saw it. It was an opening; a chink in the armor of caution that he could exploit. *You can trust me,* he wanted to tell her. *I'm not just Sovereign. I'm* yours.

It was Valen who broke the spell. "Why would Angelique put out a protection order for you, Healer Goode? And what information did she give you about the bomber?"

Margot blinked, her cheeks flushing, and hurriedly looked away. Theodore would have happily throttled the old man if only he didn't love him so much.

"I, uh..." She cleared her throat. "I started seeing people in the Market about a month into my residency at the Healing House. I just didn't have enough to *do* there, and I needed to— I needed to get out more, to meet people."

Theodore didn't bother to hide his unhappy glare. They both knew that the reason she "needed to meet people" was because she was on the lookout for her bondmate. Questions burned in the forefront of his mind, fueled not just by curiosity but by the ravenous sort of possessiveness he felt towards his witch.

Later, he promised himself once more. *We'll discuss it later.*

Margot steadily avoided looking at him as she explained, "I talked Jimmy, the troll who runs the Market off of Carolina, into letting me use one of the old storage rooms for the weekends I could spare. Almost as soon as I showed up, people came out of the woodwork. The weres especially." She shook her head, a look of helpless frustration passing over her fey features. "Broken bones, lacerations, head trauma. You name it. I swear, half my patients turned out to be weres. I knew they got into fights a lot because of the impulse problems, but I didn't know it was that bad."

"And Angelique took notice," Kaz surmised.

"Yes. A month later, she showed up at the Healing House with a scowl and a huge bag of take out." Margot shook her head again, but this time she appeared baffled. "She comes by every few weeks with more food than I know what to do with and we talk for a while. She usually asks me about the weres I've seen, and I let her know if there are any that I think may need her help. I wouldn't say we're friends, but..."

"You're allies," Theodore finished for her, not bothering to hide the note of admiration in his voice. Wryly, he added, "You've been here six months, and already you've made alliances with the alpha of the Merced pack *and* the unofficial leader of the weres. I'm beginning to feel slighted."

Margot shifted uncomfortably. He could feel the stiffness in the muscles under his palm when she answered, "People like healers. I wasn't *trying* to make any sort of alliance."

He didn't doubt that. Margot obviously had a shrewd mind, but nothing about her behavior implied she had any long-term political motives. That didn't mean those connections would be useless, though.

Valen cleared his throat, a look of impatience deepening the lines around his mouth. "What did she say about the bomber?"

"Oh." Margot licked her lips, her eyes flickering around the room until they landed on Theodore. He felt some of the tension leave her. Arching her brows, she said, "Angelique thinks she knows who made the bomb."

"What? How? Where did she get that information?" No doubt it rankled something fierce to have his elite units of information gatherers and soldiers outdone by a scrappy woman who thumbed her nose at the law.

"From the bomb-maker directly," Margot answered. "She wanted to know if I wanted to... *'get my licks in'* before she made it so he couldn't talk anymore."

All three men snapped to attention, their slit pupils expanding to swallow up their irises as the promise of a hunt sank its teeth into their instincts. Theodore removed his hand from Margot's back, afraid that his sudden tension might cause him to prick her delicate skin with his claw-caps. "She *has* him?"

"Yes. That's why I thought you might want to know."

Theodore's blood thrummed with a different sort of fire. The thrill of the hunt, the driving need to protect his consort, the desire to get revenge on her behalf; all of it made his skin itch with the need to track and claw and tear.

Reaching down to gently haul Margot out of her seat by her upper arms, he ignored her squeak of protest and grinned down at her with all his deadly fangs. "Well, my darling witch," he rasped, "what do you say we go mete out some justice together?"

Chapter Ten

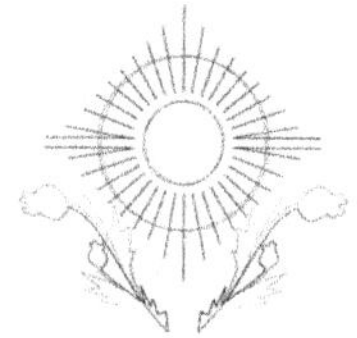

Valen was staunchly against allowing both Theodore *and* Margot to meet with Angelique, but there were certain things Theodore refused to bend on. One of those things was the need to use his own claws on the person who made his consort bleed. Another was leaving Margot.

She seemed surprised that he wanted her to come along, but it was never a question for him. Not only did Angelique stalwartly refuse to meet with any elves unless she got eyes on Margot herself, but because he *would not* be separated from her.

The pull had him in its steely grip. Even the thought of being away from her for more than a few moments made him want to gnash his teeth and start tearing at the walls.

That was how they ended up in front of a small restaurant on Geary, swaddled in coats to keep out the February chill and flanked by the Sovereign's Guard, on high alert. Margot glanced around nervously before peering into the darkened windows of the restaurant. It was closed to prepare for the dinner rush, but Theodore picked up the tenor of a few minds, buzzing with more than the usual activity within.

"I've never actually been to one of her restaurants before," Margot admitted. The wind whipped down through the narrow canyon of the street to send tendrils of her red hair flying around her bruised face.

Theodore caught a lock between his claws and carefully smoothed it behind her ear, ignoring the shy look she threw at his guards. “Neither have I. But most places don’t serve elvish food.”

Her wrinkled nose was adorable. “No, I don’t suppose they would.” Shifting a little on the sidewalk, she cast him a speculative look out of the corner of her eye. “Though, they might if elves were more open about what they actually eat.”

“The information exists,” he replied, almost missing the strained note in her voice. “Why do you bring it up?”

“No reason.”

Theodore leaned down to murmur in her ear. “Do you want to find out what happens when you lie to me, darling?”

He was close enough to hear her sharp intake of breath over the sound of cars rushing behind them. Even though her scent was dulled by city smells and the astringent sting of Noscent, he could make out the faintest thread of warm desire in it. A rumbling purr built in his chest, but he stubbornly willed it away.

If only his erection were so easily snuffed.

“I just meant that elves are notoriously secretive,” she answered, defensive despite the luscious warmth permeating her scent. “If you want to have options like the rest of us, maybe you guys should get out more. Make friends.”

Theodore considered her suggestion with more seriousness than she probably realized. It was true that elves didn’t mingle much. That was a product of the disease that nearly wiped his people out a thousand years ago. As soon as iron came into wider use by the other races, elves and fey started dying. It wasn’t until the invention of the Metallurgic Inoculation for newborns that they were freed from the grip of enforced isolation.

But old habits die hard. That tendency toward antisocial behavior was yet another holdover from a distant past that only hurt them in the present.

“Would that make you happy? If we got out more?”

Theodore caught some movement in the back of the darkened restaurant. He took a step in front of Margot, shielding her from view, as a small female figure stepped out into the main seating area and began to make her way towards the doors.

He felt Margot lean slightly around him to peer at the glass doors when she answered, "What does my happiness have to do with it?"

Everything, he wanted to tell her. *It means everything to me.*

One of the glass doors opened with a jingle. Angelique Batacan was a small, curvy woman with skin the color of rich honey and long black hair she kept out of her face with a hot pink scrunchie. She was dressed in a long floral skirt and a white t-shirt, an outfit that implied a softness at odds with the vicious scowl wearing grooves around her mouth and eyes.

"Restaurant's closed," she snapped, eyeing him up and down with open hostility. "Even for *sovereigns.*"

Theodore arched a brow. "I recall being invited."

Angelique narrowed her eyes in a shrewd glare. Her eyes were normal enough, except for the fact that they were two different colors. One was a warm brown and the other was burnished gold, the telltale sign of a dormant were. "I said *she* could come. The invitation didn't extend to you."

He wasn't ruffled by her dismissal. Theodore didn't care about her casual disrespect. His power was vast, his dominance unflinching. The were could spit at him all she liked.

What he *couldn't* abide was the suggestion that Margot should face someone responsible for her near-murder alone.

He would look that person in the eye. *He* would be responsible for her safety. *He* would be the one to make sure she got the revenge she was owed.

Letting his usual easy smile fall, Theodore straightened his shoulders and stared down the line of his nose at the small woman. "I go in with her, or my guard goes in to retrieve the captive without either of us. Your choice."

The low, purring rumble of Angelique's growl cut through

the traffic sounds around them. "I won't let even the sovereign threaten me in my own place, *elf.*"

"*Angelique.*" Margot made to step around him. "This isn't necessary. If you can just ignore him for a minute, we can talk to the guy and then be out of your hair."

Theodore clenched his jaw, the muscles of his neck straining, but turned her lack of caution into a boon for himself. Lifting his arm, he caught her as she moved to step forward and used her momentum to swing her into his side, his arm draped protectively over her shoulders.

He could feel Margot stiffen against him, but the tension was momentary. Margot loosened up immediately and offered the bad tempered were a small, closed-lipped smile. "See? He's fine."

Angelique didn't appear convinced. Eyeing Theodore's protective hold, she asked, "Everything okay, Healer Goode? That's the *sovereign* who has his arm around you."

Margot's tone was dry when she answered, "Believe me, I am well aware."

The were gave him another once-over, her expression flinty, before shaking her head and stepping aside to allow them entry. "Fine, elf, but I'm only doing this for her."

He didn't point out that he didn't *really* need her permission to enter the building. He was Sovereign; this was his city. If Theodore wanted something, he was within his rights to take it, no questions asked.

But he was smart enough to know that pissing off the leader of the weres was a bad idea. They had control of a vast underground network of information and illegal goods, not to mention that they were a viciously loyal sort. After infection with the virus that permanently altered their physiologies, most weres found themselves cast out from their families, cut loose from their jobs, and worse. Weres could be volatile, especially in their first few years, and tended to be more of a handful than most families could handle without significant time and resources.

Coming together as a tight-knit group to pool resources and

protect one another made them fiercely loyal to their kin, and Theodore was wise enough to know that pricking that sense of loyalty could bite him in the ass.

Besides, he thought, nodding to the were as he and Margot stepped into the darkened restaurant, *picking a fight might upset Margot. I want her to see me as more than just the sovereign, and that means playing nice.*

Not that it was too much of a struggle. When he wasn't under the grating influence of the pull, Theodore was a cunning but generally good natured sort of elf. Given the choice, he would prefer to make friends rather than enemies.

Angelique gave his black-clad guards by the entrance the stink eye as she locked the door behind them, but otherwise didn't comment. No doubt she already knew there were more than she could see, and a number of them posted at the back exit as well. Not that they were the biggest threat, of course.

That would always be Theodore himself.

She stepped around a small circular table and waved her hand over her shoulder, telling them to follow her as she picked her way around more tables and stacked chairs. "He's in the basement." Angelique let out a harsh breath before muttering, "Damn fool."

Margot tried to move out from under his arm, but Theodore only let her slip away enough to slide his hand down her back and onto her hip. He could feel her small shiver, could smell that familiar thread, and was tantalized by possibilities they represented.

Theodore squeezed her hip and willed the pull to be patient. Her body knew him, wanted him, even if her brain hadn't quite caught up with it yet. He would give Margot as much time to come to grips with their fate as he could. He had to.

Addressing the were, he said, "Tell me what you know."

"His name is Roger." Angelique led them through a swinging door and into a bustling kitchen. A blast of heat and fragrant steam washed over them. The smell of spices, rich tamarind and turmeric and the lush scent of fresh coconut, was almost overwhelming.

Somewhere a radio was playing tinny rock music over the sounds of frantic meal preparation and the chatter of the cooks, who cast sidelong glances at the strangers passing through their domain.

Angelique nodded curtly to the staff. They were all weres, their eyes mismatched, some covered in tattoos and thick scars, all of them bristling with the sort of wild energy that made them so very unpredictable.

Theodore tightened his hold on Margot's hip, drawing her closer. It wasn't that he didn't trust his ability to keep her safe — he was, without a doubt, the single deadliest predator in the room — but his hackles rose at the proximity of danger anyway.

They were passing by a series of massive stainless steel refrigerators when a cry of recognition went up, overly loud in the cramped space.

"Hey, Healer Goode!"

Theodore reacted instantly. Pulling her in tight against his chest, he swung around to bare his fangs at the young were who bounded toward them. Clad in a rubber apron and yellow gloves, he was a thin, sweaty youth with chestnut hair and big, downturned eyes.

In his enthusiasm, the boy glanced at Theodore and identified him too late, his arms cartwheeling as he skidded to a halt on the rubber-matted floor. The were would have knocked into Margot if Theodore hadn't lifted an arm to block the boy's clumsy stop.

That protective core of burning flame in his gut burst into an inferno.

Theodore opened his mouth and snarled, the cords of his neck pulling taut as he prepared to lunge at the threat to his consort.

"Theodore, *stop.*" Margot's voice was a cool whip across his senses, her ozone and earth smell cutting through the competing scents of the kitchen and her blockers to ground him. Her small hands settled on his arms, holding tight. "He's not a threat. I know him. He was just excited to see me, okay?"

He reared back, lip still lifted to reveal his upper fangs, and brought his other arm around his consort in a tight, protective hold. His heart slammed against his ribs. Fear and adrenaline pumped through his veins.

"*Watch it,* were," he bit out.

Angelique darted around them to grasp the straps of the shocked boy's apron and haul him out of Theodore's swiping range. "This is Frankie," she growled, running a motherly hand over his messy hair. "He's a new were and not great with his impulse control yet. He didn't mean anything by it."

"Of course he didn't. He just wanted to say hello." Margot squirmed against Theodore's chest, but he couldn't make his arms unlock from around her even if he wanted to. He didn't care what Angelique saw, or what she thought when he cupped the back of Margot's head and pressed her cheek against his thundering heart. It wasn't to comfort her, but to calm *him.*

Margot stilled. Her fists were balled against his sides, her body stiff; she didn't even breathe. For a second, he could have mistaken her for the statue of Glory in the Solbourne family shrine.

And then she relaxed.

Small fingers curled into his coat. The muscles of the shoulders under his arm unlocked. It was his turn to hold his breath as he felt the slightest shift of her weight, her body leaning into his. Her weight was familiar to him now, and more comforting than he could ever articulate.

He took in a shuddering breath. *She's okay.*

"Frankie and his brother have come to see me several times," Margot explained, tilting her head up to look at him with wide, concerned eyes. "I've healed all ten of his fingers and three of his toes. He's not a threat. I promise."

Theodore glanced between his consort and the boy, who couldn't be more than eighteen and who looked ready to collapse at any moment.

He knew that Frankie wasn't a threat. He *knew* that, but the beast in him didn't care. It recognized only split-second decisions, and once that decision was made, it would not change its mind.

Despite the rage burning in his stomach, Theodore paled.

This was what Kaz warned him about. *This* was what Valen meant when he said the pull makes even the sanest elf crazy.

Frankie isn't the only one with impulse control problems.

Theodore forced himself to slide his hand down the back of Margot's head, skimming the fall of her hair, until both of his arms were loosely wrapped around her waist. Gritting his teeth, he said, "I apologize, Frankie— Angelique. I should have reacted with less aggression."

Looks of surprise flashed across the faces of the gathered weres, but Theodore had already turned his attention away from them. Releasing a sigh, he offered Margot a wry smile. "I'm sorry if I frightened you. Your friend surprised me."

"I..." Margot's eyes darted around his face. He could feel her fingers flexing on the fabric of his coat as her throat bobbed with a hard swallow. "It's okay," she whispered, surprise making her voice and expression softer, somehow younger than before.

Except it wasn't okay.

He was *Sovereign.* More than that, he was a grown man. He knew how to control his impulses, how to keep his claws to himself. Theodore was appalled that he came so close to attacking a teenager who would have stood no chance of surviving even a glancing blow from his claws.

Elves trained their youth in combat so hard for that very reason. It wasn't about knowing how to fight. All elves were born with that instinct. It was about *controlling* that impulse, and keeping a steely grip on a strength that could destroy someone so easily.

Theodore's claws were made of an almost molecularly identical material as diamonds. He had a bite force that could snap metal. His bones were as dense as concrete and his muscle mass outstripped most other races. He *had* to be in control, to keep a rigid handle on his strength and his temper, or else he would end up just like his father — a narcissistic madman who killed without hesitation or remorse.

Angelique muttered something in Frankie's ear before turning him around by the shoulders and pushing him towards a thickly muscled cook. The cook clasped the boy's nape with a wary glance at Theodore before stepping away, taking the boy out of sight with a muttered word of reassurance.

"Apology accepted."

Theodore looked at Angelique with open surprise. She wore a no nonsense look as she began to guide them toward a small door in the farthest corner of the kitchen once more. "I didn't realize," she continued, shooting the pair a suspiciously knowing look over her shoulder. "If I had, I would have cleared the kitchen before you got here. New mates are always edgy. This was my bad."

Margot sputtered. "Oh, we're not—"

"Thank you for understanding," he firmly interjected, giving his consort a squeeze. Margot's mouth snapped shut, but she still leveled him with an indignant look.

Theodore kept his eyes trained on Angelique's back as he rearranged his flustered consort under his arm. They followed her at a brisk pace until she reached the door. Angelique's fingers were a flurry of movement as she entered a code on the attached keypad. He watched grimly, aware of the fact that every were in the room now knew exactly what Margot was to him.

The weres had their own pull, after all. They might not be born with the beast in them like he was, but they were as beholden to their instincts as any elf. Those instincts would recognize exactly why Theodore reacted the way he did. Any being who felt the call to a mate would understand.

The news was going to come out anyway, he reminded himself as Angelique pulled the door open to reveal a narrow staircase descending into a dark basement. *At least the weres appreciate the seriousness of matehood.*

He squeezed Margot's shoulder. *If only witches did the same.*

~

Margot watched Angelique disappear down the rickety wood steps into the basement and was momentarily glad for the heavy arm around her shoulders, the heat radiating through her side from the man who held her. A shudder of deep unease worked its way through her body.

Without meaning to, a confession tumbled out of her. "I'm not great in dark spaces."

No, not since she turned sixteen. Not since she spent that torturous week in that awful padded room, her ligaments pulling taut until her bones snapped and rearranged themselves. Not since strangers locked her in that dark little room and watched as madness ate her alive, only to leave without a word when clarity returned.

The memories were always worse when she gazed into the darkness. She swore she could feel her own nails raking across her skin when the shadows deepened, threatening to drag her back.

Theodore turned his attention toward her, his gaze a very real pressure against her sensitized skin. *Not that it's ever too far from me in the first place.*

He never did take his eyes off her for long, did he? Or his hands.

Margot knew that she should have panicked when he slung his arm around her, when he hauled her against his chest at the first sign of a threat, but she simply... *couldn't.* Even as an internal voice warned her that he had to be a threat, that he was playing some complex game with her she could never hope to master, she could not manage even the whisper of a fight.

The truth, no matter how pathetic, was that Margot *liked* being touched by Theodore Solbourne. And this time, she didn't even have the excuse of imbibing too much wine to fall back on.

It was such a foolhardy, outrageously dangerous impulse, but it was impossible to fight. She wanted him to touch her. She *needed* him to touch her. More than that, Margot got the uneasy feeling that with every touch, with every bone-deep craving for that touch, Theodore was being humanized, mentally declawed.

How could he not be humanized when she *felt* his heart hammering under her cheek, his shuddering breath disturbing her hair? How could she look at him and see only a predator when shame bruised his dark eyes? How could she fear him, distrust him, when she spent her first good night's sleep in a year in his arms?

Burn out is frying your brain. Theodore Solbourne is the alpha of the most predatory race on the planet. If he doesn't already know your secret, he will soon. What will you do then? Ask for another cuddle?

"Elves don't exactly enjoy it either," Theodore quietly admitted. His palm, gloved and separated from her skin by layers of clothing, skimmed up and down her arm, sending bolts of electricity through every nerve ending. "We're creatures of the light. There's a reason we build *up,* not down."

Yes, that was something she did know about elves. When Glory crafted the them from sunlight and precious stones, gifts from the heart of her husband Burden, the god on whose back all creatures lived, she didn't stop to think how creatures made of light would react to shadow.

That was why they built skyscrapers and dazzling homes of glass; why the elves had been the biggest sponsors of stained glass artisans in the middle ages; why their skin and hair shone like oil in the light.

They *were* the light. Darkness was as foreign to them as the land was to the ocean races.

Still, they both had to go down into that basement.

"The sooner we get this done, the sooner I can get out of your hair," she said, trying to bolster both of them as they edged towards the threshold. Margot wasn't entirely sure why she said it, but as soon as the words left her mouth, her stomach soured.

Theodore dropped his arm from around her shoulders to step

in front of her, a small hum in his throat. "So eager to leave me, darling?"

He was teasing her, but there was real strain under the flippant tone. *Did I...* Margot blinked. *Did I hurt his feelings?*

She didn't have time to think about it. She wasn't even sure she *wanted* to think about it.

Theodore thrust a hand behind him, the muted black leather of his gloves standing out starkly against the gleaming silver of his claw-caps, and wiggled his fingers invitingly. "Hold my hand. We can be scared together."

Margot's heart leapt out of her chest to find a new home in her throat.

Without stopping to think about why it was a bad idea, she gave into the howling impulse to touch him, to keep the steady warmth of contact. She carefully placed her fingers into his.

They stepped into the dark together.

Angelique waited for them at the bottom of the staircase, her arms folded over her chest and her narrow-eyed glare fixed on the figure huddled in a bare corner of what appeared to be a storage room. The floor was dusty concrete, the air was cool, and worryingly haphazardly stacked towers of boxes filled almost every available inch of space.

A single bulb hanging from the ceiling barely illuminated the darkness, casting liquid shadows over everything and everyone except for the figure chained to a bolt in the floor, who sat in the most direct path of its glow.

Margot scented the blood before she saw it.

Her fingers spasmed around Theodore's. He tightened his grip, enclosing her hand in butter-soft leather and warmth. A low, almost inaudible rumble raised the hair on the back of her neck. *He's purring again,* she realized, startled by the way the tension bunching her stomach into knots immediately began to dissipate. For reasons she couldn't fathom, her heart rate began to slow.

Margot licked her lips, scanning the bedraggled figure whose hands and feet were bound in cuffs and chained to the floor. His head was bowed and his shoulders hunched over his knees, so she couldn't make out where the blood was coming from, but her nose didn't lie.

She took half a step forward, her healer's heart taking over. "He's hurt. How badly? What are his injuries?"

"Oh, he could be hurt a lot worse," Angelique began, her tone biting. "Roger is a were. A damn stupid one for all that he's got a big brain, but a were nonetheless. That means he knows the rules. You step out of line, you suffer the consequences." Her lips thinned with raw displeasure. "Were justice is pretty fucking clear about what happens when you go after one of our own."

Theodore and Angelique shared a flinty look of agreement. "He's lucky he still has a head on his shoulders," he said, tone flat. "I would have taken it already."

Margot shivered. She knew that in the UTA, justice took many brutal forms. When so many beings had the capacity to cause so much harm, it had to be quick and ruthless. But actually seeing it, *hearing* them talk about it so casually, made her gorge rise.

Angelique inclined her head. "Hard to question a decapitated corpse."

Roger didn't look up, but Margot saw his head move with a slow, pained shake. "I didn't *know,*" he croaked. The nasally quality of it implied he had either been crying, or that his nose had been broken.

Margot frowned and took another step, her hands tingling with the need to heal, but was halted by Theodore's grasp.

"What didn't you know?" he asked, tugging Margot back to his side without taking his eyes off of Roger.

The huddled man tightened his hold on his bent knees, his jeans torn and splattered with dark stains. He had dark hair that was a wild mix of curls and cowlicks, and the forearms exposed by his dirty t-shirt were browned by the sun and corded with lean muscle.

Roger's breathing was labored, rasping loudly in the muffled quiet of the basement. "I didn't know the bomb was for a healer. I never would have done it if I knew. I thought it was just supposed to be the house."

Angelique let out a harsh, rumbling growl. "You never should have made a bomb to begin with, Roger. What did you think it would be used for — making rainbows?"

He flinched. Burying himself more deeply into his knees, Roger rasped, "I didn't ask any questions. I just needed the money, okay? I thought, *'it's small enough to not cause too much damage.'* The contact said it wouldn't be used to hurt anyone, anyway, and that it was just going to be for scaring someone. I didn't think—"

He cut himself off with a wheeze, his shoulders shaking. The scent of copper and salt bloomed in the air.

"Enough," Margot snapped. "Can't you see he's in too much pain to talk?" Tugging her hand out of Theodore's grip, she made to cross the distance between herself and Roger.

Heavy, claw-tipped hands closed over her shoulders. "No, Margot." Theodore's voice was a hard command. "I can't let you get close enough to heal him. I won't allow it."

Margot craned her neck to glare over her shoulder, her eyes locking with his. Her duty as a healer overrode her budding weakness for him, her anxiety, and her attraction with vicious efficiency. Pulling her shoulders back, she said, "Let me go, Sovereign."

"So we're back to Sovereign, are we?" Theodore's eyebrows drew dark slashes over his eyes, his hard expression cast in sharp relief by the single bulb. A muscle in his jaw ticked. She thought she saw a flicker of frustration in his eyes, but it was quickly overtaken by his flat glare. "The answer is still no."

Margot sucked in a sharp breath. "Don't you *dare* tell me what to do."

She felt his fingers flex on her shoulders; a warning her instincts recognized and immediately discarded. "Margot," he rumbled, voice dropped so low it sank into her blood like warm molasses, "I said no."

Anger blazed, hot and bright. The part of her that was smothered roared to life, its mental chains snapping one by one as it accepted the challenge Theodore laid at its feet. *No one,* not even the sovereign of the Elvish Protectorate, got to tell her when she could and couldn't heal someone.

Being in the basement brought back terrible memories of her own confinement, her own torture. Seeing a man suffer needlessly, criminal or not, grated hard against every healer's instinct she possessed. And being told *no,* like she was back in the Goodeland, smothered and patronized and made to fear everything that might bring her even a spark of purpose or joy? That was a step too godsdamned far.

She had so little time left, so little *life* left. Margot would be damned if she let *one more fucking person* step on her.

In an instant, electricity crackled through her veins, out through her pores to race along her skin and snap like tiny vipers in her hair. The air filled with the sharp scent of ozone and the snap of sparks as her eyes disappeared in a froth of raw power.

Margot bared her teeth and wrenched away, electricity arcing from her shoulders to sting his hands in violent rebuke.

"Shit!" Theodore hissed. He was forced to let her go, his gloves no protection from an electrical charge when they had built-in metal accents.

Before he or Angelique could try to grab her, Margot rushed to Roger's side. As soon as she was on her knees, she let the burn of electricity dissipate, the power fizzling out as it drew back into the core that kept her alive — and was steadily killing her.

Theodore stormed after her, his expression thunderous and his long black coat flapping around his knees. "Margot, do *not—*"

"Hush," she snapped. "He's chained to the damn floor and he's already injured. What do you think he's gonna do?"

Theodore stopped his furious approach barely a foot away from her, his eyes blazing and his hands flexing so hard the leather of his gloves creaked. Margot didn't let him get a word out, warning, "Grab me again, Sovereign, and I swear to Glory, I'll fry you."

Margot turned back around to face Roger and found him staring at her through a mess of knotted curls. One sky blue eye was swollen shut, his left cheekbone was black and sickly green, and dried blood crusted the skin around his mouth and chin, the clear result of a mangled nose.

He didn't even glance at the menacing elf over her shoulder when he croaked, "Are you the healer?"

Margot softened. "Yeah."

He swallowed with obvious difficulty. Tears gleamed in the eye she could see when he said, "I'm sorry. I didn't know. I don't — I never would have—"

Stretching out her hand, she simply asked, "Do you consent?"

Roger blinked at her with his one good eye. He licked his parched, battered lips. "T-to what?"

"Healing, you dumb piece of shit," Angelique chimed in. "She wants to *heal* you. Damn soft-hearted healers make just punishment impossible."

Roger's eyes darted from Margot's outstretched hand to her face and then to Angelique with obvious confusion. "Why?"

Margot could feel Theodore's eyes burning a hole in the back of her head when she answered, "Because I can. Because you want to talk. Because we need you to tell us everything you know. Because I have very limited time on this Earth and I don't want to spend a second of it witnessing unnecessary suffering. Because *he* —" she jerked her hin towards Theodore's livid form "—told me no. Take your pick."

Roger stared at her for several long seconds, disbelief written across his swollen, battered features, before he slowly leaned into her hand.

The moment the skin of his cheek made contact with her fingertips, Margot got to work. It was the simplest thing in the world for a healer of her caliber to reduce swelling, to repair broken blood vessels, to knit shattered bone. The same electricity that made her a powerful weapon also made her an excellent healer; all the commands of the body ran, to some degree, on that same explosive current.

It took five minutes at most for Roger's nose to snap back into place and for the swelling and bruises to disappear. When she was done, Margot sat back on her heels and shoved her hands into the pockets of her coat. Out of sight, they shook with a violence that made her stomach knot with dread.

Exhaustion pressed hard on her. A year ago, she could have done a simple procedure like that three dozen times in a day and not broken a sweat. Now, she had to blink away spots to read Roger's expression and fought, perhaps in vain, not to sway.

It's gotten worse, she grimly realized. *Much worse.*

Roger sucked in a deep, painless breath and rocked backwards, tears tumbling down his dirty cheeks.

"I'll tell you everything," he gasped. He sniffed hard and bent his neck to scrub his face against his bicep. In a muffled voice, he said, "I never got the name of my contact. You know how it is. I do jobs for people like this all the time. It's usually the black market m-enhanced technical stuff. I'm good at machines, and word gets around." He sniffed and looked away, a note of hollow pride in his thickened voice. "Anyway, I just got the message and followed the instructions: Make a small, low-impact bomb, leave it at the back of the Healing House, get the money."

He sniffed again and looked up from where he'd buried his face against his arm. The look he gave Margot was beseeching, hopeful that she would understand.

She didn't and couldn't. Never, ever would it be an option to play with innocent, unknown lives. But Margot nodded anyway, urging him to continue, her expression a mask of careful neutrality she perfected as an apprentice.

"I'm an idiot, but I'm not *stupid,*" he explained. "I did my homework. I had to be sure I would get paid, so I traced the message back to the IP address, but that was obviously diverted.

So I said I wouldn't do it unless we could talk in person, face to face."

Theodore's voice was a rasp of metal on metal above her when he asked, "And did they agree to it?"

Roger licked his lips and finally looked up at Margot's shadow, his eyes widening comically large. "I... Yes. That was two months ago, back when there was all that stuff going on with the dragons in town. When they closed all the streets off? I remember because we met at a bar off of Mason and it was a bitch to find parking." He sniffed hard. "I didn't see their face but..."

Roger sucked in a breath and stared at Theodore like he was looking at the goddess Grim herself. "I know for a fact that it was a woman. An *elvish* woman."

Chapter Eleven

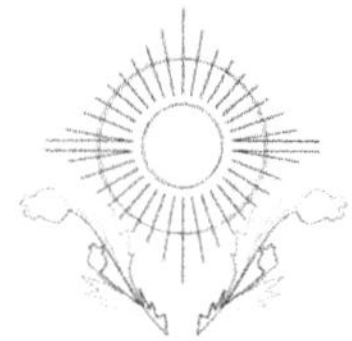

Margot could tell that Theodore was furious — with her, with the situation — and forty-eight hours ago that would have made her heave with fear, but *now...*

Now she didn't fear him. She was confused by him, painfully aware of the danger he posed, *attracted* to him, but Margot no longer felt the acid wave of fear churning in her gut when he looked at her. It was impossible to maintain that sort of thing when Theodore Solbourne wore his blue heart on his finely tailored sleeve.

Whether it was all an act or not, Margot no longer worried that he would slice her to ribbons with those silver claws. She was a tactile creature, a necessity in her line of work, and so she believed in what she could see, what she could feel.

The pounding of his heart under her cheek was real. The shame in his eyes was real. The crushing, possessive way he held her was real. The fact that he could have separated her head from her body when she shocked him was real. Those were all things she could verify with her own eyes and hands and mind; could be sure they were not simply products of her own misplaced yearning to see good in a man that made her blood hot.

Theodore was just... *good.*

Margot tucked herself against her door, the hum of the m-enhanced engine vibrating through her in time with the tremors that rattled her bones. There was no one behind the wheel this time. Kaz was busy taking Roger into Patrol custody, and the car was one of the rare luxury vehicles fully capable of self-driving. Theodore explained that he didn't trust anyone except family to drive him anywhere, and since he didn't feel like doing it himself, the m-navigation system would sync with the grid in the streets and handle it.

That didn't mean they were alone, though. Margot caught the gleam of two heavy-duty black vehicles weaving through traffic ahead of and behind them, on the lookout for threats she could only imagine.

But for now, it was just the two of them in the backseat. The interior of the spacious vehicle was dark and warm, the tinted windows blocking out the glare of the sunlight to create an intimate cocoon.

Stop shaking, she silently commanded her body. Margot couldn't afford to shake this bad when they were in an enclosed space together. *Stop it. Stop.*

But her body refused to listen.

Margot tried to breathe normally, acutely aware of the elf sitting a foot or so away. She kept her hands shoved deep into the satin lining of her coat pockets and closed her eyes. Theodore's scent filled the car, heady and familiar, *right* in a way that none had ever been before him. The caged part of her wanted to revel in it, to draw it into its pores and simply *breathe.*

It was easy to focus on that instead of the dread clawing at her insides, the fear of death that made her want to curl up and whimper.

Tears pricked at her closed eyelids. *I don't even really care about the bombing. Knowing who did it won't save my life, and I just want to live. I haven't had a chance to do that yet.*

No, she spent twenty-four and a half years locked away on Coven grounds, drilled by tutors and avoided by kids that were once friends, only let out to fulfill her apprenticeship requirements in Seattle. Even if she hadn't been physically locked down, fear of discovery was its own special prison.

It was a cruel irony that it was her impending death that finally forced her to put her foot down with her grandmother, that finally allowed her the space to *live.*

Margot wanted someone, *anyone* to blame for the massive missed opportunity that was her life, but what was the use? Margot wanted to blame Sophie. She wanted to blame her irresponsible parents, but that wasn't fair. She could have left the Goodeland. It took a massive argument to convince her grandmother, but in the end, she succeeded in winning permission to take the position at the Healing House with relatively little fanfare.

Looking back, Margot could have left at any time. She could have gotten an apartment somewhere. She could have taken a job at Luminous. She could have lived.

Damn it, I'm spiraling.

Being in the basement dredged up awful memories. The rise and inevitable crash of her temper made her want to curl up somewhere soft and cry. She didn't know how to handle Theodore's anger and she just... Margot was just *tired.*

Her nose began to tickle as a throbbing in her temples picked up a slow, painful beat. She couldn't cry in the car with Theodore Solbourne. It was bad enough that he'd seen her tipsy and then let her cuddle him close like the touch-starved creature she was. Tears were wholly unacceptable to every part of her. Her pride as a Goode, her pride as a woman, her pride as a—

Theodore's voice, low and tight, broke through her pity party. "I know you aren't going to want to do this, but you and I need to craft another statement to give to the press. My phone has been ringing nonstop since your grandmother released hers. Especially now that we know the person who planned this is an elf, it will be imperative that we show a united front."

Margot nodded, her eyes glued to the view of the street

through the tinted window. "Fine," she whispered. If it made his life easier, she would do it. Her anonymity was shot, anyway. Nothing mattered anymore.

Margot sniffed quietly, trying to keep everything in with an iron will. Her eyes burned and her sinuses felt like someone lit a match in them, so held her breath and squeezed her eyelids shut. *Do not cry,* she firmly commanded herself. *Do not!*

There was the rustle of cloth, then a hard exhale. Margot felt his warmth radiating through her clothing as he leaned closer. She didn't even need to look to know his thigh was only inches away from hers. She just *knew.*

"Margot, I am so sor— Why do I smell blood?"

Something hot trickled down over her lips.

Too surprised to remember why she was supposed to keep her hands hidden, Margot opened her eyes and lifted her fingers to her nose. *Blood,* she thought, staring at the smear of red on her trembling fingertips, smelling the sharp metallic bite of it in her nose. *I'm bleeding.*

Clawtips, cold and smooth, pressed against her jaw. She was too stunned to fight him when Theodore turned her face towards his.

He was very still, his expression blank, when he asked, "What is this, Margot?"

She knew what it was. *Second stage of burnout, triggered by high energy output. Ruptured blood vessels in thin tissues. Next will be the brain, if it hasn't begun already.*

Her estimate of weeks before a fatal magical collapse was brutally, foolishly optimistic. When she turned her inner eye towards her neural pathways, Margot was grimly unsurprised to find some of them withered, parched for the magic that was supposed to flow through them, and others so overloaded they were being charred from the inside out.

I'm burning.

Her heart slammed against her ribs. Margot opened her mouth to lie, the taste of blood on her tongue.

Theodore's hand clasped her jaw, his thumb and forefinger squeezing either side with a warning as he leaned forward to hiss, "Don't you lie to me, Margot Goode. Don't you fucking dare. You got your one, remember?" Her heart jackknifed in her chest. He was so close that she could feel every harsh exhalation of his breath on her flushed cheeks. "You and I both know that healers don't get fucking nose bleeds. This is what you've been hiding, isn't it?" The expression in his dark eyes was livid. "Tell me what's wrong. *Now.*"

I know he's been kind and I know he wants me, but I can't trust him.

But this wasn't necessarily about trust, was it? This was about the days she had left. Margot's world tilted, just a little, at the realization that there was every chance she would spend those last days in his company.

Why did that not scare her?

Margot knew that she should return to the Goodeland, to spend her last moments with her family. If not for herself, then for them and for their grief. She should not have fought Sophie so hard. She should have given in and followed her through Alric's gate.

But the more Margot spun the thought in her mind, trying desperately to *make* herself say the words that would send her home, she simply... *couldn't.*

Something painfully fundamental in her, the same force that drew her to San Francisco like a beacon, now held her firmly by Theodore Solbourne's side.

What did this secret matter, compared to the other that hung like a noose around her neck? He could use it to hurt her grandmother, but only in the emotional sense. But even then, Margot had the feeling he wouldn't do that. The look in his eyes when he apologized to the weres was burned into her mind. No man, sovereign or not, elf or not, who wore his shame so openly would use Margot's death against the people she loved.

And below that, there was that other part of her that whimpered for him, for the comfort of having the burden of fear lifted even momentarily. It was a solid core of loneliness, abandoned by the people who were supposed to love it and protect it, and it *ached* to be seen. It didn't want to die. It yearned to sink its claws into Theodore and never, ever let him go.

It craved him with everything it was. *Margot* wanted him with everything she was.

She shuddered. The truth of that acknowledgement sent a wracking, brutal wave of emotion through her as the walls around the other half of her cracked, crumbled, and fell away.

A tear slid from the corner of her eye to splash against the leather of his glove. *With the time I have left, I am choosing to trust him.*

"I'm dying," she whispered. Her voice broke. The relief of finally speaking the words was immense. "I'm dying, Theodore."

The sense of a weight lifting off of her chest was exquisite. She sucked in a harsh, wheezing breath. *Finally, someone other than me knows.*

Theodore pulled her face closer, the look in his eyes wild. In a raw, trembling voice, he demanded, "What are you talking about? Explain."

Now that the words were out, Margot felt the lock that kept them sealed inside of her shatter, allowing the rest to pour out in a deluge of grief. "I'm burning out. It's too early and I don't know why it happened this way, but I started having the symptoms six months ago. Headaches. Tremors after healing. Decreased focus. Weight loss. The bleeding is new but not unexpected. My brain hasn't begun to hemorrhage yet, but it's only a matter of time." She sniffed hard, the scent of blood thick in the air and in her lungs. "My magic is killing me."

She found it hard to look at him, so she dropped her blurry eyes to the pin holding his collar in place. "That's why I came here. That's why I need to stay so badly. If I don't bond, I'm going to die. I can't stop it. I... I'm one of those witches that can't just bond with anyone. I don't know why that is, either. I don't know anything other than that I need to find *my* bondmate and I know he's here, but I can't— I haven't been able to track him down and I thought I had more time but I don't and—"

Theodore's hand left her jaw. Margot looked up to find him pushing the sleeves of his coat and suit jacket up, revealing the pristine white shirt underneath. When he spoke, his voice was shockingly calm, a balm of pure authority that soothed that whimpering thing in her. "You are *not* going to die."

With the utmost gentleness, Theodore raised his arm to swipe at the skin beneath her nose and lips, ruining his shirt with her blood. "You are going to live a good, long life," he continued, his eyes made of the hardest, sharpest obsidian, "because I will not accept anything else. Do you hear me, Margot? *I will not let this happen.*"

She pushed at his arm, embarrassed to be taken care of like she was a messy baby by *him,* of all people, and angry that he was deliberately ignoring the truth staring him in the face. "There's no stopping it. Unless I find my bondmate soon — *very* soon — I'm dead. If I'm bleeding like this already, I have weeks at most. Probably less. Days, even. I can't..."

Theodore pressed the tips of his claws against her bottom lip, halting the frenzied outpouring of information. They pricked at her skin, demanding her complete attention.

"It's like you don't even listen to me." His voice bordered on a snarl. "I already told you, Margot."

There was a terrifying lethality in the way he held himself then, a danger that he had never displayed with her before; a monstrousness that made her want to stretch out her neck in surrender. "You *found* your bondmate. It's me. You are not going to die because *we* are going to bond. *We* are going to live long lives together. There is no alternative to look for, no surrendering to this fatalism, no negotiating for someone else. It's you and me, *forever.*"

Margot turned away from him to wipe her nose with her own sleeve, a choked laugh bubbling out of her raw throat. "You don't even *know* me! And even if you did, you're the *sovereign.* Elves don't even date outside of their race, and I'm pretty sure their sovereign doesn't either. And, what? You think I'm going to bond with you and everything will be fine? You can't just say things like that and expect me to take you seriously. Why would *you,* of all people, want me?"

She was no one, not really, and he was the sovereign. Even if they weren't two incompatible species, it could never work. He may want to use her. He may want to sleep with her. He may even like her. But a *true* bond? A marriage of magic and heart? No, that was impossible.

"If you're not looking to use me as a personal magical battery, then the only other option is that you're making a joke out of my death, because there's no way anything about what you just said could be true."

The sweet relief of unburdening herself was rapidly being replaced by stinging humiliation. Hurt thrust its blade through her, slicing her to ribbons. Did he think she was stupid? Did he think it was *funny?* Theodore had never been cruel to her before this moment, but it was the only explanation that made any sense.

Everyone knew elves didn't date outside of their race. They didn't get married to outsiders. They didn't have hybrid children. They just didn't.

Because when they did cross those lines, they left wreckage in their wake. They broke families apart. They abandoned children to live in cages of their own biting fear, with no resources, no one to ask when things weren't right, no one to explain what was happening or *why.*

Margot's chest seized, panic and anger and bitter loss wrapping like barbed wire around her lungs. In the back of her mind, she knew that the reason burn out came so early was because of her mixed blood. Another fun side effect that no one could explain to her because her elvish mother stepped out of her life as soon as the umbilical cord was cut, abandoning her to figure everything out on her own in a world that couldn't even know she existed.

Understanding why her unnamed mother did it didn't make the abandonment any easier to deal with. It didn't take the pain away. If anything, it made it worse. Better to be abandoned for selfish reasons, Margot figured. At least then she could hate the woman who brought her into the world. Knowing that Margot's very existence was unacceptable and could put the elvish part of her family at risk was a jagged shard of pain in her heart every day.

To have Theodore just... just *say* something like that to her, to so blithely suggest he would enter into a union of the very *soul* with a woman who had spent her life smothered by her own blighted identity was enough to make her want to claw his eyes out.

"Forget I said anything," she gasped, scrubbing furiously at her swollen eyes with tingling palms. "I don't want your pity and I don't want your fucked up version of a joke, either. I'm not going to be a battery and I'm not going to be mocked and I'm not—"

The click of her seatbelt releasing took her by surprise.

Margot dropped her hands to ask what the world he was doing, but the words never made it out of her mouth. In an instant, she was tipped sideways and rearranged along the length of the seat, Theodore's considerably heavier body pinning her in place.

Without preamble, he braced his forearms on either side of her head and dug his claws into her hair. "Twenty-five years," Theodore breathed against her ear, the words strung together in one grating exhalation. His hair, silky and smelling of cedar and cinnamon, slid against her cheek.

"Twenty-five years I've waited and planned and worked my way into a position where no one could take the people I love from me again. Twenty-five years I've been challenged by every fucking elf in this territory and I've fought and I've clawed my way into being the youngest sovereign in history so I could have *you.* I am not about to let you slip away from me now, Margot. Just fucking try it. See what happens."

Margot squirmed underneath him, the motion of the car pressing them both further into the cushions. Desire hummed in her veins like a low-burning fire, a furious heat beneath her anger and her grief. Her heart stuttered an erratic beat in her chest as a flush spread from her neck to her ears.

She didn't *want* to desire him, but it was a roar in her blood, that howling thing in her lunging against the surface of her mind to reach for him with the desperation of the dying.

"I don't know what you're talking about," she gritted out, trying to quell the shiver that ran down her spine when his clawtips scraped against her scalp. His weight was almost too much, but not enough, either. Margot wanted more at the same time that instinct compelled her to swipe her blunted claws down his chest for daring to pin her in the first place.

Theodore's lashes fluttered against the skin of her cheek. His breath was a hot slide against her throat, but he didn't touch her skin with his, withholding the skin contact she craved so much. Margot was caught between the overwhelming desire to just *feel* it, to break this terrible tension in her, and wanting to duck and roll out of the car altogether.

In no hurry, Theodore continued to lift his head, dragging his lashes across her cheek in a ticklish caress, before he finally looked her in the eye. Their noses were less than an inch apart when he told her, "One night when I was ten, I woke up from a dead sleep at three AM. I was sweaty and excited and my brain felt like it had been stretched like taffy."

His voice was low, a sweet crooning that curled her toes as he cupped the top of her head and settled more of his weight on her, joining them from hip to ankle. "I was an angry kid and mad at the world. I fought all the time, and I was a prick to my family because I blamed them for not having my mother or father around. I had a lot of psychic ability but thin barriers, so control was a problem. It made it so I picked up on things I shouldn't have." His lips twisted. "Seeing things in my sister's head, in Sam's, in Valen's... I grew up thinking that it would be *better* if they were still around, or maybe if I'd never been born."

He let out a shuddering breath against her ear. "The psychic strain was too much, and then picking up their worries that I was showing signs of my father's instability... Gods, it was like I was being crushed to death under it all."

Theodore shook his head as the car swayed around a corner, rocking them against one another in a way that made Margot jerk with surprise. His hands clenched in her hair as his eyelids lowered to half-mast. "That part doesn't matter as much as what happened that night when I was ten." His eyes fluttered closed, a look of something close to relief, to reverence, bunching his brows together. "Goddess, it was like a fucking *lifeline.* All my anger, all that loneliness, all that psychic instability eating away at my brain, it was just sucked out of me. Like you cut through it all with a blade and said, *Stop. I'm here now. You're not alone.*"

He bit his lip, sharp fangs pressing into soft blue flesh, before he finished in a breathless whisper, "When our minds touched, it lanced a wound that had been festering for a decade."

Margot's breath left her in small pants. Her hands curled into fists by her sides. Why wasn't she using them to push him away, to get space? He was so very close. Too close. Surely he could smell the difference in her now, the base note in her scent that marked her as a hybrid, a half-breed, with his nose an inch away from her skin. *So why am I just laying here?*

She didn't have the answer. All she could do was listen and rasp, "What? What are you talking about? We only just met. I've never had a psychic link with anyone."

No, to the despair of her tutors, she was more or less psychically blind. Margot couldn't find a telepathic link even if it smacked her in the face.

Theodore opened his eyes. The light slanting through the tinted windows was just enough to make out the difference between his dark irises and his slitted pupils, hugely expanded though they were.

In a very matter-of-fact voice, he replied, "No, I've known you for twenty-five *very* long years, Margot Goode. I've known you since three AM, March thirtieth, and you've been with me every single day since." His expression softened into pure earnestness. "We've shared a psychic link — weak, almost inaccessible, but *real* — since the day you were born. I've *looked* for you every day, but it wasn't until you came into my telepathic range that I was finally able to get a lock on you."

Theodore swallowed. A gleam of something that looked suspiciously like vulnerability entered those dark eyes. "When I say that I'm your bondmate, Margot, it's not a joke. It's not manipulation. It's not politics or blackmail or anything else you might suspect. It's the *truth.* I am your bondmate because *you* are my consort. Do you understand?"

No, she thought, *not even a little bit.*

None of that could be true. Margot could not be the *sovereign's* consort, whatever that meant. She was nothing. She was *less* than that. She was a half-breed abandoned by the two people who dared to bring her into a world that would not accept her on principle. Bonding to Theodore Solbourne, being his *consort,* was so far outside of the realm of possibility, it barely sounded like *English.*

It didn't matter that just being near him made her heart race. It didn't matter that the beast in her wanted to bite him and lick him in turn, a reaction it *never* had to anyone else. It didn't matter that she was so desperate to live that she'd take any bondmate, even Theodore Solbourne.

It was impossible.

"You're wrong," she said, sounding dazed even to her own ears. "You're *so* wrong. I don't know why you think it's me, but it can't be. I didn't even know what a consort was until this morning." She still didn't really know, actually.

"You want to test it?"

Margot stared up at him, wide-eyed and breathless. "What?"

"I bet I can prove it to you." Theodore skimmed his nose along hers, close enough to feel him but just shy of truly touching. Heat curled in her stomach. Her skin felt hyper-sensitive, every nerve firing with more intensity than they were seconds before. His voice was a low growl that made her pulse throb when he purred, "If you're so sure, then prove it."

A challenge.

The beast in her snapped its jaws and paced, the hunger to provoke and claw and test was a steady drip of lava in her veins. *What do I have to lose, anyway? If I'm going to die, I might as well go out in style.*

Death by kissing the sovereign sounded a whole lot better than burn out, at any rate.

"Fine," she gasped. "Prove it."

Theodore hovered above her, frozen, for three erratic heartbeats before a rumbling purr rattled through his chest and into hers. His fingers dragged through her hair, the clawtips catching on the soft strands. Liquid heat pooled in her belly and flowed outward as her pulse pounded between her thighs. She could see the whites all around his irises when he leaned down to growl, "You *are* my consort, Margot Goode, and I am *not* letting you go."

Theodore's head dropped. His lips pressed against hers in a scalding kiss that was neither gentle nor coaxing. It *took.*

Margot gasped, a shock of sensation blazing a trail through every nerve as he took her lower lip between his fangs and nipped her hard.

Her hands clenched in his shirt involuntarily as he swept his tongue along the stinging skin and then past it, bringing with it the taste of rain and man and something too erotic to name.

Stars exploded across the backs of her eyelids. Magic fused with pleasure, bursting through parched internal pathways in a flash flood that made her whole body jerk.

Margot didn't think about it when she lifted her head to get closer, her caution and tightly wound self-control shredded. She didn't notice the way her temples throbbed in time with her heart. She didn't consider the claws now collared around her throat, holding her in place as he slicked his hot tongue against hers.

The slow expansion of her mental walls didn't even register until it was too late.

Margot released his shirt in favor of cupping his cheeks, her palms flat against his warm skin as she demanded he move closer, that he soothe the ache that was her entire body. Now that she had a taste, a touch, it was as if she couldn't breathe without touching him, without getting more of him on her tongue and in her pores and so deep inside her that she couldn't tell where she ended and he began.

Skin, she thought, too desperate to examine anything, let alone the hot prickling in her palms. *I need skin contact. I need to touch him. I need to feel his skin and taste every inch of him. Gods, I need him to touch* me.

Theodore's growl vibrated through her as he reached down to hook her leg over his hip. He pressed his thumb into the crease behind her knee and rocked against the cradle of her thighs with one hard thrust.

Margot tore her mouth away from his to gasp for air, her body burning, magic thrumming under her skin, the shock of that single burst of pleasure tearing her up inside.

The needy beast in her bowed its back, dug its claws into him, and roared, *Mine!*

Margot would have buckled under the force of the internal transformation if she weren't already flat on her back, the hum of the car a subtle vibration along her sensitive spine. Her fingers dug into the skin of his jaw as Theodore trailed his mouth across her cheek to her ear.

"You're my consort," he snarled, "and not even Grim will take you from me." His fangs sank into delicate skin with a sharp, possessive bite, and Margot's magic *exploded.*

Chapter Twelve

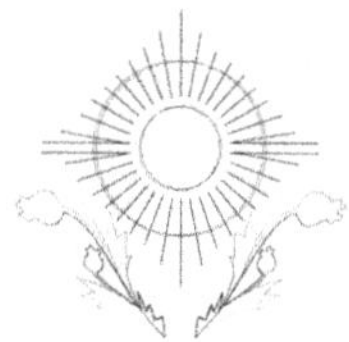

Margot stared at the roof of the car for approximately fifteen seconds before the reality of the situation — and the weight of a fully grown and currently unconscious elvish man — hit her.

She fought to free her arm from where it was pinned between their chests. Her lungs heaved against the weight of the elf crushing her. Her blood was liquid fire rushing through her veins. Her *panic* — it was unbearable.

What have I done?

Well, she knew precisely what she'd done, but that was the problem.

The car ran over a bump in the usually impeccably maintained elvish road, jostling her enough to knock the wind out of her lungs as she grappled with Theodore's bulk. It didn't help that having him draped over her, his heavy body pressing down against hers, his scent on her skin and his breath puffing through her hair, made every nerve in her body stand at attention.

Margot's arms shook as she attempted to maneuver them on the large back seat. She tried her best to be gentle, but at a certain point there was no controlling how Theodore fell off of her. The damn man was just too heavy, and she needed to get out from under him to think through the mess she made.

He landed half on the floor with a car-shaking *thunk* as she scrambled back against the seat. Margot stared at Theodore, *the sovereign,* slumped on the floor of his own car, and thought, *I'm so fucked.*

Not fucked in the way her body craved now that the floodgates were open. Not in any fun way at all. She was fucked in the very real, very dangerous way that got lesser beings turned to pulp.

Margot clenched her hands in her hair and pulled hard, trying to rein in some of her mounting hysteria with the sharp bite of pain in her scalp.

I bonded to the sovereign.

She bonded to him. Tied her fate to his. Tied her *magic* to his. Tied their souls together. Tied her *health* to his nearness, his willingness to touch her, his hitherto unexplored tolerance for half-breeds!

Worse, perhaps, than all of that, was the fact that the bonding had apparently hurt him.

Even more galling was that he was right. Just because she couldn't process them didn't mean the facts were foggy: Theodore was her bondmate. *He* was the reason she had to come to San Francisco. He was right, but Margot still couldn't understand how it could be possible.

Goddess, please tell me I didn't kill him. I can't take that on top of everything else.

Heart jammed into her throat, Margot scrambled onto her knees, her body swaying with the movement of the car, to reach for Theodore's face. His head was propped up on the seat alongside one arm and one thickly muscled thigh. If it wasn't the single most terrifying situation of her life — *including* the bombing — she might have laughed at the ridiculous pose.

The sovereign, mushed against the backseat, his long coat nearly stripped from him and tangled around his arms in the struggle to free herself from his weight, with his handsome face squished against the leather of a cushion, was somehow *more* dangerous to her now than he was before.

Margot's hand was steady as she cupped his cheek. The slide of his skin against hers, the warmth of him radiating into the fragile bones and spongy marrow of her hands — even that simple contact was exquisite.

Magic coursed through the new, white-hot bond between them; an endless feedback loop of pleasure-pain that would keep her alive for centuries to come. Tears stung the backs of her eyes. Relief mingled with guilt and a dread to close a vice around her lungs.

Theodore Solbourne was now her magical filter, his body acting as a vessel to purify and dilute the unchecked strength of her magic, prolonging her life and giving him an untold boost of power in one hit.

And it almost killed him.

Margot turned her healer's eye towards Theodore's inner landscape, painfully aware that she was breaking more boundaries, crossing even more lines by peering into the sovereign's body without his express permission. But she had to be sure she hadn't accidentally killed the damn man, and Margot didn't think he'd truly mind.

It was with immense relief that Margot discovered Theodore was not, in fact, going to die. *No,* she thought, eyeing his nervous system with awe. *He's just being completely rewired.*

No wonder he passed out on her. Her magic hit him like a tidal wave, throwing open channels and pathways that had never before seen a drop of energy. The pathways he did have were mostly linked to his cerebral cortex, which wasn't exactly a surprise, given his abilities.

Theodore wasn't a particularly magical being — most elves weren't, their pathways notoriously narrow and their inherent magic too wild to fit most spellwork — but bonding to her had *forced* him to be.

As she watched, he was being turned into her own personal magical conduit.

Margot ripped her hand away from his cheek to press herself back against the seat. “Fuck. Fuck! Glory, what the *fuck?*” She pressed the heels of her palms against her forehead and pressed hard, panic making it difficult to think of anything other than how absolutely, completely screwed she was.

I rewired the sovereign’s nervous system. I bonded to him without his consent. I bonded to him without telling him the truth. What have I done?

No matter what Theodore said, he couldn’t be her bondmate. He didn’t have all the facts, didn’t know she was something that his kind shunned, and— and she just didn’t know what the fuck to do with a sovereign as a bondmate!

A shifter she could handle. A were she could work with. Even a dragon would have been better, notorious possessiveness and nesting issues aside. But an *elf*? Not just any elf, but Sovereign of the entire Elvish Protectorate?

What in Glory’s brilliant name was she supposed to *do* with that?

What would people do when they found out? Would they find out? Or would Theodore hide her away, pretend like she didn’t exist and go on with his life knowing he would always have an endless supply of magic at his beck and call now? Would he use her and use her until she was nothing but a burnt husk, tethered to him, dependent on his goodwill as she was?

This was why the elders of the Coven always impressed caution on the younger witches. One ought to do their best to avoid bonding with someone recklessly, in case they turned out to be someone untrustworthy, or otherwise unsuitable.

Once it was done, there was no going back.

The rational witch in her would never have risked it, but the caged, feral thing in Margot had decided that Theodore belonged to her, that he wouldn’t hurt her, and it refused to wait for any reasonable assessment of the situation. It wanted to *live,* and that meant sinking her claws into the sovereign with the rabid possessiveness of a starved creature.

But no matter what Margot's other half thought, the truth of the situation was that she had no idea what Theodore was going to do now that they were tied. For all she knew, he could wake up in ten minutes and toss her in a cell. Worse, he could wake up and realize that he just... didn't want her.

Margot's throat bobbed around a shard of pure hurt. *I can't stick around to find out.*

If she went back to the Tower, she would be fully at the mercy of the elves — not just Theodore, but everyone around him. What if Theodore wanted her as a bondmate, but someone else saw their bond as an abomination? A weakness to exploit? His position was so new, his power untested. This fragile thing between them, if he even truly wanted it, could get them both killed.

And if Theodore died because of her, a territory would crumble. More than just the two of them would die. Hundreds, *thousands,* could perish in the gasping power vacuum that would follow. The Protectorate would crumble onto the heads of innocent people.

Margot tried to breathe past her feelings, each one tumbling end over end until she could hardly discern one from another. There wasn't enough time to think about it all. They would cross the bridge and be at the Tower soon, where a retinue of guards and staff would be waiting to greet them.

It wasn't like she could just explain what had happened, not without first discovering what it meant to Theodore and what, if anything, he was willing to risk. No matter what, Margot knew for a fact that showing up to the elvish stronghold with the sovereign passed out in her lap and no reasonable explanation as to *why* was a surefire way to get herself thrown in a deep, dark pit.

Can't wake him up because I don't know what he'll do. Can't stay in the car because I can't go back to the Tower with him passed out.

Margot's breath was a harsh rasp as she clambered towards the tinted window. She watched as the city sped by. They were out of the thicket of downtown, the m-enhanced luxury vehicle that was her current prison driving smoothly toward the Bay Bridge exit.

There was no way she could get away if the car got to the bridge.

Margot scrambled on hands and knees over the center console between the front seats. She did her best to keep from knocking Theodore too much, or, Glory help her, accidentally ending up with his head in her skirt, but was only partially successful on both fronts.

With her coat twisted around her, sweat dotting her forehead, and her limbs in a pretzel, Margot landed in the driver's seat.

Righting herself, she scooted to the edge of the seat so she could reach the pedals — elvish blood did *not* give her the height advantage it should have — and grasped the steering wheel.

Nothing.

Margot wasn't exactly surprised nothing happened. It wasn't like she knew how the fancy vehicles *worked,* but she had hoped there would be some sort of manual override if a person took the wheel. Cursing, Margot turned to the massive, clear-paneled console.

It was a marvel of the newest m-tech advancements, a cascade of information and readouts as the vehicle took in everything around it to guide them safely down the tightly controlled Protectorate streets. When they slid into the back seat, all Theodore needed to do to get the car moving was swipe his clawtips over the screen, activating softly glowing sigils in blue and green as he input their destination.

Margot could read sigils as well as any trained witch, of course. She was no slouch with spellwork, even if her magic wasn't always suited toward the finer elements of it. She was also perfectly capable of reading the words *IDENTIFICATION NEEDED* when she attempted to input a command.

Staring at the flashing words and accompanying PIN prompt

for a long, incredulous moment, Margot thought, *Of course it's keyed to him.*

It had to be for safety reasons — maybe even *this* very reason. If something happened to the sovereign, and if his escorts both tailed and led the way, no one could simply abscond with him.

Which is exactly what I was planning. Not intentionally, obviously. Margot had no desire to kidnap Theodore. But she *knew* she couldn't let herself be locked away in the Tower again. Not without every single assurance that no one would use the bond against her.

Or him.

With a jolt of unease, Margot realized that this was no longer just about her. No matter what Theodore's intentions were, no matter *who* he was, they were now a team. Their fates were now bound by Glory's hand, and...

Nope, not going to think about that.

Margot craned her neck to look over her shoulder. Forcing her eyes away from Theodore, she eyed the sleek black vehicle following them at a reasonable distance. Reasonable to them, at least.

A glance through the windshield told her that the car ahead of them was much the same.

"Okay," she said aloud, half to herself and half to Theodore. "Can't kidnap you. Can't go back to the Tower. Gotta get out of the car without being seen. I'd prefer not to die doing it."

Nerves made her stomach bunch up into knots. She wasn't a coward, no more than circumstances had forced her to be, anyway, but even she felt more than a twinge of unease as she peered out of the passenger side window.

I have to jump.

"Oh, I really don't want to." Margot made a face as she clumsily pulled herself into the passenger's seat, painfully aware of her thin tights and not-very-protective coat. Eyeing the quickly approaching exit, she hurriedly zipped the jacket up to her throat and pulled the hood over her head.

A bend in the road preceded the exit. It would be her only chance to slip out of the car unseen by Theodore's escorts as the escort ahead rounded the bend and the one behind them fell momentarily behind. But it was going to hurt like a sonofabitch.

Sucking in a deep breath, Margot prayed to Glory and Grim to keep her from landing on too much glass or any other gutter detritus that hadn't yet been swept up by the street bots. Not that the goddesses of magic and death made a habit of listening to her, but it never hurt to try.

I don't know why you've put me on this path, she prayed, *but I'm not looking to make too much of a mess of it. A nice, soft landing in some grass would be ideal.*

Margot rested her hand on the door handle, her muscles tensed to jump, but couldn't stop herself from looking back at the man slumped in the back seat one last time. She hesitated.

The urge to touch him one last time before she fled was an impulse she was helpless to fight. The bond was built on touch, her gifts even moreso. Margot *needed* to touch him.

She took precious seconds to skim the pads of her fingers over his cheek in a tender caress, to comb her nails through his mussed black hair — *like the thickest silk* — before she thought to snatch his bunched up coat from his arms. *I need it to protect myself from the road.*

No, it had nothing to do with that howling thing inside of her, furious and desperate at the thought of parting from its mate, and it *definitely* didn't have anything to do with the fact that it smelled deliciously familiar as she wrapped its bulk around her.

The car began its gentle turn around the bend. Before she could stall a moment longer and miss her one chance at freedom, Margot disengaged the lock, opened the door just enough to fit through, and jumped.

~

After she took her time to heal her cuts, scrapes, and fractured arm — an act as natural to her as breathing, and one she had been deprived of for almost a year — Margot wound her way through narrow streets and back alleys before using a tourist's cellphone to call Viktor.

Normally she wouldn't have dared, but she was desperate, and he was the only person in the city besides Theodore she truly trusted.

Despite the fact that it was around the time most people would be busy having dinner with their families, Viktor didn't hesitate. He was pulling up beside the curb she'd perched on not twenty minutes later. The shifter looked strangely dapper in a dark blue suit, and if she were in any other situation she would have asked him what the occasion was.

She didn't, though. Instead, she climbed into the passenger's seat and quietly asked him to take her to the Market.

Viktor didn't press her for details of what had obviously happened, though his eyes were coyote bright and flicked in her direction often. In fact, he didn't say anything at all until they pulled up to the cracked curb and killed the engine.

Turning to lean his elbow against the center console, he asked, "Did he hurt you, sunshine?"

Margot shook her head. No, now that she had a little bit of space from the disaster of their bonding, she was certain Theodore *wouldn't* hurt her.

"Then you gonna tell me why you look like you just stepped out of a warzone?"

She choked out a laugh as she scrubbed her palms over her cheeks. No doubt she did look like a mess. It was a wonder no one had called Patrol to check on her as she wandered the streets.

Her voice was reedy when she admitted, "I bonded to Theodore."

Viktor was quiet for a beat, but when Margot dared to gauge his expression, it was sympathetic, not shocked like she expected. "I figured as much. Is that why you ran?"

Margot bristled. "I didn't *run.* I just..."

"Sunshine," he calmly interjected, "it's okay. Matehood can be scary as fuck. Double for being mated to an elf. Believe me, I, of all people, get it. But I'd like to know what your plan is now."

"Plan?"

"Yeah." His blond brows dropped in a frown. "You do have one, right? You have to know he's not just going to give you up because you hoofed it."

A shudder ran down her spine. "I just needed space to figure out what I'm going to do," she answered, annoyed at a base level that he would even suggest she planned to just... never see Theodore again. That wasn't an option.

Viktor hummed a low note. "I get that, but, sunshine... Speaking from personal experience here, you should get comfortable with the idea of not having space from him for much longer." He shook his head, slow and knowing. "No, if I were in his shoes, I'd already be tracking you down." His jaw clenched hard. "I don't envy what he's probably going through right now, either. Probably worried out of his damn mind. Not knowing where my mate is? If she's hurt or scared or hungry? Yeah, I'd be fucking losing it."

"Well, he can worry for a little longer. I need space." Margot gestured out the window. "This is the only place I can get it."

"Sure, for an hour or so." Viktor reached over to give her a gentle cuff on the jaw with his knuckles. "Just don't be too hard on him if he acts crazy, alright? Teddy's a good guy. He usually means well."

Margot turned to open the door, but didn't get farther than popping the handle before she peered over her shoulder to ask, "You two have a history, don't you?"

Viktor's eyes were vivid in the darkness, reflecting with a predator's nightglow. "Yeah," he answered softly, "we do. Grew up together, if you can believe that. We were best friends."

"What happened?"

"A girl happened." Seeing her sudden tension, he released a

hoarse chuckle. "Not like that, sunshine. Not for him. He was just trying to protect one of his own. Looking back, I'm pretty sure he's always belonged to you." He nudged her elbow. "Now go on. I'd hate to have him find you here in my car and end up on the wrong side of those claws, thinking I'm aiding and abetting your daring escape from monogamy."

Margot swallowed hard. She desperately wanted to know more about what happened between him and Theodore, but he was right. She didn't need anyone else tangled up in her mess. Swinging her legs out of the car, she muttered a soft, "Thank you, Viktor."

"Any time, sunshine."

The weight of his eyes lingered on her well after she closed the door and walked away. The air was cold and wet, seeping through the impressive layers she wore to sink into her bones as Margot approached the great, ugly face of the old soap factory.

She was tired, on edge, and a part of her still shrieked to return to Theodore's side, but this place was at least familiar to her. It would be a safe place to sleep. In the morning, she could...

Well, she had no idea what she was going to do.

Margot tugged her hood up around her face and slipped through the gap in the chain link fence surrounding the property. A complex glamour on the old, squat building hid the bustling life within, but those who dared slip in and out had to be careful to avoid too much notice.

The Market wasn't nefarious, but it *was* illegal.

Tucking her arms tight around her sides, Margot burrowed into Theodore's pilfered coat and kept her head down as she passed a cluster of unhumans going in the opposite direction. They were insectoid, and she couldn't identify them at a glance in the growing darkness, but their arms were laden with tote bags full of groceries and household goods anyone would recognize, no doubt paid for with unofficial currency that didn't require the ID chips or recognized alternatives all official citizens of the Protectorate were required to have.

They chattered in a language she didn't know, but quieted down as she passed them, their steps faltering to give her plenty of room. Their caution made sense. Unofficial residents who couldn't pass the requisite background and criminal checks to enter the EVP were not allowed to stay, and the pathways to getting ID chips or accepted alternate identification were vanishingly few. If the small group ran into the wrong person, they could be booted from the territory with no warning.

As eager to avoid them as they were to avoid her, Margot hustled past them and turned right at the papered double doors that most visitors would have stepped through. Instead, she circled the squat brick building to find an abandoned loading bay.

Levering herself up onto the high ledge once used to assist in the loading of trucks, Margot pushed past a billowing sheet of yellowed plastic to skim her fingers along the metal door blocking her way. It took only a handful of seconds in the dark to find the latch, then the welded sigil in the corner.

A dull flash of light, a low creak of rusted metal, and the emergency door was open just enough for her to squeeze through.

Immediately, the sights and smells of the Market assaulted her. Unlike the morose, abandoned appearance the factory displayed for outsiders, *inside* it was a riot of color and sound and scent. Lights were strung over every available surface. Stalls crammed up against one another to sell everything you could imagine and much of what you couldn't. Heat wavered in the air, mingling with the heavy scents of bodies and cooking oil, as people of every shape and size and race went about their business as usual amongst it all.

For a long, tense moment, Margot huddled by the emergency door, obscured by several stacked crates that might have been there a day or fifty years. It was a lot warmer in the Market than outside, a product of the many fryers and bodies pushing up against one another. Sweat beaded under her layers as she waited for an opening in the flow of bodies.

Two giants, both of them wearing tool belts around their massive waists and arguing about the day's work, made a gap for her in the mass. Margot slid into the flow easily, her head down, and let it carry her around to the opposite side of the Market. When she was close enough, it took only a few creative sideways steps to exit the river of people.

The old clinic wasn't so much a *clinic,* and more of an abandoned locker room for the former soap factory workers that was — through grit and plenty of cleaning solution — retrofitted into something close to a sanitary space.

It was marked by a crudely painted sign on the old particle board door, a Healer's Hand with the open eye in the middle marking it as a place not to be disturbed and open to all who needed aid.

Fitting, she thought dryly as she jiggled the rusty knob, *since I'm the one in need of aid tonight.*

The door had expanded with the moisture in the air, but it only took a good shove with her shoulder to get it open. Margot darted inside and slammed it closed behind her.

Only when the door was firmly closed did she lean back and *breathe.*

Okay, Margot thought, I made it. *What now?*

Food first, she decided. *Then rest.* Margot slid her hand against the wall until she felt the pitted plastic of the old light switch and flicked it on.

The clinic was roughly square, with one wall made up of old, rusted lockers and the other lined with shelves that once stored safety equipment. A narrow doorway led to a communal bathroom, long defunct except for a single toilet and one rusty spigot that ran ice cold water. One high window let in the smothered light of a streetlamp, but it was so hopelessly cracked and taped back together again that Margot didn't worry about it exposing her to outsiders.

Lined up along the lockers were three cheap medical beds separated by rolling screens, and in the far corner of the room there was a workbench, a cork board, and a bookcase full of plastic containers. Beneath the cracked window, there was a single folded cot.

"Not exactly *homey,*" she muttered, wearily peeling herself away from the door, "but it'll do."

The air was at least cooler in the clinic. That was a plus. As was the lack of overwhelming food smells, which made her empty stomach protest its mistreatment even more vocally than before.

Finger combing her tangled, dirty hair away from her face, Margot trudged across the checkered floor to root around in one of the plastic bins, searching for the snacks and canned goods she kept there for emergencies. It never occurred to her that *she* may need them, but that didn't matter now.

Sitting on the edge of one of the creaky medical beds, she unwrapped a power bar and ate the pasty thing in two huge bites. That done, she forced herself to get onto her sore feet. The door wouldn't ward itself.

Her chalk was mostly dust, destroyed by her leap from the car, but she managed to get a crude set of sigils burnt into the old door anyway. They weren't neat and they wouldn't hold up to anyone who really, *really* wanted to get to her, but they would at least give her a valuable warning.

Theodore never triggered my wards, she realized dully. *I didn't notice before, but every time he entered the suite, he never... Oh.*

Which meant that he never had any intention to hurt her. No one with ill-intent could have passed through the doorway without triggering the wards.

Think about that in the morning.

Feeling too drained to do much else, Margot pushed one of the beds in front of the door for safe measure and then scrubbed her face and hands in the bathroom. The water was ice cold, but she barely felt it.

It was strange, feeling a different sort of fatigue than the one that had struck so much fear in her for so long.

This wasn't burn out. The ache in her limbs and the

pounding in her head wasn't a death knell. It was merely exhaustion, magical and physical, after a day full of impossibilities.

After sifting through her stash of secondhand clothing she kept for patients, Margot slipped on a large t-shirt better suited to someone of Theodore's size and painstakingly unfolded the rusty cot. She planned to bring extra blankets the next time she came into the clinic, so there were none besides the starched ones on the medical beds.

Not wanting to take those in the off-chance they would be needed by the sick, Margot laid her coat down on the threadbare mattress of the cot and then curled up under Theodore's.

With the dim light from the bare, flickering bulb extinguished and the muffled sounds of the vibrant Market beating like a drum through the walls, Margot closed her eyes and tried her hardest not to think.

It was surprisingly easy to push aside thoughts of the future. It was not nearly so easy to get rid of thoughts of Theodore.

I kissed the sovereign today.

She could still feel it, the firm press of his smooth lips on hers, the slide of his tongue along the seam of her mouth, the sharp bite of his fangs on sensitive skin. Margot imagined that she could still taste him.

She curled up tighter under his coat, the silk lining warm and luxurious against the bare skin of her arms and legs. Her heart beat faster.

Alone, Margot could admit to herself that she *loved* kissing Theodore — not simply because doing so had saved her life, but because it was...

It was wonderful.

It didn't matter that he was the sovereign or an elf or anything else. When he plunged his hands into her hair and kissed the breath out of her lungs, he felt like he was *hers.*

It was instinct to bury her nose in the high collar of his coat, seeking the comfort of scent her other half demanded. Cedar and Theodore and that indefinable, luxurious quality that made her bare toes curl. *If only it was real,* she thought, biting her lip hard.

The urge to be grateful for her new lease on life was strong, but so too was her bitterness at having her chance at love, at that one, great connection between magical beings, swept out from under her by a man she could never truly have. Bonding with Theodore, for all that it had saved her life, also stole her chances at a real relationship, a family. Because she could never have those things. Not with him.

I didn't even realize I still had dreams of finding that sort of thing, she thought ruefully. *But I must have, to be this broken up about it.*

No matter how *right* Theodore was, no matter how much her elvish blood keened for him, she was smart enough to know that nothing like what she wanted could exist between them.

Love. Family. Trust. A home. A feeling of safety that meant she would never have to look over her shoulder again. Maybe children, if she and her partner wanted them.

With Theodore Solbourne, son of Thaddeus Solbourne II, head of the Solbourne family and Sovereign of the Elvish Protectorate? None of that was within her grasp.

But you'll live, she reminded herself. *Isn't that enough?*

Margot turned her face into the lining of his coat, pulled it over her head, and tried not to cry.

Margot.

A fizzle of energy under her skin, a prickling awareness, and the echo of Theodore's voice woke her.

Margot squinted into the darkness of the clinic. She was still curled up in a tight ball under Theodore's coat, and although she was warm enough, her body was sore from keeping the strained position for too long.

Must have been what woke me. She groaned and turned onto

her back, careful to keep her bare toes under the hem of her makeshift blanket. *I wonder if a jail cell would have been a little bit more comfortable.*

No, she groggily decided, not if her elvish wardens decided she wasn't worth the trouble of keeping around long enough to *need* blankets.

With that grim thought in mind, Margot sighed and squeezed her eyes shut once more, determined to get as much rest as she could before the massive problems of tomorrow tumbled onto her shoulders.

Darling.

Her eyes popped open.

Darling, I know you can hear me. I can tell you're awake.

Her heart slammed against her ribs as she shot up on her cot, the old springs squealing in protest.

"Theodore?"

Margot pressed the heels of her hands into her temples, too shocked to do anything else. In the back of her mind, the electric current of their bond hummed with untold power, its size and strength quadrupled sometime while she dozed.

Margot, talk to me.

How? She didn't have any telepathic abilities! She never wanted them.

In fact, her instructors had all complained to her grandmother about her abysmal lack of talent with anything even *remotely* psychic, but Margot was pleased to know that her thoughts were never in danger of being projected to another's.

The fact that Theodore's voice rang so very clear in her head was as horrifying as it was... *Goddess, why am I actually* relieved?

The feeling lay buried under her panic, but it was there. She was relieved that she could hear his voice, that it meant he was okay. Clutching his coat around her bare legs, Margot pressed her forehead against her kneecaps and thought, *I don't know how to talk to you.*

That worked just fine.

Oh. She blinked, her chest going strangely tight at the rough warmth in his mental voice. *I don't know how we're talking.*

I have a myriad of mid-to-high level psychic abilities, he answered, clear as a bell in her mind. *And we are connected by a bond running on the equivalent of nuclear power. Connecting to you has always been easy. Now it's like breathing.*

Margot tried to swallow the lump in her throat. *Are you okay? When I left, you...*

Yes. If they had been speaking aloud, Margot imagined Theodore's response was bitten off the tip of the tongue. He didn't sound amused, but what did she expect? That he would laugh about how she knocked him out and then ditched him in a car? No doubt the only reason he was speaking to her now was to ascertain her whereabouts, like Viktor warned her he would.

Dreading the answer but needing it anyway, she asked, *Aren't you searching for me? Why haven't you asked where I am?*

There was a tiny pause, then, *Darling, I already know where you are.*

Her stomach dropped. *What?*

My consort, my... vexing witch, I'm going to have to ask you to open the window. I don't imagine you want me breaking it.

Margot gasped. Twisting around, she peered up at the single, rectangular window by the lockers. A shadow blocked out the dull yellow light. A shadow that *moved.*

A flash of metal through the twisting cracks and old tape was followed by the soft *tink-tink, tink-tink* of Theodore's claws on the glass.

It's cold out here, he rumbled. *Have some mercy on me, won't you? Let me in.*

Chapter Thirteen

For a long, taut moment, Theodore was certain she would refuse him.

His stomach, already in knots of anxiety and the sharp yank of the pull, knotted further. He didn't want to have to fetch her. He didn't want to spook her any more than she obviously was.

But if it came down to it, he would.

Not because the pull demanded it, her nearness a craving his body could not circumvent or ignore, but because her safety was his responsibility. He took her under his protection. He made a *vow.* It gutted him to think that his consort felt his word meant so little — that her fear was great enough to make *jumping out of a moving vehicle* the better option.

Margot, he said into the bond connecting their minds like a sleek electric bridge. *Please let me in.*

Theodore could almost *hear* her indecision. When she spoke, her inner voice was a rolling storm cloud in his mind; deliciously elemental, with a bite of pure power in every word.

Do you say please often?

He crouched in front of the small rectangular window, fighting the urge to pry the damn thing from the old brick wall so he could see her. It felt like she was playing for time, and that made his claws curl anxiously against the thick glass. He needed to see her. He couldn't breathe for it.

Squeezing his eyes closed, he forced himself to answer. *Why wouldn't I?*

You're the sovereign. I didn't think you would actually ask for anything.

Do you really think so little of me? Theodore shook his head. *Dominance and entitlement are weapons in the sovereign's arsenal. That's what my sister taught me, and what I had to learn to rule this territory. But I grew up with three siblings and four parental figures. Do you really think I could get away with being that sort of ass with so many family members breathing down my neck?*

There was a drawn out note of surprise in her inner voice when she answered, *No, I guess not.*

I can be high-handed, he allowed, *and I'm impatient. But I'm not above begging, if it'll get me what I want. If you want me on my knees, darling, I'm already there.*

He couldn't make out anything beyond the grimy, cracked window, but Theodore knew the moment she drew close. It should have been humiliating, crouching in the dust and detritus outside her window, the knees of his expensive suit ruined as he pressed his nose to the glass, but it was *her,* and for her he would endure anything.

What do you want?

Working to keep his inner voice calm, to not betray any of the urgency he felt pounding in his veins, Theodore answered, *You.*

Shifting shadows, an indistinct shape on the other side of the dark window. His heart jumped into his throat.

Why? So you can have my magic?

Was he imagining the yearning in her voice? That brittleness that was so at odds with the sheer magnitude of her presence?

Theodore couldn't resist sweeping his claws over the glass, wishing it was her cheek he was caressing. *No, darling. Let me in. Let's talk. Give me a chance to convince you I only want to care for you. That I'm not some monster.*

I don't think you're a monster, she said, surprising him. *Why do you think that?*

Darling, you jumped out of a moving vehicle to get away from me. What else am I supposed to think?

Oh. Yes, I guess that would give you that impression.

And they would have words about her stunt, he promised himself. Strong words. Later.

Open the window, darling, he pressed. *I need to see you with my own eyes.* He paused, suddenly gripped by a more visceral fear. *You aren't hurt, are you? I should have asked that already, but I assumed since you got here on your own...*

I'm fine. Viktor gave me a ride. Couldn't you just break in? Or send your guards in to retrieve me? Why bother to ask?

Theodore traced the seam of the window sill, his patience thinning until it was nearly nonexistent. *Of course I could, but that wouldn't exactly help your image of me, would it?* Not to mention the fact that the idea of sending in his men to retrieve her like some criminal made his spine lock. *But did you say Viktor—*

Don't worry about Viktor. Are your guards out there?

His guards were currently surrounding the Market. They were shadows melting into plain sight, their claws at the ready, and he trusted the elite group of soldiers with more than just his life. They were a selected group of elvish bastards, entitled to no family name and no inheritance, given over to Patrol at the age of fifteen to become more than nameless, hidden offspring.

The members of the Sovereign's Guard were hand picked from amongst them and, at Valen's insistence, trained alongside Theodore from the moment he could use his claws. They were his extended family, his friends and siblings-in-arms. If push came to shove, he would even trust them with Margot.

But he didn't need to. Not right then. He could coax her, gentle her. Somehow.

Yes, they are. Margot, I know you—

The sound of a rusty latch unlocking cut him off. Theodore watched, wide-eyed with disbelief, as the old, grimy window slowly rose. The hinges squealed, and it wasn't meant to open all the way even when it was new, but it was enough.

Stand back, darling.

Elves were, by nature, more graceful and flexible than most species. By dint of his lifetime of combat training, Theodore was in a league all his own. Three quick movements, a twist of his torso, a swift, silent leap, and he was in.

Even as he reached behind him to close the battered window, Theodore's eyes landed on his consort without missing a beat.

Margot stood several paces away from him in the center of a checkered floor. He didn't need light to see her with perfect clarity. Scanning her face, Theodore was immensely relieved to see all traces of her bruises and wounds from the blast erased and no new horrors from her jump at all. Her expression was wary, her rosebud mouth pinched, but the dark circles under her eyes were gone, and he could see a bright flush infusing her cheeks.

Theodore's eyes dipped reflexively, his need to reassure himself of her physical wellbeing a pounding drum in the back of his mind, and felt his heart stop.

Oh.

Of course, he *knew* she was sleeping when he finally tracked her down. The way their bond hummed low felt almost drowsy. And he understood that to sleep, one generally did not wear day clothes. Theodore was of the "no clothing is meant for sleeping" camp. Still, he was blindsided by the sight of Margot Goode in nothing more than an oversized t-shirt, her lithe legs peeking out from beneath the hem and her little, clawless toes curling against the checkered tile.

His gaze skittered down her body before running right back up to start again, slower this time, starting with the top of her sleep-mussed head and down over every tightly compact inch of her.

Her collar bones and soft shoulder peeking out from the sagging collar of the t-shirt; her small breasts, nipples pebbled with the cold air against the thin fabric; her clenching hands curled against her soft thighs; her legs, smooth and faintly muscled — all of it only a handful of feet away, ready for him to explore.

Theodore's mouth went dry in the same instant he went painfully hard.

A sharp bite of pain-pleasure told him his claws had retracted beneath his claw-caps, his body primed and ready to show her exactly how little she had to fear from him, exactly how much *he* needed *her*.

He didn't even realize he had taken a step toward her until Margot scrambled backward, her eyes huge in her startled face. "W-what are you doing?"

Theodore ran his tongue over his upper fangs as he sucked in a huge breath. The scent of the room was layered with mildew and dust and the potent mix of things from the Market beyond the door, but above all of that, he smelled *her*. Ozone and Margot; desire and sweet, delicious woman.

Three days ago, Theodore would never have imagined giving in to his baser impulses with her. There was a multi-step plan to winning her, after all. But what was the point in holding back now? Margot knew she was his, that he was hers. They shared one mind, one soul, through the goddess-given lightning crackling in the very heart of her. He kissed her until it felt like he was burning up from the inside. She kissed him back. She *bit* him back.

They were well beyond the point of propriety, of cautiousness, now.

"Come here," he rumbled, a purr building like a storm in his chest.

Margot made an indignant sound. "Why? We can have a conversation just as well with me standing here as we could with... with me closer."

"Why? Because I want to touch you." He held out his hand and curled his fingers twice, beckoning. The dim light from the street, barely enough to break through the layer of sentient fog obscuring the city, made his wicked clawtips gleam. *"Come here."*

He watched her eyes dart towards his hand. They stayed there, fixed on his claws, as he held his breath. It did terrible, wonderful things to him to see her pupils expand, almost eclipsing her coppery iris in time with her deep inhale.

"Any sane person wouldn't let those claws near their bare skin," she whispered.

A thread of heat in her sharp scent, tantalizing and familiar on an instinctive level.

Glory save me.

Swallowing hard, he replied, "Who said anything about touching bare skin?"

Margot's cheeks flushed. Her shoulders, so dainty compared to his massive frame, bunched. Before she could offer a retort, he soothed, "Would it make you feel more comfortable if I took them off?"

He watched, rapt, as her small pink tongue darted out to wet her lips. "I... I shouldn't want you to touch me at all."

"But you do." That, at least, he was certain of.

Did she realize that she was slowly inching closer, her bare feet shuffling across the checkered floor in inches? Going by the look on her face and the way she hadn't taken her eyes off of his outstretched hand, he would wager not.

Her breath hitched. Theodore had to lock his spine to keep from reaching for her as the small, stuttered inhale made her breasts move against her sleep shirt. *Wait, Teddy. She'll come to you.*

"You have no idea how dangerous this is for me," she rasped, a strangely desperate edge in her voice. "Everything in me knows that I shouldn't do this, or want to touch you *so bad,* but it's like trying to fight the need to breathe." Margot tore her eyes away from his hand at last, her expression stark, and curled her arms around her chest. "I shouldn't. I can't."

Prick her, his instincts growled. *Make her fight you. Subdue her. Show her you can't be pushed away, that she can trust you to always come back to her.*

It was an entirely elvish impulse. Humans didn't have the same courtship, the same pull that elves did. That was what his research said and the reason he'd gone out of his way to so carefully craft his plan to win her. But if coaxing would only allow her time to find reasons to fight the desire he *knew* she felt, then he would follow his instincts instead.

Dropping his hand, Theodore prowled forward. "You will," he growled, matching her backward steps with long strides. "Because you *want* to, and because my consort is no coward."

Margot sputtered. Stopping her hasty retreat, she snapped, "It's not cowardice to see how this *only* ends badly for me!"

He forced himself to shrug. "Isn't it? If you're too afraid to fight for what you want, to even *explore* it, it sounds like cowardice to me."

They were nearly chest to chest. Margot glared up at him, her head tilted back to make up for his significant height advantage. "You don't know what you're talking about. You have no *idea* what I'd be risking by entering into *any* sort of relationship with you! You have no idea what being bonded to you means for me! You're the fucking *sovereign* and I'm just— Goddess! You have no right to make any judgments about me!"

He shrugged again, and she finally appeared to notice how close they were. Making a strangled noise, she ordered, "Get out of my personal space."

Theodore held her gaze without blinking. "No."

He could feel her outrage thrumming through their bond, hot and sharp as elvish claws raking through his mind.

"No?"

"No," he calmly repeated. "If you really want me to back off, *make me."*

It was a bare challenge. If she were elvish, Margot would have gone for his throat immediately, the fury in her blood too hot to fight. The pull would be eating at her will too, demanding she make him work for their union, encouraging her to sharpen her claws against his hide to test his mettle.

Of course, Margot *wasn't* an elf, so he didn't really know how she would react to the challenge, but—

A sound startlingly like a snarl tore from her delicate throat. It was his only warning before she swiped at his cheek, her blunt little nails raking across his face with a shocking amount of force.

It was a glancing blow, nothing that could truly damage him, but he was so surprised that she reacted in the elvish way that he didn't stop to think about his response.

Theodore caught her arm on the downswing, then snagged her other as she went to claw him again with her left hand. In an instant, he had her up against the wall by the door. Pinning her hands together with one of his, he wedged his thigh between her legs and fisted his free hand in her hair, knotting the red strands around his fingers until he had a good enough grip to gently but firmly pull her head back.

The furrows in the skin of his cheek burned hot, sparking an instinct deep and dark, bred into his very DNA.

Fight. Subdue. Bind.

He closed his teeth over the soft skin of her throat. His upper and lower fangs pressed hard against the fragile barrier between their razor sharpness and her jugular. He could feel it pounding against the flat of his tongue.

Her breathing was ragged, her thighs clamped hard around the leg he pressed against her hot core, and when he dragged his fangs against her skin, Margot gasped.

Like a switch flipping, the furious tension in her vanished.

Her hands, curled into vicious little claws, unfurled. Her slight weight settled against him as she let him support her. Her head tilted back, giving him free access to the most vulnerable part of her.

Subdued.

Again, it was the right response. An elvish consort would have instinctively capitulated once their throat was bared — the main reason all elves wore high, reinforced collars. Humans, he understood, reacted negatively to this sort of handling, but Margot appeared to be different.

Theodore wondered, in some very distant part of his mind, if the bond she created was feeding some of the pull into her.

If the pull made him crave her fight, it would make an elvish consort crave his victory. It was *right* that she would melt into him, the scent of her desire blooming between them until it clouded every bit of good sense in his mind.

Fuck.

Theodore purred approvingly, letting her know how pleased he was with her trust, and ran his mouth up her throat to kiss her jaw, her ear, her chin, her cheek, her lashes, and her pert little nose. He covered every inch of her he could reach before he finally pressed his lips against hers.

She opened with a sigh. Her soft, slick tongue darted out to meet his. He was lost.

Certain that she was no longer planning on clawing his eyes out, he released her hands to cup her backside, encouraging her to slide more fully onto his muscled thigh. The heat radiating through his pants made his cock ache, but Theodore didn't care. He lavished her mouth with kisses, relishing the taste of her, his instincts crowing with victory as he began the slow binding process that would satisfy the pull.

Although they *bonded* in the way of witches, they weren't yet *bound.* Not in the elvish way.

For that to happen, and to stave off the the madness the pull inspired, they would need to keep near-constant physical contact. Sometimes it took weeks, or even months, for an elf's unique pheromones to imprint into the skin of their consort and vice versa, completing the process the pull began. Only then would the dangerous chemical imbalance that made an elf so volatile settle.

But it will be an extremely pleasurable few months if that's the case, he thought, daring to skim his hand up the outside of her deliciously bare thigh.

His claw-caps scraped gently against her soft skin, eliciting a sound from Margot's throat that made his cock throb in the confines of his pants. He desperately wanted to be rid of the leather barrier of his gloves, but that sound was so erotic, so painfully raw, that it became imperative that he make her repeat it.

Ripping his lips from hers, Theodore pressed their foreheads together and rasped, "Do you *like* my claws, darling?"

He trailed them up the outside of her thigh again and felt her shiver. *Oh, she does.* Heat licked its way up his spine. "All that talk of being afraid of them near you," he murmured, "and it turns out it's really because they make you wet, don't they?"

Margot jerked, her whole body tightening in a way that sent every drop of blood in his body below his waist. Her eyes were squeezed shut, but her lips were kiss-swollen and parted, her breaths ragged as they puffed between them, and he *knew* he was right.

Glory, give me patience.

He had always known that waiting for Margot was the right choice. It was the *only* choice, really, when one had a nascent psychic link to their soulmate from childhood. He couldn't be intimate with anyone else even if he wanted to. His body just wouldn't respond, not when his mind was so completely fixated on *her.*

And of course, Theodore fantasized about her, knew that they would have something extraordinary when they did finally touch. He spent many a long, lonely night wondering what her skin would feel like, how she would taste; *wishing.*

But in all of that, he never considered how *he* would fare when the time came. It seemed to him a given that he would be in control, that he would have no trouble lavishing her with pleasure again and again. He was raised by two straight-talking lesbians, after all. He was no slouch, and entirely unselfconscious about his needs and those of his partner.

The reality of actually *having* Margot in his arms, willing and smelling like lush desire, however, was both better than anything he could ever have imagined and much, much worse.

Calm, he mentally chanted. *Be calm. Be in control. Win her. Don't fucking blow it, Teddy.*

Sweat beaded along his spine and across his chest as he tensed his abdomen, willing his control to hold.

Sucking in a deep breath, Theodore slid his hand up beneath the bunched hem of her sleep shirt to find the crease of her thigh and the side of her panties. Plucking at the fabric with just the tips of his claws, he asked, "Are you going to answer me, darling? Or am I going to have to find out for myself?"

Margot jolted. Her eyes opened to give him an adorably indignant look. "What makes you think you have the right to that information, Sovereign? Besides, for all you know, I could like any man with claws."

She yelped when he nipped the shell of her ear, her back arching and unintentionally pressing them closer. Theodore gave her backside a hard, proprietary squeeze. "No one else is your bondmate. *I* am your bondmate, and I know you want me. I want to hear you say it."

Margot glowered at him, apparently unmoved. "It doesn't *matter.* I'm trying to tell you that this can't happen, but you're not listening! Sexual chemistry, the bond, whatever — I know what we have, but we can't take this any further."

Theodore pressed his lips against her temple before sliding them back down to her ear. *Patience, Teddy.* "Why? Explain it to me."

There was real anger in her voice when she answered, "Because you're the sovereign of the Elvish Protectorate, and elves don't have relationships with other races." A hitch, a breath that didn't flow quite right, briefly paused the flow of her words. "Not out in the open, anyway. It's great that I'm not dying anymore, sure, but I'm not going to be somebody's secret. Not anymore. Not for my bondmate, no matter *who* he is. I'm not going to be a mistress, either. *I won't fucking do it.*"

At the mention of the word *mistress,* Theodore felt all the hair on the back of his neck stand up. Scalding, familiar rage rushed up his throat and settled in his fangs, making them ache.

Pulling his hand out from under her sleep shirt, he cupped her jaw firmly, making sure she could not look away as he leaned in close to curtly inform her, "You are *never* going to be anybody's mistress. You are my consort. You are my partner. You are everything I have ever wanted and more than I ever imagined. You are my bloody *fucking* heart."

Breathing hard, he had to pause to keep himself from snarling the rest. "You're right that we don't allow ourselves to make unions with Others. We stopped mixing bloodlines a thousand fucking years ago because we thought our race was going to die out completely." He shook his head. The bite of old, helpless rage never really went away, no matter how much he fought it.

Fools. Terrified, thoughtless fools just slowed our doom down.

"But we're still dying," he confessed, watching her stricken face as she took in the magnitude of what he was revealing. "Our rough estimate is that we're only ten thousand strong now, and things are only getting worse. Mental degradation is up, fertility is plummeting, and we're all too scared and proud to admit we need help."

Theodore sucked in a deep breath. The scent of her, the feeling of her warmth pressed against him, the way she leaned into him even when she claimed she shouldn't, helped soothe the angry boy hidden below the toughened layers of a determined man.

"You're right that I'm the sovereign and that it's something we *shouldn't* do," he allowed. When Margot — stubborn, beautiful Margot — flinched, he pressed another hard kiss between her brows to soothe her, to remind her that he wasn't going anywhere. "But what you don't understand is that it's something we *have* to do. Our fertility rate is abysmal because we struggle to reproduce with people our bodies don't recognize as our consorts. We *need* the specific chemical reaction the pull — the compulsion to find our mate — creates to have healthy offspring with any consistency."

"I... *what?*" Margot sucked in a sharp breath, her mind working fast behind the copper of her eyes. "But that's— Oh, goddess, it's *hormonal,* isn't it? Like orcs."

Theodore didn't fight her on the comparison. As much as no one wanted to believe orcs and elves shared enough common traits to be of the same stock, it was the truth. Genetically speaking, studies had shown that they were very, very similar.

Not that any of those genetic studies have been published, of course.

Skimming the claw of his thumb over her jaw, he answered, "Yes. It's a hormonal change that begins when we make contact with our consorts. It rearranges things. Makes us more fertile." He swallowed. "It's... altering, to say the least."

Margot's eyes danced across his face. Some of the hard disbelief, the despair, began to leech out of her expression. He witnessed the moment it all snapped together in her mind. "And elves have been ignoring it? To try and survive?"

Theodore rubbed the pad of his thumb over the swell of her cheek. Back and forth, back and forth. *My consort, safe in my arms. My family. My love.*

"Yes. If you couldn't be with a consort that was Other, you were matched with a suitable elf, preferably with good political connections. Less than two thirds of those unions have more than one child. A good portion have none at all. It can't continue this way. We need someone to show the world we can do things differently without losing ourselves in the process."

Comprehension dawned on Margot's face. The high flush of arousal in her cheeks drained away. "You... you want *us* to be..."

"The sovereign is always the example," he gently explained. "They lead the way. *We* are going to show everyone there's a way out of this mess."

If anyone had reason to demand change, it was Theodore. His

own family had nearly been destroyed by the madness caused by a forbidden union, the unfulfilled pull.

Thaddeus II was a good man once, according to Valen. Affable and lucky to be blessed with not one, but *three* children with his chosen elvish partner, he was the very picture of a new elvish age, of what could be possible if they just held on. He was bloodthirsty and played a large part in launching the Great War, that terrible conflict that drew so many hard lines between the territories, but he wasn't a monster. Not to the elves.

The dream didn't last. Thaddeus's decline into madness and violent paranoia began after meeting his true consort.

Kaz's mother was a beautiful orcish woman, an architect he met by chance during a diplomatic visit to the New Zone and the UTA Congress. Their affair was passionate and bore fruit in the form of Theodore's younger brother, but Thaddeus resisted the pull, never fully bound Kaz's despairing mother to him when he should have. When the chemical imbalance reached a tipping point, it was far too late to stop him without bloodshed.

How many innocent people might have lived if Thaddeus felt free to be with Amira? To dissolve his political union and find happiness with his consort?

Theodore's own mother would still be alive; not moldering in an urn in their private temple because she fought to the death for her children. At least a dozen high ranking elves would be alive. Thaddeus's own brother would have lived to see his twins grow up into the thorns they were. Countless soldiers and even more household staff, forever unaccounted for, would have families, loves, *lives.*

The ripple effect of Thaddeus's downfall, and the stain it left on his family, was still being reckoned with. It would never go away.

Margot gaped at him. "I don't... Theodore, I really think you have the wrong woman for this. I'm not— there is a lot you don't know—"

Theodore narrowed his eyes. "I thought the reason you

were so afraid before was because you were burning out, but that's not it, is it? There's something else that's holding you back."

Gods, just the reminder that she came so close to slipping away from him and into Grim's arms made his heart race. Theodore knew that the sight of her pale face streaked with blood would haunt him for the rest of his life.

"No, I…" Margot shook her head as much as she was able, her expression dazed. "I mean, of course I still have secrets, but that's not— I don't even know what I'm saying. I'm having trouble processing that this could be true."

"It's true," he pressed, "and I'll prove it to you."

"How?"

He shrugged. "I'll go before the Summit and all the Families and announce our union. You'll be my consort in the eyes of *everyone,* not just me."

"That won't be enough to get them to accept it, Theodore," she argued. "A thousand years of burying your heads in the sand won't be undone just because you *say* we're together. They could deny the union is legitimate, or, I don't know, force you to give me up."

"I will *not* give you up, so don't even think it." Theodore arched his brows. "What do you propose? Someone else say it?"

Margot stared at his collar pin for several seconds, her active mind whirring through the electric connection of their bond. Slowly, halting nearly every other word, she said, "If you're serious… If you actually want to spend your life with me, then we could get married."

Theodore blinked. "Elves don't do that."

"Humans do. Witches do." Margot shook her head, as if amazed that the words were coming out of her mouth. "It would make it impossible for anyone to argue against the legitimacy of the union, and it would make my grandmother your official ally, Theodore. It would also be legally binding in every recognized territory. We could have a Gloriae marry us in the temple with witnesses to prove it, and then you could announce it at the opening of the Summit."

Theodore gently nudged her chin, urging her to meet his eyes when he asked, "Is this what you want?"

"To marry you?" A liquid sheen gleamed in Margot's eyes. "I want to live. I want to be loved. I want a family someday. A future. Can you promise to give me that?"

"Yes." He pressed his lips against the silky skin of her eyelids and tasted the salt of her tears. "Yes. I am yours, Margot. I'll give you everything you want. We're already bonded for life, but I would give you more if I could."

Her voice was an achingly soft whisper. "Then yes, Theodore. I want to marry you."

He kissed her again, softly, with all the fierce pride and hope he felt. Even dumbstruck, she leaned into him as he began to pull away, her need for touch as potent as his own. "Then we'll be married the human way," he whispered against her lips. "We're already bound for life and I'm not going to stop talking about it until everyone knows. Might as well get it out of the way now."

"You want *me.*" She still sounded baffled, as if she was trying to untangle a brutal tongue twister in a foreign language rather than accept the very simple fact that Theodore was hers — body, mind, and soul. "Not my magic. Not as a joke. Not because you just want to have sex with me. You really, *actually* want me."

"Correct." Theodore pulled his hands away from her face to haul her up by her hips. Two long strides took them across the tiny clinic he was only now glancing at — were those *lockers?* — and to the tiny cot she must have climbed out of.

Depositing her on the creaky thing, he dropped down to his knees before her bare legs and gently pulled them apart. She didn't try to stop him. She didn't even tense up.

Margot simply watched him, her breathing ragged, as she asked the most heartbreaking question he could imagine. "This is real, isn't it? You're not... this isn't some trap? A trick?" A whisper of a thought slid through their bond. *Please don't let it be a trick.*

Theodore squeezed her thighs, his insides twisted up into great, thorny knots. His voice was ragged when he answered, "Yes, darling. This is real. Now let me show you."

Margot's eyes, so brilliant and unusual, took on a shine that nearly unwound him. "Okay," she whispered. "Show me."

Chapter Fourteen

After days of non-stop, increasingly unpleasant surprises, Margot thought she was unshockable.

The sight of Theodore Solbourne, *Sovereign,* kneeling between her thighs on the checkered floor of an old soap factory locker room forced her to reevaluate.

He's going to marry me.

The thought circled her mind like a lazy buzzard, just out of reach. There were no *ifs* or *buts.* Theodore intended to marry her. He wasn't going to siphon off her magic. He wasn't going to hide her away. She could *feel* his lust, his determination, thrumming through their bond.

Theodore took up space in the back of her mind as arrogantly as he did in real life — as if he was always meant to be there, smug and deliciously, terrifyingly focused on her.

It should have bothered her that he wasn't *asking,* but Margot was a practical woman. There was no choice. There was no *asking,* because that would give the illusion that she could say no; that there was even the chance she *would.*

She wouldn't.

Because this thing he was offering her, this predator skimming his clawed hands up the insides of her thighs, was beyond price. It was beyond dreams. It was beyond *imagining.*

He was offering her a world where she no longer had to hide.

I'll be his consort, she thought, heart racing. *I'll be untouchable.*

With the might of the Solbourne family behind her, who would dare use her blood against her? Who would lay a hand on the elvish mother she didn't know? *Who?*

She had hoped to never have to hide from her bondmate, but this was beyond anything she could dare to dream up. A life where she didn't have to dunk herself in Noscent three times a day? No more skin-stripping showers? No more terror at being sniffed too much, of being looked at too closely?

The rest of what he told her would need to be digested, of course. She would need to think about what this *pull* meant for her, and what it would really mean to marry the sovereign of the EVP, but that would be—

Theodore dipped his head to press a searing, open-mouthed kiss to her inner thigh.

"I can *feel* your mind working," he murmured against her skin. His lips were hot, his tongue wet as he paused to lick a stripe up to the gusset of her panties. "Stop. We'll figure it all out later. Right now, focus on me."

"I *am* focused on you," she replied unsteadily. "You've got your head between my legs."

Theodore shot her a sharp — literally, considering the four little razors that were elvish incisors — grin that brought out his boyish dimples. His eyes, chips of obsidian in the darkness, were heavy-lidded with a look of desire that made her pulse throb between her legs.

"Yes," he agreed, amiable and totally unflustered as he pressed two fingers against the damp gusset of her panties. The sharp spike of pleasure from that simple, firm touch made her whole body jerk. "I am going to live here for a while. I am going to fuck you with my fingers and my mouth until you can't breathe, and then we're going to go somewhere with a real bed and I'm going to do it again."

Margot's chest seized. Was he allowed to talk like that? *Who* talked like that? He made it sound like he was planning a picnic, not telling her he was going to...

Arousal made her skin flush. Starved for contact she might have been, but Margot never considered herself a sexual being. Stealing kisses from her orcish neighbor behind the woodshed was exciting in a forbidden sort of way, but *this...*

"I've never done—" She forced herself to swallow before trying again. "I've never done anything like this before."

Theodore didn't stop his slow exploration of her, nor did he stop pushing her sleep shirt up her torso, revealing her breasts to the cold, damp air. Goosebumps prickled her skin.

Rocking his fingers against her core, he bent his neck to press a reverent kiss just below her belly button. "Neither have I. We might both be shit at it for a while, but enthusiasm has to count for something."

Margot only dimly processed his confession. It was impossible to focus on what he was saying when he was *touching* her.

It never feels like that when I do it, she thought, unable to stifle a whimper when he used the tips of his claws to gently scrape her nipple. They were *blades.* Why did they feel so very good on her skin?

"Fuck." Theodore removed his hand from between her legs and Margot rocked her hips, desperate to bring him back.

"Hold on." The words were bitten out from between his sharp teeth, hard and tight, before he raised his right hand between them and wiggled his fingers urgently. The hand on her breast tightened its grip. "I'm not taking my other hand off of you, so you're going to have to take off my glove."

Margot lifted herself onto her elbows to stare, wide-eyed, at the wickedly dangerous, silver-tipped claws just a handful of inches from her nose. Everything in her rebelled against just how very, very much the sight of them turned her on. That beast in her wanted those claws around her throat almost as much as it wanted his cock in her.

She bit her lip hard as that molten heat spread low, leaving her slick and wanting. *Absolute madness.*

When she hesitated for too long, he groaned and dragged his mouth along the wet seam of her panties. "Darling," he rasped, "just take the one off. Don't make me take *both* my hands off you so I can touch you properly."

The mental image of what he planned to do with his ungloved fingers was just enough to move her. Panting, she lay flat on her back so her arms would be free. Using both hands, she began to peel the black leather from his thick, sturdy wrist and then upward, over his pale blue palm, until she was revealing his long, tapered fingers one by one.

His voice was little more than a rough exhalation against her skin. "That's it."

With each inch of skin she revealed, Margot felt the ache between her legs deepen. It was, she discovered, just as erotic to take his gloves *off* as it was to see them against her skin, so very capable of danger and yet so unwilling to inflict harm.

The glove fell away from his hand with a soft clink of metal. Margot clutched it in her right fist pressed hard against her racing heart, and blurted, "You don't... you don't *have* claws?"

Something warm and wet snaked between her thighs, pressing flat against her cloth-covered clitoris with unerring precision. Pleasure scorched a path up her spine. Margot's thighs jerked upward to clamp round Theodore's pointed ears. *"Ah!"*

His husky voice was muffled against her sex when he answered, "Not when I'm with you. They retract. Only with you. S'first sign we've met our consorts." Another searing lick. "Makes pleasuring you easier."

He didn't even have the decency to move back a little to speak. Theodore rubbed his lips and teeth and tongue against her shamelessly as his gloved hand plucked at her nipple and his now naked, clawless hand slid down the center of her chest and across her belly until his fingers hit the waistband of her sensible white panties.

She half expected him to tear them off. Instead, Theodore lifted his head and ducked out from between her thighs just long enough to gently slide her clothing down her legs and onto the cold floor. He was back to his original position in a flash, though, now with nothing at all between them.

Margot felt her cheeks flush to a furious crimson, but forced herself not to cringe, not to flinch back or try to hide from his roving gaze. There was *nothing* shameful about this. She was a healer, for Glory's sake! The body was just the body. Sex was just sex. There was no reason to be shy.

But she was still a woman who had never been touched, let alone *seen,* by a sexual partner before, and Margot could admit to herself that even she felt a small twinge of uncertainty at having a man like Theodore licking his lips at the sight of her.

She was about to take yet another plunge into unknown waters. Was it really so unreasonable to feel uneasy when those waters were populated by a sharp-toothed predator waiting to devour her whole?

Theodore's rough voice broke through the cold haze of self-consciousness that had begun to push out her desire. "Do you know what it's like to dream about a woman for twenty-five years, only to find out she's... *so* much more than you could imagine?" He made a keening sound in the back of his throat — half moan, half whine. "Fuck, Margot, I want to..."

His tongue, flatter than hers and slightly rough, swept up from her core to her clitoris and back again. His ungloved hand grasped her thigh and wrenched it up and to the side, giving him unrestricted access to every slick inch of her.

Margot sucked in a choked breath and arched her back over the thin mattress. "Theodore, I—*fuck!*"

His tongue swirled around her clitoris, too rough, too fast, as the claws on her nipple pinched. A prick of pain was a spark to the kindling inside her, lighting a fire that raged out of control.

She was never this rough with herself. Margot only ever thought to touch herself when the tension got to be too much, and even then, her aim was for speed rather than intensity; a quick, hard orgasm so she could get on with her day.

Having Theodore touch her was an experience so different she could hardly even call anything before him *pleasure.*

His tongue was more enthusiastic than skillful, but what did she care? She wasn't exactly skilled herself. Besides, the sheer intensity of him, the clear desire he felt to wring as much pleasure out of her as he could, made up for any clumsiness.

Rolling her hips against his dangerous, dangerous mouth, Margot reached down with her free hand to grip a handful of his dark hair. Her eyes jumped between the painfully erotic sight of him tonguing her to the gloved hand rolling her nipple, those silver claws winking in the dim light from the cracked window.

Add to that the fact that he was still fully dressed in his fancy elvish suit... Margot let out a low whimper.

The sound made Theodore pause and lift his head just a bit. Dark eyes fringed with sooty lashes gazed up at her from between her thighs, hot and hungry. His hand left her thigh to tease her fluttering core. "You want my fingers?" he rasped against her flushed skin. "You want me to fuck you with them? Get you ready for later, when I fuck you with my cock instead?"

Glory save me. The image that presented made her ache in ways she could never have imagined. Margot shuddered, gasping, "You sure *sound* like you've done this before."

A kiss to her aching clitoris, oddly tender, accompanied his rough admission. "I've had a long time to think about it." Another kiss, another burst of white-hot pleasure up her spine. "You didn't answer me, darling. Do you want my fingers inside of you?"

A small part of her, smothered but rational, wondered if that was the smartest idea. If claws could *retract,* couldn't they slide back out just as easily?

But that voice was small and quickly hushed by the howling

beast inside of her, the one that demanded he put his mouth to work and he fill that terrible, aching emptiness that made her *burn.*

"Yes," she choked out.

When Theodore didn't immediately get to work, but instead circled her core with a lazy, proprietary touch, she made a sound of frustration and wriggled her hips. "Theodore, *please.*"

"I want you to say it," he announced, all crisp authority. "I want you to *say* you want my fingers in you, and then you want my cock. Say the words, and don't forget to use my name."

Embarrassment made her cheeks burn even hotter. "Why? You already know what I'm asking for."

"I do. But I don't want any miscommunication between us. I want to hear you say it and *know* it's the truth."

Oh. Only then did she recall the fact that he could tell immediately if someone was lying. Margot blinked owlishly down at him, taking in his wild-eyed gaze and the blue flush in his high cheekbones. Theodore's expression was hard, almost mulish, at odds with the dark desire in his eyes.

This is important, she realized.

Because if she said she wanted it but was unsure, he would know. Unspoken but crystal clear to her was the understanding that, should her answer be anything less than the unswerving truth, he would stop.

A different kind of warmth bloomed in her chest. *He's taking care of me.*

Swallowing the unwanted lump in her throat, Margot tentatively ran her fingers through his silky hair. When he tilted his head into her touch, shamelessly seeking more, that warmth in her chest expanded to a painful degree.

How could she ever look at him as anything other than this person he was now? The image of him as a cool, arrogant sovereign had been completely scrubbed from her mind. All she saw now was the tenderness under the lust, the yearning stranger she longed to know beneath the veneer of a predator.

Her answer was soft but sure. "Yes."

He waited, unmoving, until she sucked in a fortifying lungful of cold, slightly musty air to continue, barely audible, "Yes, I want your fingers and then your cock in me, Theodore."

A hiss of air from between his clenched teeth was all the warning she got before he slid two fingers inside her. Margot tensed, her muscles rippling around him as she tried to adjust to the sudden change. His fingers were considerably larger than her own, and there was a sharp bite of pain before any pleasure bled through.

It was helped along by the fact that Theodore had closed his lips around her clitoris. He teased her with the tip of his tongue, making her squirm as he slowly began to pump his fingers in and out of her, and then changed his rhythm to include hard, sucking pulls.

Without thinking about it, Margot pressed his glove against her chest, the leather sliding against her perspiration-slicked skin, and covered the hand on her breast with her own, encouraging him to squeeze her, to run the tips of his claws over the tight bud of her nipple again and again.

His clawtips were freezing and sharp enough to tear through flesh easily. She'd seen him do just that to more than a few expensive cuts of raw meat. Still, somehow, the feeling of them dragging along her skin made the tension in her wind tighter, hotter, until she was rocking hard against his mouth and fingers.

"Theodore, please, I need... I need it *harder.*" Margot arched her back, trying to press herself more firmly against his mouth, chasing that hard, delicious friction that would push her over the edge.

Picking up on her urgency, Theodore stopped his teasing licks and settled into hard swipes and pulls of his tongue. His hand moved faster and deeper, curling slightly so that the blunt tips of his fingers could rub against the rippling wall of muscle.

Margot opened her mouth, but there was no scream, no cry of pleasure. When her orgasm broke, it stole her breath, her thoughts, her very heartbeat. There was nothing except Theodore and luscious, all-consuming pleasure.

And it didn't *end.*

Her habit was to stop as soon as the initial sparks of orgasm flared, her skin too sensitive to continue, but Theodore didn't stop. He didn't let up. He continued his ruthless pace. Her orgasm came in waves, lapping constantly over her as he guided her through each swell, urging her to take more, to submit to a pleasure she could never manage on her own.

It felt like hours before she finally came down from the precipice he balanced her on. Margot sagged bonelessly into the cot as Theodore panted between her legs, his fingers still firmly, possessively held inside her.

The Gloriae said that heaven was a riverbank thronging with souls lovingly tended by the goddess Grim, but Margot thought they were bald faced liars.

Heaven was Theodore Solbourne's face between her thighs.

Echoing her thoughts, he grated, "Fucking glorious," against the skin of her inner thigh. His mouth was wet, leaving a cold trail along her overheated skin. "I'm going to eat your cunt every day for the rest of my life, Margot Goode. That's a fucking vow."

Embarrassment, and the slow fade of overwhelming lust, made her shy. Margot turned her head away from him and wiggled her hips. "You can, ah, stop touching me now. I finished."

His answering snort had a distinctly smug ring to it. "I know. That doesn't mean I want to stop touching you, though." To prove his point, he curled his fingers again, rubbing with delicious slowness until Margot saw stars. She was too sensitive, definitely not ready for another round, but it felt so *good.*

"See?" He was *absolutely* smug. "Why would I stop when I can still get you to make *that* face?"

To save her bones from melting away completely, Margot shook her head and reached down to tug at his hair. "How can I touch you if you're too busy touching me?"

That got his attention.

An avaricious look entered Theodore's dark eyes. "You want to touch me?"

~

Theodore watched Margot's elegant, sweat-slicked throat move with a hard swallow and thought, *She's going to kill me.*

Not that he minded. If surviving an attempt on his life by his father, then a childhood with Valen and Delilah as his combat instructors, and *then* six successive challenges for his throne came to his life ending between Margot Goode's thighs...

Nothing to complain about.

"Yes," she answered, adorably shy considering her taste lingered on his tongue. "I want to touch you."

The unmistakable ring of truth was a cool balm to the clinging worry in the back of his mind. Margot *wanted* to touch him. They would work everything else out later. Right now, the only thing he cared about was her.

Theodore reluctantly extracted himself from the glorious apex of her thighs to crawl over her. He still knelt on the floor, being *considerably* taller than both her and her pitiful little cot, but this way he could cover her with his bulk and kiss her until they both forgot to breathe.

"Then touch me," he murmured against her thudding pulse.

He felt Margot's small hand crawl up his side, under the lapel of his suit jacket. "But you're still wearing so many clothes."

"Undress me."

Theodore was close enough to hear the hitch in her breath, to feel the way her whole body quivered at his rough command. *She likes this,* he realized, fighting a long, pained groan. *She's perfect.*

Margot's breath was a hot rasp in his ear as she used one hand to slowly pull his shirt out from his slacks. The slide of fabric against his hyper-sensitive skin was torture. The hot bar of his aching cock in his underwear? Infinitely worse.

Unable to help himself, he braced himself on his elbows above her and, ignoring the way the cot squealed in protest, stared down the length of his torso to watch her work.

His shirt slid free from his belt and slacks, but Margot didn't take the time to unbutton it. Instead, she thrust her cold little hand beneath it to skate over the tense muscles of his abdomen, the thin trail of dark hair that disappeared beneath his belt. The touch of her fingers, the slide of her palm — Theodore had to force himself to keep still, to not react to such a simple touch with an embarrassing lack of control.

No, they wouldn't be having their first time in this hovel, on this ridiculous excuse for a bed, but he still had his pride. Like fuck he was going to come at the feeling of her fingers on his *stomach,* for Glory's sake!

To distract himself from the worrying tension pulling at the base of his spine, Theodore focused on Margot. Her expression was intensely focused. Eyebrows furrowed, her kiss-swollen lower lip tucked between her blunt little teeth, she was a potent mix of minx and innocent that threatened to drive him mad.

She was also going way too slow.

"Darling, use both hands," he gasped, fully aware of just how desperate he sounded, how close he was to the edge.

"What?" She glanced down at where her right hand was still pressed against her chest, her fingers curled around his discarded glove like a talisman. Her cheeks flushed. "Oh, right."

Putting the glove aside, she set to unbuckling his belt with quick, nervous movements. Not wanting to make her more nervous and needing to keep a tight leash on his self control, Theodore held himself frozen above her as the leather slid free from his buckle with a soft clink of metal. Her little fingers moved to the button and then the zipper of his slacks.

Sweating in earnest now, he watched, holding his breath, as those soft healer's fingers slid into his underwear.

"Fuck." His hips jerked. Electricity raced up his spine as her fingers slid against his length, a shy caress that made him want to bite her and bite her and bite her.

Theodore buried his face in her hair and breathed deep, his lungs expanding like billows as his body fought to process the overload of sensation. The pull made every part of him more sensitive to her touch, to her taste, to her scent, but this was on a completely new level.

Margot stilled, her fingers curling *away* from where he wanted them to be. "Are— are you okay? Did I do something wrong?"

Fuck. Theodore squeezed his eyes shut, fearing that if he looked at her he would just start bucking into her hand and never stop. Turning his head blindly, he pressed a hard kiss to the corner of her mouth. "No, darling," he choked out, "you're doing amazing. I'm just close."

"Oh."

That soft exhalation, breathed against his ear, combined with the way her soft fingers gripped him with more confidence? *My cause of death.*

He keened softly when Margot freed him from the confines of his underwear. "Is this right?" she asked, dragging her fist up slowly, *so* slowly. Margot's voice was husky with desire, a rough caress to his senses. With her delicious, tart flavor on his tongue and her scent in his nose, speech was entirely beyond him.

Nodding helplessly, Theodore dragged his mouth against her jaw and rocked his hips into her hand.

Margot's soft sound of pleasure was like a shot to his chest. "You're so warm and soft. You look so strong, I never thought..." Her hand tightened, increasing the pressure around his throbbing cock. Another soft sound, this one of surprise, as pre-come beaded on the crown and rolled downward, easing the slide of her palm. "I never thought I'd enjoy it this much."

Margot picked up her pace. Her hands were so soft. Her touch was as unskilled as his, but intent, focused in ways that proved she wanted him just as much as he wanted her.

"Darling." He sucked in a huge breath, taking in the scent of her desire as it built ever-thicker in the air.

"Does this feel good, Theodore?" she murmured. Margot's thighs cradled his hips as she worked him, her stomach moving as she subtly rocked in time with her strokes.

He dropped his head to rest against her temple and grit out, "You have no fucking idea how good this feels, Margot. I've been hard since the moment we met."

She paused. "Really?"

Groaning, he thrust into her hand, urging her to continue her task. "Yes, darling. I want you so much I can barely think."

Her fingers tightened around his cock. "I like that."

The tension at the base of his spine drew tighter as the muscles of his abdomen stiffened in a rippling wave. Sweat slid between his shoulder blades.

Theodore made a choked noise and desperately sought her mouth as he reached down to cover her hand with his own, tightening her grip into something that bordered on painful. He guided her to stroke him how he needed it — hard, with a firm twist at the crown — and slicked his tongue against hers in time with his thrusting hips.

He held out for a surprisingly long time, considering his threadbare control, but when Margot's thighs wrapped around his hips, squeezing him hard, pulling him until his knuckles brushed the silky skin of her belly with every pass, it was over.

Theodore rocked his hips with jagged thrusts into her fist as he came, the crown of his cock dragging against the now slick skin of her stomach — back and forth, back and forth. Stars exploded behind his eyes. Pleasure was molten honey in his veins, too hot as it rushed out of him in waves.

Ripping his mouth from hers, Theodore gasped against the warm skin of her cheek, her name escaping him on a prayer so rough it was barely understandable.

When he was finally coherent enough to process thought, Theodore lifted his head to peer into Margot's face, searching. Would she regret what they'd done? Would she feel self-conscious?

But when he looked into her eyes, Theodore was relieved to see her pupils blown up into huge, dark pools. Her lips were soft, slightly parted, and her expression was beautifully dazed. Well-pleasured and soft.

Sighing, he gently pulled their hands away from his waning erection so he could bury both of his in her hair. There would never be a time when he didn't feel like he could be closer to her, when he wouldn't feel the urge to run his hands all over her. It was built into his very DNA to want her, to adore her.

Perhaps the chemical pull started things, primed him to want her, but it was the cool touch of her mind, the aching gentleness he felt thrumming through the thin thread of their bond for so many years, that made him *love* her.

He peppered her face with kisses. "You're perfect. I knew you would be perfect, but you are so much more than I could have imagined. Just... *perfect.*"

"You just met me," she sighed, turning her face toward his, accepting the affection he lavished on her like it was her due.

"No. I've been yours for most of my life." Theodore nuzzled her cheek. There was no pleasure quite so true or perfectly catered to soothe his beast than breathing in the smell of her covered in his own scent. "The rest is incidental."

Soon, he would be able to recognize even the most subtle shifts in her scent, the layers and nuances that changed depending on her health and moods. As he breathed her in, Theodore tried to sift through it all, but was distracted by that strangely familiar note of wildness that didn't belong.

There's something familiar there, but I can't...

He didn't have the focus to follow that thread when another, far more important one grabbed his attention.

Desire.

Theodore straightened enough to look down at her, the muscles of his stomach bunching as he watched her squirm beneath him. Her cheeks were still flushed red, and when she looked up at him through her lashes, the lust in her eyes nearly unwound him.

"Darling," he breathed, skimming his ungloved hand down her slick stomach to slide possessively between her legs. "Do you want more?"

Margot rocked into his hand. A small, keening whimper shot through every nerve in his body.

Theodore breathed hard, his cock picking up a renewed throbbing that would very quickly turn into more. "Gods, I like to touch you," he whispered. "You can't imagine what it's like to feel your skin after just imagining it for so long."

It was luxurious, a privilege he would never take for granted. And if she wanted him to touch her more, if she rocked her hips into his hand so sweetly and dug her blunt little nails into the skin under his shirt like that, he would do it forever.

Groaning, he peeled himself off of her so that he could kneel between her legs once more. *My favorite place in this world or any other.*

Theodore stared up at her, over her wet stomach and heaving, pink-tipped breasts, to meet her wild-eyed gaze. He slid his hands around her waist and gave it a quick possessive squeeze. "Up, darling," he urged. "I want you to sit up while I do this. I want to see you watching me."

"Like this?" Margot propped herself up on her palms. Her long red hair, unbound and thoroughly tangled, slid over her shoulder to cover one breast. His release, pale against her rosy skin, gleamed in the low light.

The sight of her sitting above him, covered in the proof of their union, made everything in him howl. *My consort, my heart, my life — finally mine.*

Theodore pulled her legs over his shoulders and pressed a hot, open-mouthed kiss to her core. "Yes," he hissed against her skin, eyes locked with hers. "Just like that."

Chapter Fifteen

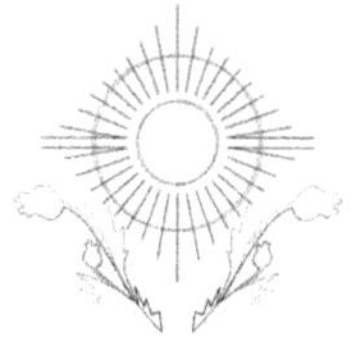

Like every elf, Theodore knew hunger. He knew deprivation. Every elf was defined by it. They were *born* hungry — not simply for food, but for everything.

They came into the world grasping for their place in the hierarchy, their own territory, their own power. Their biology demanded the violence of consumption and possession.

He thought he understood that need the day the Change hit him: When his body's chemistry tipped over into the last stage of puberty so fast, so violently, that he, like all elves, had to be contained in solitude to keep others safe from the ensuing madness. It usually lasted only a week, but that week was torture. It was seven days of gnawing hunger, rages and tears and confusion, and agony as the body adjusted to the titanic shift into adulthood.

It was nothing compared to what he felt when he touched Margot.

Theodore smoothed a trembling palm up the silky skin of her thigh. He turned his head to press his lips to a soft blue vein, his fangs sinking ever-so-gently into the fragile skin. Margot let out a quiet hiss.

"Theodore, your teeth—"

He opened his eyes to look up at her, gauging her reaction through the fringe of his lashes. Her cheeks were flushed; her penny eyes glazed. Her chest rose and feel with the quick, rapid breaths of a woman on the edge. When he scraped her skin again, her scent, already heavy in the air, bloomed with fresh desire.

Without breaking eye contact, he ran his tongue along the small surface wounds. Her skin tasted like salt and cool water and bright, electric copper — the proof of just how sharp his fangs were. Bowing to age-old instinct, Theodore closed his jaws over her inner thigh and bit down gently, careful not to puncture her delicate skin.

Above him, Margot jerked. Her spine bowed as she tossed her head back with a soft, amazed exhalation.

You're the most beautiful being in this world, he told her, luxuriating in the mental connection that made biting her and speaking to her at the same time possible. *Do you have any idea what it's like to look at you? To taste you?*

Margot shuddered. He watched, transfixed, as goosebumps erupted across her skin. With his predator's vision, she was as clear to him in the half light as she would have been in the sun. It was a good thing, too, because Theodore would never get tired of watching her. Hundreds of years could pass and he would still feel that empty gnawing, that hunger to consume her and be consumed by her.

"Theodore, I..." Her voice was thick. His name on her lips was exquisite. It didn't even matter to him that she didn't call him Teddy like the rest of his family and friends did. He liked that she called him *Theodore.* It felt special, like she had somehow stamped the name with her mark before she said it.

Tilting her head back towards him, Margot flexed her thighs around his ears. "Theodore, I'm not sure how I feel about liking the way you bite me."

No? He released her thigh to pepper her sensitive skin with more sharp little nips, leaving livid red marks up and down the length of both until they quivered around him. *I think you know how you feel, darling.*

Margot reacted perfectly to every one of his instincts. She trembled when he bit her. She went soft when he knelt for her. She clutched him hard when she worried he was about to take his hands off of her. She even scratched at him when he pushed her too far.

If he didn't know any better, he'd say she had more than a little bit of elf in her.

The reminder of her swipe made his cheek burn and his cock, only briefly satisfied, stiffen. An elvish consort would have probably raked his hide a dozen times by now. Each swipe another test, another challenge. Not that he wanted an elvish woman, of course, but that little bit of controlled, instinctive violence played havoc with his screaming instincts.

The urge to pin her there with his fangs on her throat and fuck her until she couldn't tell right from left, up from down, light from dark, was an immense, pounding urge in his mind. The pull wanted intimate skin contact — constantly. It would not be satisfied with these sweet touches, the taste of her, for long. The days of keeping himself from truly touching her were costing him dearly now.

But it was worth it.

To see the look of rapture on her face, to hear the trust in her voice, to feel the hand she raised to push his hair back from his sweaty brow — all of the suffering and savage skin hunger was worth it.

I'm going to drink my fill of you, Theodore told her as he bit his way back down her thigh and towards her slick core. *I'm going to lick this delicious cunt again and again and again. Do you know why?*

Margot's fingers clenched in his hair. That little bite of pain only made him harder. "Why?"

Theodore stroked her flushed skin with the flat of his tongue, hard and slow — savoring her. *Because I love the way you taste.*

He felt her breath hitch. Circling the tip of his tongue around her clitoris, he told her, *You know, I used to dream of you. I could never get a lock on what you looked like, but I swear in my dreams I could see and feel you.*

"R-really?"

Really.

With the sharpest edge of his urgency momentarily dulled, Theodore decided he would go slower with her this time. He would savor every reaction, every taste, every sensation. He would make her come again, harder this time, and then he would take her back to their home and do it again.

Sliding his gloved hand up to cup one delicate breast, he rolled her peaked nipple between the tips of his claws. Margot gasped, her thighs clenching, and rocked her hips into his hungry mouth.

Just like that, darling, he crooned. *You're a dream come true. Look at how beautiful you are, how much you like my touch, how much you want my mouth on you.*

Margot flushed from the roots of her hair to her chest. "I shouldn't," she gasped. "You should scare me. Why don't your claws and your fangs scare me?"

Because I'm yours. Your body knows I'm yours. It knows I'd never, ever hurt you.

He couldn't even if he wanted to. His claws retracted automatically, and the suffocating press of instinct made it impossible for him to press his fangs into her flesh, to strike or squeeze with too much force.

He could nip. He could spank. He could hold her still, but *harm* her? Never. It made him ill just to consider it.

No, everything in him was attuned to her pleasure, to her comfort and safety. It was part and parcel with that driving elvish need to know one's place in the hierarchy — in their own personal hierarchy, he was the provider, the worshiper, the protector. In turn, Margot was his anchor and his comfort, his home and his heart.

It wasn't the same for all elves, obviously. The consort relationship took on many shades, many nuances, and depended largely on the personalities involved. No two relationships were alike, just as no two families were alike.

Theodore didn't think he was above or below Margot in their hierarchy. His beast didn't either. Rather, she was his heart, his partner. It was his privilege to look after her just as it was his privilege to lead his people. His purpose in life was to do his best by them both.

Theodore took his time kissing her skin. He got to know what made her sigh and what made her buck her hips against his mouth — and promptly pulled back every time he found something new and exciting, savoring each discovery. He traced the fingers of his bare hand over the crease where her backside met her thigh until he found her center.

Breathing out hot puffs of air against her sensitive skin, he watched her face as he slowly sank two fingers into the hot, rippling core that called to him. Her silky muscles stretched around his fingers, accommodating their size with a pulsing wave that made his cock jerk, precome leaking down the shaft to meet the cool damp air.

Margot's face wasn't pinched with pleasure. Rather, she wore a surprised sort of look that made him groan. She looked at him like she couldn't believe he was real, like he was something precious and strange.

She wore her pleasure on her face openly, as if every bit of it was a sweet surprise she didn't think she'd earned, and it made Theodore want to do everything with her. He wanted to explore every inch of her. He wanted to have her in every position. He wanted to see that look of soft surprise every single day, in every single way he could, for the rest of his life.

Gently curling his fingers inside her, he began to slowly pump them in and out, creating a steady rhythm with his teasing licks. *In my dreams, I have you spread out on my bed.* He gave her nipple a light pinch with his claws. Margot made a choked sound and dropped her hand from his hair to take her weight better on the squeaky cot. *I have you in my big bed, your arms over your head and your legs spread wide as I run my hands down over your breasts, your stomach, your thighs...*

Theodore thrust his fingers hard, curling them sharply against her inner walls, and gave her clitoris a sucking pull with his lips and tongue. Margot rolled her hips forward, griding herself against his mouth, and muttered something incomprehensible as he gentled his pace once more — keeping her hovering just on the edge as he whispered his fantasies in her mind.

I knew your skin would be so soft, he told her, pausing to press a reverent kiss to her lower belly. *I knew you'd smell wonderful. I imagined that you'd taste like sunlight on my tongue when I kissed you and licked your cunt until you screamed.*

He lashed his tongue against her clitoris, pumping his fingers hard. *I was mostly right. But instead of sunlight, you taste like rain — that sharp ozone and cold water of a fresh storm.*

When he pulled both his hand and his mouth away from her center, Margot let out a keening cry of protest. Theodore took the time to stare up at her for a moment. Was there anything more beautiful than the sight of her naked above him, covered in his release, her arms shaking as she struggled to keep herself upright? No. Unequivocally *no.*

Pushing her legs open wide with both hands, Theodore kept her balanced on the edge of the cot as he dipped his head to drink directly from the source once more, a dark, rumbling purr vibrating the cords of his throat. He pressed his tongue deep, seeking more, *needing* more to satisfy the raging beast in him that demanded he finish the job with his fangs on her throat and his cock buried in all that blazing heat.

Finally unable to withstand it, Margot fell back onto the cot, the muscles of her stomach clenching and unclenching as her body chased an orgasm he refused to grant her.

Growling, Theodore grasped her by the hips and lifted her up to his mouth until only her upper half remained on the cot.

"Theodore!" Margot scrambled to grab onto something.

Lifting her arms, she curled them backward until she could clutch the edge of the cot by her head with a white-knuckled grip.

Tell me what you want.

Margot wheezed. Her hips flexed in his hands, but he wouldn't allow her any friction, any freedom to grind against his mouth as he slicked his tongue everywhere except where she needed him most. "I'm— I don't know— *Theodore!*"

You know what it does to me when you say my name like that, darling? Theodore tore his mouth away to lower her back onto the cot. Standing with jerky movements, all of his elvish grace beaten out of him by the sheer force of his lust, he stood over her naked and flushed form to grip his cock in one hand.

"You want to finish, darling?" he ground out through clenched teeth, squeezing his aching shaft. "You have to *tell* me what you want. You have to tell me you want my mouth on you, my fingers fucking you. I need to hear it." Margot met his eyes. Her chest heaved with her deep breaths as she watched him jerk his fist down his length, her legs spread in a wanton display that nearly drove him back to his knees.

He watched, pulse hammering, as her little pink tongue darted out to lick her swollen lips. "I want..." She paused, eyes huge in her delicate face. "I want you."

Theodore held his breath as Margot sat up on the cot. Kneeling on one knee, she closed her fingers around the muscle bracketing his hipbones and dragged him closer. Theodore didn't hesitate. The cot squeaked as she settled her weight down onto her folded legs, their significant height difference bringing her in line with his aching erection.

"I've never done this before," she hoarsely admitted, "but I want to."

Margot brushed his hand away, allowing her to look her fill. Theodore wasn't sure how much she could truly see in the darkness — humans were, of course, the species with the fewest survival adaptation — but he *felt* like she saw him. All of him.

"I've seen a lot of naked bodies, you know." Margot trailed a finger over the crown, flushed a deep, livid blue, and down, following a throbbing vein. "Never felt anything for a single one of them. But when I look at you, it's like..." She swallowed. "It's like I want to eat you up."

Fuck. Theodore gripped her hair with both hands, his stomach flexing as she dipped her head to give his cock a long, exploratory lick.

"Margot, you were supposed to—" The words died on his lips as his gorgeous, nefarious consort wrapped her fingers around him and squeezed. Theodore sucked in a sharp breath. This was supposed to be about *her,* about worshiping her the way he dreamed of, but if she wanted a little break to taste him, he wasn't about to refuse.

Careful with his one clawed hand, Theodore held her hair away from her face as Margot explored him with teasing kisses and tentative licks, her touches growing bolder with every one. "That's it, darling," he encouraged, watching with wide eyes as she slowly took him into her mouth.

There was something deeply erotic about watching her adjust to his size — large, obviously, compared to her — and seeing the differences between them. Her lips were rosy pink, human, but his skin was flushed blue, with a slight iridescent finish. The color stood out starkly against her lips, her cheeks, the curve of her jaw as she slowly sucked him into the hot well of her mouth.

Theodore hissed out an expletive when she dragged her lips up and down in a building rhythm, her confidence growing after each stroke. The press of her soft little tongue, the suction of her lips, the way she looked up at him as she reached into his half-undone slacks and cupped his sac — it was all too much.

"Fucking— darling, you're going to make me come," he grated. It took all his willpower to keep from meeting her mouth with hard, desperate thrusts. Sweat gathered under his stiff collar and along his hairline as he fought his instincts and that tightening coil of pleasure at the base of his spine.

He panted, each breath laden with the scent of her desire,

with the scent of his, and tipped his head down so he wouldn't miss a second of her expression. "Is that what you want?" Theodore's hips flexed, gently, as she answered his question with a firm squeeze. "Ah," he choked out, "you want... you want me to come on you again and then finish what I started. Greedy, greedy witch. You could have— you could have just told me that, you know."

He could feel her lust burning so hot and so bright in the bond between them. It scalded him from the inside out, this unfettered connection that let him into the very heart of her. It wasn't refined and she clearly had no idea how to use it yet, but it was brutally honest — an open door between their minds that let him feel the crush of his *and* her desire.

It was too much. It wasn't enough.

The pull made him ravenous, her touches, her taste only made it worse. He wanted to devour her. He wanted to debauch her. He wanted to see her covered in his release and he wanted to kiss her hard as he fucked her. He wanted to love every inch of her. He wanted to slide his tongue into her and never leave. He wanted and he wanted and he *wanted.*

Will it ever be enough? Theodore allowed himself to carefully rock his hips to meet her mouth and was rewarded with a soft, feminine moan. *No. It won't be.*

How could it, when their bodies were perfectly attuned to one another? How could this relentless, beating desire ever fade when every single part of her cried out for every single part of him?

If Theodore couldn't understand his ancestors decision to forgo non-elvish consorts before, he absolutely could not now that he knew the joy of knowing, of *touching,* his. How could anyone who felt this desire and this crushing love abandon their consort? How could any sane society ostensibly built around family make that choice?

He could never leave her. He could never choose anyone or anything above Margot Goode. She was his whole world. What madness drove a people to disregard this unfettered joy he felt when he locked eyes with her?

Of course he knew the answer was the simple, insidious fear of extermination, but Theodore could not imagine choosing the fear of death over the pleasure of a single moment with his consort. No sane person would.

Never, in all his life, had he felt like he understood Thaddeus II's madness. Not until then, when he knew that Margot was his at last. He might go mad too, forced by his position and his ego to subjugate his instincts and tear himself apart from the inside.

Theodore dug his hands into Margot's hair and held on tight as his orgasm built into a painful pressure. He gasped, hips bucking, and used their connection to warn her, *Darling, I'm going to—*

Margot's response was a streak of lighting in his mind. *Do it.*

She went soft around him, pliant and open, ready to take anything he had to give her. Theodore let out a hoarse laugh as his hips stuttered into her stroking hand and eager mouth. It made his cheek sting, her little clawmarks twinging every time he moved his jaw. "You're perfect," he babbled. "So fucking perfect. So beautiful. So fierce and soft and smart and *mine—*"

Her eyes fixed on his as her cheeks hollowed out with a long, hard pull.

Theodore came with a harsh exhalation, his lungs seizing as she wrung everything out of him. His second orgasm was somehow more powerful than the first, as if his body was only gearing up before. Now that it knew the feeling of her and had her luscious scent in its pores, there was no going back.

Coming down from the blinding pleasure, Theodore focused on Margot as she slowly pulled her mouth off of him. His throat went painfully dry when he watched her swallow hard. A pearly drop of his release escaped her pink lips to run down her chin.

Margot didn't shy away like he expected her to. Rather, she leaned forward to ruck his shirt up around his middle and laid a series of open-mouthed kisses along his abdomen, as if to say thank you.

Keening a low, yearning note, Theodore smoothed her hair back behind her ears. His voice thick, he said, "I'm going to make you come so fucking hard, darling, you'll forget your name."

"Impossible," she whispered against his skin. Her wicked little tongue drew a line over his hip. "I'm a Goode through and through. My name is all that I am."

He used his grip on her hair to pull her head back, forcing her to meet his gaze when he bit out, "That is *not* all you are. You are my everything. You are my world. Do you understand that?"

"No."

She was pliant under his hands, her throat bare and outstretched in the primal supplication his roaring instincts demanded. It was the sexiest thing she could have done, and Margot didn't even know it.

Her expression was open, guileless. In doing this, Margot had been stripped to her most vulnerable self. He saw it in the bruises in her eyes, the tender hope that glowed in them despite the sorrow there. Disbelief ran through their bond like a jagged spike, but the tenor of it didn't feel like she doubted *him,* rather that she just couldn't believe anyone would look at her and see their whole world.

Releasing her hair to drop to his knees once more, Theodore ran his hands down her sides to curl them around her naked waist. He tugged her to the edge of the cot. "Darling," he breathed, pressing one tender kiss to her swollen lips after another, "you are... you are my pride. You are my comfort. You are every sexual fantasy compressed into all five feet and three inches of you. You are my joy and my home and heart. You are more than I could have ever dreamed of — and I've had *twenty-five years* to dream."

Carefully laying her back into her pitiful little cot, he lavished her with kisses. Theodore rained them down on her face, her arms, her fingertips, her breasts and belly and thighs and ankles and tiny, defenseless toes. "My fierce little healer," he breathed, returning to pay special attention to her vulnerable throat, "who can bring the dead back to life with her soft little hands and make her sovereign beg for her soft little mouth. You have no idea how powerful you are."

Giving into instinct for just a moment, he dragged his fangs down her throat, marking her with four livid streaks of red before sliding down her body and between her legs one last time.

Margot sighed, content, as he stroked her with the backs of his claws, gentling her until she was little more than loose limbs and tumbled hair. When he glanced up at her, he found her head turned toward him but her eyes closed, her copper lashes two crescents against the swells of her flushed cheekbones.

So beautiful you make me ache, he told her, pressing his tongue flat against her clitoris in a firm, reverent stroke.

Her voice was almost drowsy with pleasure when she replied, "When I saw you for the first time, I thought you were too handsome to be real. I wanted to... I wanted to kiss you in the car. Even though I shouldn't have, I wanted to."

Theodore rewarded her confession with the fullness of his eager fingers, stroking and thrusting deep, seeking out every noise and shudder that told him he was on the right track.

You would have run if I kissed you then.

"Yes." The one word was a breath moan. Her hips rolled in a lazy rhythm with his fingers and his mouth. "But I *wanted* to."

You want me.

"*Yes,* Theodore."

He sucked hard as he pumped his fingers, his eyes on the way her eyebrows bunched, how her spine bowed with each stroke. *Then come for me, darling. You have me. You'll always have me.*

Margot's hands dug into his hair, her favorite hand-hold, apparently, as her thighs contracted around his ears. He felt her orgasm as it raced through her. Her walls clenched hard around his fingers, but he didn't stop moving, didn't stop kissing her, until she slumped, boneless, into the cot.

Out of breath and exhausted himself, Theodore extracted himself from between her legs to drape himself over her. He didn't exactly fit on the dinky little cot, but he didn't have the wherewithal to care. True contentment meant cocooning her in his arms, shielding her from the outside with his greater weight and size. When he had her safely beneath him, surrounded by him, he could finally relax.

Theodore buried his nose in her hair and let out a long sigh. It rattled his vocal cords on the way out — creating a deep, sonorous purr.

"I like that sound you make," she whispered. Margot curled her fingers into his rumpled shirt, the tip of her cold little nose rubbing against the corner of his stubbled jaw. "It's really relaxing."

"S'posed to be." He kept his weight off of her with his elbows, but that didn't stop him from slipping a forearm under her shoulders to draw her even closer. "We purr to let other elves know we're not a threat. Elvish parents purr for their kids. Consorts purr for each other. It's a sign of affection."

He felt the slight stiffening of her body under his. "Does it bother you that I've never purred?"

"Bother me?" Theodore nuzzled the crown of her head. "No, darling. Why would it? I never expected you to. You're not an elf."

Margot went rigid. "Would you prefer it if I was?"

What is this now? Theodore raised himself up just enough to peer down at her. "No," he firmly answered. "No, I would not prefer it. I want you exactly as you are."

She looked up at him warily, some of the golden glow of pleasure lost to her doubt. "You sure?"

"Yes, I'm sure." He pressed a hard kiss to her temple. "I wouldn't be the man I am today without you being *exactly* as you are, Margot Goode. Don't change a damn thing."

Margot stroked his chest through his shirt, a plaintive, apologetic sort of caress. "I hope you remember that later," she whispered, "when things get tough. I don't want you to feel like I've tricked you, or..."

"Never." Theodore squeezed her close. He luxuriated in her scent, in her warmth, in her trust, and knew that nothing would ever change his mind about her. No matter what happened, they were one.

Chapter Sixteen

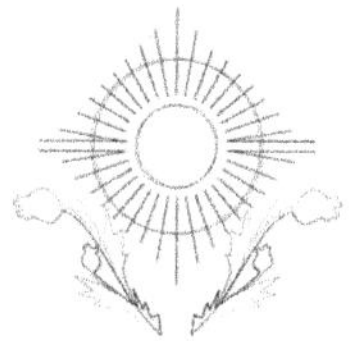

Margot shifted under him, her limbs curling tightly inward, and only then did he realize that she must be freezing. He lifted his head to scan the room.

That really *was* a wall of rusty lockers he saw. Besides a workbench and a couple unused medical beds, there was little else. The place she chose to hide out in — and didn't *that* thought make his teeth squeak — was stark, cold, and just a step above derelict.

It was not, in any way, a place fit for his consort to even *glance* at.

"Let's go," he announced, reluctantly drawing up to straighten his clothing. "We need to get back to the Tower so I can get things in order, and *you* need to eat, take a shower, and then rest."

Despite the fact that she had no visible bruising and she looked far healthier — and well-loved — than she had just days before, Theodore could not forget the fact that Margot *jumped out of his car.* He didn't think he would ever forget the terror that gripped him when he woke up as the car pulled into the Tower's underground garage and discovered that she was gone.

Worse was realizing what exactly she must have done to get out of the vehicle without either of their escorts noticing.

He shuddered just thinking about her wandering the streets, bloody and exhausted, with no money, since she was a healer and couldn't take the usual ID chip, and no way to contact anyone for help. Theodore wanted to turn the car right back around and find her, but logic — and a hard shove from Kaz — convinced him that the best way to protect her was to make sure she was safe from all other angles first.

A few hours on the streets wouldn't kill her, but ignoring the rabidly curious inquiries from the press after their joint statement as well as Sophie's public declaration of support, and the fact that he knew for certain the Solbournes had a traitor in their midst *would.*

So he briefly met with his PR team to send out a flurry of statements to the press. He took some elf-approved painkillers for the massive, full-body ache that bonding with his witch left him with. And then he set Kaz and Valen to the task of rooting out the rat in their midst, starting with the one woman who had every reason to want to hurt him.

Marian, his widowed aunt and mother to his twin cousins Camille and Cameron, was a vicious woman. Blaming his half of the family for her consort's death had led to no less than three coup attempts and one direct threat on his life over the years. The only thing that spared her from swift, brutal punishment was the fact that they were family.

No matter what Marian thought, the Solbournes didn't turn their backs on blood.

But if ever there was an elvish woman who wished him a quick, agonizing death, it was Marian Solbourne. Killing his consort before he could have her would be just the sort of thing she'd relish.

But that wasn't his problem right now. He trusted Kaz and Valen to take care of things in the short time he'd be away. Now, all that mattered was Margot.

When the said center of his universe, bloody beating heart of him, did not immediately rise to get dressed, he frowned down at her. "Come on, darling. It's too cold for you here. Let's get back home so—"

Margot braced her palms on the mattress and levered herself upright. Immediately, he recognized the mulish set of her jaw. "No."

"No?" He forced himself to keep his eyes on her stubborn expression and jutting chin, *not* the mess he made of her beautiful thighs and soft, perfectly formed stomach. *Not her breasts, either, Teddy. And not all those lovebites.* "What do you mean *no?*"

Margot shook her head. Her hair, a tumble of red silk, shone even in the blue-black shadows of the dark room. "I mean no, I don't want to go back to the Tower."

She sat up completely to reach for her discarded sleep shirt, lost at some point in their delicious tumble. Theodore's eyes followed her movements greedily. Was there a lovelier sight than watching the graceful roll of her shoulders? The soft movements of her small, rosy-tipped breasts? The fluttering of her stomach muscles as she primly cleaned herself with the wadded up shirt?

Yes, he thought, scowling, *all of this would be better if she were in my bed back in the Tower.*

"Darling, we can't stay here." He gestured to the room. "This place is barely habitable. You'll freeze to death, and even if you don't, I won't fit on that bed." Theodore added a playful note to his voice when he complained, "I'd really rather sleep with you again. It wasn't so bad last night, was it?"

Margot snagged her crumpled underwear from the floor and shimmied into them before she stood up. She wrapped her arms around herself, saying, "I figured we wouldn't stay here. But I... Listen, the Tower is safe for you, but until we—" she swallowed hard "—get married, *I'm* not safe there. That's why I ran in the first place. Not because I was panicking about you or anything... Okay, I *was* doing that, but it was mostly the Tower I was worried about."

"Not safe? The Tower is the most defensible place on the West Coast." Frowning at the goosebumps breaking out over every inch of her skin, he almost shrugged out of his suit jacket before he spotted something better. "That's where my jacket went."

Pulling it off of the bed, where she must have been using it as a blanket, he held it out for her until she slid her arms through. With practiced efficiency, he buttoned the high collared, double-breasted jacket quickly. It came to his mid-calf, but on her it touched the floor. The sleeves were already rolled up to fit her and he noticed several tears and dirty patches that were *certainly* not there when he saw it last.

Lips thinning, he asked, "Were you wearing this when you jumped out of the car?"

She looked at him through her lashes. "...Yes."

He closed his eyes and took a deep breath. *She made it. She's fine. No need to point out how easily the coat could have gotten caught in the door and dragged her onto the road. No need to tell her she could have gotten hit by any number of vehicles if she miscalculated. She's fine. She's fine.*

"Where are your shoes?" Theodore smoothed his hands over her shoulders, petting her and soothing himself.

"I'm not going back to the Tower," she insisted. Her scowl was a match for his.

"It's perfectly safe *and* it has my personal Temple *and* it has my bed. Why in the gods' names would we not go back to the Tower tonight?" He shook his head. "No, darling. The Tower is the safest place for us." Even with the traitor in their nest, Theodore was certain the Tower was safe for her.

No one but a select few could get past the hundreds of layers of sigilwork in the walls of his home — which was part of the reason it was up to Delilah to execute their father when the time came. No one else, not even Valen, could get through the security in time to save Theodore and Sam before it was too late.

He turned to hunt for her shoes, certain that things were settled, but a small hand on his arm prompted him to face her once more.

Margot's expression was beseeching, uncertain in ways that

didn't match her normal prim confidence. Fingers clenching on his sleeve, she said, "I know you don't understand, but... We have a lot to talk about, and I'll just— I'll just feel safer if we're married first, before I go back there. Please, Theodore." She paused, her gaze darting around his face like she feared his reaction. As if he could truly say *no* to her. "Please, just do this for me."

He opened his mouth to argue, but the soft look in her eyes halted anything he might have said. Searching her face for some hint as to the origin of her obvious fear, he let out a deep sigh. "Fine. We'll stay the night in my apartment."

Her eyebrows pinched together. "You have an apartment?"

They shared a look of mutual confusion. "Of course. For emergencies, or if I get caught up in meetings in the city and don't feel like going home."

Margot squinted at him, judgment in every line of her dear face. "You live, like... twenty minutes away."

Stooping to retrieve his discarded glove, he huffed, "Do you want to stay there or not?"

Her answer was lightning fast. "Yes."

Straightening, he tugged on the glove, which would *never* look the same to him now, and looked down his nose at her. "It's settled, then. We'll stay at the apartment tonight and tomorrow we'll get married. *Then* we'll go home."

Margot wheezed. "You want to get married *tomorrow?*"

He smiled. "If you're determined to keep us from my bed, darling witch, then I'm equally determined to see us married." Sliding his clawed fingers into her hair, he gave it a gentle tug, urging her to tilt her head up to him. He pressed a kiss to her forehead and breathed her in.

What a privilege it was to watch her lashes flutter against the tops of her cheeks. To feel the silk of her skin against his lips. To gaze down at her and know that she was his and he was hers and the entire godsdamned universe could look upon them in envy.

Murmuring against her skin, he said, "Apartment tonight, marriage tomorrow. Deal?"

Margot leaned into him with a low sigh. "Deal."

Margot wasn't sure what she expected from Theodore's apartment, but what she got was... exactly that.

She tried in vain not to feel awkward standing in the foyer of another palatial penthouse, this one built above the throbbing heart of the Financial District. It didn't have the Art Deco feel of the Tower, but something older, more ostentatious with its crown moldings and intricate plaster work and wallpaper stamped with flecks of gold leaf.

The Goodes were no paupers. They were ridiculously wealthy and extremely politically powerful. Her Coven created some of the most talented and sought after sigilworkers, cursebreakers, and warders in the world. The less magically talented among them went into fields of law, medicine, politics — positions that would afford them more security if ever the world decided to turn on witches again.

Much of that money went back into the Coven, which invested it on behalf of each family member. They were, to a one, *extremely* well off.

But they weren't showy. Sophie went out of her way to show that the greatest investment was in the family, not in the trappings of wealth. Their homes were comfortable, their needs taken care of, but the majority of their funds lay in wait for a time when they may need them or out into programs related to the Collective.

Elves, on the other hand, loved a display.

Margot listened with half an ear as Theodore spoke into the Met by the door. He was ordering them a meal and new clothes for her, but she felt awkward listening to him take care of her, so she paced away.

Not the only thing to feel awkward about, is it?

Margot's toes curled in her shoes. A flush heated up the skin of her neck and cheeks as she felt the satin lining of Theodore's coat brush against her bare breasts.

Nudity was just nudity, of course, but being around his *guards* while wearing only their sovereign's coat for cover? Not an experience she was eager to repeat. The rest of it could stay, though.

A heady warmth tingled in her abdomen at the thought of what *the rest of it* entailed, but she didn't want to get caught up in that distracting sexual chemistry again, so Margot turned her focus back onto the palatial suite they were spending the night.

Leaving the foyer behind to explore the sitting room, Margot turned in a slow circle to take in the lavish furniture — all in rich, jewel-toned velvets and polished wood — and the large, almost gothic windows on the far side. Not too far below them, cars whizzed past on pre-planned routes, their m-enhanced engines syncing up with a perfectly timed grid to get them where they needed to go. Buildings of every shape and design, the only *true* San Francisco style, pressed in close; their windows winked back at her in the semi-darkness of an illuminated city.

Across the street, Margot spied the glittering opulence of the Palace Hotel. It's iconic triple arch entrance glowed with golden light, welcoming the likes of celebrities and m-entrepreneurs and even Taevas Aždaja, Isand of the Draakonriik, who was rumored to have his own private suite on reserve. The golden light, the brilliantly lit letters declaring *The Palace* on the roof, and the reflection off of the crystal arches were a tantalizing hint at a world that had always been barred to her.

Until now.

Margot pulled at the lapel of her pilfered coat. *Process that later.* Padding across a thick rug, she sidestepped a low coffee table to take in one of the framed oil paintings hung on the wall.

The paint was thickly laid in the brightest areas and gossamer thin in the darkest; the subject a crystalline lake with a rough, pebbled beach, ringed by a forest that appeared to lean toward the water as if drawn.

A ping of alarm went off in the back of Margot's mind as she squinted at the painting.

With the stroke of a brush, an old dock was rendered in the far corner — almost an afterthought. A familiar red tackle box was just a dot of color.

Margot stepped closer, her heart a hammering beat in her throat.

Was that a figure sitting alone, legs dangling over the edge? It was so small that the artist had only given the form life with a stroke, a smudge, a hint of light on something orange, but—

"Do you like the painting?" Big hands, smooth leather, the faintest bite of cold claws. Her *fiancé.* Theodore slid his hands into the wide neck of her borrowed coat to rub the tense muscles of her nape.

Her throat was tight when she said, "These look like the ones in the Tower. Same artist?"

It was like he couldn't get close enough to her. If nothing else proved that Theodore was sincere in his desire to be her bondmate, her *husband,* the way he constantly tugged her closer, petted her, kissed her hair and her face and her hands, did.

Not that she could really *process* that truth yet, but...

Curling an arm around her shoulders to draw her back against his chest, he rumbled a delightfully soothing purr. "Yes. My sister painted them all."

Delilah Solbourne. A sense of foreboding swept a chill down her spine. *The Executioner.*

Theodore's sister was the former sovereign, legendary for her swift action, lack of explanations, and the cold-hearted execution of her own father. Margot had read about her in articles and heard her name mentioned on the news countless times. Her image, glossy and gorgeous, was as familiar to her as the ancient High Gloriae's was.

Personally, Margot had always found something in Delilah's dark-eyed gaze a little... wrong. Like she wasn't entirely *there.*

Now that feeling of unease came rushing back with a vengeance.

Without thinking, Margot reached up to grasp Theodore's wrist. The contact soothed the restless pacing and clawing of her other half, while the witch-forged bond between them sang a high note of pleasure.

Fighting to keep her voice even, she asked, "Do you know where this place is?"

"Hm, no." She could feel him shrug. "I don't normally ask, though. She just sends them to me with a note about where to hang them. It's an easy enough way to make her happy, so I don't think about it too hard."

"I know where it is," she croaked. "It's Goode Lake." Margot pointed at the dock, to the tiny, indistinct figure perched on the wood. The longer she looked, the more she saw. A familiar pink flip-flop, a dot of color to represent the edge of a much-loved beach towel. "Theodore, is that *me?*"

He took his time answering. Tentatively, he answered, "That is... very possible."

"Have you been watching me?" Her stomach tightened into a hard, anxious little ball. "Do you have *surveillance* on the Goodeland?"

Didn't Theodore say that he didn't know who she was until she "came into range"? But *this* — Margot couldn't recall the last time she sat on the dock. She had no time to relax like she once did, not with the apprenticeship and her studies and getting her papers published anonymously so no one could track them back to her, something that took way more work than one would think.

Her mind raced, trying to place when she would have owned that pair of bright pink flip-flops with a time when she would have had a moment to spare. A nervous sweat broke across her chest. *I would have been nineteen.*

"Margot, no." Theodore turned her around with firm hands. His expression was thunderous, his eyebrows sharply angled over dark, troubled eyes. "Don't get upset, darling. It's not what you think."

She made a high noise in the back of her throat just as she spotted another painting across the room. Margot didn't need to get close to it to recognize the familiar lines of a white-washed house almost overgrown with climbing roses. "That's my *grandma's house,"* she gasped, horrified. "That's— you can see my curtains!"

Yellow. Her curtains were yellow. Delilah rendered them with a jaunty splash of color peeking out from behind a fringe of wild roses about to bloom. Was Margot standing just inside that window, unsuspecting? Just how long did the Solbournes have the Goodeland under surveillance? Their wards were the best in the world. *How* could they have managed such a feat?

Why?

Warm, leather-covered hands on her cheeks pulled her attention away from the painting of her grandmother's house. Theodore fixed her with a hard look. A deep rumbling in his chest made the other half of her settle into a watchful crouch. "Hush now, darling. Let me answer your questions before you start jumping to the worst possible scenario."

He ran the pads of his thumbs over her cheeks in a soothing rhythm as he explained, "This is a secret I can only share with you. This is a *family* secret. I need to know that you won't share it with anyone before I tell you."

Margot gave him the look the words deserved. "If it's a secret that jeopardizes the safety of my Coven, I absolutely *will not* keep it to myself, Theodore."

His lips curled in a slight smile. "I'm not asking you to. This isn't what you think. But this isn't just my secret. I need you to understand that if I tell you this, it's a lot of trust I'm giving you. It's about my *family*. Do you understand?"

A little bit of her horror, her panic, began to lose its grip on her heart. Margot inwardly touched the bond. She tested the strength of it, the sincerity thrumming through it, and understood that this was a step toward something she could have only dreamed of before.

Total trust.

With the sovereign? Yes. Because he was her bondmate, and because she wanted to trust the man who looked at her like she shaped the world with her hands.

Sucking in a deep breath, she nodded haltingly. "Okay. I won't share it. Just... please explain. You have to know how terrifying it is to walk in here and see this."

Theodore pursed his lips. A look of consternation made him seem very young when it crossed his expressive face. "Yeah, I can imagine. I wouldn't have them up if I knew, but Delilah doesn't —" He let out a huffing sigh. "What she chooses to tell us and why has always been a mystery. Why she lets certain things happen, why she doesn't, none of us knows. My sister doesn't explain herself to anyone. Not even her consort."

Winnie Solbourne, Margot recalled, vividly reminded of pop culture feeds and the fashion programs her cousins liked to watch. Winnie was famous. Really, *really* famous. There was a whole industry devoted to following her fashionable exploits, her latest shoe choice or which up and coming designer she chose to sponsor that season.

Yes, I know her. She's the most beautiful elf in the world.

Dropping his hands to guide her toward one of the velvet loveseats, he continued, "My sister has Foresight. That's the big secret. She can see up to twelve futures at once."

Delilah Solbourne had *Foresight?* Margot rubbed her forehead. *Of course.*

That explained the slightly unhinged, distant look in her eyes. So too did the number twelve. Most foreseers could only manage three to six time streams at once. Twelve was on the upper end of the rarest of the rare.

Margot couldn't imagine how valuable she would be, how sought after, if the news got out that she could handle so many time streams at once. The odds of a failed prediction lessened dramatically with each stream, after all. A foreseer with the ability to balance a paltry four had a roughly sixty percent success rate. Margot could only imagine what Delilah's rate was.

Sitting down heavily on the squishy cushion, Margot gestured vaguely to the paintings. "So, these are..."

"Another way for her to get predications out," he finished for her. Theodore sat down beside her on the loveseat, his greater bulk taking up most of the space, and gathered her into his lap shamelessly. Margot's other half preened, while the rest of her froze, uncertain about so much casual affection so soon. She certainly craved it, but that didn't mean she was used to it.

In the middle of arranging her legs so she was draped across his thighs, Theodore paused. In a worried voice, he said, "I'm sorry, I didn't ask. Are you okay with me touching you like this? Do you want me to stop?"

Margot considered his question for a moment, her thoughts and feelings tangled by more than her fatigue or a couple bone-melting orgasms. Her competing natures dueled it out, too. The elvish half of her wanted to strip naked and rub itself all over him until... until *something* happened, but the witch half of her was shy, touch-starved, still wigged out by the way her life had taken such a dramatic heel-turn in a matter of days.

It felt a bit like going from famine to feast with Theodore, and she wasn't yet sure if that was a good thing.

At least he doesn't seem to notice I smell weird, she thought, forcing the tight muscles bracketing her spine to unlock so she could relax into his embrace. *Amazing that the one man I actually need to tell my secret to is the only person on the planet who can't seem to tell something is off about me.*

Which made it somehow harder to get the words out, didn't it? He didn't notice, and if he did, Theodore didn't seem to *care.* That was nice. Really nice. Margot was loath to ruin any part of this fever dream with the introduction of cold reality.

So she didn't tell him. Instead, she tentatively tucked herself under his chin as she toed off her shoes. That done, Margot curled her legs up and braced her bare feet on his thickly muscled thigh. "No," she whispered, "this is nice. I'm just not used to it. No one touches me outside of healing. All this contact is..." She let out a shuddering breath. "Nice."

His collar pin dug into the side of her head, and his high collar was stiff against her cheek, but the sound of his hard swallow? The thunder of his pulse? Margot could have sat there for days, listening to him breathe, basking in his glow.

"Well, I need contact with my consort and I *want* to touch my witch, so you'll never go without again." Theodore rubbed the underside of his chin across the top of her head. His arms curled around her, tucking her close. "Anyway, to answer your questions, *no,* we aren't watching the Goodes and *no,* we don't use Delilah's ability for nefarious purposes. Mostly."

He scoffed, muttering, "For Glory's sake, I didn't even know these paintings were about you. You know how I would have obsessed over them if I did? I would have had them moved to some place I could look at them every day, not *here.*"

Warmth, golden and sweet, spread through her chest to infuse every cell in her body. Theodore's affection, his honest, unvarnished yearning, came through their bond like a burst of sunlight.

Compelled to put her hand against his heart, she felt it's steady beat under her palm as she asked, "Does this mean she knew who I was this whole time?"

"I learned a long time ago that it's useless to try and get information out of my sister if she doesn't want to give it."

Old bitterness colored his voice, telling her a story without words. How many times did he ask his sister about his consort? How many times did he feel desperate enough to beg, to yell? In his place, could she forgive a sister for withholding information like that?

It struck her then that Margot, too, had reason to be bitter.

If this was true, if this was all real, then Delilah had deprived *both* of them of something life-changing. It was hard not to wonder what her life would have been like if Theodore had showed up on her grandmother's porch when she was just a bit younger, ready to tell her she *did* have a place in the world, if only she could be brave enough to accept it.

No more fear. No more suffocation. No more shame. No more burn out.

Sensing her sudden tension, Theodore distracted her by unbuttoning several of the topmost buttons of her pilfered coat. Warm, dry air filtered through the gap to kiss the naked skin of her collarbones and chest.

"I don't want to talk about my sister anymore," he muttered. Theodore slid his hand into the gap to stroke his gloved fingertips over her skin. "I've got my consort in my lap, a marriage tomorrow, and a speech to make in front of the entire Protectorate the next day. I've got to win over my in-laws so they don't kidnap my wife-to-be from under my nose, and I've got to convince my myopic brethren to abandon a practice that's killing us. My sister has been a thorn in my side for my entire life. She's not going anywhere."

Margot shuddered at the feeling of his claws dragging over her skin. "Th-that's a lot on your plate."

He inclined his head, sending a lock of inky hair tumbling over his forehead. "It is. I planned to introduce myself to you *after* the Summit so this kind of thing wouldn't happen, but..." Theodore shrugged again. His big shoulders moved under his elvish suit and rumpled white shirt in ways that tantalized her. "I have you now. Nothing else matters."

Warmth was a slow drip in her veins, spreading outward from his touch with bursts of feel-good hormones she knew, clinically, were natural, but felt like a new, delicious drug. When he stopped to pull off his gloves and set them on the arm of the loveseat, she watched from under half-lidded eyes.

Theodore had lovely hands. Long-fingered and sturdy, the knuckles toughened, his skin a pale blue. The claws she was so worried about? Nowhere in sight. His fingers looked human enough, the diamond-hard tips pulled back to be flush against his skin.

When he ran those callused knuckles over her sternum, she sighed and closed her eyes.

"You should eat something before you go to sleep." His voice was a purr against her cheek.

I should do a lot of things before I go to sleep, she thought. *Like tell him he's marrying a half-breed.*

A pang of guilt, barbed with anxiety, shook off some of her drowsy haze.

Bile churned in her mostly-empty stomach. Really, she *should* have told him before she bonded to him, but that was out of her control. The marriage, though, wasn't. She had plenty of time to tell him, to make sure he was okay with it, but when she thought of revealing it to him, Margot's chest tightened painfully, that sick feeling tracing a fiery path up her throat.

What if he's disgusted? What if he doesn't want you anymore?

Was it silly to worry so much when she'd only just accepted this might be real? Probably. But Margot was sensible enough to not beat herself up about it. After all, wouldn't any reasonable person cling to such an impossible dream if it was presented to them? After a lifetime of hiding in plain sight, she was loath to give up the sweetness of his touch, the heady scent of him in her nose, the affectionate purr rumbling in her ear.

But she had to tell him. He wanted to marry her tomorrow. He wanted to tell the whole world about their... relationship, and it wouldn't be right to start things out with such a massive secret between them.

Even if it ruined things, Margot had to tell the truth.

She opened her mouth to say it, but when Theodore rose in one smooth motion, taking her with him like she weighed nothing, all that came out was a squeak.

His laugh was husky. "Don't worry, I won't drop you."

Margot wrapped her arms around his neck anyway, relieved and disappointed to be interrupted. "Where are you taking me?"

"To the shower," he answered, like that was normal, as he strode across the sitting room to head down a narrow, high-ceilinged hallway lined with more suspiciously Pacific North-western landscapes. "We both need one, and I don't want you going to sleep before I get some food in you."

"I had a protein bar."

"That's not food."

No, she supposed, to him it wouldn't be. Elves were almost entirely carnivorous, with stomachs that could handle raw meat better than any human could. She wondered if watching her eat greens and carbs was as strange to him as watching him eat raw steak was for her.

But that stray thought couldn't completely distract her from the fact that Theodore very much appeared to be suggesting that they shower *together*, nor that he had swept them into a massive bedroom dominated by a huge, elf-sized bed.

Margot's heart lurched at the sight of it. Four-poster, with luxurious velvet curtains, and planted in the center of the room — it was utterly unmissable.

Am I going to sleep there? With him?

Margot hadn't slept next to anyone since she was a kid. She didn't really count their night on the couch, since Margot spent most of it pretending to sleep but actually agonizing about how nice it was, and how stupid she was for doing it. But it made sense that they would sleep together now, considering what transpired in the clinic and what they planned for tomorrow, but she couldn't tell whether she dreaded the idea or worried it wouldn't happen.

What if he didn't *want* to sleep next to her? The sharp bite of hurt was as unexpected as it was painful.

Theodore was stepping over the threshold into a glittering, marble-floored bathroom when he froze. His eyes swung down to pin her in place. "What's wrong?"

Margot raised her head to look at him, taken aback. "I— oh, you felt that?"

Just how sensitive *was* the bond, anyway? Was that normal, or did it have something to do with Theodore and his abilities? It frustrated her that she didn't know, when knowing things was about all she was good for.

"Yes," he answered, staring down his nose at her with an uncompromising look. "Now you tell me what made you hurt that way."

Embarrassment sent a rush of blood to her cheeks. Looking away, she muttered, "I just... I had the thought that I wasn't sure we'd share a bed, is all."

Grim, take me now.

She wanted to cringe. Gods, would he think she was clingy? Too attached, too soon? They had only just met, after all, and she had been nothing but trouble for him from minute one. What would he think of her if she started pining after things he had no intention of giving her, when he already gave her so much?

Warm, firm lips sealed over hers in a bruising kiss, startling her out of her spiral.

"So long as we are in the same territory, Margot Goode, we are sleeping in the same bed, skin to skin," he breathed against her mouth. His fangs scraped gently at her lower lip in a soft reprimand. "Do you understand?"

Her answer was automatic, strangely breathless, and *pleased.* "Yes."

Theodore hummed and kissed her twice more before he continued on into the bathroom. Setting her down onto the cool marble floor, he turned to a massive, glass-enclosed shower and pulled open the door.

Margot eyed it critically, trying to distract herself from the knot of anticipation winding tighter in her belly. It was big enough to fit at least four people, with three walls of black and white, veined marble leading to a floor of what appeared to be cedar planks. A bench sat at one end, and tiny silver vents winked in regular intervals around the walls.

It wasn't until Theodore fiddled with the sleek silver panel by the door that she realized they were for steam.

With a low chime, a cascade of warm water fell from the ceiling to join a slow release of steam from the walls. The smell of cedar — *Theodore's* smell, she realized — filled the room alongside the bright, clean scent of water.

The rustle of clothing drew her attention away from the jaw-dropping shower.

Margot turned her head without thinking, but by the time she realized what was happening, it was too late.

Theodore Solbourne stood by the door, his suit jacket shrugged off and tossed aside, his chin tilted high into the air as he flicked the latch of the tie pin at his throat. Setting that on the nearby counter without looking, it took only a few more deft, cat-like movements for him to remove his stiff collar.

Holy Glory.

Was it *normal* for men to have throats so sinfully, beautifully made? Margot felt a now-familiar heat pool in her belly as she watched him unbutton his wrinkled shirt with those pretty hands. Her mouth went painfully dry.

Goddess, his skin... Theodore had strikingly beautiful blue skin.

When he pulled the sides of his shirt apart and slid it down his corded arms, Margot's heart thumped wildly in her chest. The urge to step up to him, drop to her knees and run her tongue over every inch of his chest and stomach was so visceral, she took half a step before she caught herself.

Theodore's eyes darted up to meet hers just as he reached for the silver buckle of his belt, his gaze hot and hungry, but Margot was already turning away, her breath short.

"Shy now, darling? After what we did?"

She squeezed her eyes shut. "No."

"No?" The clink of metal had the distinct ring of cheekiness in it. The slithering sound of a belt sliding clear of loops came next, followed by the slow drag of a zipper. "Then why won't my consort look at me?"

Because I want to bite you, she thought, squeezing her thighs together.

His internal voice rang in her mind. *Then do it.*

Chapter Seventeen

Margot turned redder than her hair. *That was private!*

Not when you think at *me,* he answered, even his internal voice smug. There was a whisper of fabric, the sound of fine leather shoes being toed off, and then bare feet on cold marble, moving closer.

I didn't mean to, she groused.

Theodore's hands skimmed her shoulders and down over her arms. *You'll get the hang of the connection soon enough, but until then, certain things may slip through — especially if those thoughts are about me.*

Margot swallowed the lump of embarrassment in her throat to say aloud, "What about you? Am I going to accidentally hear your thoughts, too?" At least then they would be equal.

"No," he answered. "I have more telepathic control than you do. I'm used to keeping my thoughts to myself." His lips skimmed the curve of her ear. His breath was hot, the awareness that he was entirely naked behind her even hotter. "I don't *have* to, though. Do you want me to share all the thoughts I have about you, darling?"

Her breath stuttered as it left her. "I don't know if I could handle that."

"Mm. We'll see." Theodore's hands fell away. She felt it when he stepped back, even the rising temperature of the moist air in the bathroom feeling cold when he left her to step into the shower.

Don't just stand there staring at the wall, you wimp. Margot sucked in a deep breath. She was aware that this was another challenge, and it irked her that it worked to prick at her other half so well. That part of her wanted to hiss at him even as it threw off the jacket to strut proudly, nakedly into the enormous shower.

Too bad the rest of her felt ten kinds of awkward.

He's had his tongue between your legs, she thought, very careful to keep the words directed at herself, not him. *There's nothing to be shy about.*

But she was shy. For all that she saw naked bodies almost every day of her working life, Margot hadn't been naked in a room with another being in... decades.

Her instinct was to deny him this casual intimacy, but she didn't *want* to. Besides, she wasn't a coward. She didn't back down from challenges. He *had* already seen her most intimate parts — up close and personal. What was there to lose?

Theodore's coat slid off of her shoulders easily. The silk of the lining was a deep violet, the same color of the thistles in the Solbourne crest, and it stood out starkly against her skin as it traveled down to pool around her legs.

Anticipation hummed like a livewire in her mind, and it took her a moment to figure out that it wasn't just her. It was Theodore, too.

Margot blinked at the wall. *He's excited. He... wants to see me. Oh.*

That helped. A lot.

Sucking in a deep breath, she turned slowly toward the shower. Margot didn't make it more than a step before her spine locked.

The door was left open for her, letting out great clouds of rolling, fragrant steam. Theodore stood in the center of the stall, his pale blue body made only vaguely fuzzy by the steam, his shape almost dreamlike, as a curtain of rain fell from the ceiling to spill across his upturned face and slicked back hair.

Margot stood before the open shower door, awestruck.

He was gorgeous. There was no other word for it.

Handsome wasn't right. Beautiful implied a certain delicacy that his dense build lacked. He certainly had a pretty face, but the rest of him was rendered by an expert hand, a divine sculptor that knew their way around a muscled, agile frame. The stretch of his jewel-toned skin, the breadth of his shoulders, the tapered shape of his lean waist — Theodore Solbourne was a stunningly packaged predator.

But it wasn't the lean muscle of his stomach or his corded arms that made her knees weak. It was the way he turned his head, opened his eyes, and grinned at her with a smile so wide it brought both his dimples out.

"Are you coming in, or are you going to ogle me all night?"

Margot didn't feel like she had much of a choice in the matter. Who could resist that look?

"Maybe if you weren't posing," she muttered, stepping onto the warm cedar planks of the shower floor. She pulled the door shut behind her. Immediately, the steam thickened, now trapped in what previously felt like a very large shower, but what she now realized was a normal-sized space for him.

Because Theodore was fucking *massive.*

Why hadn't she noticed it before? Well, she supposed, she had, but it was only in terms of how threatening he might be, how close he was to her. Standing in the warm, damp space, buck naked with Theodore was a very different experience than sitting in the back of a car with him.

The steam was so thick that even standing three feet away, she struggled to make out his facial features. All she saw was the occasional flash of blue skin, jet black hair, and dark, hooded eyes.

The voice that cut through the fog and patter of water between them was a low, masculine purr. "Why are you so far away?"

Hands, *big* hands, closed over her naked hips to draw her under the water. This close, the steam parted to reveal her elf, his expression full of a certain type of hunger that had, as far as she was aware, never been directed her way before.

Warm water soaked her hair, slicking it against the column of her spine as she tilted her head back to look at him.

"You're very tall." *Good goddess, Margot, is that the best you've got?*

Theodore's smile curved wider as he drew her in by inches, his thumbs pressing against the bows of her hip bones. "Noticed that, huh? Is that a problem for you?"

His smug expression didn't convey the smallest hint of worry. "No," she answered anyway. "But I'm awfully short compared to you. I don't want you getting a crick in your neck."

Margot usually didn't dwell on the things she didn't inherit from her mother. Her height was one of those things. Becoming bitter about it wouldn't have solved a single one of her problems, but just then, Margot might have liked to be elf-tall, so she could run her nose along the swell of Theodore's cheek without having to ask him to bend down first.

"I like your size," he assured her. "I don't mind if I have to get on my knees to kiss you. I *get* to kiss you."

Margot's insides twisted, everything in her tangling for one heart-stopping instant before the tension released with a rush of pure affection. Water gathered in droplets on the fringe of her eyelashes as she let him pull her against his slick skin. His erection prodded her hip, but she barely noticed it.

Theodore had her complete attention; he held it in his hands with a single look of pure, boyish joy.

You love me, she thought, her throat too tight to say the words aloud. The realization, the recognition of just what was flowing through their bond like liquid sunlight, staggered her.

Theodore's glowing expression didn't dim. It didn't even flicker. His hands traced up the wet contours of her sides, over her ribs, and then around to her back to cradle her with infinite care as he replied, *Yes. Does that scare you?*

Did it? Maybe it should have. They barely knew each other. A day ago she was terrified he'd eat her for breakfast. But now he lived in her head, he held her life in his hands, and... he *loved* her. She could feel it running through their bond, making it stronger, tying them together in ways deeper than magic ever could.

Margot flattened her palms against his chest as another stab of guilt stole her breath. *Does it bother you that I don't love you?*

Yet. You don't love me yet.

You're very sure of yourself. But he had every right to be, didn't he? Theodore was the sovereign, he was gorgeous, and so far, he'd been right about everything. If his ego was a little inflated, Margot could hardly blame him. That didn't mean she would let him know that, though.

His snort echoed against the marble. "With the way you're looking at me? I give it a month, tops."

Margot made to argue with him, for her pride's sake, but didn't even get so far as opening her mouth.

He was right.

Days. They'd known each other for days, and already they were bonded, she had almost completely let her guard down, and she was currently standing naked in a shower with him, debating about how quickly she'd fall in love with him. A week ago, this kind of casual intimacy would have seemed impossible.

Privately putting her pride aside, Margot could admit to herself that she'd be lucky if she lasted a month.

She swallowed hard. Her gaze slid away from his adoring expression to stare sightlessly at the wings of his delectable collarbones.

I have to tell him. I can't fall in love with him and not tell him.

If he rejected her after she got in so deep she could no longer tell up from down, it would break her.

Panic burned away the soft glow of her realization. It was sharp, acrid, familiar in the most unpleasant ways. "Theodore," she rasped, shoving the words out before they could be swallowed again, "I'm not what you think I am."

~

Theodore blinked water out of his eyes. "What?" He frowned down at Margot, so small and beautiful tucked against him, and growled, "I thought we had this figured out. You are my consort. What—"

"It's not that." Her fingers, with their blunt little nails, scratched nervously at his chest. The touch sent ripples of pleasure down his spine, but not enough to distract him from her clear distress.

Theodore tightened his arms around her. Eyes narrowing, he asked slowly, "Are you finally going to tell me what has you so scared?"

Margot's head dipped in a nod. Red hair, dark with water, slid against her cheek. Her voice was faint under the patter of droplets and hiss of steam. "Yes."

"Now?"

She lifted her head to glower at him. "Yes, now."

"I'm not complaining," he rushed to explain. "I'm just... I mean, a shower seems like a weird time, is all."

Gods, but she was cute when she stuck out her little jaw like that. It made him want to bite her all over. "Do you *want* me to tell you, or do you want me to keep it to myself some more?"

Forcing himself to be serious, and to push the hyper awareness of her naked body against his to the back of his mind for the moment, he nodded. "Of course I want you to tell me."

He wanted to know everything about her — even the parts she kept hidden from the rest of the world. Maybe *especially* those parts. Her secrets were his to keep, his to guard. Soon, she would understand that, above all else, Theodore's loyalty belonged to her and her alone.

When Margot hesitated, her expression contorted with distress, he smoothed his bands up her delicate spine and reminded her, "I've already shared my secrets with you. I trust you. Are you going to trust me?"

"It's hard for me," she reluctantly answered, petting his chest in the same rhythm he used to stroke her back. He wondered if she knew she was doing it.

"Okay. Can you explain why it's hard? That might be an easier place to start. We can circle backwards." Her look of surprise was both endearing and a little insulting. Dryly, he informed her, "I have a big family and I'm the leader of an entire territory, darling. I know how to listen."

"Right." She swallowed again, her eyes lowering until all he could see was the sweep of wet lashes against the tops of her flushed cheeks. "So... It's like this: My whole life, my grandma has kept me safe. Very safe. The reason I'm not in line to become Matriarch? Because it wouldn't be safe. The reason I'm not head of my own Ward by now, making huge strides in healing? It's not safe. Nowhere is safe. Even the Goodeland."

Theodore's fingers flexed on her back, instinct driving him to bring her closer, to protect her from whatever threat she perceived but he could not. "I don't understand. You're from the most powerful Coven in the UTA. You're a *healer,* and I saw what you're capable of in that basement. What could you possibly have to fear?"

Margot might be small, but his consort was fierce. The memory of her bolt of electricity running through his gloves to snap up his arms was bitingly fresh.

Her eyes lifted to meet his. They were beautiful, unusual. Bright, almost reflective copper that shone with old hurt and the clear anticipation of oncoming pain. "You," she answered, the word bouncing off of the marble like a chorus of accusation.

Theodore's brows bunched hard. A bruise settled into his

heart. Even now, after everything, she saw *him* as a threat? "That's what your grandmother said, too, but..." He swallowed hard, afraid his voice would break. "You have to know by now that I would never hurt you, Margot. You're all I've ever wanted. You're everything to me."

Her fingers were a soft pressure on his jaw, her expression going stark with the realization that she'd caused him pain. "No, no," she hurried on, "not *you.* I meant *you* as in *elves.* I see now that you wouldn't hurt me, I swear." Margot dropped a small, apologetic kiss to his sternum before she continued. "But the rest of your kind? Theodore, you have to understand that my whole life I've been taught — it's been *drilled into me* — that if I ever find myself caught in a room with one of you, my life is over."

Some of his hurt eased, his beast satisfied knowing that she didn't distrust *him,* but his confusion lingered. "What? Why? That doesn't make any sense."

Elves, as a rule, had nothing against witches. Sure, they might have eaten them as snacks for a while, but that stopped hundreds of years ago. If anything, elves had a grudging respect for the Collective's bargaining power and political acumen.

Besides, witches and elves shared the favor of Glory. They were spiritual siblings, if not friends. There was no reason for a witch to fear elves, let alone have their entire life dictated by that fear.

He could see, now, where that hunted look in her eyes came from. Tension made every line of her lovely, fey face rigid, her lips pressing hard together into a bloodless grimace. Her pulse throbbed in her neck, and when he took in a deep breath, even the sweet water of the steam was tinged with the acrid scent of anxiety.

Margot's fingers slid from his jaw to rest against his throat. His beast purred a contented song in his soul, its devotion to her a foundational, unshakable thing.

The throat was the most vulnerable place on an elf, where diamond-hard claws could so easily end a life that should last centuries. Did she know that the baring of his throat to her was a sign of absolute trust? That his lack of reaction, his total acceptance of her blunt nails on his pounding jugular, meant he was *hers?*

"My love," he whispered raggedly, torn up by the sight of so much pain in her, by the poison churning through their bond. "I'm here. You can tell me anything. I'll protect you from the world if I have to."

It was a shock to see a liquid sheen of tears in her eyes. Worse, to see those tears overflow, dripping down her cheeks in rivulets that mixed with warm, sweet water. In an achingly soft voice, she confessed, "I'm afraid that if I tell you, you won't look at me like that anymore. I only just got you and I don't... I don't want to lose you."

It was his turn to cup her cheeks. His sorrow was like gravel under his skin, grating against every fine nerve. "You won't," he swore. "You couldn't."

Margot tilted her head into his hands. Her eyes closed. For a long, taut moment, the only sound in the shower was the fall of water from the grate over their heads and the low hiss of steam.

When she finally spoke, Margot's voice was so soft, it was nearly lost in the small space between them. "I'm a half-breed."

Theodore blinked. "I... what?"

In a stronger voice, but with her eyes still firmly shut, she said, "My mother is an elf. My dad is a witch, a brightling. My parents left me with my grandma and Noni Tula when I was born, and they raised me. They taught me everything. And... they made sure no one ever found out." Margot opened her eyes to stare bleakly at him. "That's my secret. I shouldn't exist."

"I..." Theodore struggled to connect her words with what he knew, with the woman he held in his arms, with everything he valued. Confusion snarled those connections into a tangled mess. *"Half-breed?"* he repeated dumbly.

Margot's expression took on its own look of confusion. "Yes?"

He took half a step back, extending his arms so he could scan her slight build with his critical gaze. No, she couldn't be a halfling. Not because they didn't exist, but because she looked so very, entirely *human.*

"Darling," he cautiously began, "I don't know why someone would tell you a lie like that, but you can't be a halfling."

Margot snatched her hands away from him to tuck her arms against her naked chest in a defensive move that made his hackles rise. "Yes, I *can,* because I am!"

"No, darling, you *can't* be," he argued. "For one thing, you look *nothing* like an elf. For another, no one, not even the cruelest among us, would abandon young. We just don't do that. Ever."

"Maybe you don't *know* that people do that because the people who *have* don't talk about it," she snapped, her temper returning in a flash. *"Because we're not supposed to exist!"*

"Who says?" Theodore lifted his hands in a universal gesture of confusion. "Margot, darling, of *course* halflings exist! You met one this morning! You've been surrounded by them all day. Nearly all of the Sovereign's Guard are halflings."

Margot rocked back on her heels. Swiping water out of her eyes, she asked, "What? Who did I meet?"

"My brother Kaz. *He's* a halfling." And he looked it, too, although orcs and elves appeared so similar that most people didn't give his elvish traits a second thought. Margot, on the other hand, could be nothing except human. Her size, her blunt teeth and nails, her round ears — not a single elvish trait among them.

While she processed his revelation, Theodore closed the distance between them and ran his hands up and down her arms in swift, soothing strokes. "My love, I know you *think* this is true, but it can't be. You would have some elvish traits if you were a halfling, but you don't. You don't even smell like..." He paused.

You don't even smell like one. That's what he meant to say, except—

Theodore's brows snapped together. *No.* She couldn't be elvish. Margot was so small, so defenseless. Her skin was too soft, her nails too blunt, her pupils too round, her scent too...

Wild. Familiar.

Theodore choked on air, his eyes widening comically large as he stooped to bury his nose in her hair. He breathed deep, ran his nose along her forehead and down her cheek, until he was bending nearly double to sniff hard at the juncture of her throat and jaw.

There it was: that strange, familiar note that teased him. Gone was the astringent punch of Noscent. Gone was the artificial sweetness of soap. This late in the day, and after standing under the water for a few minutes, there was nothing on her skin except her own delicious scent — layers of femininity and power and a distinctly familiar wildness he was so used to, it slid under his radar completely.

"Ho-ly Glory," he breathed, leaning back to stare at her with new eyes. "You're a godsdamned halfling."

Margot threw up her hands. "Yes, thank you, that's what I *said!*"

"But... how?" He shook his head hard, sending water in every direction. Scrubbing his wet hands over his eyes, Theodore continued, "I've met dozens of halflings. Most of the Guard is halfling! My *brother* is a halfling. All of them, except maybe Kaz, look more elf than whatever else they are."

He dropped his hands to ogle her lovely, fragile frame, her soft cream skin, her distinctly human build. "The only thing different about you is your scent. Are you *sure* you're not just the descendant of a halfling? Maybe third generation? Fourth?"

Margot scowled at him, her arms crossing over her pretty, rosy-tipped and well-loved breasts. "Yes, I'm sure. I don't have my mother's name, but I know she exists." She hesitated. An uncertain look replaced some of her annoyance when she continued, "And... I was born looking a little different. My grandma thought I'd be safer if I changed things."

The world around him stalled. "Changed things?" he echoed, a nameless, gnawing horror running cold fingers up his spine to grip him hard.

She nodded. With a sweep of her fingers, Margot brushed her lips, then moved up to push her wet hair back behind her ears. "When my adult teeth came in, grandma took me to a specialist to have my... fangs filed down. They weren't super noticeable, and we considered coming up with a hybrid ancestor to pass them off as a surprise recessive trait, but she thought it was too risky, so..." She cleared her throat and turned her head slightly.

Using her thumb, Margot pushed her round ear forward until it was pressed almost flat. With her hair pulled back and her ear out of the way, a small mark was clearly visible against her creamy skin — a tiny, light blue X with hooked ends that looked a little fuzzy with age.

A sigil, he dully realized.

"See this? My auntie did it when I was a baby. She's an extremely powerful illusionist. These tattoos keep my ears hidden so well that even when you touch them, the brain is fooled into thinking they're normal."

Theodore couldn't speak. He could only stare in horror as Margot continued, her words coming faster, as if a dam had broken now that the truth was out. She dropped her hands into the space between them and wiggled her fingers, saying in a rush, "And I *do* have claws, but I keep them filed down. Normally I do it every night after my shower, but..." She clenched her fingers into fists and dropped them to her sides. "See? The only human things about me, really, are my height, my eyes, and my coloring. I might have been taller, too, but it took a long time to realize my diet wasn't right for my metabolism, so my family healer thinks my growth was stunted."

Margot licked her lips and stared up at him, clearly waiting for him to say something, anything, but he couldn't find the words.

A fist squeezed his throat. *My consort filed her fangs down,* he thought, so full of black rage it made spots float in front of his eyes.

My consort underwent sigilwork to hide her ears. My consort has lived in fear her whole life because she was abandoned with people who made her feel like she wasn't normal, like one wrong look would sign her death warrant.

He couldn't breathe. He couldn't feel his heartbeat as it thundered in his chest. He couldn't even *see* her. All Theodore saw and felt and heard was the roar of the brutal injustice done to the woman he loved.

But he had to say something. He had to. The longer he stood there silent, speechless with rage, the more damage he would do to the fragile trust between them.

Forcing himself into the moment, to take care of her first and his howling, protective fury second, Theodore caught her just as Margot was beginning to fold into herself, her copper eyes taking on a bruised look that cut him to the quick.

No, not copper, he thought, *topaz. Glory crafted her from sun-kissed topaz.*

The goddess responsible for the creation of elves crafted them of the sunlight she ferried to the Earth each day, striking it against the precious stones gifted to her by her long-suffering but adoring consort, Burden, the god of all the Earth. It was the stones that gave elves their colors.

Theodore held sapphires in his veins. Kaz, emeralds. Their reclusive older brother Samuel, who looked most like their father, carried the fire of citrine. Valen and Andy's daughter, Theodore's surrogate mother and Delilah's consort, Winnie, was one of the rare elves lucky enough to boast a skin tone of dark, rich garnet.

Margot — *his* Margot — was cut from topaz. Pure sunlight, caught in a gem so luminous, it was often referred to as *Glory's Stone.*

Theodore squeezed his eyes shut. Shame bit at him from a hundred different angles.

Glory, you gave me all the signs, but I ignored them.

Was there ever a woman so clearly in the goddess's care? A witch, a *gloriana,* a healer, crafted from Glory's own stone; given to *his* care from the moment she was born, their link forged with her first breath.

And I failed her.

Theodore felt more than heard Margot shuffle backwards. "I'm sorry, I knew this would be bad. I should have told you before we... I'm— I can go."

His eyes snapped open just in time to see her slim back turning towards him as she reached for the door, her shoulders hunched. Hurt soured the electric current of their bond. It filled him up, scouring his veins to wash away the worst bite of his anger. *Oh, goddess, I'm making this worse.*

Theodore snagged her around her waist just as her fingertips brushed the silver handle of the door. "No," he bit out, pressing his lips against the crown of her head. "No, darling, I'm not upset with you. I'm— Glory help me, I'm *furious* on your behalf. I can't even breathe through the anger. Hearing how you've been treated makes me want to tear this world apart."

"Oh." She stood rigid against him, her arms stiff at her sides. Margot didn't believe him. No wonder, considering how he reacted.

Drawing her back under the warmth of the water, Theodore did the only thing he could think of to show her he meant it. Grabbing a bottle of unscented but very expensive shampoo from the nook cut into the marble, he poured a dollop into his hand and began to work it into her long hair.

"Now listen to me," he growled as he worked, ignoring the stiffness of her spine as he scraped his retracted claws against her scalp. "You are a *halfling*, not a *half-breed*. That's derogatory and I will not tolerate anyone, least of all you, insulting my consort. Hybrid is fine, I suppose, but pedestrian. Elves call their mixed offspring halflings."

Smoothing his shampoo-slick fingers through the long strands of her hair, Theodore worked out any knots he found as he continued, "As that implies, darling, we do have halflings. They are an accepted part of our society. We banned unions with Others, but of course that never stopped people from seeking out companionship elsewhere. But without binding a consort, the chance of producing offspring with those companions is slim, so halflings are rare."

He tilted her head back into the spray. As he painstakingly washed the suds free, Theodore gazed down at her pale face, at her closed eyes and hard mouth. He knew she was listening, but her expression was cautious, as if she expected him to bring the axe down at any moment.

Reaching for the conditioner, he continued, "We don't advertise them, obviously, but when do we advertise anything about us? I suppose it makes sense that your grandmother would just... *assume* we did something horrible to our young, since she would never be allowed to see any, but that's not true."

Not for the first time, Theodore cursed the elvish tendency to use secrecy to their advantage. If people *assumed* they were more brutal than they were, if they filled in the gaps of their knowledge with horror, then all the better for their reputations as predators, right?

Except that reputation meant people like Margot slid through the cracks. If she'd been properly cared for by her elvish family, she wouldn't have been mutilated, starved, or left to suffer on her own.

His voice taking on a razor's edge, he said, "Family is the bedrock on which elvish society rests. We take care of our young. Goddess, darling, we don't have the numbers *not* to, mixed blood or not."

Smoothing the conditioner into the tips of her hair, Theodore watched the bunched muscles of Margot's shoulder gradually begin to loosen. Her voice was small when she asked, "Then why did my mother leave me with my grandma? She said it was safer that way."

Theodore slathered his hands in body wash as he waited for the conditioner to set. With tremendous care, he began to rub the tension out of her shoulders and neck. "I don't know. Elvish life *isn't* safe, but abandoning a child is unthinkable. Wouldn't you be safer with a mother who would tear the throats out of your enemies? Who would at the very least know what to feed you when you were hungry?" He shook his head. "I don't have those answers. What I *do* have is this: You are perfect as you are, Margot Goode. You are a halfling, you are blessed by Glory, and *you are mine."*

She turned her head to look at him over her shoulder. It did something to him to see her lower lip quiver, to see his fierce halfling look at him like he could shatter her any moment. "Do you promise?"

His voice was thick with tears when he answered, "I promise."

Chapter Eighteen

"Why are so many of your guards halflings?"

Margot watched Theodore turn down the blankets of the enormous bed. She stood by one of the bedside tables, cast in the warm glow of the lamp perched on its surface, and curled her bare toes into the lush rug under her feet. They were both swaddled in thick robes — Margot's far, far too long — and their bellies were full from the late dinner that had been delivered to their door.

It was late enough to be considered early, but Margot couldn't bring herself to give into the exhaustion tugging her towards the bed. They'd been talking for hours now and she didn't want to stop.

Ever-patient, Theodore flipped the plush comforter over and adjusted the chunky pillows to lie flat as he explained, "Because it's a good place for them. Families want to keep them close and give them purpose, but I'm not going to pretend like it's an easy life when the rest of elvish society still turns its nose up at Others. Being in Patrol, moving up the ranks to join the elite forces like my guard, it gives them a sense of identity and kinship a lot of them lack. Halflings stick together, make their own families, have their own traditions. That sort of family loyalty — the hierarchy of family — is important to us. It's what keeps us grounded."

"Would I have gone into Patrol?"

Theodore cast her an assessing look. "Mm, probably not. Fierce as you are, darling, you're still fragile." He shook his head, his full mouth pursing with the anger that rippled through their bond. "Besides, you would still be a healer. You know how rare that is for witches? It's even more rare for elves. You would have been fast-tracked into a specialized program and swaddled in wool."

Margot rubbed her toes into the carpet, her chest aching. "So I wasn't ever in any danger."

If there was no danger, then it really was just that my mother didn't want me. Her greatest fear, her deepest insecurity come to vivid, terrible life. It wasn't enough to not be normal — she was also *unwanted.*

Theodore stopped fluffing a pillow to send her a conflicted look. "I... can't say that for sure. We are a brutal people, Margot. I won't pretend we're not. I defend my seat with my own claws, and there's more than a few people who would be happy to see my throat slit. But..." He looked down and took a deep breath. "But I can't imagine you would have been in a precarious situation. We're dying out, darling. Any child is too valuable to lose."

Apparently not, Margot thought, pushing away the sting of tears. With effort, she said, "I suppose it doesn't matter. I've lived without understanding them my whole life. I don't need to now. Right?"

Theodore's reply was tight with barely leashed fury. "Right."

When he indicated she should crawl into bed, Margot didn't think twice about shucking off her robe and sliding between the silky sheets. Her eyes never left him. It was not simply that Theodore was handsome. He wasn't just her future husband, or her bondmate, or the sovereign. For the first time in her life, Margot was presented with the only thing she had ever truly lacked: an endless font of *information.*

Removing his own much more reasonably sized robe, Theodore slid under the covers with all the grace of a big cat.

Margot turned on her side and scooted closer to him, her hands tucked under her cheek.

Theodore chuckled. "If I'd known it would be so easy to get your attention, I would have told you our secrets back at the Healing House."

"I'm not trying to use you," she explained, suddenly bashful. "It's just that everything I've been able to figure out about myself, I've had to either piece together on my own or pick up from the few academic sources out there. It's exciting to finally have *answers.*"

His expression gentled. "I know, darling. I'm just teasing you."

Theodore settled into his side of the bed. Pulling up the covers so they were both firmly ensconced in warmth, he snapped his fingers. The room darkened instantly.

"There," he whispered, wrapping an arm around her middle to draw her closer, "now that we're cozy, ask away."

"It's really not a problem that Kaz is half orc? I thought the elves and the orcs didn't get along."

"It's more unusual than a half witch might be," he allowed, "but Kaz is a Solbourne first. If anyone questioned that, they'd be questioning *all* of us, and that's not a very healthy thing to do."

Margot sighed wistfully. It was delightfully warm under the blankets, with all of Theodore's skin sliding along hers as he subtly drew her closer and closer, until they were plastered together from chest to knees, their legs tangled in a loose embrace.

"Can I talk to him about it?" Margot pictured the man she'd met only briefly, with his striking face and luminous skin. He looked like every orc she knew and had a crush on as a teen. Familiar. It felt natural to go to him with her questions about being a halfling in this world that was so new to her.

Margot could practically hear Theodore's frown when he answered, "Of course you can. Don't know why you'd want to, though. Just because he's pretty doesn't mean he's not a surly bastard."

"I'm more comfortable with orcs than I am with elves," she explained. "The Goodeland is right up against the Orclind, you know."

Theodore's knuckles followed the line of her spine in a slow, sensual drag. "Did you have orcish friends growing up?"

"A few, yeah."

"Just a few?"

"Well," she admitted, giving in to the urge to run her fingers over his collarbones in the semi-darkness. His skin was smooth, but tougher than hers. His bones were sturdier, too. She couldn't begrudge him for dismissing her question about becoming a soldier in Patrol when he was built with steel bones but she could crack like an egg with one wrongly placed elbow.

Theodore made a soft sound in his chest, the beginnings of a low, shiver-inducing purr. "Well?"

Margot licked her lips. "Well, I mainly had just the one friend. His name was Luke."

"Luke."

"Yes," she answered, distracted by the fascinating line of his trapezius. Every muscle, every bit of his skin, every breath he took called to her. "He lived in town, but his mother was my grandma's accountant, so he came over a lot. They didn't follow the migration, so he was always around. We used to swim in the lake all the time. Catch frogs and things." A painful twisting in her heart accompanied the sun-soaked memories.

Sometimes she missed Luke, and the sting of his mother's command to stay away from her never really faded. "We were really close. When there were other kids around, he always made sure I could keep up with the games even though I wasn't as strong or fast as them."

She grinned into the darkness, her fingers falling away to explore the fascinating slopes of his bicep. "Once, when we were twelve, he picked me two full buckets of blackberries before anyone else could get to them. I was eating blackberries for *weeks.*"

Theodore's hand spasmed on her back. "Do you like blackberries?"

"They're my favorite fruit, yes."

"Then *I'll* get you more blackberries than you could dream of," he declared, sniffing haughtily. "More than this *Luke* did."

Margot snorted. "Do you even know what blackberries are?"

"I can find out."

Warmth took wing in her belly, fluttering until she felt too giddy to contain her laughter. "You don't have any reason to be jealous," Margot assured him, pleased by it anyway, "we only kissed once. He was my first and last. Until you, of course."

Theodore let out a low, pained whine. "You *kissed* him?"

"Once. Behind the woodshed."

A warm hand clasped the nape of her neck. Theodore's fingers tangled in her hair as he angled her head upward against the pillow. "I'm the only one who should get your kisses," he groused. "Not some orcish boy named *Luke.*"

Margot's pulse jumped. Would this constant, burning desire for him ever fade? "You can have my kisses," she breathed, "if you want them."

There was a small pause. Margot thought she could *just* make out the reflective backing of Theodore's cat-slit pupils as they expanded in the dim glow from the street lights below the lavish apartment. "Can I?"

Her answer was soft but sure. "Yes. Whenever you want."

And *goddess,* wasn't it a delightful thing, knowing she could be kissed at any moment! It was enough to make her touch-starved soul drunk on giddiness. It was something a much younger, more hopeful Margot dreamed of, but something she'd left the day she entered the dark little room. To have that precious dream made real? It was a gift beyond price.

Margot felt him hovering close, his breath puffing against her cheek as he traced a line down the bridge of her nose with his lips. "Now?"

"Now's good."

The kiss was gentle, hardly a whisper against the corner of her mouth, a tantalizing tease that made her follow his retreat. "I think," he rasped, pulling her over until she was nearly draped over his chest, "I would like *you* to kiss *me* this time, darling."

Margot felt her neck heat up with embarrassment. It was harder to be bold when the reins were in her hands. "I'm not sure I'd be as good at it as you are."

"You've had more practice than me, apparently," he tartly replied.

She huffed. "It was *one* kiss!"

"It was your *first* kiss."

"So?" Margot shook her head. "It's not like *you* didn't kiss anyone before me."

There was no sharp reply to that. There was simply loaded silence as Margot stared into the vague shape of his face, comprehension dawning slowly.

"Wait..." Bracing palms on his chest, she sat up a little. Disbelief made her words slow when Margot asked, "You... I know you said you hadn't done *other stuff* with people before, but you kissed someone before me, right?"

Theodore's hands drifted to her bare hips. The blankets slid off her back as he pulled her completely on top of him, her legs straddling his waist and her hands sinking into the pillow beside his ears.

"No," Theodore answered, utterly unashamed. "I've known you for twenty-five years, darling. Kissing anyone else when your soulmate *lives in your head* would have felt wrong." He said it so matter-of-factly. Even his internal voice, when it filled up her mind a second later, was clear of self-consciousness or artifice when he informed her, *I wouldn't kiss anyone else when I knew you were mine.*

"Oh, *Theodore,*" she groaned, "you are just so..." Sweet? Soft?

So vulnerable it made her heart ache? How did she *ever* think this man meant her harm?

Margot leaned down onto her elbows to kiss his cheeks, his forehead, his eyelids, his chin, his nose. She peppered him with slow, affectionate kisses, and when he turned his face up for more, she covered his mouth with hers and showed him exactly how much his tenderness unwound her.

When she felt the hard, hot bar of his erection pressing insistently between her thighs, Margot pulled her mouth away from his to breathe, "Oh, that's—"

Theodore curled his fingers around the nape of her neck to drag her back, his tongue slicking against hers with a smooth, sensuous glide. Margot clenched her fingers in the pillowcase as he slowly lifted his hips, grinding them together in a way that shot sparks up her spine.

Her heart pounded in time with the aching pulse between her legs. The silky heat of his erection, so foreign and exciting, made her stomach flip with taut anticipation.

Margot untangled herself from his grip to sit up completely, her weight settling against him in a way that made them both gasp. She licked her lips and wondered, with a forbidden sort of thrill, *Will it feel this good inside of me, too?*

"Fuck, darling, you can't just think those things at me," he gritted out. The wonderful, talented hands she so admired closed around her thighs, his fingers digging into the soft skin as Theodore bucked his hips against her.

Margot's breath came out as small, panting gasps as she rocked her hips in time with his, the movements becoming smoother with each pass as her core softened for him. Pleasure, wonderful but yet unfulfilling, made her clench with a needy ache.

Now that her secret was out, now that she *knew* she was safe with him, Margot wanted to let go. She wanted to chase all the things that were forbidden for so long. She wanted to know what it was like to have Theodore inside of her, to feed that touch hunger that dogged her for so very long.

"Theodore," she murmured, pleading for something she had only ever dreamed of. She pressed her hands down onto the tense muscles of his stomach. A buzz took up residence under her skin: the madness of instinct she only barely understood. Margot curled her fingers into his skin to satisfy the urge to claw, to bite, to provoke him into the frenzy her other half demanded.

Her legs locked, her breathing sharpened. *Yes,* she thought, *that's what I want to do. But I can't do that. That's not normal.*

No, normal witches didn't want to close their teeth around their lover's throat as they slammed into them, their claws digging into tender, sweat-slick skin as they struggled to define who would make the rules, who would be on top. Normal witches liked soft kisses and slow, gentle exploration. They didn't want *violence.*

Margot pulled her hands away from Theodore's stomach, horrified by the possibility that she might have left furrows in his skin. She was vividly reminded of her loss of control in the clinic, when she struck him. What had come over her? What madness would drive her to strike a man she was rapidly falling in love with?

"I'm sorry," Margot yelped, "I don't know what's wrong with me. I—"

"Do you want to bite me, darling?" Theodore smoothed his hands up her thighs and over her hips until he could circle her waist. With a simple movement of his wrists, he pushed and pulled her against him, rocking them in time. "You want to use your claws on me? You want to test me? See if I'm worth a damn?"

She shuddered as he slid smoothly against her slick skin, her clitoris throbbing with each tantalizing pass. "I s-shouldn't. That's not normal. You shouldn't want to fight the person you want to..."

"Fuck?" Theodore's voice was a velvety purr in the darkness. "You want to fuck, darling. You want to bite me and scratch me and mark me up, make me work for it, because you're a fierce little halfling, and that's what *we* do."

Margot's hips jerked involuntarily. A bolt of lightning-hot lust slammed through her, making the ache almost unbearable. She shook her head, her long, half-dry hair flying over bare shoulders. "No, I'm a healer, I shouldn't want to do that. We don't hurt anyone. We definitely don't hurt the people we love."

"You're the woman who justifiably clawed my face a few hours ago," he reminded her, "and you're the woman who shocked me *and* you're the woman who fearlessly jumped out of a moving car. I think you're capable of a lot more than you realize."

All of that was true, of course, but she'd spent a lifetime suppressing the other half of herself, the one that *howled,* and Margot wasn't entirely sold on letting it out. Her grandmother drilled control, the need to hide anything beyond the bounds of *normal,* from the moment Margot was able to comprehend speech. To suddenly defy a lifetime of that conditioning felt impossible.

And desperately, tantalizingly freeing.

"Do you want to stop?" Theodore asked, concern humming through their bond as he brought their moving hips to a slow halt. "If you're uncomfortable, you just have to say so. I won't ever push you into something you're not ready for."

Did she want to stop? *No.*

No, she didn't. Margot wanted to live, and living meant facing the parts of herself she didn't necessarily understand. It meant that maybe her grandmother was wrong. It meant that maybe, if she could trust this man who looked at her like she was Glory's own flesh, that howling part of herself deserved to live, too.

Margot sucked in a deep breath. "You'll tell me if I do something you don't like, right?"

Theodore rubbed her sides with slow, tender strokes. There was a husky note of pride in his voice when he answered, "Yes, darling."

"And if I... I get too rough, you'll stop me?"

"Yes, darling." He gave her waist a gentle squeeze. "You won't get too rough with me, though. We're consorts. Half of the pull is fighting one another." He paused long enough to find one of her nipples. Smoothing his thumb around the tight bud, Theodore added thoughtfully, "Thinking about it now, that's probably why my gloves turn you on so much. They seem dangerous to you, don't they?"

A flood of warmth trickled through her veins as he conjured the image of his gloves in her mind: The black leather stretched tight over his knuckles, the dangerous shine of the claws, the smooth glide of them over her skin — and yes, the very, very dangerous appeal of knowing he could so easily harm her with those wicked silver tips.

Margot shuddered, her hips moving in slow circles over him as he plucked at her nipple. "Yes."

"And you want to bite me. You said so yourself."

"Yes."

"Do you want to claw me, darling?"

Margot bit her lip, her lashes fluttering. Yes, she did want to rake her nails across the tight skin of his stomach until she hit that line of crisp black hair below his navel. Then she'd be gentle. She'd handle him with care as she stroked the hot length of him currently grinding against her slick core.

But she couldn't *say* that.

"Well?" When she still didn't answer, a rumbling growl built in the darkness between them. He was too fast and the light from the street too dim to give her any warning before the hand on her waist slid back to deliver a swift, sharp swat to the back of her thigh.

The reaction of her other half was so fast, so overwhelming, that Margot didn't have any hope in fighting it.

The thrill of a challenge, the indignation of being *swatted,* the boiling lust turning her veins into rivers of heat — all of it combined to crack the walls holding her elvish blood at bay.

Instinct was a haze slamming down over her mind. It moved her hands, it pulled her lips back in a snarl, and it said, *We have claws, too!*

Her hands lashed out on their own, swiping at his chest and stomach in vicious reprisal.

Margot didn't have time to be horrified. The instant her nails made contact with his skin, Theodore was flipping them over, his weight pinning her down as he fought to wrangle her arms over her head. Instinct compelled her to make it as difficult as possible. Her teeth snapped whenever he dared bring his throat too close, and when he couldn't get a good grip on her, she ran her nails down his vulnerable sides and twisted her hips, trying to buck him off.

Not too much, though, her other half whispered gleefully. *Just enough to make it difficult for him. What will he do if I fight? Does he know his own strength? Will he lash out? Or will he seduce, gentle, show me he's willing to work for it? Will he play?*

Oh.

Margot's struggles paused as she processed that thought. *It's... play.*

That's what the elvish blood wanted: a partner to play with, to test, to fight and know, without any doubt, that they would never, *ever* hurt them. It wasn't weird, or unnatural. It was just... courtship.

The relief of the revelation was overwhelming, but it was almost immediately washed away when Theodore successfully pinned her arms over her head with one hand, his hips wedged against the cradle of her thighs as he purred against the line of her throat. A slow, deliberate lick along the throbbing pulse of her jugular told her that she had lost this round.

"Ah, darling," he whispered against her skin, "I love it when you use your claws on me." His fangs left a line of fire in their wake as he dragged them down her throat, over her collarbones, to nip at the valley between her breasts. "It shows you trust me. Each little bite and scratch means you think I can take you, that you want me to prove I can subdue you without hurting you, that I'll *take care* of you. It means you *want* me."

Her fingers clenched uselessly in the air. "I do." Margot tried to breathe, but the air felt thinner, less essential than everything that was Theodore. "I do want you. So much it makes me feel crazy."

"You have me. You have me, darling." He placed a hot, open-mouthed kiss to the tip of her breast, sending a streak of pleasure straight to her core. "But I'm not going to fuck you here. I'm saving that for *our* bed, in *our* home."

It took a second for the words to penetrate. Margot lifted her head to blink owlishly at his shadowed face. "What? You're not going to touch me?"

She could feel his smile curve against the soft skin of her breast. "Now, I never said *that.* I am going to touch you, darling. Don't worry." Theodore released her hands with a slow drag of his fingertips down her arms, her breasts, her stomach, to slide down the bed.

When he grasped her thighs and hooked them over his wide shoulders, she sucked in a sharp breath of disbelief. "Again?"

"Yes," he purred, *"again."*

Again, as it turned out, did not mean *once more.*

It meant several times, enough to leave her boneless and deliciously sore from the insistent stretch of his talented fingers when she woke up a handful of hours later.

Theodore's voice was a low murmur from the next room. Margot heard him, felt his warmth in the back of her mind, before she opened her eyes. Why should she hurry waking up, anyway? She knew instinctively that she lay in his spot, her nose turned into the pillow that smelled like cedar and cinnamon and *him,* the sheets so silky against her skin.

Most mornings of her life were dreadfully early, rigidly regimented things.

Wake up, shower, get dressed, eat, work. All before sunrise, and before a long, exhausting day of working in Healer Mason's Ward, or, in her childhood, before an endless day of advanced tutoring. Or, most recently, in her own Healing House.

Which is destroyed, she reminded herself with a grimace.

Was it wrong to feel so... *relaxed* when everything she had ever defined her life by — her secret, her work, her staunchly guarded privacy — now lay in shambles? Maybe.

But Margot couldn't summon the will to fight the languid peace that settled over her like a blanket. For the first time in memory, she was *free.*

Theodore's voice, low and almost unintelligible, lilted upward in a question before dropping with what she assumed was a goodbye. There was a moment of silence, but she didn't need to hear his feet on the floor to sense him moving closer. The awareness of him was just *there,* baked into the bond keeping her alive and healthy, as well as the part of her that purred whenever he was near.

Familiar arms came down around her, dipping the mattress as they took Theodore's considerable weight. The sense that something was blocking the soft light of the morning followed. Body heat radiated over her as a pair of soft, plush lips skimmed the side of her neck. A low purr made her stomach flutter.

"Good morning, darling."

Margot curled into him as best she could. Gripping the front of his shirt with gentle fingers, she turned to nuzzle her nose against his throat.

"Ow!" Margot recoiled, her eyes opening to squint at the starchy thing barring her from him. The bridge of her nose smarted from the glancing blow against his offensive clothing. Theodore's collar looked like it was made of regular, if very stiff fabric, but when she bumped up against it, Margot discovered it was bafflingly rigid. "Why are you wearing that? And what's it made of, anyway? Steel?"

Theodore snickered. "It's reinforced with a proprietary blend of armored fabric."

She hooked her finger under the edge of the high collar and gave it a tiny tug. "Why are you wearing it? Doesn't it suffocate you?"

The idea that he might be uncomfortable stuck in her craw. Margot frowned at the offending article, a feral sort of protectiveness prickling under her skin. *She* would certainly hate wearing something like that. The idea of him feeling strangled, even mildly uncomfortable, made her want to throw the damn thing away.

"I'm used to it," he soothed, petting her mussed hair out of her face. When she glanced up, Margot found him grinning that big, boyish smile that made her insides melt. "It's traditional to cover the throat. Most people don't go to this length — they just wear scarves or ties or whatever they want — but I'm the sovereign, so I have to take extra precautions."

Her brows furrowed. "Extra precautions?"

Theodore's smile dimmed. In a voice she was coming to recognize as his *soothing tone,* he explained, "Someone will always want my seat, darling. I've already met six challenges since Delilah abdicated. And those were just the public ones. I'll always need to take extra care with my safety."

Margot stared at him blankly for a long moment. When what he *wasn't* saying finally dawned on her, she made an appalled sound in the back of her throat and cried, "You wear that so no one can *slit your throat?*"

"Shh," he soothed, gathering her up into a sitting position so he could run his palm up and down her bare back. "Don't worry about it, darling. No one's ever come close. I haven't worked all my life to get *here,* only to have some upstart claw me when I'm not looking."

Margot clutched at his shoulders, her heart pounding in her ears. *I could lose him.*

The thought, clear and sharp, was a blade cutting through her contentment. It never occurred to her to be afraid *for* him, but now that the thought was there, now that she could look at his collar and know the threat it represented, Margot found herself dizzy with the fear of his loss.

Losing a bondmate wouldn't kill her. She would have to find another one, but it wouldn't necessarily be a death sentence.

But losing *Theodore,* who made her feel safe for the first time in her life, who looked at her like she was the whole world, the man she wanted to wake up and see every day for the rest of her life, would *shatter* her.

Someone could take him from me, she thought, breathing hard. *I could lose him. I just found him and I could lose him.*

You will not lose me. Theodore's inner voice was hard-edged, steely in its certainty. *My love, I have trained all my life for this. No one will take me from you except Grim herself.*

But what if marrying me— what if doing this thing, breaking all these rules, puts you in more danger? Cold sweat dotted her hairline as she buried her face in his shoulder. *Would it be safer for you to not acknowledge me? We could—*

Abso-fucking-lutely not. Theodore's arms were a cage around her, his muscles suddenly rigid. *I don't care if it paints a massive target on my back, Margot. I'm marrying you. I'm telling everyone you're my consort. I am not ever, ever hiding you. I'll face every challenge, every threat, as I always have: with my own claws.*

Margot pulled her head back to stare at him, horrified. "Theodore... you have allies, right? Amongst the five families? People who will back you in this decision of yours. Right?"

Of course he would have allies. He was Sovereign. He knew politics better than even she did. That wasn't to say she was some expert, of course, but being attached to Sophie's hip for most of her life made her no novice.

Organizing the Covens in the Collective was a massive political endeavor. Managing the Goode Coven, with its wide net of business interests and sprawling family structure, was a feat.

Doing that many times over, with the ten Covens in the Collective? An astonishing testament to Sophie's skill.

Margot witnessed firsthand the necessity of having one's ducks all in a row before throwing yourself into something. She watched good *and* bad resolutions die swift, brutal deaths in the meeting chamber of the Collective headquarters due to a lack of assured allies and support.

Surely Theodore, who had this planned for so long, would have his sworn allies, his confidants who would back him when the time came. Surely...

Theodore's jaw set at a stubborn, almost mutinous angle that made all the blood rush from her head in a dizzying wave. "They'll accept it," he ground out, giving her the answer she dreaded. "I don't care how many challenges I have to face. They'll accept it or they'll die — one way or another."

Chapter Nineteen

His consort sank into a chair across from him and put her head in her hands.

"Baby," she groaned, "you can't do this without allies."

Theodore scowled down at her untouched breakfast. In the back of his mind, a thousand undone tasks buzzed in time with the incessant notifications hitting his phone, each one demanding his attention.

None of it mattered when his consort was upset.

"I have allies," he insisted, pushing a plate of curled bread-things toward her. Now that he knew she'd gone without proper nutrition for so much of her life, Theodore couldn't stop himself from insisting she eat at every opportunity. When she flatly refused to entertain his assertions that she should eat good, healthy meat, he settled on shoving human food her way instead.

"I have my family. We're the most powerful name in the Protectorate. My sister has Foresight, Patrol is loyal to me and Valen, Sam runs most of the EVP economy from his estate, and I can cut down any challenger who threatens my seat. We don't *need* anyone."

Margot dropped her hands to the small, circular table, her slight frame gilded by the warm light spilling from the window next to her. Her face was lined with exasperation when she sighed out, "Theodore, you..." Without looking at him, she sought out his hand, seeking his touch even when her temper made little electric sparks flare around her eyes.

She began again. "Okay, I'll grant you that those are all strengths. I'm not arguing that. What I *am* arguing is that you are currently in the middle of a brewing disaster, threatening to make it worse by upending a thousand years of dogma with no backing, no warning, no friends to stand by you when your enemies decide to use the ensuing instability to cut you down."

"There's no reason to view this as creating instability." He cupped her hand in both of his, soothing himself with the necessary skin contact. "I'm telling them the truth. If we don't change, we die. I'm not taking their money or their traditions or their children from them. I'm just marrying the woman I love and making a point while I do it. After that, it's up to them."

Margot flushed an endearing pink, her topaz eyes softening for a second before they snapped back to temper. "Yes, but those articles you showed me— Theodore, you've pissed off the Collective, the Temple, *and* you're about to blindside the five families that could, if they got their acts together, depose you. Even with the entirety of Patrol on your side..." She shook her head. "You already have someone out to get you. What happens if they decide this is the perfect time to gather support? If nothing else, going into this without warning any of the power players will be viewed as massively arrogant, if not outright insulting."

Theodore fought the urge to bristle. He'd done things on his own for so long, his family's steel will behind him every step of the way, that it went against the grain to stoop to politics to ensure his place. It was his strength — his *family's* strength — that got them where they were, not petty politicking or currying favor.

Elves, as a rule, didn't play nice with one another. Their society was built on insular family groups, on the pride of their names and their kin; the vicious sharpness of their claws. He was proud of who he was. He was proud of his family. He was proud to say he'd fought and clawed for his place in the world, so he could have the woman he loved in his arms and know she was safe.

To hear her questioning that strength stung, but Theodore was smart enough to know that didn't mean Margot was wrong.

Theodore's phone buzzed in his pocket. Another important call. Another irate message from the Gloriae demanding an audience, or the pissed off family representatives wondering why he wasn't in the Tower to greet them as they arrived for the Summit. Perhaps it was another request for a follow-up statement about Margot's safety, about what he intended to do with the Healing Houses in his territory now that he overstepped his bounds, or a thinly-veiled threat from the Collective, reminding him that Margot's choice to stay by his side was the only reason they weren't howling for his blood.

Things were, put simply, a mess.

Theodore knew he could hold on to power. Nothing and no one would take the future of his people from his hands, not when the cost of it might be their extinction. Nothing and no one would take Margot from him, either.

But I don't want bloodshed. We can't afford it.

Even one lost life was too much. Their numbers were pitifully small. If a full war broke out? His people would wipe themselves from Burden's Earth.

Rubbing his eyes with his free hand, Theodore asked, "So what do you propose?" Before she could respond, he added, "And no, I will not accept any answer that involves hiding our relationship for any length of time, darling."

"Fine." Margot looked out the window for a moment, her eyebrows drawn tight together as she lifted her cup of coffee to her lips for a long, slow sip. "So you don't have any families you can get to back you up? None of the big five?"

"We have families with business interests in common," he answered, "but no, none that I would trust this information with ahead of time." Glory knew what they would do with it. Take the advanced warning to consolidate their own power, organize a coup? Try to take him out before the announcement could be made? Something more nefarious?

Besides, the idea of groveling to even the second most powerful family in the hierarchy, the du Soleils, made his stomach turn. They were as secretive as his own family, but arrogant, quarrelsome, and a general pain in his ass. Perhaps he wouldn't have so much against them if Olivier du Soleil, the scion of the family, didn't act like Theodore had mortally wronged him at some point in their lives.

No doubt Olivier penned one of those irate messages currently buzzing away in his pocket. Theodore could just about imagine what the whipcord lean, white-blond elf would have to say if he was informed Theodore preferred eating breakfast with a witch — a witch *halfling* — to dealing with whatever his problem was.

"So what about people not in the hierarchy?"

Theodore blinked, the image of Olivier's aristocratic sneer vanishing from his mind's eye in an instant. "Others?"

"Yes," Margot answered, squeezing his hand. Her gaze was intent, shrewd. His halfling knew what she was doing, and that sense of calm authority was deeply attractive. *My consort is fierce, intelligent, and proud. I'm damn lucky she's mine.* "What about allies outside of the five?"

"Elves don't make alliances." The answer came automatically. "Well," he amended, thinking of the stubborn prick that was Taevas Aždaja, "not officially."

Taevas was the *Isand* of Clan Aždaja, the leader of all the dragons in the UTA, and at some point after making a brief acquaintance at a meeting of the United Congress, he decided Theodore was to become his *protégé* — whether the elf agreed or not. After a decade of enduring his high-handed lectures, snark, and unexpected visits, Theodore still wasn't quite sure what to make of him.

What he could say but never *would,* however, was that it was Taevas who first put the idea of banishing the moratorium on taking Others as consorts entirely. Initially, Theodore's only goal had been to have Margot to himself. After a memorable evening of sullen drinking with the devilish dragon, wherein Taevas outlined *exactly* how the dragons nearly went extinct five hundred years before, the idea of true change took root.

He still wouldn't call the man an ally, though. Theodore shuddered imagining Taevas meeting Margot. The man was a menace and a self-proclaimed "enemy of panties and sobriety." He could only imagine how Taevas would act with his prim, deceptively fragile consort in the room. Likely, the dragon would take her dignity as a challenge.

Margot's honeyed voice cut through his sour musings, drawing him back to her presence, to the feel of her delicate, blunted claws in his grasp. "Okay, but you're already planning on changing the world, Theodore. Why not in this way, too? Allies can only make you stronger, if you pick them carefully."

He brought her hand up to his lips to press a kiss to her knuckles, pleased and chagrined by her faith in him. "My love, you vastly overestimate the number of people who like me."

"*I* like you," she replied instantly.

Another sharp-edged shard of worry, lodged deeper with every shadow that lingered in her eyes, melted away. "That's all I care about." He smiled and tilted his cheek into the ridge line of her knuckles. "You and my family — I have all I need."

"Not if you die."

His scowl snapped back into place. "I'm not going to die."

"Not if you have a laundry list of powerful allies, no. Witches learned that lesson seven hundred years ago. Why do you think we formed the Collective?" Margot cast him another shrewd look. "What about Viktor?"

"What about him?"

She blew out an exasperated huff. "You were friends once, right? Why can't he be an ally? The Merced pack is powerful and stupidly wealthy. They've got pull with the major players in the Packlands."

Theodore made a face. "We haven't been friends for a long time."

"Why?"

It had been ten years. Theodore was surprised that the sting of Viktor's lost friendship lingered still. Shaking his head, he answered, "We had a falling out when we were teenagers."

Margot tilted her head, her perceptive gaze catching every flicker of emotion in his expression. The bond, too, he was sure. No doubt she could *feel* the dull ache that never really went away. Stroking the palm of his hand, she asked, "What happened? Viktor said you fought over a girl." Margot's tone took on a tartness that made him preen, just a little. "He *assured* me it wasn't what it sounded like."

Theodore reached across the table to rub her cheek with the pad of his thumb. "He didn't lie. It's really not what it sounds like. You are my one and only, darling."

Her smile was brief but full of warmth. "Then what happened?"

"It's not really a story I can tell," he hedged. Loyalty to his cousin held his tongue, their blood bond strong despite the animosity Cammie's mother held for the main branch of the Solbourne family. "But I *can* tell you that despite being considered a ruffian unfit to grace the halls of the Tower by more than a few, we always considered him family. Some of us... more than others." He sent her a look from beneath his brows, heavy with implication. "He was *very* close to one of my cousins."

Margot's eyes widened. "Oh. I see."

"Things went sour, and when I confronted him about it, Viktor and I..." Theodore sighed, the bitter clarity of hindsight making his stomach twist. "I lost my temper. We both said things that we shouldn't have. After that, he stopped coming around. We went our separate ways. He took on the responsibility of the pack when the previous alpha got into one scrap too many and I became sovereign."

"So, Viktor and your cousin..."

"Haven't had any contact since, as far as I'm aware." He smothered a growl. "Not for lack of trying on my part. I've talked to them both, but they're stubborn, heartbroken fools."

Margot winced. "Messy."

"Extremely."

Using her free hand to pick up one of the bread-things, Margot took her time nibbling the flaky edges as she thought. "Is that a barrier to asking him for help, though?"

Theodore fought his pride in silence for several beats. "No," he begrudgingly allowed, "no. He... would probably jump at the chance to help."

Because Viktor was a loyal sort, despite how he'd broken Cammie's heart. He was also a good, strong leader who would understand the benefits of finally securing a real alliance with the Solbourne family. The Merced pack would become functionally untouchable as long as Theodore wore the crown, so to speak, and the Solbournes would gain sway with the notoriously suspicious Packland alphas.

It was a good idea, even if his pride smarted at the thought of being the one to reach out first.

Margot waited for him to say something else, her expression softly encouraging. In the end, Theodore knew he could deny her nothing. It was a waste of time to try. "Fine," he sighed, "I'll call him."

"Now."

"Now?" He gave their breakfast — his own good, bloody meal only half eaten — a longing look. "But I'm having breakfast with my consort. And we're getting married this afternoon. At least let me call him *tonight.*"

"No," she pressed, entirely unmoved, "you need to call him now, so he can be at the wedding."

Theodore gawked at her. "Why in Glory's name would we invite him to our wedding?"

Elves didn't even *do* weddings. He planned on inviting Kaz, and that was only because Margot explained the need for two witnesses — one for the bride and one for the groom.

"Because shifters are all about family events," Margot patiently explained. "Huge dinners. Birthdays. Mating celebrations and anniversaries and graduations. Inviting him to be a witness at our wedding will be a display of trust that he'll understand immediately." She paused, a flicker of uncertainty in her eyes. "Besides... he's the only friend I have in the city. It'd mean a lot to me if he was my witness."

It occurred to him that perhaps this thing that meant very little to him meant something much greater to her. Was Margot sacrificing a dream for him? An uncomfortable twisting sensation took up residence in his chest.

"Darling," he began, searching her expression with mounting dread, "this wedding... Is this what you really want to do? I didn't stop to think that maybe this wasn't what you had in mind when you imagined getting married someday."

Surprise flashed through their bond, quickly followed by a heady rush of pure, golden tenderness. Margot offered him a heartbreaking smile when she answered, "Baby, I'm just happy it's you. I don't care how or when we do it. Truly."

Just like that, the terrible twisting guilt evaporated. In its place, a swarm of butterflies filled his stomach, each one a longing fulfilled. "Are you sure?" he asked, voice thick.

"Yeah." Her grin widened. "Besides, once Grandma's temper dies down, I'm sure we'll have a massive Goode wedding to make up for it."

It was Theodore's turn to wince. "Oh, but that doesn't sound—"

"Poor baby," she crooned, wiggling her bread-thing at him sympathetically, "you only just realized what you got yourself into, didn't you?"

~

Obviously, no one at Glory's Saint Emaine Cathedral, the main place of worship in the city, expected the sovereign to show up with a retinue of grim-faced, black-clad guards, an orc, and a witch. Margot almost felt sorry for the poor man at the desk currently sweating bullets as he struggled to dial a number on the intercom again and again.

"I'm sorry," he gasped, his round gut pushing against the brilliant scarlet and gold robes of his Gloriae uniform. "We didn't expect— Her Grace is visiting from out of town and has been busy trying to get an audience with—" The acolyte cut himself off, his eyes bulging as he realized exactly *who* this visiting priestess must have been hard at working trying to get an audience with.

For his part, Theodore's bland expression didn't so much as twitch. Despite the amusement she could feel flowing through their bond, his arm was steady under her hand, his eyes half-mast as they took in the sweating acolyte with disinterest.

Standing in front of a man who looked like he might pass out at any moment, Margot felt her pre-wedding nerves melting away. "It's all right," she soothed, "we can wait a moment."

"No, no," he wheezed. Pushing his rolling chair away from his desk, the squat man ran a shaking hand over his balding head and backed away, towards a door that presumably led to a private wing of the Cathedral's complex. "I'm just— I'll go find her now. It will only be a second. I'll find her!"

The acolyte was gone in a flash of scarlet, the door opening and slamming shut with a rattle.

Margot made a small sound of concern in the back of her throat. "Do you think he's going to be okay?"

Theodore shrugged. The end of his cape, part of the traditional elvish finery his brother brought with him when he met them at the apartment, tickled the back of her bare calf. "As long as he doesn't have a heart attack while he's looking, sure."

She pinched his forearm. "That's not funny!"

Kaz's voice was a low, sensual rumble from behind them. "My bet is he pissed his pants as soon as the door closed. He'll have to stop to get a new pair before he comes back, so it might take a while."

This time, neither Margot nor Theodore could stifle their snorts. Peering around Theodore's shoulder, she gave her future-brother-in-law a speculative look. "Do you think it's Theodore or you that really put the fear of Grim in him?"

Personally, she didn't think Kaz looked scary at all. Or, if he *did,* it was in the good, deliciously rakish sort of way.

Kaz didn't wear elvish regalia like Theodore, but he still dressed up for the occasion: his powerful, jewel green frame was swathed in a black on black suit, his long black hair tied in a high ponytail, and he'd even gone so far as to swipe traditional orcish kohl around his eyes and across the bridge of his nose. With his pouty face and wide-legged stance, he looked like he just stepped off of a runway.

Kaz leveled his dark, kohl-rimmed eyes on her. "Funny that you didn't put yourself in there. Don't think you're scary enough to send an acolyte running?"

"Me?" She waved her free hand. "I'm not scary at all."

A laugh bubbled out of Theodore — a real, hearty belly laugh — as Kaz dryly replied, "Sister-mine, in three days you've managed to not only survive a bombing and a swift trip out of a moving car, but you've successfully bamboozled the sovereign into standing for a human wedding." He arched a dark, perfectly-shaped brow. "Also, didn't I hear something about you being able to stop a heart with a fingertip a while ago?"

Margot flushed scarlet and hastily turned away, muttering, "Yeah, but *he* doesn't know any of that."

"Don't worry, darling," Theodore interjected, patting the hand tucked protectively into the crook of his elbow. "He's just jealous. Kaz would love to find a consort even half as fierce as my beautiful, genius halfling."

Kaz grunted.

Margot dared to peek at him again, her interest piqued. "Are you on the lookout?"

The half-orc favored her with a slight smile. *Glory save me,* she thought, briefly stunned, *he could level cities with that face.*

"Why? You think I need some help?"

"With your looks?" She shook her head, ignoring Theodore's annoyed rumbling. "No, probably not. But I *do* have a lot of cousins who'd be interested."

If Kaz ever came to a Coven gathering, they would eat him up with a spoon.

He'd be lucky if there was anything left of him afterward, she thought, smiling wryly. Coven witches were not, as a rule, particularly hung up on sexuality or its expression. He'd have more offers than any single being could handle.

Perhaps seeing the gleam of humor in her eye, Kaz's smug look turned wary. "And risk bringing home another tiny hellion? No, thanks."

Margot quite liked the idea of being a hellion. Preening a little, she opened her mouth to tell Theodore so when the door through which the acolyte disappeared opened once more.

A woman stepped out into the reception hall, her gate smooth and her long, white gold hair flowing like silk down her back. Besides the symbol of Glory she wore around her neck, the priestess was shockingly unadorned. She wore a black pencil skirt, stilettos, and a simple cream blouse under her robes of office — yards of topaz silk crafted into a long-sleeved garment that fluttered around her slim ankles.

"Good afternoon," the priestess smoothly greeted them, her voice fascinatingly smoky. "My name is Petra Zaskodna, High Priestess. What a happy coincidence it is to find you here, Sovereign. I've been trying to reach you since I flew in last night."

"I've been busy," he blithely answered.

Petra's eyes, cornflower blue and sharply intelligent, flicked down to where Theodore still clasped Margot's hand on his arm. "I see. Am I to assume this meeting is not to discuss your infringement on Glory's domain?"

"Is that what the Temple is calling it?" Theodore's amusement bled through the bond and into his voice. "Fascinating."

Petra's cool expression didn't change. "Indeed." Gesturing to the room at large with an elegant twist of her wrist, she continued, "I am not the Priestess in residence here, obviously, but since there still hasn't been a member of the Gloriae picked to fill the empty seat, I was sent by the Temple to speak to you about your edict."

"We had a Priest until recently," Theodore coolly replied. "I would have been more than happy to speak to him."

"Yes. Priest Maximilian Dooraker. He passed away a year ago. He was a good man." Petra said the name in the same even tone she said everything else, except Margot caught the slight tightening around her eyes that hinted at hidden feeling. "Unfortunately, filling a position as important as this one is tricky. Perhaps the vacancy is why you felt comfortable stretching your authority."

Margot raised her eyebrows. *She cuts right to the heart, doesn't she?*

A bit like someone I know, Theodore replied, squeezing her hand. Aloud, he said, "This is my Protectorate, Your Grace. I can stretch my authority as far as I wish."

Petra hummed. Tucking her hands into the pockets of her long robe, she glanced between the couple with cold-eyed calculation. "Is that so? I'd inquire, then, as to the nature of your visit, if the sovereign is so certain of his authority over the dominion of a goddess."

Margot's eyebrows hit her hairline, but Theodore wasn't fazed. A slow smile stretched his mouth, revealing a hint of deadly fang. Drawing Margot closer to his side, he answered, "Why, Priestess, I should think that's obvious."

To her credit, Petra didn't gawk at the sight of the sovereign draping an arm around a witch's shoulders, his gloved hand skimming down her side in a blatant caress, a statement of proud ownership. "Oh?"

Theodore's grin widened, dimpling his cheeks. "We're here to be married."

"Married." The word was flat, hardly a question. Petra's gaze lingered on Theodore's broad smile for a beat before sliding to Margot. "You wish to marry this elf, sister?"

Margot tactfully refrained from mentioning that, officially, the Goodes and the entire Collective did not recognize the "family" that was the Temple and its devotees. They worshipped Glory, certainly, but in their own ways, and not at the behest of an organization that had been brainwashing children for hundreds of years.

"Yes," she answered, her heart beating faster at the renewed realization that it was the truth. Would she have preferred to marry him under the sky, without the blessing of an institution her family had feuded with for generations? Of course, but Margot didn't care enough about bad blood to pass up the opportunity when it presented itself to her. "Yes, I want to marry him. I want a real ceremony, too. It has to be legal."

Petra searched her face for several seconds, but Margot didn't see any judgment there. Another unusual thing. Most High Gloriae of the Temple tended to look down their noses at people, whether or not they actually disagreed with them. It was a certain inherent smugness that could make even the most even-keeled person puff up with indignation if they endured it for too long.

Petra, however, looked at her with a shade of real concern in her eyes, a warmth that some might miss under the layers of cool professionalism she wore like a her robes of rich topaz.

The Priestess's gaze slid back to Theodore. They lost a little bit of their warmth as that calculating gleam returned. "Tell me, Sovereign, why should the Temple consent to marry you when you have shown no respect for the sanctity of our mission thus far?"

Theodore's smile blew up into a full grin. Staring down his nose at the Priestess, he asked baldly, "What do you want, Your Grace?"

Petra rocked back on her pencil-thin heels, her eyebrows arching. "What are you willing to give?"

"For my consort?" His smile fell. In an instant, he was not Margot's Theodore, but the deadly predator who claimed her as its own; he was the elf who would tear his own kingdom apart before he let her go. Margot felt his conviction, his unwavering loyalty, like the twang of a bowstring snapping in her soul. *Absolutely lethal, absolutely uncompromising, and all mine.* "Anything."

Amusement quirked the corners of Petra's full mouth. "How romantic." She canted her head to one side, her waist-length hair falling over one shoulder. "It's a good thing for you, then, that I only have a small thing to ask of you in return for this favor."

Margot tensed, her hackles raising, but Theodore didn't blink. "Ask."

"I want this position," the Priestess announced, tilting her chin up. "I want to be High Priestess of the Protectorate."

That, at last, took Theodore by surprise. "Why would the Temple consider my opinion on that sort of thing? They never have before."

"If you agree to sit down for talks with them on the issue of the Healing Houses, they will take your interest in filling the position as a sign of some... repentance." Petra smiled, showing off blindingly white teeth. "Besides, if they believe you like me, they will leap at the opportunity to influence you. I'll be transferred here within the day."

"Did the Temple really feel that threatened by the edict?" Margot asked, amazed. They'd weathered criticism and censure — and worse, when evidence occasionally came out about what exactly the Temple did to get so many bright young witches in its ranks — but they'd never seemed truly *threatened* before. Not too long ago they had their own military arm, after all.

Petra nodded. "They don't like it when someone thinks to reveal just how thin their authority really is these days." She snapped her fingers. "Like that, you showed the world that, if one so chose, the Temple's influence could be brushed aside. That rankles the High Gloriae, as I'm sure you can imagine."

Margot narrowed her eyes. *They, huh?* It was interesting that a woman of Petra's rank would refer to her own organization as *they* and not *we.*

Turning back to Theodore, the Priestess continued, "If you feign an interest in having a closer relationship with the Temple, they will call off the boycott of Solbourne tech and save your image from an overzealous beating so soon after your ascension. A meeting or two with the Temple leadership to discuss the Healing Houses, a request for my transfer? Hardly a steep price for something so precious as your... marriage, don't you think?"

"A marriage is an awfully simple thing to do, though," he shot back. "Whereas sitting with Temple leadership for even a minute will cost me years of my life."

Petra shrugged. "A marriage is not so simple, especially when you've given me no time to prepare. The sigilwork alone takes an expert hand." Leveling him with a blandly pleasant look, she added, "Of course, you are free to go to any two-bit Priest to get your sigils done, but I warn you that the results may not be exactly as desired."

Theodore held her gaze for a long moment before conceding defeat with a shrug and an easy smile. "Fine. I'll play nice just long enough to get you transferred here."

Petra's smile, when she turned it on, was bright enough to blind. Looking like the cat who got the cream, she swept her arm toward the grand door that led to the main cathedral. "Fabulous. Shall we begin, then?"

Theodore and Margot shared a glance, their answers blending into one. "Yes, we're ready."

Chapter Twenty

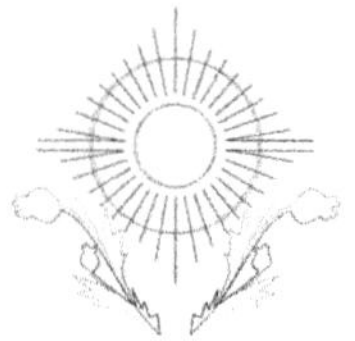

"Nervous?"

Theodore wiped his palms on his thighs, remembered too late that he was wearing gloves, and aborted the movement in such a way that left him patting his legs like a buffoon. "No," he growled.

"Uh-huh." Viktor crossed his arms. His white dress shirt stretched across broad, sun-tanned shoulders. The shifter was as dressed up as Theodore had ever seen him, wearing a shirt with buttons and dark jeans, his sandy blond hair scraped back with either claws or a comb.

Honestly, what Cammie ever saw in him, I'll never understand.

Sure, Viktor was handsome in a carefree sort of way, but compared to the meticulous grooming and style of an elf or orc? He was positively unkempt.

And I'm fixating on this because... Theodore rubbed the back of his neck, his eyes darting to the small door behind the altar. The Priestess and Margot had disappeared through there some time ago. The itch to be near her, to feel her smooth skin under his fingers and breathe her in, grew harder to ignore with every long minute that dragged by.

"You know how many men would kill to be in your place right now?" Viktor asked, a sly, coyote's grin stretching across his mouth. "About half my pack was mooning after our little healer. And the *weres—*"

"Do you *want* me to kill you?" he snapped, turning on his former friend with a snarl.

Viktor didn't even tense. He shrugged, his smile unabated. "Just reminding you that you're damn lucky to have snagged the witch you did. In case you were getting cold feet, I mean."

Theodore shared a look with his brother, who arched his eyebrows as if to say, *I don't know.* "Cold feet? What are you talking about?"

"I mean, if you're getting second thoughts about marrying Margot." Viktor's smile never faded, but something cold and predator-bright entered his gaze. Theodore wasn't surprised to see it, only that it took so long to come out.

"Careful," Theodore warned. "It's a dangerous thing to question an elf's devotion to their consort."

"Just checking." Viktor's sharp smile remained fixed in place. "Someone has to look out for her, you know."

"Of course. Me." His family would look out for her too, of course, but Margot was *his* responsibility in the same way he was now hers. They were a single unit, a family. What hurt her, hurt him.

"You really want to marry her, then? The human way?" The shifter cocked his head to one side, assessing the tense set of Theodore's jaw as he ground his fangs together. "Because if you're just doing this to make her your mistress anyway, I'm going to beat the shit out of you."

Both Kaz and Theodore froze, their outrage a mutual thing. Theodore narrowed his eyes at the shifter, hissing from between clenched teeth, "Are you doubting my reasons for—"

Viktor put up his hands. "Listen, I just have to ask these things, okay? She asked me to be here because you're in a rush and her family couldn't be invited. Her family would be grilling you right now if they were."

That, Theodore allowed, was true. He shuddered to think what he would be going through if Sophie and Alric Goode emerged from another m-gate, dressed and ready for a ceremony he only had a vague understanding of.

"Fine," he sighed, "I'll allow it because you're my consort's friend."

"Yours too, idiot." Viktor reached out to playfully punch Theodore's shoulder. "Always will be."

Theodore looked away. "Yeah, I guess." He traced the backs of his fangs with the tip of his tongue before adding, "Thank you. For coming, I mean."

Viktor shrugged. "Of course. We're family. Doesn't matter that you and I are both assholes who can't communicate to save our lives."

Kaz snorted, his massive shoulders settling into a smooth line. "The new family motto."

Theodore paced away from the two men with a grunt. Shoving his hands in his pockets, he walked up and down the long aisle, the massive dome of stained glass arching high over his head and the marble statue of Glory, her arms upraised, at his back.

It wasn't as beautiful as his family's temple, but it was passable, he supposed. A fine enough place to get married to the woman his entire universe revolved around. If only she'd come *out.*

Theodore turned on his heel to march back down the aisle. His eyes were laser focused on the door behind Glory's altar. *What's taking so long?*

Was Petra trying to convince Margot this wasn't a good idea? Had something happened to her while she was out of his sight? Anxiety gnawed at him.

Theodore, are you okay? Margot's voice was a cool breeze in his mind, the touch of her mind to his a bone-deep comfort.

He closed his eyes for just a moment, savoring it. *Yes,* he answered, *just anxious to see you. Is everything alright in there?*

Yes, we're just putting the finishing touches on the sigil. I want it to be perfect.

He tried not to feel like an ass. Of course she wanted it to be perfect. This *meant* something to her, and she was already sacrificing so much of her traditions to do this *now,* without her family present and without warning.

Take as much time as you need, darling, he told her, giving their bond a slow mental caress of apology.

Theodore did another circuit up and down the long aisle, trying to get the restlessness out. He would never, ever admit it to Viktor, but he *was* nervous. Not because he was afraid to officially join with his consort — they had, of course, already done as much on their own — but because...

Because this was *it.* This moment, when Margot publicly declared herself as his and he declared himself as hers — it was finally, after so many years, *here.* His consort was bonded to him. He bound himself to her. In the eyes of Glory and the law, they would be considered one.

The excitement, and the dread that at the last moment some terrible thing would happen to tear her from his grasp, made him feel as though his bones might jump out of his skin and run away without the rest of him. He wanted this over with. He wanted Margot in his bed *now* so that no one and nothing could deny them what they were owed.

A heavy hand clasped his shoulder. Theodore craned his neck to see his brother standing behind him, one hand casually tucked into a pocket of his slacks. "Hey," he muttered, too low for even shifter ears to pick up. "You okay?"

Theodore's throat was tight when he admitted, "I'm scared."

Kaz's dark brows drew together with confusion. Slowly, he asked, "Are you... unsure about the witch? I thought—"

"No." Theodore shook his head and blew out a long, shuddering breath. Quieter, he continued, "No, never. She's mine. I'm

just..." Fear made his chest tight, his fingertips tingle as his claws flexed against the insides of his claw-caps. "I'm just afraid that something will go wrong. I've waited for so long. To have this so close... I'm..." He swallowed.

Kaz squeezed his shoulder before sliding one heavily muscled arm around Theodore's neck, drawing him in close to whisper in his ear, "Nothing is going to take this from you, Teddy. You've fought for this every single day for twenty-five years — and I'm damn proud of you for it. You might be older than me by a month, but I think we both know who the big brother is here." A low, husky chuckle, as familiar to him as the scent of home and the embrace of the people he loved most in the world. "I've got your back, Teddy. Always. Everything is going to be fine."

Theodore rested his forehead on Kaz's shoulder for just a moment, his eyes closing as he breathed in his brother's smoky scent and the aura of pure, quiet strength he radiated.

Pride was a dull ache in his chest: for himself, for the woman he was lucky enough to call his own, for the brother who stood by him always, for the family they shared. Theodore was terribly, painfully proud to call himself a Solbourne. For all that they'd survived, for all that they'd clung to one another with love instead of bitterness or lust for power. They were a *family.*

Margot was part of that family. Kaz would fight to the death to protect her, to make sure his brother would know the happiness he longed for.

If Theodore knew anything for certain, it was that his family would go to any length, would endure any hardship, would cross any line, to ensure his happiness. Just as he would do the same for him.

Loyalty to family meant more than just blood. It meant doing what needed to be done to see the people you loved *thrive.*

Something niggled at the back of his mind. Not the bond, which burned with sweet electricity through his soul, but suspicion. Raising his head, Theodore took a step back to look into his brother's face when he asked, "Have you heard from Delilah?"

Kaz shook his head, his normally impassive face giving away nothing. "Plan is to arrive tomorrow morning to be here in time for your address. Why?"

Theodore swallowed. Looking away, he muttered, "Just... Why didn't she say anything about the bomb? If Marian was behind it, she had to see it, Kaz."

"You know just as well as I do that questioning Delilah is useless." Kaz pressed his hand between Theodore's shoulder blades and pushed him back toward the altar. "Don't get yourself worked into a knot about it, Teddy. It's not worth it. Just focus on the now."

"But what about Marian?" he pressed, voice echoing off of the cathedral walls. "Have you—"

"*After,* Teddy." Kaz's expression was hard, utterly implacable. "Please don't make me spoil your wedding. I really don't want to."

"I've heard it's bad luck to discuss a bombing before a mating celebration," Viktor chimed in from where he leaned casually against the armrest of a mahogany pew.

That sounded like bullshit, but Theodore bit back his acerbic reply. Straightening his cape and the buckles across his chest made to look like two entwined thistles, he sent his brother a significant look. "Fine, but we are discussing it *after.*"

Kaz smiled, slow and knowing. "If you aren't too busy, of course."

Margot stared at the sketch on the small square table by the stained glass window. The office behind the altar, presumably where the Gloriae worked when they were not speaking the words of Glory to the devotees who sought succor in her light, was warm, the air heavy with the scent of incense. Drapes of paper-thin red silk hung next to the stained glass windows, the cloth brightened into translucency as sunlight streamed through scenes of the creation of the races and their acceptance of Glory's gifts.

"Is it everything you want it to be?" Petra asked. She stood beside Margot, their hips nearly touching, a pencil in her long-fingered, perfectly manicured hand.

Margot swallowed the knot in her throat. The image on the paper was slightly blurry, but she could see it well enough through her tears.

"Yes." The word was choked, barely understandable, so she tried again. "Yes, it's perfect."

Soft fingers skimmed her bare elbow. "Are you sure about this, sister?"

Margot sucked in a deep breath. When she turned to look at the Priestess, her smile was wobbly but sincere. "I am."

Petra set down her pencil, her bemusement open. Alone with her fellow witch, she'd softened, her icy perfection melting away to reveal a quiet, perceptive woman who didn't once complain when Margot rejected the first five iterations of their marriage sigil.

"I won't question you further, then." Petra caught her gaze, held it. "But... this is a big thing. Perhaps the biggest union in a century. More, even. I'm sure you know this already, but... this is going to change things, sister. For better and worse."

Margot didn't look away. Perhaps she should have been scared, or at least *intimidated* by the path that lay before her, but she couldn't muster it. How could she, when fear and death were her companions for so long? If she didn't do this, there would be countless more people like her in the world, without a place, wondering if every shadow hid danger.

Marrying Theodore Solbourne, her bondmate and her... *consort,* was the right thing to do. Not just for herself, but for the world. If even one person saw their union and thought, *That could be me,* then it would be worth it.

Besides, she didn't want anyone else. The knowledge that he

was *right* made its way into the marrow of her bones, settling like glittering silt in her veins.

"I can do this," she assured Petra. Margot straightened her spine. "I'm a Goode. We can do anything."

The Priestess's smile was slight, but more genuine than the grin from the reception hall. "You Coven witches," she muttered, "always so arrogant."

Margot didn't bother denying it. "True. It's the only way we survived." She looked askance at the Priestess, but suspected she knew the answer to her question before the words left her mouth. "Do you belong to a Coven?"

Petra smoothed a hand down the front of her blouse, her lashes lowering to create crescent moons against the tops of her high cheekbones. "No. My parents were arrant."

"Oh." Margot swallowed. There appeared a small fissure between them, a gap in understanding. What would it be like to grow up in an arrant family, to be one of those witches whose m-gene appeared spontaneously, with no support structure built around them to understand their abilities, their *legacy?*

Sometimes, the only thing Margot could understand about herself was that history, that storied arrogance. When nothing else made sense, at least she had that.

The audacity of continued survival, her grandma called it. The arrogance of thumbing your nose at a world that thought it could step on you simply because you lacked claws or wings or tough skin. The pride in knowing that they could not burn or slaughter or eat every witch even if they *tried.*

Covens carried that legacy, but witches like Petra were unfortunately disconnected from that righteous arrogance, that rich vein of pride in their survival. So many never learned how to use their abilities. So many fell into the hands of those who would abuse them. So many, like Petra, ended up in institutions like the Temple, who offered them some semblance of community in exchange for their unerring loyalty.

No matter how the Collective, with Sophie at the helm,

fought on the Congress floor, no matter how many laws they passed through and institutions they exposed for being corrupt, they couldn't catch them all.

Brushing a lock of Margot's hair over her shoulder with a fingertip, Petra met Margot's stark gaze with an expression of solemn warmth. Her blue eyes glowed with a ring of pure light around the pupil — the mark of a born luminist, those rare few who could bend light to their will.

In an instant, Margot got the impression that she was no longer talking to a fellow witch, but a High Priestess of Glory.

"Whatever happens with your elf, sister," the Priestess murmured, "don't ever forget that you were forged in the fury of Glory's fiery heart. Be strong. And if you should ever need me, I will be there." The light in her eyes, two perfect, razor-thin circles of white, burned brighter. "Witches don't walk alone."

A buzzing warmth passed down her spine and across her cheeks. A caress from a hand unseen.

Margot gasped, the magic in her veins *singing* with awareness. "Was that—"

Petra touched the heavy gold necklace around her throat, her buffed nails gleaming against the sun and its beams, stretching out to warm the Earth. She leveled Margot with an intense look; one of deep, unshakable *knowing.* The light disappeared with a slow blink. "Glory has her eye on us, sister." Her lips quirked. "Perhaps she's urging us to get on with the ceremony."

A nervous laugh bubbled up from Margot's throat as she smoothed her hands down the bodice of her white cocktail dress, the kiss of heat lingering in her cheeks. "Yes, I suppose we should get on with it, shouldn't we?"

Petra hummed, her hair sliding over her shoulder to catch the light with her slow nod. "It's no good to keep a goddess waiting."

No, Margot thought, the sense of some great weight settling heavily on her shoulders. *It's not.*

~

The ceremony didn't take long.

They did not have a procession. Her Coven didn't line the aisle, welcoming her into the marriage. Neither Margot nor Theodore had vows prepared. There was no exchanging of family gifts before the altar.

There was only the ritual lighting of the hearth built into Glory's statue, their hands joined by a golden ribbon as they dipped the long match into the flame cupped in Petra's hands, then into the kindling. There was only hushed expectation as the flame crept higher, burning hotter, to burn in the heart of the goddess, the red glow building in the hollows of the statue's eyes as she came to life.

There were no cheers when Petra asked whether they consented to be wed in the eyes of Glory and Burden, the divine union of Earth and sunlight, and Light and Darkness, the couple who created all things. There was no music.

There was only the great, solemn silence of a nearly empty cathedral built to shelter hundreds, the fragrant smoke of the hearth curling from the cutouts in Glory's forehead, and the light of the sun passing through the dome of stained glass over their heads, a shattering brilliance of color so lovely it stole the breath from Margot's lungs.

There was only Kaz, who stood behind Theodore with the plain silver box that awaited their marriage ember in his huge hands, and Viktor, who solemnly placed their offering in the fire for them.

There was only Margot and Theodore, their hands clasped, with Glory's eyes trained upon them.

I love you, he whispered to her, holding her gaze as Petra reached up to burn the marriage sigil between his brows with a fingertip gone pure, blazing white — forever branding him as *hers.*

I'm yours, she answered, taking the pain of the burning sigil gladly. The smells of burned flesh, smoke, and incense mingled. *Always.*

The burning of the sigil hurt, of course, but she took the pain with an open heart, knowing that it would tie them together in the eyes of the world forevermore. Her gaze lingered on his mark, on the sigil burning a livid dark blue in his elvish skin. Margot's heart thumped unevenly in her chest. Tears stung the backs of her eyes.

Depending on how one looked at it, their marriage sigil could be a Healer's Hand, a rising sun, or a blooming thistle — an amalgam of all that they were, and all that they wished to be.

She didn't hear Petra confirm with the witnesses that the union was complete. She didn't feel the silky tug of the ribbon releasing their hands. She didn't see or hear or feel anything besides *him,* drawing her in by their clasped hands, until Theodore's lips covered her own.

We're married. The thought bubbled up, a sparkling, brilliant thing. *I married my bondmate. I'm going to live. I'm going to love.*

I married my consort, he smartly replied, kissing her again and again and again, those big hands on her cheeks and his breath in her lungs. *Now all the world will know she's mine and see how proud I am to call myself hers.*

Margot broke away, grinning too hard to continue, and pressed her smarting forehead against his own. When their sigils touched, magic popped between them like a burst of fleeting starlight.

"You're my husband," she whispered, equal parts awed and shy.

Theodore nudged her nose with his own. There was laughter in his voice when he replied, "You're my wife." *Finally.*

Finally? She skimmed her fingertips over the line of his jaw. *You only met me a few days ago, remember?*

She expected him to reply privately, his voice clear and strong in her mind, but Theodore surprised her. Straightening, he turned to look into Glory's eyes, glowing red and yellow with the fire inside her. "No," he said, voice thick, "Glory made me yours twenty-five years ago and I'm going to thank her every day for it."

Margot's throat seized when he turned dark eyes gone shiny with tears back to her. He cupped her cheek, smiling crookedly. "My fierce halfling, I was made to love you."

Falling in love, Margot thought, was not what she thought it was. A private person by nature and circumstance, she always assumed that the feeling came on in inches, a slow creep of Tempest's rising tide one didn't notice until it was too late to escape it.

Standing before Glory's altar, Margot realized that it wasn't always like that. Sometimes love was like walking down a dark staircase and missing a step — terrifying, unexpected, with a quick drop and breathless landing. Sometimes love didn't wait for you to be ready. Sometimes it came into being fully formed, beautiful and new and strong.

Too overcome with feeling to say anything, Margot wordlessly accepted the ornate silver tongs Petra handed to her and knelt with Theodore before the altar to choose the ember they would carry with them for the rest of their lives. His hand was huge and warm and leather-smooth over her own unsteady one; his much bigger body enfolding itself around hers from behind to block out the world.

I don't get this part, he said, a note of endearing confusion in his inner voice. *How are we supposed to choose which one is the right one?*

Even the voice in her mind was watery with emotion when she answered, *You're just supposed to go with what feels right.*

He pressed a kiss to the crown of her head. *You choose, then. You're the blessed one, remember?*

Margot had never really considered being a gloriana a blessing, but... *I guess I am,* she allowed, letting intuition guide their hands toward an ember that burned white-hot beneath several others.

Being a gloriana seemed like a burden and then a curse for most of her life, a designation that did her no good when she couldn't live up to her full potential and did even less for her when it began to kill her. But without it, she would never have met Theodore. Without the cold breath of Grim on her shoulder, she would not have run off to San Francisco. She would not have their marriage sigil burning the skin of her forehead, nor would she have his arms around her, steadying her, guarding her from all the world.

In that light, it was the greatest blessing of her life.

Margot turned to deposit the crackling ember into the small silver box Kaz held out to her. His expression was deeply grooved with indecipherable emotion, his gaze lowered as she gently lowered the symbol of their union into his hands. Rising from his kneeling position, he offered it to Petra, who covered the open box with both hands.

There was a shift in the air, a sudden warmth like a stifling summer breeze, as the rings of light in her eyes blazed. It only lasted a moment. Almost as soon as it arrived, that foreign warmth disappeared, leaving the incense-heavy air of the cathedral chilly in comparison.

"There," Petra announced, indicating the couple should rise with an elegant twist of her wrist. She shut the silver box with a definitive *clack.* "Your sigils are burnt. Your ember will blaze." A small, genuine smile stole across her beautiful face, transforming it into something heart-stoppingly radiant. "Your marriage is sealed. May you walk forevermore in Glory's light. Congratulations."

A howl went up, low but ecstatic, the haunting sound bouncing off the cathedral walls to multiply and transform itself into a melody of celebration. Margot grinned even as a hot blush stole across the skin of her chest and neck.

When she peered at him, she found Viktor with his head back, his sandy hair falling out of its carefully combed position as he let the whole Temple and all of San Francisco know of his approval.

Theodore shook his head, but he couldn't stop the grin from twisting the corners of his mouth upward. *Coyotes,* he mentally sighed. *The loudest shifters in the world.*

Viktor's howl ended with a hoot of very *human* delight. Snapping his head back to grin at the couple, he bounced forward on long, muscular legs and gave Theodore several wallops on the back. "I'll be damned! I'm going to be honest, there was a part of me that definitely thought you were going to chicken out when the sigil part came up."

Slinging an arm around her shoulders, Theodore used drawing her in close as an excuse to evade any more of Viktor's thumps. "I *told* you not to question me," he archly replied.

Viktor backed off with his hands up, an unrepentant look on his handsome face. "I was just doing my job, Teddy. It's nothing personal."

"Your job?" Margot lifted her eyebrows. "What job?"

With painstaking care, Kaz tucked the ember into the inner pocket of his suit, saying, "The one where he nearly made my brother tear his hair out by questioning his motives for marrying you and threatening to end him if he treated you poorly."

"Oh, that's all?" She lifted her shoulders in a shrug, ignoring the incredulous look her new husband aimed her way. "Of course. That's what my family would have done."

"See?" Viktor pointed at Margot, vindicated. "I told you!"

Theodore moved his arm from around her shoulders to cup the back of her neck. Twisting to give Petra an appreciative nod, he announced, "I think this has been enough socializing. My wife and I have a celebration waiting for us."

Margot's heart kicked as a slow, steady burn of desire sparked where his leather-covered palm massaged the back of her neck.

Falling into step with the couple as they moved to step down from the altar and down the aisle, Viktor teased, "Is there food involved? You know, most weddings have a big dinner for everyone afterwards."

Margot's steps stuttered when Theodore's silky inner voice whispered, *I have dinner plans, but not the kind I'm willing to share with him.*

Flushing a furious pink, she shot back, *Stop that! We are with people!*

There was laughter in his voice when he firmly replied, *No, I don't think I will. I like you bothered, wife of mine.*

While she stewed on that, he answered Viktor with a bland question of his own, "If we did, would you join us? I'm sure the family would love to see you again. Cammie specifically—"

Margot watched, fascinated, as the men locked eyes. In an instant, all playfulness evaporated from Viktor's demeanor. His eyes were coyote amber when he replied, "I think I'll pass."

Theodore shook his head slowly, disappointment bleeding into their bond. Not for himself, she felt, but for another. A sympathetic sort of pain. "You'll be at the Summit tomorrow, though."

Viktor looked away. His normally open expression shuttered. "Yes. Of course I will."

"Good."

Her husband cast a look over his shoulder, calling out, "And you, Priestess?"

"I cannot imagine a thing the Temple would like me to do more," Petra replied, her dry tone echoing off of the cathedral's walls. "I would not miss it for anything, Sovereign."

Satisfied, Theodore pulled Margot in close to press a hard kiss to the top of her head. Desire thrummed a steady, throbbing beat in the electric current of their bond. It warmed her from the inside out and made the beast in her stretch languidly, readying itself for the promise of pleasure.

"Good. It's about time I took my wife home, then."

Margot's thighs clenched reflexively. *For a post-wedding lunch?*

The sharp tip of a silver claw traced the line of her pounding jugular. *Only if you're willing to eat in bed.*

Why would we do that? She hid a smile as the bright, early afternoon light slanted through the open doors. Theodore urged her onward, down the steep steps, moving a little bit faster than before. Opening the door of their strategically placed get-away vehicle, he nudged her in.

Because, he answered, a growl rumbling in his chest, *once we're home, I'm not letting you out of my bed, wife.*

Margot let him usher her into the dim interior of the sleek vehicle, her pulse pounding between her legs in time with the throb of their bond. *Who says you can keep me there?*

Kaz snapped the door shut as soon as Theodore had his legs in. He was taking his own car back to the Tower, leaving them alone in the self-driving vehicle. Viktor would return to his pack until the Summit opened. Until then, it was just her and her new husband.

...Who currently had a hand up her skirt.

Theodore bent over her, crowding her against the door as he blindly reached toward the center console. The car came to life with a low purr.

Rasping in her ear, he asked, "I think the real question is: Do you honestly think you'll want to leave?"

Chapter Twenty-One

Theodore's life could be split into three epochs: *before* Margot, *waiting* for Margot, and *loving* Margot.

The last was, by a wide margin, the most pleasurable.

Theodore watched her step into his suite with a curious tightness in his chest, his eyes glued to the soft line of her back. Her long red hair fell in a mess of waves down her spine, thoroughly mussed by his searching fingers in the nearly thirty minutes it took them to drive back to the Tower and then slip unseen up to his floor. The color stood out in a flash of copper against the cream of her simple wedding gown, the cocktail dress he insisted she buy the night of their date. *I promised I'd find her a reason to wear it,* he thought, admiring the fitted bodice and a full skirt that brushed her knees. So simple, so lovely.

He felt overdressed in comparison. Stuffy even, next to her simple elegance and all that silky skin.

Goddess, he thought, watching her stride to the wall of windows that faced his large, free-floating bed. Margot was limned in the light bouncing off of the slate gray waves churning below. *She's the most beautiful woman in the world.*

She needed nothing. No adornments, no glamours or powders. She needed only to feel comfortable, to lose that knot of tension that kept her rigidly at attention, and Margot became a woman of unmatched loveliness.

And she's mine.

The woman who made him who he was, who set the course for his life, who held his bloody heart in her capable, compassionate hands — *his,* finally.

It was almost too much to bear.

Theodore leaned heavily against the closed door of his bedroom, his heart pounding a furious beat in his ears. All of his life came down to this moment and suddenly... suddenly he worried that he wasn't going to be enough for her.

Anxiety, cold and barbed, wrapped itself around his heart and *squeezed.*

Now what?

Now that Theodore *had* her, he wasn't sure what to do. What if he disappointed her? What if he failed her? What if their plan didn't work and he couldn't protect her?

His family would look after her. He knew that. He took comfort in that. But that knowledge didn't alleviate the immediate concern that he might simply disappoint the woman who was his everything. In the marathon of hard focus and determination that was his journey to get to this very moment, Theodore never considered the practicalities of *after.*

In an instant, all of the anticipation and aching desire he felt leading up to this moment transformed into brutal anxiety. *What if I can't make this good for her?* The shame of that thought, after so much build up, threatened to choke him. He wanted to bring her so much pleasure. He wanted this moment to be something she remembered all their long lives. *What if she thinks this is a mistake?*

"Hey." Theodore snapped his eyes up to meet Margot's concerned frown. She stood by the window, the pads of her fingers pressed lightly against the impenetrable glass. Half-turned to him, she reached out her free hand to beckon him over. "Hey, come here. What's wrong, baby?"

Baby. Had ever a sovereign allowed someone to call them baby before? He didn't know and didn't particularly care. Theodore *loved* it.

He crossed the room in several long strides. His trembling hand sought hers immediately, and that band of anxiety around his heart eased a little.

Drawing her into his arms so he could bury his face in her sweet-smelling hair, he shakily admitted, "Now that I have everything I've ever wanted, I'm... I'm scared I'm going to disappoint you somehow. What if I can't please you? What if you regret this? I never thought—"

Margot slid her arms under his ceremonial silk-lined cape to run her palms up and down his back. "Shh, it's okay." Pulling back a little to look into his eyes, she summed up everything he felt in one short, matter-of-fact sentence. "It's a lot of pressure, huh?"

Yes. That was it. It was an enormous amount of pressure — pressure he'd pushed on himself for so long, he no longer felt the crushing weight of it. To have that pressure suddenly *gone...* He felt unmoored, without direction, expecting to know what to do and how to succeed in this infinitely precious thing and failing.

He wanted to be perfect for her. He wanted to take the reins and step into that role he had so far occupied in their most private moments, but the ability to be assertive, to act on the driving need to win her, fled, leaving anxiety to pin him in place.

Theodore *wanted* her. He wanted to show her how much he loved her now that he finally could, but in that enormous wanting, he was paralyzed.

What if I don't do it right? What if I hurt her? What does she think of me now, when I was all over her just a few moments ago but now I can barely look at her?

His answer came when Margot stretched onto her tiptoes to circle his neck with her arms. She drew him down into the crook of her neck, whispering, "Baby, it's okay. There's no expectation here. I'm just... so happy to be with you." A small kiss to the pointed tip of his ear. "If you want me to take the lead here, I will. If you just want to lay down and cuddle with me, we will. If you want to— if you want me to bend over the couch over there, I will."

Fuck. Theodore squeezed his eyes shut against the painfully erotic image, his need and his anxiety tangling. He pressed his branded forehead against the cool skin of her exposed shoulder and sucked in a shuddering breath. The touch of the raw wound to her skin was a sharp bite of pain — bracing, erotic, a reminder that they were bound on every level.

She's mine. I'm hers. Why is this so hard all of a sudden?

"Glory help me, I want you so much I can hardly breathe," he choked out. "But I'm terrified of disappointing you now."

The fingers of one hand tangled in his hair, sending a rush of sparks down his spine. "You are not going to disappoint me. Not in anything. Certainly not in the bedroom, if that's what's worrying you. Are you not the man who made me come so hard I saw stars last night?"

He groaned. She wasn't the only one. When Margot slithered down the bed to lick a hot stripe down his stomach and then lower, until she took as much of him into her mouth as she could, Theodore thought he would never get his brain to work again.

The memory, along with the feeling of her soft, deliciously familiar body pressing hard against him, made his cock ache. Everything else about her made his chest constrict, as if it struggled to expand wide enough to hold all the love he had for her. "*Margot.*" He ran his fangs over her shoulder, too grateful for her, too awed by her for words. "I..."

"I can take the lead here, baby," she quietly reassured him, her voice soft. "Do you want me to talk to you like..."

The unsaid *like you talk to me* sent warmth through every tense muscle and overwrought nerve. Tenderness squeezed his throat until he couldn't breathe.

His halfling liked it when he whispered raw words in her ear. Theodore figured that out quickly enough, with the scent of her desire growing stronger each time he dared to provoke her, to tell her how much he wanted her. But Margot was prim, polite; she was used to hiding herself. No doubt turning the tables and taking the lead, being *verbal,* was hard for her. He could feel that sweet shyness fluttering through their bond.

But she was willing to do it for him, to take that enormous pressure off of his shoulders without hesitation.

"I love you," he told her, voice ragged. "I love you and I want you more than anything in the world. I'd follow you anywhere."

Fingers tightening in his hair, she used her free hand to stroke his shoulders, his chest, and down over the tense muscles of his abdomen to rest on the top of his belt. "Do you know what it does to me to hear your voice like that?"

Her fingers danced downward to trace the outline of his cock through his formal pants. Every nerve jolted at the slight touch. Her voice began soft, tentative, but built into a husky murmur as her confidence grew. "There's this part of me, baby, that looks at you and wants you to take me by the throat, flip my skirt up, and slam into me until I can't breathe or think or feel anything else."

Theodore's heart battered against his ribs. The image seared his mind, made it impossible to think of anything else.

Margot, bent over the back of the couch, her creamy thighs spread for him as he flipped up the skirt of her dress. His gloved hand clasped around her throat as he slid into her slick heat. The taste of her skin on his tongue as he thrust hard and fast. Her soft cries in his ear as he—

Theodore slid his hands around her waist, circling it until his clawtips touched, and breathed hot and hard against the shell of her ear. His voice was barely audible when he rasped, *"Fuck."*

Squeezing him gently, Margot continued, "But then there's this other part of me that wants to just... lay you down on that bed over there and climb on top of you like we did last night, except this time you're inside of me and I get to have you there for as long as I want." A slow, agonizing stroke. "Mostly, though, I just *want* you. I want you so bad it feels like a bruise, baby. There's no need to feel anxious about this. About us. I would have you any way I could."

"Margot, I—" His throat closed around a ragged groan. He bit her throat, instinct and need working in tandem to push aside his worry. When she gasped, her fingers curling hard around his cock through his pants, Theodore bucked into her hand. Pressure built, pulling the muscles of his spine taut.

He froze, choking back a cry. *Too much!*

Gods, but he could *not* finish before they even got to the good part. He *could not.* The shame of that, of disappointing his consort, his wife, that way *the first time* made his stomach curdle.

No, her clear inner voice, as refreshing as cool rain on his fevered skin, rang in his mind. *No, baby, it's okay. We need to take the edge off. You can't expect to have perfect stamina the first go-around. I promise, it's okay. We're both new at this, remember? It's okay.*

He shuddered. *Take the edge off?*

"Yes." Using her grip in his hair, Margot guided his head up until they locked eyes. Her expression was glazed but determined, her cheeks flushed with color and her lips bruised. "We do it quick first, then we practice. A lot."

He could only stare at her. Numbly, he repeated, "Quick first. Take the edge off."

"Right." Margot hauled him down for a hard kiss before stating in her prim healer's voice, "I'm going to take this dress off, climb onto that big bed, and then get on my knees. You're going to fuck me. No theatrics, no pressure. I want you inside me. Nothing else matters."

Before he could get his brain working enough to respond, Margot was slipping out of his arms and striding toward the bed, all business. Turning to meet his wide-eyed gaze, she reached for the hidden zipper along her ribs and pulled it down. The rest of the dress came next.

A puddle of creamy fabric lay around her feet as she toed off her little black slippers. Theodore watched, every muscle in his body locked, as her breasts moved against her simple black bra; the shape of her svelte hips, encased in matching underwear; the supple shape of her thighs as she stepped out of the circle of fabric. It took only moments for her undergarments to fall away. The sight of the black fabric sliding against her unblemished skin to drop carelessly on the floor was something even his neediest fantasies couldn't conjure.

The scent of her desire, like molten honey with a sharp bite of ozone, filled the room. Theodore breathed deeply, unable to do anything more than stand there, watching and aching as she turned to climb onto his bed. Her backside was perfectly shaped for his hands, her spine an elegant bow, and her hair, when she pushed it out of her eyes to look at him over her shoulder, was a copper ribbon he wanted to curl around his fist and *pull.*

Instinct overcame anxiety in one great, snarling heave.

Theodore was beside the bed before he realized he was moving. Wedging his thigh between her spread legs, he trapped her underneath him, anchoring them together, locking them tight. Curling the length of her hair around his gloved fist, he turned her head to one side so he could give her a ravaging, open-mouthed kiss.

He was wearing far too many clothes, but the feeling of her bare body beneath his, the sound of the whimper caught in her throat, the sight of all that naked skin against his traditional elvish suit — all of it triggered a need so deep, so fierce, it eclipsed all the sensible thoughts in his head.

That need demanded he pin her there, subdue her, make her purr for him as he showed her just how gentle he could be, how much he wanted to please her even as he refused to let her go.

Sinking his teeth into the plush cushion of her lower lip, he used their bond to say, *You're mine.*

Margot pressed back against him, the damp heat of her core soaking through the fabric stretched thin over his muscled thigh. *You're mine.*

Theodore thrust his hips against her backside, seeking relief from the terrible pressure. *I want to hear you say it, darling,* he replied, tearing his mouth from hers to bite her unmarked shoulder. *I need to hear it.*

She arched under him, a sound of surprise and pleasure bursting from her lips as he bit her again and again. It wasn't gentle, but it was what instinct told him she needed — that threat of danger, that understanding that it would never, ever be fulfilled. His halfling wanted him to be rough with her, needed the intensity that called to their basest instincts.

Her hips pressed backward, seeking. "I'm yours," she gasped.

Theodore drew himself up abruptly. His chest heaved as he scrambled to unlock the clasps on his shoulders, his eyes glued to the wanton creature beneath him. Margot turned her head to watch him. With her cheek pillowed against the comforter and her hips arched in the air, waiting for him, she embodied something wild, primal, too erotic to name.

"I love to watch you undress," she admitted, voice husky and eyes gone heavy-lidded.

A keening sound built in his throat. His fingers flew, discarding the cape thoughtlessly, then the suit jacket, then the damned collar and pressed shirt. All the while, Margot's greedy gaze traced every inch of skin he revealed, her lust a tangible pressure on his overheated flesh.

By the time he got to the buckle of his belt, he was fumbling, his aching cock too hard and too demanding to ignore. Instinct howled for her and the luscious heat waiting for him.

Unable to stop touching her, Theodore tore at his belt at the same time that he ran his left hand down her spine, tracing the bumps and valleys with the tips of his claws until he reached the swell of her backside. He gave it a firm, appreciative squeeze. The sight of his black gloves and wicked silver claws against her delicate skin was almost obscene.

She looked so delicate in comparison to his huge, dangerous claws. So breakable. Through gritted teeth, he said, "I need to take off the gloves. I don't want to—"

Margot made a soft sound of protest. When he was able to tear his eyes away from the gorgeous sight of her slick and ready for him, Theodore saw her staring back at him with eyes half-mast, pupils blown wide, her lashes casting shadows against her soft cheeks. A lock of red hair lay like a streak of copper against her jaw when she said, "No, keep them on. Just this once. I like the way they feel."

Breathe, Teddy. He had to stop for a moment and grasp his erection hard, trying to stem the build-up of furious pressure there before it was too late. *Breathe.*

Swallowing hard, he slowly lifted his lashes to find her hips swaying, urging him on. He gripped her hips automatically, instinct snapping to the fore at the hint that she might be trying to get away, to challenge him.

I'm not letting you go, he told her, raw and implacable.

Then I need you inside me, she tartly replied. *Now.*

Pulling her hips back hard against his sagging belt and half-undone slacks, Theodore leaned down to nip at her shoulder blades. His fangs left trails of red welts on her perfect healer's skin — never enough to draw more than a pinprick of blood, but enough to leave a mark. Her back arched. Her small, blunt claws dug into the comforter as he soothed the scratches with his tongue. "Theodore!"

My consort, in my bed, in my territory, calling my name. Satisfaction roared through him in a searing wave.

Dropping his hands to her thighs, Theodore spread her legs wider, accommodating his considerably larger size, and massaged the sensitive, well-loved skin there with his gloved hands.

A shudder rippled down her spine as he trailed his claws upward. Carefully using the smooth backs of his claw-caps, he brushed her soft red curls, her warm, wet skin, and the bud of her clitoris with the utmost care.

Margot's hips jerked. He watched, fascinated, as her shoulder blades drew together, the muscles bracketing her spine flexing as desire rippled through their bond. His name was a broken murmur into the comforter.

Breathe.

Theodore leaned back just enough to push his slacks and stupid, restrictive underwear down around his thighs. It wasn't dignified and he would have preferred to at least not be wearing *shoes* when he made love to his consort for the first time, but he was not about to waste even a second bothering with them when she lay before him, hips up, thighs spread, breathing soft pleas for him to give her more.

Trying to marshal even a shred of composure, Theodore gave himself a hard squeeze and breathed deeply three times. *It'll be fast, but you can still make it good, Teddy. Come on.*

"Tell me to stop if I'm hurting you," he rasped, gripping one of her thighs to spread her wider still. "You've got to tell me, darling. I can't do this if I think I might be hurting you and not know it."

Margot nodded quickly against the comforter. "I'll tell you. Promise."

Relief was immediately followed by hot, brutal anticipation. Slowly easing forward, Theodore lined himself up with her and pushed.

"Fuck!" The clasp was so tight, so hot, he had to stop almost immediately to tilt his head back and breathe, his chest expanding to its full capacity with each deep breath.

Beneath him, Margot trembled. Her fingers clawed at the comforter. She held perfectly still, the muscles of her inner thighs and shoulders rigid. Theodore blinked hard to rid himself of the stars exploding behind his eyes.

"Godsdamn it, darling." Theodore smoothed his hands over her thighs, up her backside, to clasp her around the waist. "You're so tight, it's—" He cut himself off with a groan as her muscles fluttered around him, their tense, choking grip easing ever-so-slightly to allow him a little deeper.

Theodore moved slowly, terrified of causing her more pain

than strictly necessary. Sweat slicked a path down his back. "Are you okay?"

Margot peeked at him from over her shoulder. Her cheeks were flushed red, her eyes glazed. "Yes," she whispered hoarsely. "It hurts, but it's a good hurt." Biting her lip, she leaned back into him, taking more. "Please, Theodore. I want all of you."

He groaned. Dropping onto his elbows, he pressed his chest against her sweat-slicked back and kissed her hard, desperate, with everything he had. When she parted her lips for him, Theodore thrust hard.

"Ah!" Margot lurched forward as he buried himself to the hilt, her muscles locked around him in a vice of liquid fire.

I can't take this. There was no way. Nothing, in all his life, could compare to this brutal pleasure. He'd branded himself for her, wore their marriage sigil proudly, but *this* — this was a mark on his soul, a searing brand that would be at the forefront of his mind always.

"Theodore, *please.*" Her voice was a raw plea.

Theodore forced himself to hold still, fighting the battering instinct to move, to alleviate the throbbing ache and painful pressure, as Margot gasped for air beneath him. Dragging one arm around, he clasped her throat, just like she said she wanted, and slid his lips over her cheek, her ear, her jaw.

"You're so beautiful." He pressed himself closer, nearly flattening her into the mattress, and *felt* her clench around him. Panting, he continued, "You are perfect. More than I could have ever dreamed of. This is— this is everything, Margot. Everything."

He felt the hard press of her blunted claws in his thigh a moment before she rolled her hips forward and back, barely moving in the tiny space he allowed her but enough to make them both lose their breath.

Theodore tentatively moved his hips, almost afraid of the intensity of the friction, of that liquid rippling of hot muscle around him.

Pleasure speared through him. The hand around her throat

spasmed. The need to move, to let go, was a thunderous drum beat in his head.

"Margot," he choked out, "are you—"

I can't speak. Her inner voice was bright, a flash of pure heat through his mind. *It's too much.*

Dread trickled down his spine. *Do you need me to stop?*

No! Margot's fingers clawed at his thigh. *No. I need you to* move.

I don't want to hurt you. I can't.

She shook her head. *It doesn't hurt much any more — and it was good. I told you it was good. I liked it.* He felt her hips move, rolling slightly like she was testing the fit. *I want...*

Theodore closed his teeth around the side of her neck, knowing instinctively that she would freeze, her instinct working in concert with his. It was the ultimate sign of trust, the most intimate position: Locked together, fangs pressing against paper-thin skin of a partner's jugular, holding life and pleasure in one embrace.

Do you want me to fuck you? He was painfully aware of how desperate he sounded.

It seemed impossible, but she somehow went *softer* beneath him, her body loose and open, begging him to do anything he wanted to her, trusting him to take care of everything she needed. Margot's pulse pounded against his tongue. She arched her neck, giving him more access, giving him that most primal trust.

Yes!

That was all he needed to hear.

Gripping her throat — carefully — and using his free hand to hold her hips still, Theodore let go of everything except that huge, pulsing instinct, the beast that knew *exactly* what to do.

His undone belt rattled with a musical tinkling sound as he snapped his hips forward and back, trying to find the angle and depth that would make her cry out. He knew now that Margot wasn't a particularly vocal lover, but when he did things *just* right, she made a precious, sexy little whine that filled him with pure satisfaction.

Seeking that sound, knowing that he wouldn't have long before he lost control completely, Theodore followed his instincts. Pausing long enough to haul her up, he knelt with her in his lap, one arm a band across her breasts as his claws cupped her delicate jaw.

Margot scrambled to hold on. Her hands clutched his arm as he drove into her. He couldn't move freely in this position, but he could go *deep,* and that, he discovered, was what she needed.

Her hips moved erratically against his, her thoughts a broken cascade of begging and appreciation in his mind. In this moment, all of her pitiful telepathic walls slid away, leaving her stripped bare before him, able to witness firsthand how badly she wanted him, how good he felt inside her.

Theodore knew immediately when he hit the right place inside her. He knew how much she loved the overwhelming stretch of him. He knew that the feeling of his gloved hand on her throat, his heavy arm across her chest, made her feel safe on the deepest level. He knew she never, ever wanted to do this with anyone but him.

It was too much. It would have been too much for anyone, let alone a man who had eschewed the usual elvish practice of losing his virginity when he came of age at thirty.

Her gasps, the sounds of their bodies meeting, the scent of her in his lungs, the bright streak of her pleasure in his mind — it threw him over the edge with a choked exclamation.

Pleasure exploded across every nerve, his hips moving on their own. Theodore's ears rang as that tight band of tension at the base of his spine snapped. He barely felt Margot take his hand from her hip to stroke herself, her heat gliding against the smooth leather of his gloves. He *did* feel it when she came around him, though. The rhythmic clenching of her inner walls drew another round of brutal release from him, his hips jerking hard as she tossed her head back onto his shoulder.

For several long, breathless moments, they simply sat there, their hard exhalations and pounding heartbeats the only sounds in the bedroom.

Theodore clutched her close and sagged, his muscles turned to mush, to bury his face in her hair. Aftershocks of pleasure continued to ripple up and down his spine. Every time she moved — even *twitched* — he could feel it. What's more, he could feel *her* feel it. The pleasure was almost too much for both of them, but neither were willing to move.

You know, she said, sounding sated and a little smug, *for a couple of first-timers, I think we did pretty good. Maybe could have gone a little longer, but that just means we can start again sooner, right?*

It was all he could do to huff a laugh against the hot skin of her reddened, well-bitten throat. *We need more practice.*

He felt the shiver that ran through her; could feel the desire that triggered it. The euphoria of making love with her melded with the joy of their bond, crystal clear and strong, to make his eyes prickle with unshed tears.

Margot reached up to cradle the side of his head. *You okay, baby?*

Yes, he answered. Even his inner voice was thick with tears. *I'm just happy.*

A rush of tenderness and pure adoration coursed through the bond to fill every empty, yearning place inside him. *I'm happy too. More than happy. This is so much more than I could ever... You don't understand what this means to me. A few days ago I thought I'd be lucky if I got to live. Now I'm here.*

He placed a reverent kiss against a livid bite mark. *With me?*

With you. Always.

There was nothing in the world he wouldn't do for her. *Nothing.* Theodore hugged her close, gratefulness a flame in his chest, and let time pass at a leisurely crawl.

Elves were proprietary by nature. He knew from the moment their whisper-thin bond snapped into being that Margot was *his,* but more than that, Theodore's furious determination to have her was born from gratitude. If not for the cool brush of her mind against his, her even-keeled compassion that flowed endlessly through him, he would have destroyed himself and his family.

Rage at the injustice that was his father's crimes; rage at the loss of a woman who died so brutally for him before he could know her; rage at being shackled to a people who, through their sickly fear, had put the wheels of tragedy in motion; the guilt and horror of seeing his sister's and Sam's memories of that bloody day — all of it made for a poison that coursed through him for ten long years.

All of the intensity and focus he honed into becoming the sovereign once lived in that rage. It didn't matter how much Winnie and Delilah loved him. It didn't matter that Sam held him when he suffered under the psychic weight of too many clamoring minds before he learned to shield himself. It didn't matter that Valen thought he could channel that anger into martial skill. It didn't matter that Andy lavished affection on him, that Kaz needed Theodore to be there for him as they grappled with their father's legacy, that he was enormously lucky to be alive.

His fury was a raw, living thing. It had no outlet, no recourse, no conduit. It would have consumed him — might have pushed him into the same madness that claimed his father — if not for the woman in his arms.

A psychic lancing. An infection excised from his heart. His healer, doing what she was born for: Taking the pain from him with a soft touch of her mind until it simply bled away into nothing.

It seemed almost cruel to him now, thinking about her own suffering. If only the bond were stronger. He might have been able to help her in return, to offer her the same comfort she offered him when he was at his lowest. Horror about what her family did to her in a misguided attempt to protect her remained a hot stone in his throat.

Abruptly, he asked, *Can you reverse the sigilwork on your ears?*

Margot's thoughts were sleepy, surprised. *Huh? Maybe. Why?*

Theodore skimmed his palm up her belly in a soothing stroke. *Just wondering. I want you to have the option now that you don't have to hide.*

Now fully awake, she petted his arm, her conflicting feelings a pulse in the bond. "I'm not sure I want to. I've never even seen them before." Margot paused. "Are we going to tell everyone I'm a half-b— halfling?"

Using his hand on her jaw, Theodore gently turned her head so he could meet her eyes when he answered, "I had no intention of hiding it, but it's up to you, darling. What do you want to do?"

Margot moved to disentangle herself from him. Although his first instinct was to keep her close, to continue all that luscious, necessary skin contact, he understood her need for space.

Grabbing one of his — *their* — pillows to clutch to her chest, she turned and tucked her legs underneath her. "I didn't really think about it," Margot quietly admitted. Her eyes lingered on his naked chest and lower. A hungry pulsing in the bond told him they were not yet done *practicing*. "I've been distracted."

The muscles of his stomach tightened under her scrutiny, but he kept himself from being derailed with sheer force of will. "It's up to you, darling."

"Do you think I *should*, though?"

He hesitated, not wanting to push her one way or the other. Running a hand through his mussed, slightly sweaty hair, he answered, "I think it would be good to have the sovereign's consort be openly witch *and* elf, but I never want you to do something that makes you uncomfortable. I know how you've carried this secret for so long. Expecting you to come out and tell the world right away isn't fair."

Margot chewed her swollen lower lip, her eyes downcast. "I just... I don't mind it for *me*, but I don't know who my mother is. What if she gave me up because she was ashamed of me?"

Hot fury threatened to make him see red. Voice dropping into a growl, he told her, "Darling, that's *her* problem, not yours.

Besides, if she's so ashamed, she will never see the need to associate with you, will she? No one will be able to magically divine who you're related to. This doesn't mean you have to interact with her, or even know her name." He flicked his wrist, his lip curling. "Besides, you'll outrank her."

When she met his eyes, her expression was bruised. "But what if I want to know her?"

Smothering the desire to tear the world apart for putting that look in her eyes, he promised, "Then we'll do whatever it takes to track her down. Either way it's your call."

Margot was quiet for a moment, her lower lip caught between her teeth, before she blinked hard and set aside the pillow. Crawling back to him, she curled her arms around his waist and hid her face against his chest. Theodore hugged her hard. Her trust was a gift too precious for words.

"If I could take this pain from you, I would," he confessed. "I would do it in a heartbeat."

"I know." Her breathing hitched. "I'm just— I know I need to do this. It's just going to be hard. My grandmother will lose her mind." A small pause. "More. She'll lose her mind more."

Theodore stroked her back. "I think we can handle that."

"I know we can." She pressed a small kiss to his sternum, then another to the dip between his collarbones. "I just wish I knew—"

Margot was interrupted by the insistent buzzing of his phone, still tucked into his pocket. Hissing an expletive, Theodore fished it out, fully intending on sending whatever pressing issue it represented to *mute.* Only the flash of an urgent alert stopped him.

"What?" Margot peered at the screen, her worry obvious. "What's wrong?"

Theodore squeezed his eyes shut and tried to get his breathing under control. Through clenched teeth, he answered, "We have visitors."

Chapter Twenty-Two

On the list of things Margot wanted to do in the hours immediately following her wedding, frantically urging her frustrated new husband to get into the shower and then into a fresh suit so he could meet with the second most powerful elvish family in the Protectorate, unsurprisingly, fell quite low.

Not that it mattered. Margot was a practical sort of person, and able to see the long-game even if it made her present less than ideal.

Shrugging on a soft white turtleneck over a fitted black skirt, she spared only a moment to think about the sharp ache between her legs and her longing for the huge, Theodore-scented bed. *We'll have all the time in the world after this is done,* she promised herself. Once things were settled and the Summit was over, they could have a real honeymoon and plenty of time to be together.

She said as much to Theodore, but his sulky expression told her he was even less pleased by the interruption than she was.

Adjusting his collar with quick, irritated flicks of his claws, he muttered, "I've never given Olivier the time of day before now. I don't see why I have to start on my damn wedding day."

"Because," she calmly replied, "you can't afford to make *any* enemies right now. Besides, it's just until the Summit is over.

Once it's done, maybe we can take a honeymoon somewhere, or..." She trailed off, her thoughts derailed when he turned away from the mirror to pin her with a heated look.

It's not fair how attractive he is in a suit, she thought, a coil of heat tightening her belly.

"Honeymoon?" A slow, wicked smile curled Theodore's lips.

Oh. The sight of his dimples made her heart clench. "I didn't think about that when you asked me to marry you, but we are supposed to have one of those, aren't we?"

Margot let him clasp her hips and draw her closer. Even knowing it was only delaying the inevitable, she was helpless in the face of that smile, those hands, all that naked affection in his gaze. "Do elves not have honeymoons?"

He stroked the bows of her hip bones with the pads of his thumbs. "Mm, sort of. The pull varies from couple to couple, but the rule of thumb is that an elf should be excused from public life for at least a month after courtship."

"You can't afford to be out of the public eye for that long."

Theodore shook his head, the heat in his eyes fading to something softer. "No, I can't. But we could manage a week or two."

Looking down at the buttons of his suit jacket, Margot felt strangely shy. "Maybe... we could go to the Goodeland?"

"That's... not the most private getaway."

She tugged on a button. "Well, no, but we have lots of empty cabins around the lake and in the forest. We could have our own space. And when we're ready we could have a family celebration for our wedding." Margot risked a glance through her lashes and found him staring down at her with a heart-stopping look of tenderness.

Cupping her cheek, he promised, "Darling, I will do anything you ask me to."

What heady power it was, to have the sovereign at her mercy. Margot tilted her head into his hand, the memory of his kisses and the weight of him pressing her into the mattress lingering on her skin.

Theodore Solbourne knelt at her feet, true, but Margot knew she would only ever use that power to love him bigger, better, with all she had.

Overwhelmed by the enormity of her feelings, Margot stretched up on her tiptoes to press a quick kiss to his lips. "Then let's get this over with," she announced, darting away before he could reel her back in for more. Margot fished a tiny stub of chalk from her skirt pocket — no witch in their right mind *didn't* carry something to write with in every article of clothing — and wiggled it at him. "C'mere."

With a beleaguered sigh, Theodore bent to let Margot trace a chalk sigil high on his forehead. There was a small flash of heat before both it and their marriage sigil disappeared.

"Oh." Margot blinked, surprised by the force of her displeasure at the sight of bare skin between his brows.

Theodore turned to glance in the floor length mirror in the center of his dressing room. His thick eyebrows first rose high, then dropped low in a deep scowl. Whirling around to face her, he growled, "I hate this."

Avoiding the sight of his sigil-less forehead by repeating the procedure on herself before dusting off her hands, Margot forced a shrug. "It's only for today. You get to show everyone at the opening of the Summit tomorrow, right?"

His tone was biting. "Yes, but a day is too long. Hiding it feels like an insult."

She agreed that it sure *felt* wrong. Margot got an awful little shiver when she looked at him, and she had no desire to peer at her own reflection. His face looked bare, wrong. The magic infused in that sigil, unique to them in all the world, did not appreciate being hidden beneath a glamour any more than they did.

A rumbling sound of displeasure spilled from Theodore's chest, but when he bent to press his forehead against hers, the sweet *zing* of pleasure-pain made them both sigh. It was a kiss of magic, of the promise they made to one another. It didn't go away just because his sigil was momentarily hidden.

Neither of them had to *like* it, though.

"Go," she urged, giving his chest a pat. "Your guest awaits."

"You'll be in the next room. Door cracked, so I can hear you if you need me." Theodore didn't move until she nodded. "Fine, then. Let's get this over with."

Margot settled into the sitting room beside Theodore's enormous study. It was more like a small library than a living room, with walls covered in enormous, custom-built shelves. The Tower had an Art Nouveau aesthetic on the outside, but within it was a curious mix of natural woods and streamlined, modern furniture.

She sat on an angular gray sofa that didn't look particularly comfortable, but proved to be as plush as any heavily padded couch she knew. The rug under her feet was thick and well-made, the furnishings scattered around the room all dark wood polished to a high finish. The chrome and finely-wrought glass light fixtures were unnecessary on such a bright day, especially with the wall of windows that, somehow, every room in the Tower managed to boast. The room was, like everything else, a mix of the new and the old that struck her as distinctly *elvish.*

Settling into her seat, Margot tried to ignore the door to her left, the one tucked between two towering bookshelves that connected the sitting room with Theodore's study. Someone had laid out a spread of fruit, bread, and cheeses on the low table by the sofa. Probably Andy, who had remained discreetly out of sight but whose touch Margot could see in the vase of white roses and the faint scent of soft perfume in the air.

Margot was hungry, certainly. Their afternoon activities left her ravenous, but... She glanced at the door reflexively. *I want to eat with him.*

But that was silly. He had extremely important business to

attend to — business she could hear coming his way, as a man's low, angry voice carried down the hall — and it wasn't like there was anything he would enjoy on the table anyway.

It's normal. Theodore's inner voice was a stroke in the back of her mind, a loving touch that soothed a tension she didn't even know she carried. *The pull makes separation difficult, darling. Don't worry about it. We'll be back together soon enough.*

Margot shook her head to clear it and stood up from the sofa to pace the room, scanning the shelves without really seeing them. Despite Theodore taking the time to explain what she was going through, what the elvish half of her kept trying to tell her, Margot struggled to reconcile the urges with the rational, human part of herself.

It just feels weird to miss you this much when we've only been separated for a minute. She ran her fingertips along the glass encasing a row of leatherbound books, walking aimlessly. *I'm not a particularly clingy person, usually.*

I like you clingy, he replied. *I hope that never changes.*

Margot didn't fight the besotted smile that stole across her mouth. It didn't surprise her to find that she'd wandered toward the door. Stopping to lean her forehead against the edge of a shelf, Margot imagined him standing on the other side. Her stomach fluttered.

Sending a surge of pure affection through the bond, she answered, *I don't mind it. It's just different. But you'll have to tell me more about how the pull—*

A sharp knock cut her off.

Straightening, Margot grasped the edge of the bookcase and leaned toward the door, terribly curious about what the heir to the du Soleil family would have to say to Theodore. Although she'd never met them, they were the only elvish family she was truly familiar with — mainly through old business records that she spent one long, stifling summer organizing as a teenager.

At one point, the du Soleil family and the Goodes had several lucrative business deals between them; mainly property investments and joint ventures in m-tech, including the development of the first ID chips. Elves were legendary for trying to poach Coven talent for their m-tech R&D, just as the Collective was coldly practical about keeping that talent in-house.

A joint venture where both parties benefited and no one gave up total rights to their intellectual property was rare, but they managed it beautifully for a decade before the du Soleils abruptly ended their contracts.

Theodore's voice was coolly distant when he called out, "Come in, Laurence."

Who's Laurence?

The captain of my guard, he answered easily, the warmth of his inner voice in stark contrast to the chill he projected for his guest. *Non-family guests have to be escorted onto the family floors and supervised by a guard at all times. Mr. du Soleil wants only the best, so he gets a captain.*

The sound of the study door opening prompted her to lean a little closer to the door, her curiosity impossible to ignore.

A man's voice, low and velvety, came through the small opening between the door and the jamb. "Mr. du Soleil, Sovereign. Would you like for me to stay?"

Theodore's answer was immediate and blasé. "No, I'm sure we won't need a chaperone. Thank you, Laurence."

"Of course." There was a small pause, the faintest sound of shoes on hardwood floors, before the door opened and closed again.

"What can I do for you, Olivi—"

"What fucking game are you playing?" Margot reared back, shocked by the pure vitriol in that cultured snarl. She could feel Theodore's surprise through their bond, a small burst of emotion that set her teeth on edge.

In a mild voice, her husband replied, "I'm afraid you're going to have to elaborate."

Hackles raised, Margot pressed herself as close to the door as she dared. A hint of the man's scent filtered through the gap in the door, carried by a draft of warm air from the vents above.

Being half-elvish had a few distinct benefits, and one of those was her sense of smell. She knew by scent alone that Olivier du Soleil was a man who liked expensive things. In his scent there was a thread of rich, amber cologne. Leather polish. Beeswax. The hint of musk particular to him alone.

That last thread, nearly hidden by all the rest, triggered an immediate physical reaction.

Cold sweat broke out across her chest and behind her bare knees. Her stomach knotted so tightly it felt like her insides were being squeezed in a vice. Her hands, steady since her bonding, began to shake once more.

I know that scent.

A fragment of memory she did her best to bury burst to life behind her eyes. She barely registered Olivier's biting reply. "Do I? Really? You don't think I know *exactly* what you're doing? You think you can come after our most vulnerable and we'll just stand by and *let you do it?*"

A dark room. Too dark to see anything except the shapes her mind conjured. Soft walls, soft floor, but spongy, like the weird stuff they put on playgrounds so kids don't scrape their knees too bad when they fall. The sense of time passing in between bouts of screaming hysteria and the snap of her bones breaking themselves, over and over, her muscles shriveling and expanding in agonizing bursts. And hunger. So much terrible hunger.

A muffled voice from far away: "...not eating enough. It's not good for her. I'm going... help the..."

"Olivier." Theodore's voice was hard, his authority snapping like a whip through the fog of an agonizing memory. Margot shook herself.

No, she had to be wrong. Her memories of that time were shattered. A week of hell, existing in total darkness as her body turned on itself in a process that no witch could explain to her; the only time in her life when she had contact with her elvish relatives as they took over her care for what she later learned was called *the change.*

What did it say about her family that the only time they bothered with her was when it required locking her, hysterical, terrified and without explanation, in a padded pitch-black cell for a week?

Margot never saw their faces. She couldn't remember a kind word. All she recalled was someone forcing water down her throat periodically. The scent of iron in her nose as her blunt claws tore through her skin, desperate to end the pain.

The endless, pressing darkness.

She was sixteen when the change hit her like a truck. It only took a week, but that week wiped away any fantasies Margot might have harbored about one day walking openly as a half-breed. If *that* was what being an elf was, she doubted she could survive any more of it.

The scars of that week lingered still if not in the flesh, then in the way she *still* couldn't stand the dark.

"I have no idea what you're talking about. I promise you, I haven't spared you more than a passing thought in months. I *definitely* haven't been plotting to hurt you *or* your family." Theodore snorted. "I have been pleasurably distracted."

"Really?" The single word was laced with so much contempt, it made even Margot recoil.

There was a rustle of paper, then the sound of something slapping against a hard surface. "What do you call this, then, *Sovereign?*" Olivier didn't give Theodore time to answer. "This is how you're getting back at us for opposing Delilah's abdication. You found her, and now you're using her to hurt us. You know, I've never liked you, Solbourne, but *this*— I didn't know you were capable of this kind of cruelty. She's an innocent, for Glory's sake!" A sharp intake of breath followed. In a voice that trembled with rage, Olivier continued, "If you don't release her to our custody this instant, I swear, I will tear your throat out where you stand."

There was a curious stillness in the bond, as if Theodore was *so* surprised that nothing, not even annoyance or worry or amusement filtered through it. In an odd voice, he said, "I can assure you that she is *not* a prisoner."

The sound of paper crunching, as if it was snatched up quickly and crumpled in a fist, came with an unfamiliar, hair-raising growl. "First, you stage a bombing to send a message. Then you take her into your custody and shove her in a hole somewhere so we can't get to her. I don't know what you're holding over the Collective to get them to put out that farce of a statement but— *Now* you say to my face that she isn't your prisoner? What are you doing with her, then, hm? What the fuck else could you want with her other than to try and keep us in line?"

Darling. Theodore's voice was cautious, indecipherable. *Will you join us for a moment?*

Margot's heart slammed against her ribs. *Is he... Is he talking about me?*

It was a stupid question, but her brain couldn't process what she overheard. Of course Olivier had to be talking about her. But... *why?*

Just come in, darling, Theodore coaxed. *I don't think he's going to listen to a thing I say, so this may be the most expedient option.* He paused before speaking again, his mental tone hardening. *You don't have to worry. I won't let him hurt you.*

Her answer was immediate. *I know.*

Good. Will you come in before he tries something foolish?

"What are you doing? Where are you going?" Olivier's voice rose, his fury beating at the walls in a raw, magical wave. "Don't walk away from me, damn it! Fucking *answer* me!"

Margot jumped. That raw bellow, full of rage and tightly bound worry, hit her like a hammer-blow. She stood, frozen, as her husband pulled the door to the study open. Reaching out to cup the side of her head, Theodore half-turned to arch a brow at a man she couldn't yet see. "Olivier du Soleil, meet Margot Elloise Goode. My consort."

Margot took half a step into the room, her heart in her throat.

Theodore stepped with her. His hand slid down to cup the back of her neck as she stood face to face with one of the most powerful elves in the country.

She knew Olivier's face in passing. For all that he was young, Olivier was known the world over for his startling financial acumen and ruthless business practices. Although the businesses he owned were prosperous and his many, many employees never had a bad word to say about how he handled things to the media, the elf was also known for burning down rivals with cold efficiency.

Every few months, the news would run some story or another featuring the latest du Soleil conquest. Usually they would throw up a grim-faced headshot clearly torn from the du Soleil's own PR department, but sometimes they caught him exiting an m-jet or train, or climbing into a car no doubt headed for the du Soleil territory of Malibu.

She was passingly familiar, then, with the stark, bone-white hair carefully combed behind pointed ears. She knew the aristocratic features, elegant in all the ways Theodore was hard, almost blocky. She knew the copper skin tone, a shade off from true topaz. She even knew the bright, burnished gold eyes, though they were often concealed by dark sunglasses.

What she didn't expect was his towering height, greater even than her husband's, nor the expression of slack-jawed shock on his severe face.

The crumpled newspaper hanging loosely from his limp fingers and featuring a grainy photo of her and Theodore climbing into a car, their hands intertwined, was also unexpected. Above the photo, she could just make out a headline that read, ***SOVEREIGN AND HEALER? THE MATCH OF THE CENTURY!***

Olivier's eyes, wide enough to show the white all the way around his gold irises, locked onto her face. For a long, tense minute, no one spoke. No one except Theodore, who stood with a relaxed sort of readiness that hid the tension she *knew* he felt, seemed capable of it.

Finally, with a reflexive crunching of the newspaper in his hand, Olivier choked out, "Gods, Solbourne, *what have you done to her?*"

Unease was a tangled knot in her belly, the sense of familiarity between her and Olivier increasing with every word, with every draw of his scent into her lungs. The implication of what that might mean made her knees weak.

Baby, I know him.

Theodore's voice was so gentle. *Tell me how.*

He was there. In the dark. During my change, I swear, I heard his voice.

She leaned into Theodore just as he slid his arm around her shoulders, drawing her into the study. Nothing would soothe away the scars of that time in the dark, not even the gentle explanation that her experience with the change wasn't at all unusual. The memories bit at her heels, more real than when she explained the terror of that week to Theodore the previous night.

Margot's voice trembled. "He hasn't done anything to me. Theodore's my..." The words fell from numb lips.

Olivier wasn't listening. His eyes were fixated on the point at which she and Theodore were connected — his big, gloved hand curving to hold the dip in her waist like it was made to fit there.

Slowly, the surprise bled out of Olivier's expression. It was replaced with the cold type of rage that would terrify any sentient being with a shred of self-preservation.

With his white hair and hard, pitiless gaze, Olivier du Soleil looked like a man carved from pure ice. When he spoke, there was no inflection, none of the raw intensity of before. His voice was flat, hard. "Take your hands off of her. Now."

Theodore didn't stop drawing her slowly around his huge, live edge desk. His posture was totally relaxed as he put the hulking piece of furniture between them. "No."

Olivier didn't blink. He held Theodore's stare even as the

newspaper slid from his hand. His gloves, Margot noticed, were silver-tipped too, but made of gray suede to match his charcoal, pin-striped suit and light overcoat.

In that inflectionless voice, Olivier asked, "So this is your scheme? To repeat history and strike at the heart of us at the same time?"

Theodore didn't rise to the bait. Still, she felt his claws flexing over her ribs, his only tell. "You always had an overblown sense of your own importance, Olivier." He pulled her closer, nearly tucking her under his arm. *I'm safe,* she thought, the shadows of her nightmares receding. *I'm safe with him.*

Theodore stroked her side, his protectiveness a steady current in their bond. "But in this I can *absolutely* assure you, neither you nor your family played any role in my relationship with my consort."

"Bullshit." The single word was cutting; almost as sharp as the look he leveled at Margot when he snapped, "Come here."

She stared, astonished, as Olivier lifted one of his gloved hands and crooked his fingers — *beckoning her.*

Margot's eyebrows hit her hairline. "Excuse me?"

"I don't know what he's told you, but whatever it is, he's lying to you. Step away from him." Olivier curled his fingers sharply. "Come *here.*"

Theodore let out a low whistle. "Big mistake."

Margot acknowledged Theodore with an absent wave of her hand, her indignation rising to a boiling point the longer she stared at Olivier du Soleil's imperious little sneer.

"Who do you think you are?" Margot felt the crackle of electricity in her veins, in her hair, as her temper snapped. "You think you can call me over like a *dog?* You don't even know me!"

Olivier blinked, his arm lowering a fraction as he took in the crackle of electricity around her eyes. He almost looked startled — for a moment. "I don't have time for this. I need you to step away from the sovereign *now,* Margot! Don't make me come over there and separate you."

Oh, she wanted to swipe that cold, imperious look off of his sharply handsome face! It was bad enough that he thought he could order her around — *her,* a healer, a gloriana, a fucking *Goode!* — but threatening to get between her and her husband? It snapped what few chains remained on that clawing thing inside her.

Theodore warned her that increased aggression was one of the main reasons elves in the grip of the pull were generally left alone, but until then, she couldn't have comprehended the whiplash of fury that scorched a path through her at the *idea* of being separated from him.

Margot lunged, fingers curled into claws, and might have made it across the desk if Theodore didn't already have his arm around her waist, restraining her easily. She snarled, fighting to be free so she could get rid of the man who wanted to take her husband from her, who dredged up all those terrible, scarring memories like they were nothing.

"Shh, darling," Theodore soothed. He ignored the startled elf on the other side of the desk. Petting her hair, he leaned down to murmur in her ear. "It's okay. I'm not going anywhere." When she stopped fighting him, her chest heaving, he pressed a hard kiss to the crown of her head. "There now. Everything is okay. He doesn't know."

Lifting his head to send Olivier a wide, sharp-toothed smile, Theodore explained, "You're lucky I was here. If my consort got to you, there'd be nothing left to find." He cocked his head to one side, his playfulness barely concealing an anger that roared through their bond. "The only reason I didn't let her do it, by the way, is because *she* would regret it. I might actually enjoy seeing you torn apart. My consort is softhearted, though."

"She is *not* your consort." Olivier's voice hadn't changed, but the way he held himself, the shifting of his weight on his expensive Italian shoes, gave the air of tightly restrained menace.

Theodore didn't argue like Margot expected him to. Instead, he stroked her hair calmly and asked, "Then what is she?"

Olivier slammed a hand on the polished surface of Theodore's desk, his claw-caps raking across the wood with a terrible ripping sound. "She's my *sister!*"

~

On the list of things he wanted to do in the hours after marrying the woman of his dreams, sitting across from Olivier du Soleil as he glared holes in the side of his head didn't even make it onto the page.

Theodore rubbed his eyes in time with the soothing circles he drew on Margot's tense back. *Of all the families, she* had *to be a du Soleil.*

What a price to pay for an otherwise perfect partner! In-laws who not only hated him on principle, but who he would happily see tied to the pylons at the bottom of the Golden Gate.

It was not just because they made his life as difficult as they possibly could in the months leading up to Delilah's abdication, but because he now knew they put the shadows in Margot's eyes; were responsible for the hurt she wore so close to her heart. The political machinations he could accept. The treatment of his consort he could *never* forgive.

But Margot needed him to be the level head in the room right now. Olivier was still entirely convinced that Theodore was plotting to ruin his family by destroying Margot, and *she* was... not entirely present.

Worry gnawed at Theodore when he glanced at her. Margot was pale, her eyes locked on her kneecaps, her soothing inner voice distressingly silent. Instinct urged him to pull her into his lap and nuzzle her until that icy distance shattered, but man and sovereign knew that wasn't the answer.

Dropping his hands to dangle his fingers between his bent knees, he said, "Explain, Olivier. Don't just stare."

He could feel that icy glare trying to drill holes in him, but

Theodore was made of sterner stuff than the lean, handsome elf sitting in the gray arm chair across from him.

Olivier's sharp jaw worked, the muscles clenching and unclenching as he no doubt fought the instinctive urge to snap back. Theodore caught his quick glance at Margot and watched, fascinated, as the man swallowed his acerbic response.

Keeping his eyes on Margot, Olivier said, "My mother Tatiana had an affair with George Goode twenty-five years ago. Margot is the result of that affair."

He felt Margot stiffen as a streak of horror passed through their bond. *Oh, gods, my mother was married?*

Unlikely, he assured her. *I believe she has a union with the du Soleils, but like most unions, it's for business and procreative purposes. Affairs are very common amongst our kind, darling, remember?*

Margot's fingers clenched in the hem of her skirt. *How common?*

Cursing himself, he ran his hand up and down her back with more urgency, like that might take the sting out of his words. *Amongst unions? Very. Amongst consorts? Never.*

So you won't...

Theodore's heart ached for the soft, tremulous sound of her inner voice. *Never. Never, darling.*

Reining in the temper that wanted to take a swipe at the whelp for bringing up a subject that neither he nor his consort enjoyed, Theodore bit out, "Explain to me why she was left with her human family and not, as is the standard, raised in seclusion with those who would *protect* her."

Olivier crossed his arms over his chest. Everything in his posture and expression screamed that he did not want to answer, but when his gaze flicked in Margot's direction, he took in the pallid state of her skin, her distant gaze, her white-knuckled fists, and gave in. "Mother isn't... she's not well," he admitted. "She hasn't been well for a long time. After my birth, she suffered through many losses. Too many. Her and my father struggled to have another child for too long."

Olivier paused long enough to meet Theodore's eye. A silent understanding passed between them. No one spoke about those great, tearing losses, but everyone knew someone who suffered them. *Another reason to end this suicidal experiment in self-preservation.*

"Mother was happy when she spent time with her lover," Olivier continued. He closed his eyes, the ripples of painful memories bleeding across his face.

Damn, Theodore thought sourly, *I hate to sympathize with him.*

"I was too young to understand it at the time, but I remember her coming home from business trips in the Goodeland and being... better. Lighter." He shook his head. "When she discovered she was pregnant? It was a miracle. Father was overjoyed, of course. He only ever wanted her to be happy. When they found out she was pregnant, he was ecstatic."

Theodore felt Margot jolt with surprise. No doubt it was a shock to her that Marcus would eagerly anticipate the birth of a child he didn't father, but it made sense to Theodore. *Any* child was a gift — a child born to the woman he loved even moreso. After all, a union didn't mean there was no love between them. In all likelihood, Marcus cared deeply for Tatiana and would have loved her daughter just as much. Any self-respecting elf would.

Olivier rolled his tense shoulders, as if the memories made him restless. "But Mother... Mother was afraid. Every day, she lived in terror that it would be another loss."

He swallowed hard. "I remember those days clearly. The fear was a kind of madness. She'd shut herself up one day, convinced too much exertion would poison the pregnancy, and then refuse to sleep indoors the next night, telling us only fresh air would keep the baby healthy. It went on like that until the day..." His eyes opened to fix on Margot with a soft, longing look that shocked Theodore. "Until the day you were born."

Theodore felt Margot unthaw a little, her eyes lifting to focus on her half-brother with all the cautiousness of a bruised creature.

Olivier leaned forward in his chair, apparently forgetting Theodore for the moment, and clasped his hands between his knees. "Margot," he said, earnest, "I was there. Your grandmother invited us to use a cabin in the Goodeland for your birth. We stayed there for a week, and when you came, my father was the one to cut the cord. He was so proud." Olivier's voice broke. "But I was the first to hold you, after Mother. You were so small, I... I've never loved anything so fiercely as I love you."

Margot's voice was surprisingly steady when she asked, "Why did you leave me there, then?"

A flash of pain and stark concern pulled the skin tight over Olivier's cheekbones. "Were you mistreated in the Coven? Father was in contact, and we were assured you'd be treated no different from any other child. We thought—"

"No, I had a good life," she interjected. "I was loved. I had everything I wanted. I got a good education and I grew up proud to be a witch." A tremor entered her voice as she lifted her chin to finish, "But I grew up thinking that I was *wrong*. That someone would lock me up or— or worse for just being what I was. And I... and I would have done *anything* to know I was wanted by my mother. By any of you."

Olivier was silent for several beats. Theodore wondered if, like him, he felt his heart tearing in his chest. If the wet sheen in his averted eyes was any indication, he thought so.

When he spoke, Olivier's voice was a hard rasp of old pain. "Mother was... She was adamant that the only way you could grow up healthy was to be raised outside of the Protectorate." He raked his claws through his hair. It was disturbing to see the icy, tightly controlled thorn in Theodore's side so disheveled, off his guard.

"In some ways she was right. If you'd been raised in the household, you would never have had *any* freedom. You would have been kept out of sight and wrapped in cotton wool, never allowed to roam or live freely. You might have been contracted in a loveless union." Theodore let loose a warning growl. Olivier scowled, allowing begrudgingly, "Or perhaps not. Either way, Mother was adamant that you should be raised by the Goodes. But if anyone in the upper tiers of the hierarchy were to discover you..."

Theodore leaned back into the sofa's cushions, a bitter taste taking root in his mouth. "They would have reported your existence and removed you from their care, no matter what your mother wanted."

She turned to blink big, wet eyes at him. "But *why?*"

"Because we're dying, darling," he gently reminded her. "Every elf, halfling or not, is too valuable to lose."

"Mother's greatest fear was that you wouldn't get the chance to live." Olivier's voice was equally gentle, his sorrow shockingly open. "She was willing to sacrifice anything to secure that chance, even if it meant not being a part of your life."

Margot shuddered. Circling her back with his arm, Theodore drew her in close as the tears came. Her voice was rough when she asked, "Where is she now?"

Olivier sighed, long and full of feeling. "She stays in our estate. The stress of the pregnancy, then giving you up... She was already unwell, but she got worse after that. These days, she is much happier when she stays inside her peaceful bubble."

"O-oh." Margot clutched his shirt. "Do you think she will want to see me someday?"

The chill returned to Olivier's expression with frightening speed. Spearing Theodore with a hard look, he said, "I imagine she will demand it as soon as the news reaches her that you've been taken prisoner."

Theodore blew out an astonished breath. "Back to this? Olivier, she's my *consort.*"

"I don't believe you." His handsome face twisted in a sneer. "This *would* be just the sort of twisted scheme you would use to get revenge on us for our valid concerns over—"

Enough of this. Using his free hand, Theodore swiped hard at the chalk mark on his forehead, smearing it until the magic could no longer hold. Immediately, his skin prickled with intense relief.

"For Glory's sake," he exclaimed, gesturing to his forehead with a sharp twist of his wrist, "if she wasn't my consort, do you think I would have *married* her?"

Chapter Twenty-Three

Margot wasn't sure how she felt about having a brother. She wasn't sure how she felt about suddenly having a father, either.

Actually, she wasn't sure about having *three* new brothers, grandparents, and whatever Winnie Solbourne née Yadav was to her.

She might have adjusted to having in-laws easily enough — they had, after all, known her far longer than she knew them and treated her accordingly — but they weren't the only ones who now claimed Margot as their own. It turned out that the du Soleils, now free of their self-imposed isolation order, were a viciously possessive family.

In the hours after her first, tense meeting with Olivier, Margot found herself swept into one luxurious suite of guest rooms after another. The du Soleil delegation was large and every single member of the family wanted to meet her. If she wasn't so used to dealing with a massive Coven, Margot might have crumbled under the pressure and emotional stress of so much, so soon, but she leaned on her lifetime of Goode family politics and the soothing touch of Theodore's mind to get her through it.

He offered to accompany her, of course, but she knew he had

too many fires to put out and too many people to see before the Summit to make that a practical choice. As much as it pained both of them, she grimly reapplied his glamour and sent him on his way.

The du Soleils were a snooty lot, but their acceptance of her felt genuine. They peppered her with questions about her upbringing, about healing, about what Margot liked and whether she would spend time in their Malibu estate now that the secret was out.

Margot answered their questions to the best of her ability, but demurred on making any plans to see them. Truthfully, she wasn't sure she was ready for that yet.

She wasn't ready for *any* of it, really, but fate didn't care to wait for her to adjust to her new life with Theodore before thrusting everything else her way. Exhausted to her marrow, Margot only narrowly escaped being trapped into sleeping in Marcus du Soleil's suite — the man who seemed to wear his fatherly solemnity like a cloak and who looked almost identical to Olivier — by Kaz, who extracted her from the possessive clutches of her new family with a firm order from the sovereign.

She crawled into Theodore's massive bed bonelessly, her emotions buzzing under her skin like static. Theodore came in sometime later, when she was half-asleep and curled around one of his pillows, her nose buried in the spot that smelled most like him.

"What's this?" he murmured, pulling the comforter back to reveal a simple, strappy nightgown.

"S'jamas." Margot blinked blearily up at him, relieved to feel his ungloved hands sliding over her shoulders and down her arms — beautiful, vital skin contact at last.

He *tsk*ed. "I thought we agreed on no clothes in bed." Theodore pulled the comforter all the way down, revealing her bare legs to the slightly colder air of the room.

Only then did she realize he was nearly undressed himself. Squinting in the dark — why couldn't she have gotten the famed elvish night vision? — Margot could just make out his bare chest and undone slacks sagging around his narrow hips.

Very much awake, Margot turned onto her back to allow him better access to her nightgown. Theodore immediately pushed it up and over her head. Watching his shadow throw it aside like it offended him, she replied, "You weren't here. Didn't think it counted."

Shucking his slacks and underwear, Theodore made quick work of joining her in bed. "You knew I would come."

She smiled into the dark, shy but pleased. "Maybe I just like it when you undress me."

Theodore drew her close, sealing them together from chest to thigh as he tilted her chin up for a long, thorough kiss. *I missed you,* he told her as he nibbled on her lower lip. *I hated leaving you with strangers. I hate having you out of my sight.*

Margot smoothed her palms over his back. The play of his muscles under his smooth, blue skin was a delight she doubted would *ever* get old. *I missed you, too. Not having you next to me feels wrong.*

Even knowing he was but a thought away, being physically separated became harder to bear as time went on. The discomfort began as an itch under her skin, but grew into an ache that spread inward, settling into her bones and teeth and fingernails until she could think of little else *except* finding him, touching him in any way she could.

Although it made Olivier's handsome face pucker, even he had to accept that she and Theodore were consorts when the symptoms of the pull became so obvious. It was, she thought, probably the only reason he and Marcus agreed to let her return to Theodore at all.

Not that she would have tolerated them keeping her from Theodore for much longer, anyway. A flare of indignation *still* raised her hackles when she thought of Olivier's high-handed command in Theodore's study. Brother or not, best of intentions or not, *no* one got to order her around.

Well, maybe Theodore, she allowed. But that was only because he enjoyed pricking her temper.

Clutching him close, Margot arched her back when he rolled a nipple between his fingers, pinching gently. His tongue slid along hers in slow, languorous strokes, petting her, soothing the ache that built and built in the hours since their frantic joining. His scent of cedar and cinnamon and man mingled with her own, creating a heady perfume that wiped away all rational thought.

When he rocked her against the hot bar of his erection, she met him eagerly, her pulse a heavy, distracting beat between her thighs. Theodore hoisted her leg over his hip before asking, *Are you too sore?*

For you? Never.

Theodore ripped his mouth away from hers to bury his face in her neck with a grating sound of pure want. His fangs closed over her throat. Once again, Margot was shocked by the pure eroticism of the hold, by the way her body fell limp and languid under him when he rolled them over.

Safe, her other half purred. *Cared for. Loved. Pleasured. His.*

Her arms fell over her head in a boneless slump as he spread her thighs wide around his hips. She knew for a fact that it would take only the slightest amount of pressure for Theodore to slice her jugular with those wicked fangs. Even without knowing that the average elf had a bite force that outstripped a human's by the *hundreds,* even a simple turn of his head could send those sharp incisors slicing through delicate skin and tissue.

Safe, her instincts purred. *He'd never hurt me.*

Margot's other half pressed close to the surface, luxuriating in the dangerous hold. She didn't care to fight it. It felt *good* to give him her absolute trust, to feel her bones and muscles melt into pure warmth as he slid the hot, silky length of his cock into her aching center.

It *did* hurt a little. Margot considered healing the small tears in the untried muscle, but quickly decided against it. Some discomforts were necessary. Some, like this one, even felt *good.*

His thrusts were slow and deep, each one marked by a fresh nip to her throat and shoulders. Margot tangled her fingers in his hair as her hips lifted to meet him in an instinctive rhythm. Every part of her belonged to him. The witch, the woman, the elf — she belonged to this man who loved her so much, it came through their bond like *sunlight*.

His hips stuttered. Panting against her throat, Theodore replied to her thoughts with a rawness that unwound her. *I belong to you, too. Always. Always. I'm yours.*

Margot used her grip on his silky hair to draw him up, seeking a kiss as his thrusts picked up speed. The tension of impending release made her needy. When she could no longer keep up with his pace, Margot sealed her mouth over his at the same time that she guided his hand between them, using his fingers to stroke and pet her into her own brilliant release.

Theodore didn't need any more prompting. Slicking his tongue against hers, scraping his fangs against her lip, breathing her in, he pressed the pad of his thumb against her clitoris and slowly, ruthlessly stroked her.

Pleasure was a golden haze, the feeling of Theodore's erratic thrusts and hard exhalations in her ear a sweet, distant song. Nothing compared to the pleasure of being with him. Nothing was so perfect as his taste on her tongue, his hands on her skin, the stretch of him filling her, the weight of him on top of her. *Nothing.*

A while later, they both caught their breath in the blue-black darkness of their bedroom. They lay side by side, their marriage sigils kissing, and breathed in one another as the night deepened around them.

"Did I ever say thank you?"

Theodore nudged her nose with his. "For what?"

Her throat tightened. "For saving my life. For loving me. It would have been easier not to."

When she thought of all he had done for her, to *have* her, Margot wondered what she'd done to deserve a man like him. If not for her, he would not have clawed his way to the top of the hierarchy. He would not have taken on the responsibilities of a sovereign so very young. He could have been free. He could have been anything he wanted.

Instead, he chose *her*.

"Oh, darling," he murmured, cupping her cheek, "there was never any choice. You saved me first, remember?"

The Summit was nothing and everything that she thought it would be.

Margot watched from a discreet balcony as delegations from the five families entered the massive meeting hall, followed by the much smaller but more numerous representatives from the families further down the hierarchy. The meeting hall itself was a huge, semi-circular room filled with rows of mahogany and leather seats. A dais stood at the front of the room, set with a tall mahogany podium. Behind it, a banner with the Solbourne twin thistles and rising sun hung proudly.

And above it all, a domed ceiling soared — every inch of it magically enforced stained glass designed to look like a glorious sun set in a deep violet and navy sky speckled with stars.

Balconies ran along the walls, filled with elves, she was informed, who were too low on the hierarchy to have assigned seating on the ground floor but who still retained the right to vote.

That was the main purpose of the Summit, Margot learned. Every year, the Families and representatives of smaller elvish enclaves came to vote on issues that pertained to them — as well as the petitions pushed through by neighborhood committees and city councils, and what agendas they would push in the UTA Congress. This was where change came to pass in the Protectorate, and where Theodore would make his stance on elvish isolationism known to all.

Margot curled her fingers in the deep violet skirt of her fitted dress, the twin of the simple gown she wore to her wedding, her palms sweaty.

The politics didn't scare her. She dealt with that all her life, both from the shadows and within the Coven. No, what made Margot nervous was how this massive group of predators, already backed into a corner by their dwindling population, would handle the surprise of Theodore's announcement that he not only married a witch halfling, but made not one but *two* outside alliances.

"He'll be fine." Marcus du Soleil's deep voice rumbled behind her.

Margot turned to see the tall, aristocratic elf a few steps away, his lean body swathed in layers of fine velvet and crisply tailored Italian wool. The peculiar mix of old regalia and modern business wear was so distinctly elvish, it made her smile.

Marcus didn't return the expression, but she didn't expect him to. Although they had only officially known each other for a day, she got the impression that he was a man of little expression but great depth.

Offering her his arm, he said, "Let me escort you back to the waiting room. We don't want your consort's grand surprise being spoiled by someone stumbling upon you up here, do we?"

She slipped her hand into the curve of his arm and let him lead her into the shadowy hall and down the stairs. "I just wanted to see. Andy said that was the best place to get a good look at everything."

Marcus hummed. The sleeve of his suit was warm under her hand, the hem of his half-cape a velvet brush against her back when it swayed with his long gait.

Margot glanced up at him from under her lashes, considering the strong, sharply featured profile and silver hair he kept out of his face with a gold pin.

He was a stately, severe man; hard to look at for too long without feeling as though she was inviting a scolding and yet still somehow intensely handsome. He was also the man who "caught" her, according to Olivier.

In a traditional elvish birth, her half-brother explained, the partner eased the baby into the world, not the midwife or the healer or the arrant doctor. It was the partner who rubbed life into the baby, who cut the cord with their own claws and welcomed the child into the world before handing them off to their mother.

It was *that* which made Marcus du Soleil, one of the most powerful men in the UTA, consider himself her father.

Considering Margot's biological father had never been around — too flighty, too caught up in his research, not ready to be a parent until recently, when he married an arrant professor and welcomed a son with all the baffled joy of a man who acted as though he didn't already have a child — it was... strange to be the focus of real paternal scrutiny.

Nearing the private, guarded entrance to the waiting area where the rest of the Solbournes, Petra, and Viktor mingled, Margot was unsurprised when Marcus pulled them to a gentle stop in a shadowed alcove.

Turning to face her, he said, "Before we go in, I wanted to speak with you privately."

Margot raised her eyebrows, girding herself for some fresh revelation. Perhaps seeing the resigned dread on her face, the smallest, wryest smile twisted the corners of Marcus's mouth. "Don't worry. I don't have any bad news for you. I just want to be sure this is what you really want to do."

Her first response was annoyance. Margot had lost track of the number of people who asked her whether or not she *really* wanted to be with Theodore. Every single du Soleil had asked her that exact question. She might have begun to snap at them, except she understood where their concern came from.

For one thing, the power imbalance between herself and Theodore, at least from the outside, was tremendous. For another... they *really* didn't like the Solbournes.

Margot gave Marcus's arm a tentative pat. "I do," she answered. "I'm the one who asked *him* to marry *me,* remember?"

"Yes." His eyes, pure amber, flicked to the marriage sigil branded between her eyebrows. "But that doesn't mean there can't be second thoughts."

"Do consorts normally have second thoughts?"

The smallest grimace creased his mouth. "No."

"Then you have your answer." She examined his face, taking in the severe lines and ageless, mature quality of it, and felt a pang of pity for him. Tatiana, her faceless mother, was not Marcus's consort. Theirs was a union built of practicality, but the way Olivier told the story, it sounded as though Marcus cared deeply for his partner.

And, despite being a stranger, she couldn't dismiss the evidence that he cared deeply for her, too.

Wanting to show how much she appreciated that, Margot grasped his gloved hand between both of hers and gave it a small squeeze. "Can I ask... *why* do you disapprove of Theodore so much? It would mean a lot to me to understand where you're coming from."

Lines fanned out around Marcus's eyes when he answered, "I don't dislike your consort. We voted against him taking Delilah's seat because he's too young. His determination to take sovereignty seemed... troubling, in light of his father's crimes." Marcus surprised her by bringing their joined hands up to his lips for a soft kiss to her knuckles. His voice gentled, losing some of the forbidding quality that made her want to show him her perfect GPA. "However, if we had known his motivation was your safety and happiness, perhaps we would not have fought so hard."

Lowering their hands, he gave her an imperious look that exactly mirrored his son's. "Still, that does not excuse him from the fact that he did not properly court you, *nor* the fact that any self-respecting elf would seek permission from a family *before* moving their child into his territory."

Margot sputtered. "But he didn't even know who I was related to! And it wasn't like it was normal circumstances."

Tucking her hand back into the crook of his arm, Marcus stared down his nose at her. "All the same, you *are* a du Soleil. He will treat you like it or face the consequences."

Her feelings on having gained so many new family members were complicated and contradictory, but *that...*

That felt nice.

The scene in the waiting room was strange, to say the least. Not simply because the alpha of the Merced pack was currently all but plastered to one wall, his back ramrod straight and his eyes riveted to a small, black-haired elvish woman across the room. Nor was it strange because High Priestess Petra Zaskodna stood beside Kaz, who looked viscerally uncomfortable in traditional elvish finery.

Impossibly, not even the sight of Delilah Solbourne and her world famous consort made the list of weirdest happenings.

It was the fact that the tiny elvish woman — tiny for an elf, anyway — stood toe-to-toe with Theodore, her svelte body vibrating with rage, as a young man stood behind her, a restraining hand on her petite shoulder.

"...think you're doing, trying to interrogate my mother?!" she snarled, stomping one stiletto-clad foot. She wore a sheath of pure, ice blue silk with a high, mother of pearl buttoned collar and translucent sleeves. Her hair was shorn close to her head in a cut that emphasized her striking cheekbones and full mouth. She was lovely, except she was baring her fangs at Margot's husband, and that was *unacceptable.*

"My mother had *nothing* to do with—"

A crack of pure electricity cut through the air, silencing whatever it was the woman was about to say. Every eye turned toward Margot, except, she noticed, Viktor's.

Keeping her eyes locked on the elvish woman, Margot asked in her chilliest voice, "What's going on here?"

Theodore stepped around the pair of what had to be siblings

to extract her from Marcus's light hold. Placing a hand low on her back, he grimly introduced them. "Darling, this is my cousin Camille and her brother Cameron. Cousins, this is my consort, Margot Goode."

"Margot *du Soleil* Goode," Olivier interjected, only a shade away from openly gleeful.

Shooting the young man a dark look, Theodore corrected himself. "Margot du Soleil Goode. My wife."

Both Camille and Cameron, who looked almost identical to his sister except for the heavy silver jewelry he wore up and down the length of his pointed ears, froze momentarily, their catlike eyes fixed on Margot and the sigil between her brows.

Camille recovered first. "I... Are you *kidding?*" Turning furious violet eyes on her cousin, she gestured sharply to Margot with diamond-clad claws. "She's the reason you tried to have Valen and Kaz take my mother in for questioning? Why on Burden's green Earth would she care about you shacking up with a witch?"

Theodore rubbed his forehead, carefully avoiding the place where his new chalk sigil lay. "Cammie, your mother has tried to kill me *three times* in six months. The person who set up the bombing was a woman, and the money came from a Solbourne account. You think it's unreasonable that she would go after my consort? Really?"

Camille narrowed her eyes. His cousin was lovely in a doll-like way, but when she jutted out her chin like that, Margot got the impression that she was made of far stronger stuff than porcelain. Behind her, Cameron crossed his arms and peered at Margot from under thick black lashes, like he was trying to put together a particularly troublesome puzzle.

"Mother did not put a bomb in your consort's house," Camille announced, each word bitten off with the utmost contempt.

Theodore arched his brows. "Can you prove it?"

Taking half a step closer, she hissed, "Yes, I can. You know why Mother hasn't tried anything stupid the past two months?" She swept a glittering hand up, gesturing to her temple with a flick of her wrist. "Because she hasn't been *lucid.*"

"What?" There was a chorus of low, astonished questions, but Theodore's voice cut through them all. "Cammie, what happened—"

In a stiff, flat voice, Cameron answered, "Mother is sick."

But elves didn't get sick. Not like humans and other races did. The copper in their blood was a nasty surprise for most pathogens, making them immune to all but a select few diseases. Margot shot a questioning look at her husband. *Baby, what are they talking about?*

Theodore put a hand on her shoulder, the fight draining out of his expression to leave him — and everyone in the room except herself and Petra — pale.

It's not sickness like you know it, he replied, his inner voice strained. *But something that's become increasingly common among our parents' generation. Mental degradation, then physical weakness and rapid aging. Our healers think it's a symptom of the generational lack of pheromone binding among consorts.*

A light clicked on in the back of her mind. *Like the madness that hits if the pull starts and isn't finished?*

Very similar, yes, but this is slower. It can take years to show.

Margot stared at Camille and Cameron with new eyes, her heart squeezing as she spied the lines of stress around their mouths, the shadows in their eyes. No wonder Camille acted so outraged at the possibility of her mother being the bomber. If she was that unwell, there was no chance that it could be true.

Margot's healer's heart ached for them, but a quick glance and small shake of Theodore's head told her there was nothing she could do to help.

Heaving a sigh, he said, "I didn't know that, Cammie. You should have said something. We would have helped you."

Camille's violet eyes, striking against her pale lavender skin, took on a wet sheen even as she lifted her chin into a stubborn angle. "Mother wouldn't have wanted your help."

"No," Theodore allowed. "She probably wouldn't have."

Why?

There was a note of raw sorrow in his inner voice when he answered, *Because my father killed Cammie and Cameron's father. He was Marian's consort. That's a wound nothing can heal.*

Valen's voice was a hard, grating rumble when he said, "Then we're back to square one. Someone with access to the Solbourne accounts paid the bomber, but we have no trail to—"

"Oh, that was me."

Every head turned to look at the statuesque woman in a crisp suit, unquestionably a Solbourne in looks and the way she held herself, standing by the table of refreshments. Her skin was pale blue, her eyes heavy-lidded and her lips full. A double thistle pin held her high collar closed, and she had one leg crossed over the other, displaying a silver-tipped leather boot. Her hip was casually propped up against a chair occupied by a woman Margot immediately recognized from years of entertainment feeds and magazine covers: the most beautiful woman in the world, Winnie Yadav.

Dark-skinned, with a head of electric, corkscrew curls and a face wrought so delicately, so strikingly, it almost hurt to look at, Winnie was one of the most arresting people on the planet.

At that moment, though, she wore a stiff-lipped look of resignation that was at odds with the way her consort, standing over her chair, addressed the room: utterly unbothered, her curvy body relaxed, her dark Solbourne eyes just a little... off. Despite Winnie's fame, Margot's eyes barely touched on her before they bounced back to the standing woman. A deep, primal part of her recognized an unfathomable danger in the blue-skinned woman's familiar face.

Delilah Solbourne, The Executioner.

Theodore's voice was a croak. "Delilah, *no.*"

Margot shot a quick glance at Kaz, noting how he closed his eyes and dropped his chin, his hands braced on his hips. In the expressions of everyone else, there was a note of shock, perhaps disappointment. In Kaz, there was only resignation.

He knew, she thought.

Yes, Theodore answered. Even his inner voice sounded strangled. Pain rippled down the electric bridge of their bond. *And that explains why he didn't want to tell me yesterday.*

Margot stepped closer and wrapped her arm around his back, her arm gliding underneath the short, violet silk-lined cape to hug him close.

"I thought you would know by now," Delilah said, blinking owlishly at the astonished room. Winnie, meanwhile, slumped further. "Of course it was me. Who else would have access to our accounts? I didn't exactly hide it."

A choked sound erupted from Theodore's throat at the same instant that a series of low, furious rumbles built in the chests of Marcus and Olivier. Margot paled, her eyes darting. They looked ready to take Delilah's head off her shoulders.

More pain snapped across the bond. Betrayal, hot like the splash of acid, scorched a path through it. "Why would you do this?" Theodore demanded. "Why would you try to kill her? You *knew* what she was to me! You knew! Why would you *do* this, Delilah?"

The air in the room crackled with barely leashed violence. Camille stepped forward, clearly intending to step between Theodore and Delilah should he lunge, but the small elf was intercepted before she could take more than a step or two. One tanned, corded arm in a familiar navy suit jacket hauled her out of the way. *Viktor.*

Camille tried to lunge out of his arms, her legs kicking as he lifted her off of her feet. "Do *not* touch me, you godsdamned piece of—"

Viktor dragged her away, his eyes gone amber and coyote-bright. Her furious hiss was cut off with a short, sharp, "Hush, Cam. This isn't your fight."

Delilah canted her head to one side, the look in her eyes just shy of being dreamy. Long, thick hair of the deepest black swayed around her back. She wore a suit similar to the men's, except she apparently rejected the use of a cape and merely attached two bejeweled thistle cape pins to her shoulders, giving them the look of strange, spiked epaulets.

"Sweetheart," she gently admonished, "if I tried to kill our girl, she would not be standing here now."

Theodore tensed, the bones of his face standing out starkly against his pale blue skin. "Delilah, *explain.* For once in your life, *explain* this."

Delilah's eyes roved over Theodore to meet Margot's. They stared at one another for a long, silent moment. An enigmatic smile curled her mouth. Margot knew instantly that she had no intention of explaining just as another light flicked on in her mind.

Closing her eyes, Margot reached up to press the heel of her hand into her forehead. Her marriage sigil twinged as the skin wrinkled around the scab. "Because she knew."

Every eye swung in her direction. Margot gestured toward Delilah with a flick of her wrist. "She *knew.* I saw the paintings in the apartment. She's been keeping tabs on me for years." Margot cast her a narrow-eyed look. "Probably my whole life, huh? You *knew* I was dying."

Both she and Delilah ignored the burst of questions that went up in response to that admission.

"Yes," Delilah answered, looking very pleased with herself. She shrugged. "Of course I ran the odds of every scenario, but *this* one was the only path that led to this moment — when Teddy would get what he wanted *and* change the world. Every other path either ended up with him being forced to abdicate or, regrettably, Margot's untimely death." She fixed Margot with a small, distant smile that sent a shiver down her spine. "You usually died alone, in case you were wondering. But most ended with both of you dying. My least favorite choice, obviously."

Delilah looked at her watch, a sleek silver timepiece that

matched the silver accents on her boots and shoulder pieces. "I did what needed to be done. Now it's your turn, sweetheart. It's time for your speech, Teddy." Grasping Winnie's hand, she ignored her consort's aggrieved expression as she gently hauled Winnie out of her chair and began towing her toward the door. She tossed a grin over her shoulder. "Come along, everyone. It's time for my boy to make history."

She made to pass Theodore with breezy efficiency, but was stopped by his hand on her elbow. With a thunderous look, he warned her, "We're going to talk about this later."

Delilah's smile was untroubled. "Of course. You don't think I know that?" She skimmed her knuckles over the swell of Theodore's cheek as she passed. "I know everything, sweetheart."

Chapter Twenty-Four

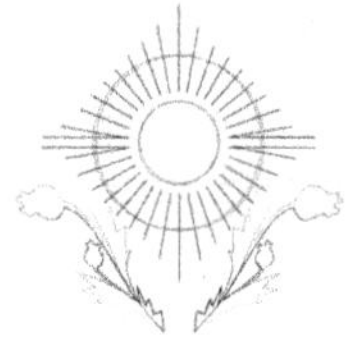

Margot watched from her place beside the podium as the world changed.

Theodore's speech lasted ten minutes and forty-eight seconds, but it was only the last handful of moments that really made a difference. It took approximately four seconds for him to swipe off the chalk keeping his glamour in place, and about ten seconds for the entire meeting hall to explode into a riot of furious debate.

It didn't appear to matter much that she was a halfling. To all the world she was a Goode, a witch. Theodore's detractors didn't appear to have much interest in her personally at all. Rather, they balked at the precedent their relationship set for a younger generation of elves, as well as the message it sent to the world — that the Protectorate was not the bastion of elvish culture it once was, untouched and safe from the dangers of the world. That they were *vulnerable.* That they were dying. That they needed help from the Others they had shunned for so long if they wanted even the barest chance of survival.

Although there was a hardline faction within the Parliament that demanded Theodore be unseated, after two hours of furious debate and the assurance that the Solbournes had not only the Merced pack behind them, but the surprising support of Glory's

Temple and the du Soleils, as well as, through Margot, the Goodes — there was no contest. But even if Theodore didn't have a shocking amount of outside support, there was a wave of internal agreement that ending the moratorium on outside interaction was the only sensible choice left to them.

Supporters came out of the woodwork to shout down the hardline believers. The air in the room was charged with a current of desperation. The expressions on the faces of the younger elves were drawn tight, the gleams in their eyes almost fanatical now that the seal on speaking of breaking free from a thousand years of tradition was broken. Margot got the impression that they were a generation starved for air, for food, for light, and now that they caught a hint of a life beyond deprivation on the breeze, there would be no stopping them.

Change had finally come for the Protectorate.

Margot watched Theodore field volleys of accusation and snarling challenges to his authority with cool, measured dominance, his confidence in his place unchanged. She wondered, as she stood beside him, what it would be like to be married to a man who would so easily take on his entire world for her.

Good, she decided. *It will be good.*

The press release that they'd already drafted, outlining their marriage in clear, impossible-to-misinterpret language, went out almost immediately after the opening meeting of the Summit ended — with a slight alteration.

At the bottom, Valen tactfully added, *"This comes on the heels of the discovery that the presumed 'bombing' of the St. Francis Woods Healing House was, in fact, an accident related to defunct twenty-first century gas lines. Patrol has officially closed the case and will resume normal security after the Summit has concluded. However, the sovereign's edict for enhanced protections for healers will remain until representatives meet with the Temple to discuss the changes."*

Margot knew that Theodore struggled with what his sister did. She wasn't a huge fan of Delilah herself. But prosecuting the former sovereign, let alone Theodore's own family, was out of the question. It would be a political disaster, a PR nightmare, and something a devoted little brother couldn't stomach. They would simply have to deal with Delilah on their own terms, something the former sovereign seemed to expect when, after they all retired to the family floors, Theodore dragged her into his study.

They did not emerge for a long, long time.

Scanning the richly decorated living room scattered with tables of food, a surprising amount of which catered to her own tastes, Margot took in the people she now called family.

Andy and Valen were curled up together on a loveseat, their heads bent as they silently watched the sunset streaming through the windows. Cameron was engaged in low conversation with Kaz by a table of refreshments, cups in their hands. Camille appeared to be missing, as did Viktor. Petra had been invited up as well, her presence having been vital to calming some of the more overzealous, more religiously devoted elves during the meeting, but politely declined in favor of returning to the cathedral. The du Soleils also bowed out, claiming the need to consult with their allies about the state of things post-announcement before they left her with soft touches to Margot's hair and cheeks.

Winnie sat on a couch beside a man Margot had yet to meet. Her stunning face was tired, but when she lifted a hand to smooth a lock of fiery hair out of the unfamiliar man's eyes, her expression softened with motherly affection.

Margot stood by a bookcase, longing for Theodore and feeling awkward amongst so many people she was now related to but still unfamiliar with. She might have hovered forever, waiting for her husband to return and take the awkwardness away, if Winnie didn't seek her out.

Ushering her over with a wave, Winnie's expression was gentle, almost hesitant. Margot steeled herself and, clutching a glass of sparkling cider with white-knuckled fingers, made her way over to the couch.

"Margot." Winnie's voice was as soft as her eyes, the complete opposite of the steely countenance her father, Valen, projected. But Margot could see the lines of her father's face in Winnie's striking bone structure, the gentle curve of Andy's mouth and big, catlike eyes. Somehow, the two opposing personalities had come together to create a woman so stunning, it almost hurt to look at her.

Smiling with sharp, beautifully white teeth, she reached out to take Margot's free hand and give it a delicate squeeze. "It is so good to finally meet you. I feel like I already know you, of course, but it's taken such a long time to come to this moment."

Unable to help herself, Margot arched her brows. "You probably had more advanced notice than some."

Winnie's smile dimmed a bit. Fingers tightening, she reluctantly replied, "Yes, but only a little." She shared a glance with the red-headed elf sitting beside her. "I promise you, though, I didn't know anything about Delilah's plan until we got on the jet to come here. If I'd known..."

Margot shook her head. "No, I'm glad it worked out the way it did. I could have gone without getting blown up, of course, and I feel awful about the Healing House, but it's a lot better than being dead — which I might be right now, if not for her."

That didn't make it right. It certainly made Margot look at Delilah as the predator she was — a woman who would go to any lengths to get what she wanted, without regard for the collateral damage she willfully created — but it was also the truth. If the alternative was death or a life without Theodore, then Margot would take being blown up a thousand times over.

"Yes, I..." Winnie trailed off, her fingers sliding away from Margot's to rest on her knees. "Lilah and I have been together since we were teenagers." She slanted a look at Valen, who was whispering something in Andy's ear with a small, barely perceptible smile quirking the corners of his hard mouth upward. "My father was the captain of Thaddeus's guard, so we basically grew up together. When the pull hit, it seemed perfect. Meant to be."

Winnie gave her a small, sad smile. "But even *I* struggle with her gifts sometimes. It's not easy loving a woman who lives ten steps ahead of everyone around her." She paused, the sadness in her eyes dimming to a kind of stubborn pride Margot admired. "But you should know that Lilah does everything — *everything* — for her family. I don't always agree with her methods, but the fact remains that she would never willingly cause any one of us harm. Our happiness is everything to her."

Margot considered her grandmother and the lengths she would go to protect her kin, her Coven. "I understand."

"No, you don't, but that's okay. Hopefully you'll never have to see the full extent of Delilah's devotion." Knowing what she did about how Thaddeus II died, Margot emphatically hoped she was right.

"Well, now that *that's* out of the way!" Winnie's smile brightened as she changed the subject. Twisting to curl one arm around the shoulders of her companion, she announced, "Forgive me for not introducing you to your other brother-in-law yet! Margot, this is Sam."

She knew the name, but Margot was surprised to see him. Theodore mentioned that he lived an entirely secluded life somewhere in Nevada and barely ever ventured into the heart of the Protectorate. "Oh, I'm sorry. I didn't see you at the meeting." She held out a hand. "It's lovely to meet you."

From a distance, she thought that she could be forgiven for not immediately picking up the fact that he was related to her husband. Sam, Margot decided, had the Solbourne handsomeness, the thickly muscled build and sultry eyes, but the coloring of the blazing sunset touching the choppy water of the Bay behind her.

His hair was a thousand colors of ruby and carnelian and amber. His skin was a soft gold. His eyes were Solbourne dark and large, soulful, set in a face of angles offset by a sensitive, plush mouth. The bone structure reminded her of Theodore and Kaz, but the rest of him looked exactly like— Margot blinked hard, a shiver of unease rippling across her skin.

Thaddeus. The mad sovereign stared up at her as he took her hand and gave it a firm shake.

No, he's dead. Margot knew that. Everyone knew that. Theodore had gone so far as to tell her the true story of what happened the night Thaddeus finally lost his crown — and his head — but seeing Sam was still a shock.

"It's a pleasure to finally meet you," he replied in a voice that was all pleasant raspiness and soft syllables. "Don't worry about thinking you missed me. I skipped the meeting and watched from a live feed in my suite."

"Ah." Margot forced a smile. Thaddeus was ten years dead by the time she came into the world and *still* his likeness inspired a churning dread in her. "If I knew that was an option, I might have joined you."

"I don't know. You looked pretty at home up in front of the horde." He let her hand go with a small squeeze. She was surprised to see that, unlike every other elf in the room, Sam didn't bother with gloves. His claws stood out against the gold of his skin, their diamond-hard tips gleaming in the light.

"I'm used to that sort of thing," she replied. "Collective meetings aren't that different, really, and being from a big Coven involves a lot more shouting than you might think."

Theodore's older brother offered her a small, shy smile. "I'm glad you were prepared. I would have folded under all that scrutiny."

"Sam is the Head of the Treasury," Winnie proudly explained. She pressed an errant wave of red hair back against his head with a loving caress of her claws. "He runs nearly the entire Protectorate economy from his lab, all custom built and incredibly advanced. I swear, he can work miracles with all those numbers and codes."

Margot eyed Sam closely, the understanding of where he fit into the hierarchy snapping into place. This man, with his soft eyes and rueful smile, held a staggering amount of power. How was it that she didn't know him? Surely, if his role was public knowledge, everyone would know the face of the man who kept one of the biggest economies in the UTA going. "Theodore mentioned that you live in Nevada. Do you live close to Vegas?"

Sam shook his head. "No, I own property in the high desert, several hours away from any major city. I have to go there occasionally, but I don't make a habit of it."

"Doesn't the Luz family control Vegas?"

"Yes, but I rarely have any trouble with them," he answered, shrugging. "They don't notice me, generally, and when they do, they know I'm not going to be in their territory long. I own the land around a small lake called Fort Ruby and I prefer to be there above just about anywhere else. Life's simple and quiet there."

Margot blinked, surprised once again. Elves didn't often venture too deep into the wilderness, as they generally preferred their tall towers of glass and metal, as well as the comforts of city life. Theodore mentioned Sam lived in seclusion, but she assumed it was in some sort of high tech elvish enclave. The way he spoke, it sounded more like a ranch. Or a bunker.

Eventually, Margot settled in beside Sam on the couch. She, Sam, and Winnie spoke for a long time, trading stories about their homes — Sam was very proud of the hot springs around his property, just as she was proud to say the Goode lake would freeze his toes off in the winter and yet offer a breathtaking view all year round — before Kaz and Cameron wandered over.

At some point in the evening, Margot forgot to be self-conscious and just... enjoyed herself.

The elves were different, sure, and Kaz liked to tease her about what a hellion she was in his deadpan way, but talking to them, letting their voices wash over her as they traded stories and jokes back and forth, felt natural. Like home.

I missed this. I missed being in a family, she thought, just as Delilah meandered back into the room. Their eyes met. Delilah tipped her head toward the door, mouthing, *Teddy.*

Margot set her empty glass of cider down on the coffee table. *But I miss him more.*

Rising from the couch, Margot made her excuses and hurried

out of the room. She shared another look with Delilah as she passed her in the doorway, but Margot couldn't make heads or tails out of the inscrutable expression in the former sovereign's dark, dark eyes. Nor could she decipher the small, knowing smile.

Doesn't matter.

She found Theodore in his study. The sight of him leaning against his desk, his head bent and his hair in disarray like he'd run his claws through it again and again, made her heart squeeze.

Touch hunger ran like razors over her skin. It made her want to cross the distance between them at a run. It made her want to lock the door and keep him to herself for as long as it took to satisfy the beast in her gut that craved him so violently. Margot the witch understood that they had to make certain sacrifices for their long-term relationship, but that other part of her couldn't take the interruptions, the distance, the distractions from the one thing she wanted above all else — *him.*

Closing the door behind her, Margot quietly flipped the lock before making her way across the room. Her voice was husky when she said, "Hey, baby."

Theodore lifted his head. His eyes, normally full of humor and warmth, were dull with the sadness that permeated their bond. "Hey."

Margot pushed aside some papers and a sleek tablet to perch on his desk. Drawing him into the circle of her arms and legs, she cupped his cheeks. "This hurt you," she whispered, his pain settling under her skin like tiny pieces of glass. "Do you want to talk about it?"

He let out a ragged sigh. "I just... I can understand why she did it. I can understand that you were never in any danger. I can even appreciate the ruthlessness of it." He shook his head slowly. Theodore's hands, ungloved, settled on the desk by her hips as he bent to touch their sigils together. "But none of that means this doesn't feel like a betrayal."

Margot stroked his cheeks, his jaw, wishing there was more she could do to help him. "I know. That's a terrible feeling."

"Yes." He breathed deeply. "Yes, it is. I'll get past it. I have to. She's my sister. She and Winnie *raised* me, and without her, I wouldn't have you right now. But I'm going to need a while to forgive her for it."

"Did you tell her that?"

He huffed. "Yes. She was as understanding as always — which is to say she just nodded and said, *I know.*"

Margot stroked the soft wisps of hair that tickled his ears. "Well, in her defense, she *does* know."

"Doesn't make it easier."

"No," she agreed. "It doesn't."

Margot took a long look at her husband's face. This man who changed the world for her had lines of stress around his mouth. His dark eyes were bruised. Even his proud, gorgeous shoulders were rounded with the weight of the day.

Unacceptable.

Lifting her hands to his cape, the same one he wore to their wedding, she made quick work of unfastening the thistle clasps. Theodore opened his eyes, bemused, and watched as she tossed the thing onto his desk chair and then went to work on his reinforced collar, followed quickly by the complicated fastenings of his suit jacket.

"What are you doing?"

"We're going to have sex on your desk." Margot pushed his jacket over his shoulders. As soon as it slid away, she turned to the many buttons of his formal shirt.

Theodore jolted with surprise, his bare hands curling around the edge of the desk. "What? Now?"

"Yes, now." She tugged his shirt out of his slacks before finishing with the buttons. That job done, she left him to take it all the way off while she turned her attention to his belt.

"But— *ah!*" Most of her attention went to his belt, while the rest of it went to leaning forward to run her tongue over one flat nipple and scraping it with her blunt fangs.

Peering up at him through her lashes, Margot stopped

fiddling with his belt buckle long enough to stroke the tense muscles of his abdomen and the line of crisp black hair there. "Do you want to?"

Theodore grasped her thighs and pushed them further apart. A seam of her tight violet cocktail dress ripped, but she couldn't care less when one of his hands found the gusset of her satin panties. "Fuck," he breathed, finding her soft and ready for him. "Of course I do. But I don't... What brought this on? You're already wet."

That she was. No use denying it. Margot hadn't had a moment's reprieve from the constant, grinding hunger for him since their quick, desperate joining in the shower that morning. Every twinge of her sore muscles and fresh lovebites was a reminder of what she could have. Every glance in his direction as he calmly took on the world for her was a tease. Every hint of his cedar and cinnamon scent was a temptation.

It was a miracle she'd managed to keep her cool the entire, hideous day.

Margot pulled his belt free and dropped it to the floor. Working on the button of his fly with both hands, she answered, "Remember when I said I was a little sore this morning?"

"Yes," Theodore gritted out. He breathed deeply and dipped his head to watch her progress as she pulled down his zipper and tugged his slacks down to reveal his briefs.

"Well, imagine me going through this whole, high-stress day without being able to really touch you, but having that little ache remind me of what I *could* have every single time I took a step." She hooked her thumbs in the elastic band of his briefs to gently tug them down as well. He sprung free, hard and ready for her.

Theodore groaned. Almost absentmindedly, he ran a knuckle back and forth along the gusset of her panties, making her squirm. "That's..." He swallowed. "Quite the image." Cracking his eyes open to give her a heated look, he added, "Although, not so different from me watching you walk around in this tight little skirt all day. I thought I was going to go insane."

Margot flattened her palms on his stomach and leaned forward to tease, "Then take it off of me."

For a moment, he stared down at her, his chest and shoulders moving with deep, ragged breaths. Finally, when she was about to lose patience with the unmoving hand up her skirt, he grinned. "Good idea."

Being so close to her meant he didn't have claws with which to menace her clothing, but he *did* have enough strength to make up for it. Without a hint of remorse, Theodore grasped her skirt and tore it clean in half. He didn't bother doing the same to the bodice. That, he merely tore down the button-up center and pushed aside until the cups of her bra came into view. Pushing those down with one hand, he snapped the elastic of her panties and threw them aside.

Margot laughed as he palmed her breasts, her heart thumping in her ears. "What am I going to wear to walk out of here?"

"My shirt will work."

"What if someone sees me?"

Theodore's eyes gleamed wickedly as he knelt on the floor, putting his head squarely between her spread thighs. "Then they'll know I've done a good job pleasing my consort, won't they?"

She screwed up her face. "No, that's not something I want people to— *Oh!*"

Damn, but Theodore had gotten good at this. Margot's thighs shook as he ran his tongue over her hot skin, seeking out all the places that would make her arch her back and gasp. Throwing her legs over his shoulders, he used one hand to hold her in place and the other to thrust his fingers inside of her, stretching muscles that were so wonderfully sore.

It didn't take long for her to orgasm. Theodore was too good with his tongue, too determined to see her release hard and fast. He didn't let up until she was gently pushing his head aside.

Enough of that, she told him. *I want you now.*

You have me.

Theodore rose, his mouth kiss-swollen and gleaming, to kiss her hard and hot and beautifully messy. She dug her fingers into his hair and whimpered, locking her legs around his waist as he slowly eased inside of her — a perfect fit, an easy glide. Two people made for each other.

Reluctantly ending the kiss, Theodore gently eased her back onto the desk so she lay flat beneath him. His hungry gaze roved over her, taking in her free breasts and destroyed dress, her spread legs and flushed face.

"Gorgeous," he panted, pressing one of her knees upward so it almost touched her shoulder. The other he hooked over his forearm as he began a slow, relentless beat that sent sparks shooting up her spine.

Margot raised her arms to clutch at the edge of the desk by her head, her eyes glued to the hypnotic movement of his chest and stomach, the flexing muscles of his arms, the look of rapture on his face as he slowly picked up the pace.

When he drove deep and fast into her, Margot couldn't hold on anymore. She squeezed her eyes shut and threw her head back, her spine a taut bow. It was too much. It was not *enough.* It was everything she wanted and more than she knew how to ask for.

Theodore let out a hoarse groan and abruptly pushed her other leg up as well before he bent over her. Slapping his hands onto the desk, he fastened his fangs over her throat in that wonderful, possessive hold and thrust so deep, so hard, it felt like he was trying to rattle her bones apart.

The feeling of his fangs closing around her jugular as he slammed hard into her? Pure, wild bliss.

Margot came with a shattered gasp, her claws digging into the smooth skin of his back, and felt his pace stutter before turning somehow *more* ferocious, harder and faster, until he followed her over with a grated cry.

They lay there for a while, Theodore's face pressed into her throat and her hands lazily stroking his back as he softened inside of her. Neither was particularly eager to move. It didn't matter that she was pretty sure a pen was stuck in her ribs, or that Theodore weighed about as much as a building. It was perfect.

Pressing a reverent kiss to her throat, he whispered, "Thank you, darling."

Margot didn't play coy. "You're welcome."

He peeked up at her from under the curtain of her mussed hair. "Can I count on you to be around *every* time I have a bad day?"

She nudged his forehead with her chin. "If cheering you up means I get *multiple* orgasms, I don't see the downside. Consider me your personal pick-me-up."

His smile was unrestrained, boyish in the way that she associated only with him. "You already are."

"Even without sex?"

"Yes." No hesitation. No hint of a lie in their bond. It was the pure truth, straight from the heart of him. "Even if we never had sex again, I'd love you every second of every day, darling."

Margot's heart was a wonderful ache in her chest. "How did I get so lucky?" she wondered aloud.

He dimpled. "I don't know. That's a question you'd have to ask Glory."

Some of Margot's humor melted into thoughtfulness. Recalling the heat, the feeling of being *seen* from Petra's office, she asked, "Do you think this is what the goddess wanted?"

Theodore lifted himself up a little to prop his chin on his hand. "Glory?"

"Yes."

Stroking her from collar to bellybutton with one hand, he answered slowly, "I think that if Glory *didn't* approve of our union, she would never have tied us together in the first place." He looked into her eyes, his expression thoughtful. "You're a gloriana, darling. Blessed by the goddess from birth. You wear her colors. You use her gifts for good. She entrusted me with your safekeeping for a reason. Why wouldn't she want us to be happy together?"

"I think she does," Margot admitted. Stroking his cheek with the tip of one finger, she quietly added, "But I also feel like she's watching, and that makes me nervous. The gods only watch those they have plans for."

And those plans weren't always pleasant, or safe, or kind. More often than not, those who became the fixation of the gods ended up dying young, or simply disappearing altogether.

Theodore smiled crookedly and turned to kiss the tip of her finger. "Could her plan not just be us living happily ever after?"

Margot swallowed. "You changed the world with a ten minute speech today. Somehow, I doubt that our marital bliss is all Glory has in mind."

He conceded the point with a nod. "True." Ducking his head to kiss her, Theodore scattered her heavy thoughts before whispering, "But all we have control over is our own happiness, darling. And you're mine."

Margot clutched him close, that howling thing in her settling, at last, into quiet contentment. "And you're mine."

Epilogue

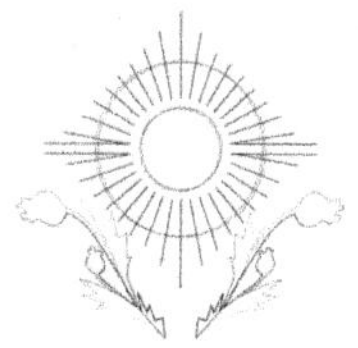

June 2045 - The Goodeland, Coven Collective

"It's a little small."

Theodore set their luggage down by the door. Turning to wrinkle his nose at the low-hanging light he had to step *around* to get into the cabin, he muttered, "Who builds houses this small?"

"Not everyone is elvish," Margot reminded him from the tiny kitchen, where she was gleefully unwrapping container after container of homemade treats left for them by the Coven.

"I'm not asking everyone to be elvish." Theodore closed the front door with his foot before striding down the narrow hall to find his wife. He leaned against the door jamb — something that was *necessary,* because he couldn't actually stand up straight beneath it without slamming his head into the wood. "I'm simply asking people to make reasonably-sized homes."

"Hush." Margot propped her hip against a steel-basin sink and took a bite out of what he had been informed by her great aunt was "an extra gooey brownie with double the nuts". Personally, he thought it sounded revolting, but he couldn't deny his consort her pleasures.

And they *were* pleasures, going by the look of bliss on her face when she savored another bite.

Theodore shifted his weight, his blood rushing south as he watched the familiar look of rapture cross his consort's face. She usually only looked like that when he had his head between her legs, or, most recently, when he bent her over the bathroom sink and watched her reflection in the mirror as he fucked her until she let out a cry that still rang in his ears.

Was that only three and a half hours ago? Theodore watched her hungrily. *Feels like a lifetime.*

But then again, that made a certain amount of sense. It only took an hour to get to the Goodeland via jet, but the chilly meeting with Sophie and then the hours of introductions to Margot's kaleidoscope of family members might as well have been an eternity.

Kaz had come along as moral support and security detail, but he hadn't fared any better than Theodore. The Goode Coven was warm, welcoming, but voraciously curious about their new member and viciously protective of Margot. They wanted to know everything about the two interlopers in their midst, and it felt like every member of the Coven was prepared to interrogate them individually.

It was a relief to finally be shown the way to their cabin — a secluded one bedroom home well away from the main cluster of homes around the crystalline lake. Margot had specifically requested that they stay in the cabin she was born in rather than her grandmother's home, which was Sophie and Tula's firm desire, and for that, Theodore was deeply grateful.

He liked Tula. She was warm, her love an open, generous thing, and when Margot hugged her Noni, there was no doubting how much relief she felt to be home. That didn't mean he wanted to sleep under the same roof as her, though.

Though they were warm, and though he tried his best to be reasonable for his wife's sake, it was all Theodore could do to stomach the sight of the elder Goodes, who so profoundly harmed his consort for so very long. It didn't matter that their intentions were noble. It didn't even matter that, in their place, he might have done the same. He wanted to track down every last one of the people who knew her secret and make their last living moments on Burden's Earth as miserable as possible.

He didn't and he wouldn't. Margot wasn't ready to face the justice she was owed. Until she was, he could grin and bear whatever she needed him to.

The day she gave the word, though, he would let his rage loose on the whole damn lot of them.

Margot drifted over to him. Dressed in loose pants and a soft, baby blue blouse, she had the air of a woman who was entirely comfortable in her skin. Happiness flowed through their bond unchecked.

"Where do you think Kaz has gone?" she asked, slipping her arms around Theodore's waist. She leaned her weight onto him with easy familiarity.

"He was probably kidnapped by one of your aunts." Theodore cupped the sides of her head with his ungloved hands. Gently guiding her head back, he pressed a series of lingering kisses to her lips, each one a promise for more and payment for those that couldn't be exchanged in polite company.

Margot stroked her hands up his back, tracing her favorite path down the muscles bracketing his spine. "I tried to warn him," she sighed. "I said, *If you're not prepared to end up bonded to a Goode cousin, don't go.* Remember? I even said we should bring Laurence instead."

"Do you think Laurence would be less likely to end up married?"

"Not even a little." Margot grinned impishly up at him, her cheeks flushed and her eyes sparkling. "But the difference is that Laurence would love it. Kaz looks like he's going to be ill every time someone hits on him."

Theodore snorted. "He's shy."

That didn't mean she was totally wrong, though. Laurence

would have loved all the attention. A quiet, serious halfling, he was as deadly as they came and intensely interested in his newfound freedom to seek out his own consort, no matter her race. No doubt that interest was spurred on by the sudden flurry of bindings and marriages that flowed into the Protectorate on the heels of their declaration.

Barely three months had passed since he and Margot went public with their marriage and every day more announcements came across his desk — the dissolution of unions, the formal recognition of bindings, petitions to have halflings legally allowed to inherit family seats and property, and, most importantly, the proud announcements of pregnancies.

His people, once freed from their self-imposed restrictions, were charging full speed into the future.

"No, he's just awkward." Margot rested her cheek against his chest. "Maybe he'll meet someone even more awkward and fall in love."

Theodore shrugged. He had hope that Kaz would meet his match. Perhaps not in the Coven, but elsewhere. He needed someone who would smooth his rough edges, but who would understand the vicious need to protect that made Kaz who he was. Whoever it was that his brother finally clicked with, Theodore wished them all the luck in the world. They'd need it.

"Speaking of love..." Margot propped her chin on his chest to look up at him. "Any word from Cammie?"

He shook his head. Worry beat at the back of his mind like a steady fist. "No. Not since Marian's funeral. Cameron says she's not speaking to anyone."

"Not even to Viktor?"

"Especially not to Viktor." Theodore grimaced. Something happened between those two at the Summit, but whatever it was, neither would speak about it. He had his suspicions, of course, but without prying into their private lives, Theodore couldn't confirm it.

But if Cammie continued her isolation, he would be forced to intervene. Family didn't let family wither away under a cloud of grief, and family *definitely* didn't let family drive themselves slowly insane by denying a connection that both the coyote shifter and his cousin knew existed.

Theodore had already decided to give Cammie and Viktor until the end of his visit with the Goodes before he stepped in. It was only his respect for Cammie's grief over the loss of her mother that stayed his hand so far.

"Do you think it's Marian's death or the bad blood that's making this such a big mess?"

"Both," he answered. Twenty years was a long time to nurse a broken heart, after all. Solbournes weren't the most forgiving family on a good day. What Viktor did to Cammie, how he courted her and gentled her, only to shatter her heart when it was fullest, would not be easy for anyone to forgive, let alone an elvish woman with a vindictive streak as wide as the Orclind.

Theodore pressed a gentle kiss to Margot's marriage sigil and felt the sweet bite of her magic against his lips. "It will work out," he muttered against her skin. "Even if I have to force the issue."

"Let's not worry about it right now." Margot curled her fingers into his black button down and slowly began to pull it out from under his belt. "We're on our honeymoon, remember? And we only have so long before my family drags us back to the square to get ready for our ceremony tonight. I want to enjoy my husband before then."

Shutting away his worry for the time being, Theodore grinned down at his consort. "You'll hear no complaints from me, darling."

She smiled back, her soft fingers gliding over his sides to lay flat against his stomach. "Didn't think so."

~

Margot always knew that she was a Goode. Even when she didn't understand anything else about herself, she understood her place within her Coven, within her family, and clung tight to the feeling of identity it gave her.

Still, she would be lying if she said that she had never felt just a *little* bit on the outside of things. It played hand in hand with her sense of purposelessness, her feeling of squandered potential. Under different circumstances, she would have been Sophie's protégé. She would have been groomed to lead the Coven, to carry their legacy into the future.

Instead, Margot was forced to hide. She had to sit on the side-lines and in the shadows, contributing only anonymously or strictly within the family bounds. No matter how much they showered her with love, there was no escaping the reality that was her fringe status.

How could she relate to her cultured, ambitious cousins when she could barely get permission to work in a Ward only forty-five minutes from the Goodeland? How could she participate in discussion about the Coven's future if she couldn't expose herself to meetings with outsiders? How could she use her abilities to bring prestige and respect to her Coven if she couldn't even sign her name to her work?

Over the years, Margot did her best to be useful. She used her abilities to take care of her elderly Covenmates. She helped bring new ones into the world. She assisted her grandmother in the shadows. She organized gatherings and checked in on those who didn't live in Goodeland, made sure even the farthest flung members of the Coven knew they were cared for.

It wasn't enough, though. Not to feel like she was a fully contributing member of her Coven, and not enough to erase her hyper-awareness of her differences. Certainly it wasn't enough for her to feel comfortable admitting her problems to even her closest family members before she fled to San Francisco, and that, she realized, was telling.

But when she returned to the Goodeland a full nine months after accepting the post at the Healing House, her elvish husband in tow, Margot was shocked by how *normal* it felt. Gone were her fears of being useless. Gone were her sneaking suspicions that behind every indulgent smile there was worry, disappointment. Gone was her tension and the feeling of being collared in the dark, cursed by her own blood.

Not even the brittle, unspoken tension between herself and Sophie took that sense of wholeness from her. It would take Sophie a long time to forgive Margot for keeping her condition a secret, but so too would Margot for being kept in the dark. They would work it out, though. Having the ceremony on Goode soil, being part of the Coven in vow as well as in blood, went a long way toward that.

Mistakes were made. Scars would linger. But the strength of a witch lay in her Coven, in her ability to lean on and forgive others. Though she was conscious of a dam deep in her mind, holding back a torrent of rage and confusion and flailing, helpless hurt, Margot leaned on those tenets. She would do it for however long she needed to; until the day she felt strong enough to knock that dam down.

Margot walked into the lush forest compound with her head held high, her husband's hand on her back, and felt like she *belonged.*

She felt her family's joy and astonishment, their pride and their concern radiate through her as they gathered outside of her grandmother's house. She embraced every aunt and uncle, smothered babies in kisses, and accepted their rapid fire inquiries with a smile. When Noni Tula fussed over how skinny she was, Margot didn't flinch. When they pestered her about her new job as a junior healer at Solbourne General, she didn't worry that they would try to talk her out of it.

For the first time in memory, Margot loved her life and everyone in it without reserve or dread. There was no more axe over her head or shoe waiting to drop.

There was only the soft, sticky faces of her baby cousins and too much food and the cold breeze kicking off of the lake in the evening and *Theodore,* who endured all the cautious looks and invasive questions her family could throw at him with his practiced aplomb.

Their first night in the Goodeland, the Goode Coven and all the surrounding Covens came to celebrate Margot's marriage in their own way: outside, with overflowing food, music, and a bonfire so tall it dwarfed the trees.

Under the crescent moon set in a velvet sky, Theodore and Margot were married once more. Standing before the roaring bonfire crackling with spiced wood and purifying salt, they made their vows in front of three hundred witches, arrants, hybrids, orcs, and every god that lurked in the shadows of the forest.

Sophie bound their hands. Alric and Kaz exchanged the family gifts — a priceless heirloom from the Goode family vault and a large offering bowl carved from a single piece of paper-thin tektite for the family altar from the Solbournes — while Ruby, dressed in a flowing dress covered in glittering, bejeweled flowers, fed an offering to the fire.

They didn't pick a new ember, as they already had theirs safely tucked away in the Solbourne vault, but Margot and Theodore knelt in the grass anyway, their eyes on the roaring flames, and sent their thanks to the goddess of elves and magic for bringing them together.

When they rose to face the crowd, the roar of their approval was deafening. Margot beamed and stepped into Theodore's arms, her heart too full and her pride too intense to do anything more than grin.

Music filled the square. Children in their best outfits ran past, screaming their joy as they chased one another, and someone called out to say that all the food on the assembled banquet tables was now officially fair game, but not to touch the blackberry chocolate wedding cake, made by Noni Tula herself.

It was perfect.

"Hey," Theodore whispered, his lips pressed against the shell of her ear. "Look over by the drink table."

Margot craned her neck to peer over her shoulder just in time to see Kaz melting into the shadows between the trees, his strides quick and purposeful. "Where do you think he's going?"

"Mm." He swayed with her to the beat of the song and the chorus of excited voices around them. "My first guess is that he's running away from the horde. Second guess is that maybe he has somewhere else he'd rather be."

"Interesting. He *was* moving pretty fast, wasn't he?" Margot turned her attention back to her husband. Melting into his arms, she gave his handsome face and healed marriage sigil an appreciative sigh. "Can't imagine wanting to be anywhere other than here, personally."

Theodore dimpled. "Yeah?"

"Yeah."

He bent to touch their sigils together. Both of their eyes fluttered closed as they savored the bite of magic, the heat of the bonfire, the scent of the forest, and the bond that arced between them.

I love you, darling.

Margot felt his voice, the raw feeling behind it, in her marrow. *I love you, Theodore.*

Theodore met her gentle kiss with an aching softness of his own. A howl of approval went up around them. *You ready to spend forever with me?*

Yes, she answered, *I won't accept anything less.*

Epilogue II

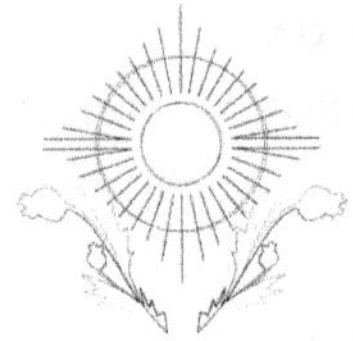

Margot's great-aunt was a wizened woman. She was beautiful but frail, her skin paper-thin and her hair a closely shorn cap of snowy white. Theodore could see hints of his wife in her dainty chin and the cunning, very *witchy* look in her steel gray eyes, but the resemblance didn't soothe him.

She was a Goode, and all the Goodes were, as far he was concerned, his enemies. And if there was a list of Goodes Theodore wished he could sharpen his claws on, Fara definitely cracked the top five.

"How long will it take?"

"The glamour has been embedded in her skin for twenty-six years," Fara answered, barely paying any attention to him. Like every elder Goode he'd met, she lacked even a hint of warmth under her aloof expression. "It will take as long as it takes."

Gods, it was like she didn't even *care* that it was her great-niece she was working on, that she mutilated. Elves were vicious, but they at least cared about their kin. The same could not be said for the generation of witches Fara and Sophie Goode hailed from.

Theodore adjusted his grip on Margot's shoulders. She sat in a chair in front of him, perfectly composed, but he could feel her anxiety running like a jagged current through their bond. Prickles settled under his skin, an itch to soothe and to eliminate the source of his consort's distress that was bred into his very DNA.

"Will it hurt her?" His temper bled into his voice, but he didn't care if he offended the old witch. It was her bony hands that mutilated Margot in the first place, though he tried valiantly not to think about that, for his wife's sake. She didn't want him to seek justice on her behalf.

Yet.

"Theodore..." Margot's voice was a gentle reproach. One of her soft hands came up to cover his.

He sucked in a deep breath and became aware of the fact that he was letting out a low, threatening rumble. Theodore managed to squelch it – not for Fara's sake, but for Margot's. The last thing he wanted was for her to feel like *she* needed to look after *him*.

If he'd learned anything about his wife in the four months they'd been married, it was that she couldn't fight the instinct to comfort even when she was drowning in her own pain. Whether it was a healer's trait or something more intrinsic to her, he didn't know.

Theodore turned his hand around so he could entwine their fingers. He wasn't entirely certain who was giving strength to whom, but that was the way with them. Their relationship was constant give and take. Something raw and unchecked flowed between them; a current of gratefulness, of love, of protectiveness and pride.

Every day he woke up surprised to find her there with him, a purr rattling his chest, and every night he thanked the gods for his fate. Twenty-five years of constant, grinding determination and yearning were nothing compared to the joy of his daily existence. He wouldn't trade Margot for anything.

That didn't mean he had to like her relatives, though. He counted himself lucky that she had so far kept the du Soleils at a distance. Even Theodore wasn't certain he could handle both Olivier and Sophie at once. Not even his patience could stretch *that* far.

"There will be some discomfort," Fara answered as she slowly lowered herself into the chair beside Margot's. Two dainty needles gleamed in her wizened hands. They looked terribly sinister in her grip, and out of place amongst the finery of their suite's lavish sitting room.

The room was too big for what they were doing. It felt more appropriate to have the procedure done in a back alley, or perhaps a dank basement. A setting that fit the crime the Goodes had committed, however well intentioned, against his consort.

But of course, he refused to entertain the idea of Margot undergoing the procedure anywhere but in their home. He'd gone to the trouble of flying Fara into San Francisco just so Margot didn't have to travel back to the Goodeland for the procedure. There wasn't a chance on Burden's Earth he would let her travel back to Sophie's territory to undo the wrong they'd done to her, no matter what the old, wretched woman insisted. If Margot needed the comfort of family, she would ask for it. Until then, Theodore would keep her in his territory, where he knew she was safe and well cared for, without a single care for what any of the elder Goodes thought of it.

"It's okay, baby," she murmured, staring up at him with the sort of serene confidence only a healer could manage. "I'll be fine. If you can't stand it, maybe you should—"

"If you ask me if I want to stand outside one more time, Margot Elloise Solbourne, I'm going to bite you."

A smile curled the corner of her mouth upward. *You're going to do that anyway.*

He huffed and, leaning down to press a hard kiss to the crown of her head, muttered, "Don't tempt me, witch."

"Are you ready, Margot?"

They both turned their attention back to Fara, who sat poised, needles raised. A crackle of energy bounced between the sharp tips — electric blue twined with vivid teal. The metallic tang of magic seeped into the air, coating his tongue in a taste very close to blood.

"Yes, Auntie," his wife answered, quick and easy, like she was agreeing to take a pie out of the oven rather than having her skin burned off.

Theodore clenched his jaw and heard his fangs squeak against one another. *Calm. It will be over soon.*

Not that the thought made it easier. He didn't think he would ever be able to stomach her suffering. Even the necessary kind.

Margot had already secured her hair in a tight bun, leaving plenty of room for her great-aunt to work. When she tilted her head in Fara's direction, a single strand of red hair fell against her forehead, flirting with the edge of their marriage sigil. The scab was long gone, but the skin was still a faintly puckered lavender; a living chronicle of just how long they'd been together.

Heart clenching, Theodore crouched down in front of her and gently brushed her hair back into place with the pad of his thumb. "Keep your eyes on me, my love," he whispered.

Their twined hands fell into her lap. Margot covered them with her free hand and squeezed tightly as Fara pressed her needles into the skin behind her ear. Immediately, the faint but stomach turning scent of burning skin filled the room, mingling with the elemental smell of magic.

Margot stiffened, but otherwise didn't seem troubled by it. When he touched their bond, he found her emotions muted, as if she had retreated somewhere so deep inside herself that not even the pain of having a sigil removed could reach her. She'd once called it her *Healer Zone* and had described it as a sort of flow state, where she could turn all her focus away from her own body. It was a useful tool when you were using every ounce of your ability to save the life of another – or when you needed to hide from pain.

And yet, even in that faraway place, Theodore felt her connection to him.

I'm here, he told her, his inner voice echoing deep into that placid part of her. *Squeeze my hands as hard as you want. And don't be afraid to cry if you need to.*

You know I hate crying, she replied.

Even her inner voice was a little farther away than normal. That worried him, but he tried not to let it leak into the bond. Another thing he'd learned in the months they'd been married was that Margot was an excellent compartmentalizer. When she couldn't handle something, she merely set it aside, or retreated from it until she could better deal with it. She claimed it came from her training as a healer, but Theodore suspected it had a lot more to do with her upbringing.

Coming to grips with what her family had done to her — both sides of them, witch and elvish — was one of those things she had neatly compartmentalized. She had to, growing up as she did. Squirreling away the other, unacceptable and dangerous half of herself was the only way to survive.

While Theodore wanted nothing more than to cut the family who'd done that to her out of her life completely, Margot had only just begun to wake up to her own anger, her own sense of vicious injustice. It was as if she couldn't face the enormity of it head on. Instead, she could only look at it in pieces — her anger coming in small flare ups and flashes, one realization bubbling up into another, faster and faster.

He tried to be understanding. He even made nice with the Goodes when she asked it of him, but Theodore knew the reckoning was on the horizon. One day, Margot would wake up and have to deal with all the wrongs Sophie and her inner circle had done to her. He vacillated between hoping it would come soon and dreading its arrival.

Theodore knew that when she finally accepted her anger, the weight of so much wrong, it would crush her.

His wife, his incredible consort, had built her entire identity around her Coven pride. Asking her to face so much betrayal and neglect from the people she'd worshipped and strove to please for so long was no easy task.

All he could do was be there for her whenever she took a step in that direction. The day she felt ready to face the weight of her trauma, he would be there, too.

Theodore knelt before her and brought their joined hands up to his lips. He kissed the delicate line of her knuckles and tried not to breathe through his nose as the smell of burning skin grew more pungent. Magic hummed in the air, thick and cloying.

I bet you are going to have the cutest little ears, he told her, attempting to distract them both. *The prettiest little points. I'm going to love seeing them every day.*

Margot's expression didn't change, but he felt her wince when Fara leaned forward, using more pressure to uproot the sigil from her skin. Her inner voice was strained when she answered, *I can't even imagine what they'll look like. I never considered finding out until I met you.*

I think they're going to look like a newborn's ears.

Oh?

Yes, he replied, hoping she couldn't read how sick he felt at the sight of her pain, the smell of it. *I think they're not going to be very pointed, not like mine. Maybe with a cute little roll at the tip. They'll be cute.*

Margot's eyes moved across his face, looking for something. *What if they're not?*

Impossible. Everything about you is beautiful, Margot.

She squeezed his fingers. *When we have kids, do you think they'll get your ears or mine?*

Theodore shifted closer, his heart beating fast. They hadn't talked about children yet. Not that they didn't want any, but rather that there just hadn't been any time to sit down and have the conversation. Between the upheaval created by their wedding, his duties as sovereign, and her new job as a junior healer, it simply hadn't come up.

I think they'll probably have my big, ugly ears, he answered, strangely breathless. His chest ached at the thought of being blessed with her children. Not yet. Not when they were so young and their lives so in flux, but eventually. *Hopefully they get your coloring. Our colors would clash, I think, if they took too much from both of us. Why do you ask?*

I've just been thinking about babies lately.

The response might have sent his alarm bells ringing, if there wasn't a note of pure sorrow in it. Theodore swallowed. *What have you been thinking about, my love?*

Margot's eyes drifted down to her lap. *I guess I just... with the procedure coming up, I've been thinking a lot about my parents. About why they did what they did. Why Sophie raised me like she did. I know they all had reasons that made sense to them, but... I've been trying to wrap my head around the idea that someone could leave their baby, and then that they could do* this *to them. I wouldn't be able to do it.*

If you thought it might save your child's life, I think you would, he replied, picking his words carefully.

Theodore didn't like coming to the defense of the du Soleils and the Goodes, but he knew the road Margot walked could very easily lead to blaming *herself* for what was done to her. Reminding her that there were reasons for her treatment didn't absolve them of guilt. It merely reinforced the fact that none of it was her fault.

But you will never have to make that choice, he told her. *When we choose to have children, we won't make the mistakes our parents made.* He smiled wryly. *It shouldn't be hard to do better. They set the bar on the floor.*

Margot's eyes, the stunning topaz he'd mistaken for copper, misted. When Fara leaned in closer, pushing her head down at an awkward angle, she barely seemed to notice. The stench of burning skin got worse.

I never thought I'd get to be a mother, she told him. In her way, it was a simple, direct statement, but one so laden with unspoken pain, it shattered him all over again. *I never thought I'd get the chance to meet someone who could keep my secret, and then I didn't think I'd have the time. But now the whole world is open for me and things I never thought were possible are happening. I can't... I can't process it all.*

Her chin wobbled as she valiantly blinked away tears. The sight broke his damn heart.

His witch, so brilliant at compartmentalizing, was also a practical, determined sort of woman. She did not let misfortune or fear or circumstance drag her down. Even when the end closed in around her, she kept going.

Margot Solbourne was no weeper, but in that moment, when her skin was blistered to undo a profound wrong, she struggled to hold on to her usual composure.

He could see it beginning to crash down on her, the first bits of shattered rock that would soon turn into a landslide, and knew that this moment was the start of a long and painful process.

My love, he crooned, pouring as much of his adoration and his pride into their bond as he was physically and psychically capable of. *Oh, my love. You are so strong. So, so strong. You don't need to process everything at once. We take steps one at a time, remember? And we do it together.*

The metallic scent in the air got sharper until, with a great burst of magic, it became more than just energy. Margot made a small sound of distress, her shoulders jumping with a full body jolt. A bloom of warm copper and salt flooded his senses, drawing his outraged gaze to the vivid tracks of blood sliding down the creamy column of her throat.

Fara sat back in her seat, apparently satisfied with her work, as Theodore barked out, "What have you *done?*"

"Blood's normal for a sigil as deeply embedded as that. Nothing to get your panties in a twist about." The old woman sent him a cool look as she gave Margot a single, conciliatory pat on the shoulder. "That's one done, then. Want to look?"

Fara held out a small compact mirror, but Margot didn't take it. Her face had gone ashen and her eyes remained fixed on his, as if she couldn't bear to even glance at the reflective glass for fear of what she'd find there.

Margot sucked in a shuddering breath. A single tear escaped her stubborn grip as she locked eyes with him. Her voice was barely even a whisper when she asked, "How does it look?"

He squeezed her hands and held his breath. Theodore's eyes followed the trail of vivid, iron-rich blood up her throat and was, for just a moment, taken back to the first time he saw her in the flesh. Like that night in front of the bombed shell of the Healing House, she looked stricken, blooded, but determined. The only difference was that now she didn't look at him like he came to ruin what was left of her life.

She looked at him like he was the only being she could trust.

Theodore swallowed, his throat thickened by his worry, by his fierce pride in his consort, and beheld her elvish ears for the first time.

He was staggered by the picture she made: bloodied, sitting stiff in a chair by herself, tears clinging to her lashes, and one ear as round as any humans and the other a perfect, dainty point. A striking image that encapsulated everything she was and all that could be, had been, and would never be again.

The point of her ear was not nearly as large as his own, but held a gentle curve like the end of a plum leaf. He hadn't worried that she would look strange with her glamour removed, but he knew she'd entertained the stray thought that the effect might be similar to what happened when one wore glasses for so long, people forgot what one looked like without them. Theodore was happy to report that Margot's ears, like the rest of her, were perfect.

Overwhelmed, he kissed their clasped hands three times before he could manage to get a word out. "It's beautiful," he rasped.

Another tear slid out from under her control even as she asked, "No little curl?"

He kissed their hands again. "No," Theodore breathed against her skin. "No curl."

She nodded, blinking fast. Relief flowed through their bond, mingling with a profound grief that knew no name, no place of purchase. It merely *was.*

Even when it felt like she was unraveling inside the safety of their bond, the shelter he so willingly provided, Margot didn't miss a beat. Turning her head toward Fara, she said plainly, "I'm ready for the next one, Auntie."

~

The entire procedure only took forty-five minutes. They were among the longest minutes of his life.

By the time Fara declared Margot officially free of the glamour she'd laid twenty-six years prior, Theodore felt stripped raw. Despite the fact that Margot healed the wounds behind her ears immediately, and even with all traces of blood gone, he felt her pain echoing on a loop in his mind, tearing at him with each pass.

And yet it was nothing compared to how Margot felt.

At first, as they retreated into their bedroom, she was still. Her head was empty; her thoughts slightly fuzzy from emotion and adrenaline and the lingering buzz of pain. And then she caught her reflection in the glass of the huge, floor to ceiling windows behind their bed.

Margot, so strong for so very long, shattered.

Theodore caught her when her knees buckled. They slid onto the floor together, his arms looped around her middle as she bent over and heaved great, silent sobs into the floor. It was as if the breath had left her body. The avalanche buried her under a lifetime of pain, knocking the strength from her limbs and crushing her ability to cry out, to *breathe.*

Her blunt claws scraped at the floor as her fingers curled, seeking purchase. Theodore held her tighter and squeezed his eyes shut. Helplessness churned like acid in his stomach, mingling uneasily with an immense relief. Each wracking sob was a lash on his soul, but he knew this was necessary.

Like the burning away of the sigils, the stubborn block on Margot's grief and pain needed to be removed.

I'm here, he whispered to her, over and over, as he nuzzled the back of her neck. *I'm here. You're not alone, my love. Never alone.*

He felt her reaching for him in the bond, though she did not seem capable of physically doing so. It didn't matter. She could cry as much as she wanted. He would hold her until the tears stopped, and even then, he would not let her go without a fight.

I love you, she cried out, a clear, high note amongst the storm of chaos that was her normally painfully organized mind. *I love you. I love you.*

I love you, he answered every time. *I love you, Margot. Just as you are.*

He didn't know how long it took for her weeping to subside, nor for the wracking tremors to fade from her limbs. He didn't know how long they sat there on the floor, though he suspected it was over an hour. The sun was beginning to set beyond the choppy waves of the bay when Margot finally slumped back against him, spent.

Theodore cradled her against his chest and, laying his legs out on either side of her, pressed their cheeks together. As one, they stared at their reflections in the glass.

"I thought I might feel more like an elf," she mumbled, nasally and raw. Her eyes were bloodshot and her nose was flushed pink. To him, she looked very human. "How come I still just feel like a witch?"

"How many times do I have to tell you that you're not *just* anything?" He asked it playfully, but his voice was similarly hoarse, as if he too had spent the last hour crying out decades of pain. "You can be both an elf and witch, darling. You *are* both."

Unwrapping one arm from around her middle, Theodore fumbled with his suit jacket for a moment before he was able to pull out the long, velvet box he stashed in the inner pocket that morning, just in case. Flipping the lid with his thumb, he extracted the contents and held it out for her in the palm of his hand.

Margot sucked in a sharp, shuddering gasp. "Theodore, what..."

"I know you don't do jewels unless you have to," he said, "but I felt like you might accept some on this important occasion." He angled his hand to catch the light, letting it bounce through hundreds of perfectly cut diamonds and deep, dark sapphires. Light burst around them, spraying the floor with tiny rainbows. "My family thought it was a bit old fashioned of me, but I had this union necklace made for you. Initially, I had it made to represent the future — elves and Others, our two families moving forward as one."

Theodore examined the familiar facets of the jewels and the wide, collar-like width of the necklace, such an elvish combination of luxury and vital protection. It didn't just represent their families, of course. Tradition demanded he choose jewels that echoed his own coloring, so that whenever she donned the necklace, it was as if they were skin to skin, always.

He smoothed his thumb over the cool stones, tracing the smaller, square cut diamonds with the edge of a retracted claw when he continued, "Now it means so much more. Not just our future, but your past. The part of you that should never have been locked away in the first place."

Margot's fingers trembled as she traced the sapphire thistles, rendered in a flat, art deco style, that ran around the width of the jeweled choker. Along the top and bottom, carefully selected diamonds swirled in geometric curls that, when looked at just right, brought to mind the famous Healer's Hand.

She said nothing, but when she held her hair away from her neck, Theodore's heart soared. Carefully, he secured the choker around her elegant throat, explaining in a hushed whisper, "These days we usually give these to someone we've contracted a union with, but for generations it was a traditional gift for a consort. A public declaration for a people who don't do marriage sigils."

He dipped his head to kiss the nape of her neck, right above the platinum clasp. "I requested it be made the day I learned who you were. I've carried it with me for weeks, waiting for the right time. I'm giving it to you today because I want you to always remember this moment, Margot."

Her hands came up to touch the cool platinum and glittering stones. He watched her reflection as a fresh wave of tears slid down her cheeks. A weak smile flitted across her mouth — there and gone in a moment. "You mean the moment I had a breakdown on the floor?"

Theodore pressed a fierce kiss to the side of her head. Gods, she had no idea how resilient she was. The strength hidden in her soul could move mountains. "No," he rumbled. "No. When you were the strongest you've ever been."

He felt her shudder. Margot was silent for several minutes. Her tears dried into salty tracks on her cheeks as they watched the sunset together. Orange and pink and brilliant yellow light streaked over the cold, gray water. In the distance, a fog bank began to roll in. Soon, night would fall like a curtain over their territory, opening up the world for all those who could not dwell in Glory's light.

In his arms, Margot breathed easier. Although he left her thoughts to herself, knowing she would share them with him in time, he felt even the tumult inside of her begin to subside.

Finally, as the first stars began to glitter in the navy dome of the sky, she said, "I *am* strong."

Theodore closed his eyes and leaned his jaw against her temple, savoring the moment, when his pride in her felt like it might burn him to ash. "Yes," he murmured. "Yes, you are. By all the gods, Margot, you are *astonishing.*"

She took in a deep, cleansing breath. Their bond thrummed between them, full of life and power beyond reckoning. The soft overhead lights hit the jewels of her necklace and bounced back, shattering in rainbows around her face.

"Thank you." Margot stared at her reflection, her gaze

unflinching even when it landed on the soft points of her ears. "For reminding me." She raised her chin. The prim, determined tone he loved so very much began to bleed back into her voice. "And for setting me free."

"You freed me first," he replied, kissing her beautiful little ear. "I'm just returning the favor."

Margot reached up to gently touch the spot he kissed. Her fingers lingered on the unfamiliar curve. Her eyes, so human and so elvish, met his in the glass. Theodore smiled, his dimples deepening with the force of his joy.

Finally, he thought. *Now we can really begin.*

A sneak peek of Courtship's Conquest...

February 2045 - San Francisco, The Elvish Protectorate

Camille Solbourne, first cousin to the sovereign ruler of the Elvish Protectorate and one of the last three living descendants of the Dia family, turned a corner so sharply, she nearly lost a heel.

Somewhere else in the cavernous warren of the Summit Hall, a crowd's roar went up, shaking the walls and bouncing off of fine marble floors. She didn't hear it. All she was aware of, all she could feel and hear and taste, was *him.*

And that meant she had to run.

The Hall wasn't particularly familiar to her. She rarely left her mother's Napa estate, and even when she spent time with her cousins in San Francisco, they didn't care to pass the time in the awe inspiring labyrinth where the elvish government made their laws.

It didn't matter, though. She didn't need to know where she was going. She just needed to get *out.*

Camille's skin burned as pheromones washed through her veins. Her heart stuttered a wild, uneven beat. Sweat beaded along her spine beneath the silk of her ice blue dress. Her bones felt ill-suited to their muscled confines. The beds of her claws ached. Even her vision was sharper.

All it took was one deep breath of his scent, one touch of his fingers to the soft, vulnerable underside of her chin, and she was changed.

Fuck!

Camille made another wild turn into an unfamiliar corridor, her heels clattering against the black marble floor, and spotted a door to a small, unused meeting room. Her preference was to get outside and as far away from Solbourne Tower as she possibly could, but what if *he* was out there? What if he waited for her by the steps or lingered in the shadows of the parking garage? She thought he darted after her when she fled the green room behind the sovereign's podium, but if he pursued her, wouldn't he have already caught her?

A more insidious inner voice than that of her anxiety whispered, *What if he isn't waiting? What if he's already forgotten you, like he did before?*

She shook the crushing doubt loose and kept going. She would not turn around. She would not look to see if he followed. She would not take *any* unnecessary risk.

It was much smarter to lie low until she was absolutely certain he was no longer on the small spit of land that was the elvish stronghold. Even if he wasn't looking for her, she couldn't risk it.

Intuition pulled her in another direction, away from any exits. *Don't expose yourself outside. Hiding is smarter.*

Camille darted down the hall, her breaths rasping in a throat that felt like sandpaper, and attempted to pry open the door. Her first try didn't do anything productive. Her hand shook too badly. Her glove, white silk with diamond-tipped claw-caps, slid against the bronze handle. Growling, she just managed it on her second try.

The room was small and dark, with a single, shuttered window in the far right corner. A wooden table sat in the center, framed by four chairs and overlooked by a large feed screen on one wall. It was a room that would have looked at home in any corporate office or government building, but to her it was a refuge. She would hide away until the day's meetings were over and her brother sought her out to give her the all-clear.

Camille dove in, her mind in a wild tangle of fear and desire, fury and desperation, yearning and revulsion.

How had she survived this once, only to succumb again? Why *now?* If her mother found out that she'd been in the same room with him, it would kill her — or, knowing Marian Dia Solbourne, she would try to kill *him* first.

Everything in Camille balked at the thought. Not that her mother stood a chance in her deteriorated state, but the idea of Viktor being injured made her stomach *roil—*

The door was on its return swing, sailing toward the jamb with all the force of a desperate woman's shove, when a tanned hand slid into the gap. Camille made a sharp sound of alarm and jumped back. She stumbled into a chair, knocking it onto the floor with a clatter.

She *knew* that hand. She knew that skin. She knew that tantalizing scent of salt and musk and clean, sweet sweat like she knew her own soul.

Gods, she thought, furious at the wash of relief and pleasure that swept through her, *he followed me.*

With a small push, the door swung open.

Viktor Hamilton, alpha of the Merced pack and figure of her sweetest nightmares, stood in the doorway. His beautiful face was cast half in shadow by the light from the hall, obscuring the fine lines of his features, the luminous quality of his cornflower blue eyes.

But she didn't need the light to see him, to *know* him. Camille's soul had been branded by the shifter nearly twenty years prior. She could never forget him, no matter how hard she tried.

"Cam..." Viktor's voice was a deep, jagged rumble. It lacked his usual lackadaisical cheer and was softer, gentler than it had any right to be. "I didn't mean to scare you off. I'm sorry about what happened in there."

He was apologizing for manhandling her, pulling her away from interceding in what could have been a politically catastrophic fight between her cousins, but all she heard was the bass rumble of his voice, that sensual shifter purr that made even the most sensible people beg for more.

Everything in her, instinct *and* soul, snapped to attention. Without intending to, she sucked in a deep breath, bringing more of him into her lungs until it felt like there were millions of tiny bubbles popping in her veins.

No! Run!

Her logical mind, the part of her that was all raw, wounded fury, had no plans to give into the pull that had rearranged her hormones and stolen her good sense. She'd done it once and suffered the consequences.

Camille gripped the edge of the table to steady herself — and keep herself *away* from Viktor — straightened her shoulders, and hoarsely demanded, "What part of me trying to get away from you as fast as possible told you to *follow* me? Get out!"

"I wouldn't have if you didn't look like you were ready to shatter into a thousand pieces," he shot back. "Did you really think I was going to let you run off after all that without even checking to make sure you were okay?"

Camille let out a distinctly elvish hiss. "I'm fine. Now get *out.*"

In an instant, Viktor's eyes went from human to coyote. In the dark, his pupils suddenly expanded and glowed with the vivid green of a predator's vision.

With a flick of his wrist, the door shut with a resounding *bang.*

"Cam," he tried again, moving a step closer.

Acknowledgments

For all that writing is a solitary endeavor, a book does not come into being in a vacuum. This book would not be in your hands without the support of an incredible number of people.

Consort's Glory took nearly ten years to write. It began as drawings in my sketchbook penned during long classes in art school. It has lived in countless iterations throughout the years — believe it or not, this story actually began as YA, with Theodore as the heartless villain (yes, really) — and met with several dozen rejections. In the time it took to write five, seven, *ten* drafts, I dropped out of art school, became a bookseller, and started the *Kingdom of Thirst Podcast.* Other things happened, too, but those are the important bits.

In all of that time, from those first sketches to the completion of the book you now hold, I have been blessed with the support and understanding of friends and family. I wrote the first 700 page draft of *Consort's Glory* in secret, with only my best friend, Paige, cheering me on. She truly got the worst of the agony of self-doubt, bad prose, and wild woman muttering. The book would not have made it past its first stumbling steps without her and the apparently endless font of patience she possesses. Full stop.

When I was ready to say, *"Yes, this is what I want to do"* I found endless encouragement from my mother (sorry about all the smut!) as well as my bookshop family — Kat, Jessica, Brendan, and Ali. Their advice, support, and voracious reading of my work have been a bright spot in some of my darkest moments.

My family took my career pivot in stride. My dreams would

not exist without my mother's careful tending and reckless encouragement. My Nana, despite her disapproval of my use of the word *fuck,* braved the first drafts and came back asking for more. My brother, poor romance-ambivalent soul that he is, has been a backbone of strength when I felt like crumbling.

This book would not be nearly as good, nearly as loved, without the incredible author and human being Amalia Dillin, who took a chance on friendship with a weird podcaster and ended up bringing so much sound advice, humor, and warmth with her. Similarly, Victoria Aveline graciously took my fangirling in stride and decided, perhaps against her better judgment, to become a friend. I am grateful that I have her dry humor, support, and extremely good taste in entertainment in my life.

Without my fearless copy editor and friend, Gwen, it would be damn near unreadable. Without my podcast family, all my listeners who indulge me and offer their boundless support, I'm not sure I'd have the courage to do this thing at all.

KoT has brought a tremendous bounty of wonderful people into my world, including CM Nascosta, who listened to me ramble for five minutes and thought my silly book might actually be something good.

Without *KoT* and the *Works by Abigail Patreon,* I never would have met Seth, Anne, Diesis, Shelby, Meg, Aelia, Krista, Whoop, Drusilla, Erin (our local hammock queen), and many more, who help me beat back the demons of self-doubt whenever they arise. You are all a gift I am impossibly grateful to have, and your creativity, kindness, and laughter bring me so much joy.

Consort's Glory would not be what it is today without the support of all of these people, as well as the inspiration and kindness of the authors who have blazed the trail ahead of me. My sincerest gratitude goes to Ruby Dixon, one of the most gracious and skilled writers this side of the universe, for her support and the comfort her books have brought me over the years. Ruby, you are a rockstar, and your reputation for kindness and generosity is well earned. Thank you for taking a chance on my funky little book.

To author duo Tiffany Roberts, thank you for laughing at my dumb jokes and for your fabulous work — no one does weird and wonderful like you two.

To Abigail Owen, thank you for you for taking the time to talk dragons with me and for writing such a complex, delightful world.

To Laurel Cremant, thank you for being my mentor. I truly don't know what I did to earn the guidance of someone as talented, witty, and compassionate as you. I wouldn't be the writer I am now without you.

There are so many more people I can and should thank, including every single Patron and every author who has ever leant me their encouragement and listening ear, but alas, we are in a paper shortage. So to all of you who I cannot thank personally on this page, know that I am thinking of you now, my heart full. I cannot imagine my life without you in it.

Thank you.

Find out more about how this book came to be by reading or listening to the Consort's Glory: Then, Today, and Tomorrow essay on the Works by Abigail Patreon.

About the Author

Abigail Kelly is a writer of alternate histories, love stories, and women with drive. Her work is heavily influenced by both her modest family roots and her passion for history. A former illustrator, she is now a bookseller at an independent bookshop where she gets to badly influence impressionable young minds and put her favorite books in eager hands. She is also the host of the Kingdom of Thirst podcast, a show all about romance novels and why they matter.

Her favorite authors are Shirley Jackson, V. E. Schwab, Ursula K. Le Guin, Kresley Cole, Nalini Singh, and just about anyone who writes about the weird and wonderful. She lives in San Francisco with her dog, Babs, who remains stubbornly illiterate.

Glossary

A full character directory and map can be found at Abigailkkelly.com

Places

United Territories and Allies: What we would consider the continental USA. A loose federation of sovereign states established after the Great War. The UTA capital is United Washington, in the Neutral Zone.

The Elvish Protectorate: Also known as the EVP. Stretches from Oregon to New Mexico. Capital city is San Francisco. Led by the elvish sovereign Theodore Thaddeus Solbourne.

The Coven Collective: Also known as the Collective. Encompasses Washington state. Capital city is Seattle. Led by a large coalition of witch covens, with Sophie Goode acting as their leader.

The Orclind: Encompasses much of the Midwest. Led by the Iron Chain, a close-knit government made up of orcish clans and family groups. Capital city is Boulder.

Shifter Alliance: Takes up a section of the midwest and all of the south. (Unfortunately includes Florida.) Run by a very, very loose alliance of shifter packs from three capital cities — Minneapolis, Oklahoma City, and Atlanta.

The Draakonriik: Also known as the 'Riik. The second smallest territory, it takes up all of the Great Lakes region and stretches to New York. Led by Taevas Aždaja, the *Isand* (ee-zand) of the dragon clans. Pronounced: *dra-kon-reek*

The Neutral Zone: Also known as the New Zone. Technically it is held by a coalition government consisting of representatives from the UTA, but in reality it is run by a syndicate of feuding vampire families. It is a small strip of land squeezed between the Draakonriik and the Shifter Alliance.

Gods

Light & Darkness: The primordial gods who created all the others. Also known as The Lovers and First Union. Both are generally represented as female.

Loft: God of the sky and creator of flying beings. Twin sibling to Tempest. They know no gender. Also known as the Boundless One.

Tempest: God of the ocean and creator of all water beings. Also known as the Hungry God and the god of love.

Burden: God of the Earth, creator of all beings who live within it — most notably the orcs. Husband of Glory.

Glory: Goddess of sunlight, magic, and creator of elves. Worshipped by witches for giving the gift of magic to humanity.

Blight: God of forested places and disease. He works in partnership with his daughter Grim and shares her dominion over demons and all reviled creatures.

Grim: Goddess of death. Known as the Merciful One and the Brilliant Lady. She is widely beloved.

Craft: God of change, newness, and messengers. Creator of humanity and viewed warily by non-worshippers as the Chaos Maker. They change their gender frequently, but generally is referred to using he/him pronouns.

TERMS

Arrant: someone born without m-paths, or the ability to channel and use magic.

Dragon: a person with a dual form. In their bipedal form, they have claw-tipped wings, horns, and a tail. In their quadrupedal form, they are roughly the size of a standard SUV and can fly at extremely high altitudes for weeks at a time. They come in a variety of extremely saturated colors that shift with the time of day (light to dark). They breathe cold blue fire and can see the Earth's magnetic field. Identifying mating feature is marked change in behavior, including the overwhelming urge to nest.

Elemental: a being created by a spontaneous magical eruption. They often take on the attributes of whatever weather they happen to be born into, *i.e.* a lightning storm might produce a lightning elemental, or a blizzard might make a snow elemental.

Elf: someone born with jewel-toned skin, claws, pointed ears, and four fangs. Very secretive and considered apex predators who require a strict hierarchy to function. Average height of 6-7ft. Identifying mating feature is the retraction of claws.

Fey: a person with nearly vestigial, insect-like wings, small fangs, and claws. Usually live in large groups. Identifying mating feature is bioluminescence.

Foresight: the ability to see multiple possible futures. The average number is between 2-4, with the likelihood mental instability increasing with each subsequent possible future.

Healer: a person who possesses the ability to see into and heal bodies through touch.

M- : M- is frequently used as shorthand to denote when something is infused or otherwise combined with a magical element.

Met: acronym for *magically enhanced tech.* A branded home assistant that can do everything your Alexa can, as well as small, low-level magic to help around the house.

M-siphon: a containment device used to imprison a magical being and siphon off their magic. Highly illegal.

R-siphon: also known as *reverse siphon.* New technology that redistributes magic away from the siphon instead of into it.

M-lev: a play on *maglev,* meaning a high speed train that levitates using magnets. In this case, magnets *and* magic.

M-weather: magic weather. Very common, but can result in "clusters" or storms that wreak havoc if not properly contained. In rare circumstances, it can also produce a sapient being known as an *elemental.*

Orc: a person with green, gray, russet, or blue skin, two fangs, and claws. Widely renowned for their strength and beautiful voices.

Identifying mating feature is "the kohl", or altered, dark pigmentation of the hands and feet developed after meeting their mate.

Pixie: a small, winged creature with compound eyes with about the same level of intelligence as a rat. In the wild they live in trees and in burrows, but have adapted to living in walls, pipes, mailboxes, etc.

Shifter: a person who can shift into an animal form. They can partially shift (changing only parts of their bodies at will) and often take on characteristics of their other half. Famous for their strength and tenacity, as well as their dual-voiced "shifter purr" which many people find deeply attractive. Usually found in packs.

Sigil: a symbol used to channel magic. Western countries use the alchemical alphabet formally codified in the 1800's, though many, many variations are used all over the world.

Vampire: a person who drinks blood to survive and cannot go out in sunlight. Vampirism can only be "caught" with the exchange of fresh blood, and as of 2045 is much more widely spread through procreation. Vampires can only breed with their *anchors.* Identifying mating feature is marked change in behavior, including overwhelming desire and need for total isolation.

Were: a person infected with the were virus, a much mutated strain of the vampirism virus, resulting in altered physiology and magical ability. They can be identified by their heterochromia, or different colored eyes. They are the newest magical race and viewed warily by the general public for a variety of earned and unearned reasons. Identifying mating feature is marked change in behavior, including highly increased territorial instinct and the urge to nest.

Pronunciation guide for names of important characters in this book

Margot Goode: mar-goh good

Theodore Solbourne: thee-oh-door soul-born

Viktor Hamilton: vick-tor ham-uhl-ton

Sophie: soh-fee

Alric: awl-rick

Valen Yadav: vah-len yah-dahv

Andy Yadav-Coran: an-dee yah-dahv cohr-an

Kazimier Rione: kaz-eh-meer ree-own

Samuel: sam-yool

Taevas Aždaja: tay-vahs ash-DIE-ah

Petra Zaskodna: peh-trah zas-code-nah

Olivier du Soleil: oh-liv-ee-ay doo soh-lay

Marcus: mark-us

Also by Abigail Kelly

Find all new releases, bonus chapters, and exclusive content on the Works by Abigail Patreon!

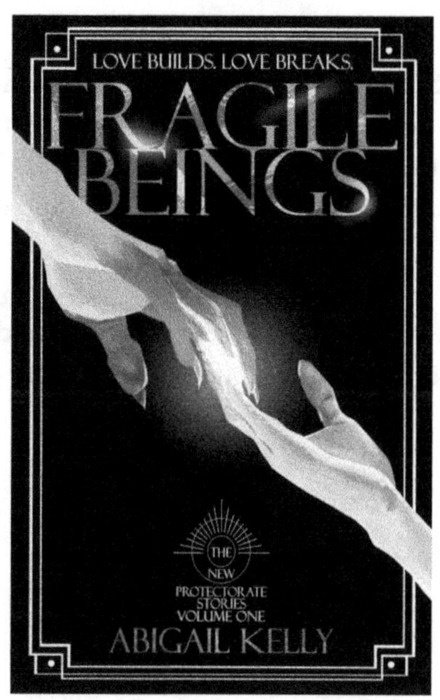

Fragile Beings: A New Protectorate Novella Collection

In the first volume of The New Protectorate Stories...

Fate can't be contained.

#376: A fey Changeling is rescued from captivity by a reluctant demon on a quest to find his fate. Of course Dom expects trouble, but he is shocked to discover his fate is tied to an imprisoned fey woman. Charlotte's a kicking, spitting, hissing little Changeling — and she's his.

A dragon's kiss burns cold.

Astray: When Paloma Contreras, arrant scientist, accidentally dooms a rogue dragon to death, she'll do anything to save his life. If that means giving up the mountaintop she's called home her entire life, so be it. Too bad Artem Aždaja has no plans to steal her roost. He only wants one thing: *her.*

Desire fogs the mind.

Weathering: Elise Sasini, an intrepid reporter and weather witch, sets out to uncover the story of San Francisco's legendary sentient fog and gets a lot more than she bargained for. The mysterious elemental agrees to tell his story in exchange for a taste of the life — and the woman — he craves.

Three novellas. Three couples. One fractured world. Step into a magical near-future where love builds, breaks, and defies boundaries.

Available in Kindle Unlimited, ebook, and paperback!

Courtship's Conquest: The New Protectorate Book Two

Their future hinges on a promise.

In the wake of her mother's death, Camille Solbourne is determined to follow through with her deathbed promise to arrange a union with a suitable partner and get out of the Solbourne family. A union is cold, more business than love, and negotiating them is a dangerous political dance. It's not what she wants, but sometimes happiness is found in compromise – and keeping one's promises.

Their choices haunt their past.

Nearly twenty years ago, Viktor Hamilton, alpha of San Francisco's lone coyote shifter pack, let his mate go. Becoming someone his pack could rely on for safety and guidance is the only thing that kept him sane in the long, lonely years that followed. When the opportunity to make a life-altering choice for the betterment of his people arises, he makes a promise to see it through.

What he doesn't expect is for the world to change around him in the blink of an eye. After a volatile run-in with Camille reignites the flame between them, he knows he can't leave the past alone. The only thing standing between them is their fraught past and Camille's furious determination to tie herself to another man. Pursuing Camille means gambling with the future of his pack, but Viktor won't let his mate go a second time – even if it means he has to put his life on the line to keep her.

Available in Kindle Unlimited, ebook, and paperback!

Empire: The New Protectorate Stories Volume Two

Love blooms in the dark.

After a lifetime of service to the Amauri vampire family, retired assassin Harlan Bounds lives his life exactly as it pleases him – on his private estate, surrounded by beauty, and unbothered by the bloody politics of the criminal underworld he left behind. He doesn't need or want for anything… except, perhaps, the tantalizing witch hired to look after the acclaimed rose garden on his grounds.

Zia North has nursed a crush on the mysterious vampire that is her boss for nearly a year. They've never spoken, and she knows the rules by heart: never stay on Empire Estate's grounds after sundown and never, *ever* bother Mr. Bounds. There's no chance for her to fulfill her sensual fantasies, so what's the harm in indulging a crush that will never see the light of day – or the kiss of darkness?

It's all daydreams until she makes a mistake that finally brings her face to face with the intimidating vampire. Harlan's dark intensity draws her in, and Zia's light sparks a craving that can't be denied. Fantasy clashes with reality when his dangerous past threatens to bite them both, but not even the violent conflicts of the vampire syndicate can sever a bond forged in blood.

Available in Kindle Unlimited, ebook, and paperback!

Content warnings

Content warnings: death, illness, familial estrangement, parental death, brief mentions of minor character infertility and infidelity, explicit sexual situations, biting, minor body modification, and violence.